The Rose Amongst the Thorns

Laura Johnson-Smith

The Book Guild

First published in Great Britain in 2026 by
The Book Guild Ltd
Unit E2 Airfield Business Park,
Harrison Road, Market Harborough,
Leicestershire. LE16 7UL
Tel: 0116 2792299
www.bookguild.co.uk
Email: info@bookguild.co.uk

The manufacturer's authorised representative in the EU for product safety is Authorised Rep Compliance Ltd, 71 Lower Baggot Street, Dublin D02 P593 Ireland (www.arccompliance.com)

Typeset in 11pt Minion Pro

Printed and bound by CPI Group (UK) Ltd, Croydon, CR0 4YY

ISBN 978 1835743 775

British Library Cataloguing in Publication Data.
A catalogue record for this book is available from the British Library.

FSC www.fsc.org
MIX
Paper | Supporting responsible forestry
FSC® C013604

For you. All of you.

A note from the author

This is a work of fiction inspired by the past, referencing real places and historical characters. Our main heroine is an amalgamation of women who were denied a platform to voice their story. A story about love, power and finding a voice amongst the thorns, life is reimagined to show what could have taken place if one woman was given equal power, wealth, and status as the men around her. This is Katherine's story.

Leicester

Late-Medieval England

One

My dreams are broken by a gentle voice calling my name. I slowly open my eyes, heavy from much-needed sleep, and I search the darkness for the source. The room comes into focus by a flicker of candlelight suspended in the air. I turn my head and find a man standing over me, smiling.

At first, I think it's my father, reaching out to me as if from a dream. But then the voice calls my name: "Katherine?"

I scramble to sit up, shaking my head to rid it from the heaviness of sleep.

"William? It is not yet dawn… you are leaving now?" My voice is thick and croaky from lack of use. Standing, I grab the nearest blanket and wrap myself up against the cold of the morning, the long sleeves of my chemise getting caught amongst the heavy material. I reach for his hand. "You cannot go."

"I don't want to go either, Katherine. No matter how many times I wish I could stay here with you, I have been entrusted by King Edward to make sure his treaty with France is still honoured."

"But…"

"No, Katherine, you know I must. We have to travel before first light if we want to reach the coast by tomorrow evening." My brother lets go of my hand and sits on the edge of the bed.

I can already feel the darkness suffocating me.

"Sir Francis is preparing the horses as we speak, but I wanted to see you before we left."

I nod my head, trying to digest his words.

"Our uncle and aunt promise to look after you, just like before."

The twitter of early morning birds filters through from outside, which is broken by the sound of agitated hooves on the frosty ground and the voices of nervous men talking below.

"What about Smith or Taylor? Are they going too?" I try to stall him with questions.

"No, they are here to look after the castle walls." He smiles. "And you, of course." He tickles my chin with his finger.

I stare into his eyes – so similar to our father's – and try to think of another question to delay him further, but words fail me. Just as he goes to stand, I say, "Promise me that you will return." I reach for him. "I need to know that you will be safe." My hand touches the ring on his finger, the indents that mark our family crest: a flower in the centre of two lions. It was once my father's signet ring.

William squeezes my hand, though his gaze doesn't meet mine. "Of course, Katherine, I promise. I never break my promises, do I?"

I shake my head. With a resigned smile, he stands, stretching his arms high above his head as he makes his way towards the door.

I follow him to the top of the staircase. Just before he descends into the dark abyss below, he turns and hugs me tightly, holding me close longer than usual. The stubble on his cheek grazes against my soft skin, tickling me like it always does. I breathe in the smell of him, trying to commit every inch of him to memory, his dark brown curly hair as soft as it has always been.

"Come back to me in one piece, big brother," I whisper, tears that I refuse to let fall stinging the corners of my eyes.

William loosens his grip and releases me. "I promise. Look out towards the road where the forest meets the sky and you will see me riding back home." He takes a small step down.

All I can do is nod. I feel like this every time he has to leave me here, all alone, with only my aunt and uncle to talk to, no friends.

"I love you, Katherine."

"I love you too." My voice cracks. We smile at each other for only a brief second before he disappears into the blackness of the spiralling stairs.

I rush to my bedchamber window and rub the morning's frost away from the glass with the edge of the blanket still cocooning me. As I force the window open, the frame pops slightly, breaking away from the night's icy grip. I look down into the courtyard. William is with Sir Francis Grey and his men, riding out towards the rising sun. My breath freezes as it hits the early morning air, as if time itself is stopping it from leaving my lungs. The portcullis rises and then falls along with the sound of horses' hooves clattering away into the distance until all is quiet and the air is still.

The castle sounds so different now that William is no longer here. It is as if a change has overcome the whole county, a change that makes me shudder when my mind wanders to the coast of England and across the deep dark sea. There is no use in sleeping; instead, I get dressed and pass my day walking through each room and corridor of Leicester Castle. I run my fingers across its cold damp stone, feeling every dent and ridge as I glide aimlessly from the north to the south wing, lifting my eyes towards the horizon, expecting my brother to appear.

Descending the battle-worn stairs, I walk into my mother's rose garden. I had visited this place so many times before, smelt all the sweet scents that each rose possessed, felt each thorn that tried to catch at my pale skin. I stop at the centre of the rose's maze and gaze upon the blunt stems that hide from the winter's icy breath.

William, my father and I planted these in memory of my mother's passing. I chose the red rose, William the white and my father the deep purple. I caress the blunt stems with my frozen fingers as if by doing so they will bloom into beautiful roses once more, but they do not. A sound of rustling leaves wakes me from my winter daydream, and from behind the dark bush, Thomas Moore, our head gardener, pushes his wheelbarrow filled with all of the tools he needs to keep this beautiful garden alive. He is too busy to notice me at first, concentrating on a rogue tuft of grass that refuses to stay within its boundary, but when I attempt to move away unseen, he looks up in slight panic.

"My lady!" He quickly drops his scissors into the

wheelbarrow with a clatter. "I am sorry I didn't see you there!"

I smile warmly at him, as much as I can in the bitter cold.

He leans onto the tall brush in his hand. "It is very cold, my lady. You should be inside where it is warm." He smiles.

"I will, thank you, Thomas." I nod and turn to leave my mother's garden, heading for the warmth of the castle's fires. As I trace my fingers across the stems, a sharp sting forces me to look down at my hands. A rogue thorn sticks through my leather glove, clinging onto me. Something troublesome crosses my mind as I remove the stubborn thorn from my hand. Blood begins to trickle down my fingers and splashes onto the icy grass below.

***

A letter arrives for me just over a week after William's departure.

My Dearest Sister, Katherine,

I have arrived in Brittany as promised. I apologise for not being able to write any sooner. The sea was against us and tried to shatter our ships and drown our men with every wave that hit. King Edward's youngest brother, Richard, made the crossing one day earlier; it is a comfort to have him amongst us. Do not worry, little sister, I will be back home tormenting you soon! Sir Francis sends his regards and promises to look after me.

Your loving brother,
William

I read this letter over and over again, hearing his voice echo in my mind with every word. Once finished, I fold it neatly and lock it into my small wooden box that William gave me a few Christmases ago.

"He is safe," I mutter to myself.

As I walk into the library, I am greeted by my aunt. Sitting in the chair closest to the fire in all her old finery, her hair scraped back in a tight bun underneath a pretty little hair net, she studies me with a deep frown, which is something I have got used to. "I have received a letter from your brother. He is well and will return soon." She throws the letter onto the empty chair beside her.

"Thank you, Aunt. Is there anything I can help you with today?" I fold my hands behind my back and purse my lips.

Since William left for France along with Sir Francis, there is no one else to talk to. I have no friends here; I never have; it was always just me and William. Sir Francis Grey has been a loyal family friend all our lives, but he normally does not stay long in Leicester.

Aunt Golding lifts her head. "No, thank you, Katherine. Maybe you could help your uncle with running the estate."

"Is there any need? William is the Earl of Leicester now, and I am just his sister…"

"Never undersell yourself, Katherine. You need to be able to show all of your greatest assets if you are to marry one day, but not too well… men hate a clever wife."

"But William will be running the estate whilst I get carted off to whomever it is I am to be married off to." I sigh, looking out of the window at a little bird flying in the sky above.

"The time will come when your brother needs you, as he is yet not married, only betrothed. The running of this castle falls to you when he is away from home, just like I have taught you."

I let out a groan of annoyance, which regularly occurs when my aunt talks of marriage, something that I do not wish to be a part of just yet.

"Lady Warrington is a beautiful young lady. It would suffice if you showed the same care and attention to your appearance, Katherine."

I roll my eyes but face away from my aunt so that she cannot see.

"How is it that I've never met her?"

"Have you not?" she questions, raising one eyebrow. "Hmm... I'm sure you will meet her in time. Lord Warrington and your father arranged the match long before your uncle and I ever came to live with you."

Silence fills the room again, until my aunt looks up at me, catching me yearning for the outdoors as I gaze out of the window. "Well, why don't you go and practise? I see that you left the target outside again in the wet weather! It won't do you leaving everything lying around, Katherine. We don't have enough money to keep replacing those things." She shakes her head, adding, "Once you are married you won't have time for all of that, so enjoy it whilst you can." She lowers her gaze towards her embroidery again – the signal for me to leave her in peace.

I remember the first weeks of my aunt's arrival: she loved to order me about and keep me locked up in the North Tower where she held my lessons. I never wanted to be sent away from home to learn, so my aunt agreed to teach me here. She kept telling me that, when I marry, my husband will expect me to be highly accomplished. I always argued that an accomplished woman is not one who can recite pretty poetry, but one who is strong and hold her own against those who wish to do her harm! That never went down well. Her lips would always tighten when an important guest would visit, her eyes narrowing down at me whenever it was my turn to speak. My experience with prestige and noble guests is limited. My father protected me and William from the prying eyes of court, something that I secretly thank him for. I don't think someone like me would ever fit in at court, anyway. William ran in the mud, climbed trees, shot arrows, played with swords… so I wanted to do the same.

When William gave me the bow I use now, I started to practise more and more, neglecting my lessons and Latin words. My aunt wasn't so sure to begin with, as it is frowned upon for a lady to practise with such things, but when my uncle and brother saw how good I was with it, they persuaded my aunt to let me keep practising – something I intend to carry on. She comes across as a harsh woman, but she is the only mother figure I know and I cannot help but love her.

I take my aunt's advice and bring myself to the west of the castle. I begin shooting my arrows at the round target that I neglected from my last practice. The sun rises above the walls, warming my skin against the new year's fading winter weather. I pull back my bow and release, watching it slice the cold air and sink into the target at the end of the range. Mr Sutton, our gamekeeper, plucks the arrows from the target and hands them back to me.

"Move the target further down the range, Mr Sutton," I command.

He lifts the heavy circle back a few yards.

I check the quiver on my back by running my fingers over the tips, counting the remaining arrows I have left: two. I plant my feet in line with the target, lift my bow just above it, pull back as much as I can (careful not to scrape my cheek), aim and release. The arrow flies through the air, curving then landing in the outer blue ring. I want nothing more than perfect, so I eagerly load the next arrow. I must concentrate every time I aim at the target, oblivious to the world around me. A strand of hair tickles my cheek, forcing my aim off the centre of the target.

"Mr Sutton, please pass me another arrow." I place my palm outwards but nothing appears. "Mr Sutton?"

Confused, I look up. My eyes are drawn towards his hands as he drops the arrows to the ground with an eerie clatter, his lips parted and his eyes drawn to something behind me.

I turn with caution. "My lady." Sir Francis bows and raises his head. His voice is quiet; his gaze does not meet mine. Various scars, old and new, stretch across his face, his hair even more grey than before. I look down as he holds out a letter and a gold ring. I frown in confusion. If Sir Francis is home, then so must be my brother!

"Sir Francis… what is this? Is my brother with you?" I look around for William to jump out and surprise me, but there is no sign of him. Instead, my eyes land on two men either side of Sir Francis, David Johnson and Christopher Giles, two of our most trusted men who help guard this castle and the people within. They avoid my eyes, faces drawn into a deep expression.

"Katherine…" Sir Francis swallows and motions his eyes towards the letter in my hand.

I gaze down at the ring: it is William's ring. The one he always wears, the one with the seal of our family crest embossed into the top of it. It does not match the design in the seal on the letter. "Why have you given me my brother's ring, Sir Francis? He will be needing it." I try to ignore the stillness in the air and the heavy beating of my heart as I look down at the parchment again, which has been sealed with a red-wax blob. "King Edward's seal?" I choke, ignoring all of the alarm bells in my head.

Sir Francis nods. "Yes, my lady." The lump in his throat is evident.

Deep inside, I know what is coming, but I am battling against the voice in my mind. I quickly open the letter.

Lady Turner,

I regret to inform you that your brother, the Earl of Leicester, has been killed. I am sorry for your loss. He was a great knight and a loyal friend to the crown and country…

I drop the letter along with my bow, which clatters on the ground, time stopping altogether. I think I will fall too, but Sir Francis leaps forward and holds my arms, Johnson just behind him. A tear falls down his cheek. His lips move, but I hear nothing. My heart beats against my chest, my ears ringing with the words that burnt my eyes as I read them. I lift my head and his words become clearer to me.

I open my mouth to scream, but I am silent.

Eventually, I stand and shake his hands off me, anger taking hold of everything inside. I look around at Johnson, Giles, Sir Francis and then up at the castle, which now overshadows the ground I stand on. "It is not true," I whisper. Disbelief swells in my chest. "It is not true!" I shout, clenching the ring in my hand. Looking up, I ask, "It is not true?" Tears sting my eyes.

"I am so very sorry… I… I am afraid to tell you that… it is. William is dead." A single tear rolls down Sir Francis's cheek and then another.

William is dead. He is too young to die, and I need him. I will not be left alone again. "How?" I manage to gather my strength and repeat, "How? We are supposed to be at peace with France!" My voice shakes with anger as I clench my hands into fists at my side.

Sir Francis looks at the ground and then into my eyes. "We should go inside, my lady."

My eyes search his face for answers. The last time I saw him he looked ten years younger, but now his face shows the fatigue of battle and the loss of those dear to him. I do not know what to feel. Angry. Hurt. Tired. Then I remember my brother's promise to me.

"He promised that he would come back. He promised!" I take a step closer, but Sir Francis cannot look me in the eye. "He promised!" I look away. Tears start to fall down my cheeks, then something changes in me. "You promised to keep watch over him!" I hit him on the chest with my fist, William's ring held tightly in my grasp. "You promised to keep him safe!" I hit him harder. "You said that you would always come back to me with

William…" I hit him so hard that I hurt my hand and he stumbles backwards.

I sink to my knees. I cry and scream. I unclench my fist and find that the ring has left a pattern in my palm. Why is the ring here, but not William?

The walk back inside the castle is the longest I have ever had to take in my life. As I make my way into the Great Hall, I am vaguely aware of the people lining up as I walk by, but all I can do is focus on putting one foot in front of the other. I somehow find myself at the front of the room. My head is heavy as I lift my gaze, my vision finally focussing on those who are gathered before me. I squeeze the ring in my cold, pale hands. I guess it is up to me now to stand out of my brother's shadow and start from where he left off.

I am the sole heir. I am the Countess of Leicester.

Two

A faint knock on the door of the Council Chamber interrupts my thoughts.

I clear my throat. "Enter."

Sir Francis pushes the door ajar and greets me with a thin smile. "My lady, I thought I would check in on you, make sure you are well… considering." He fumbles at his words.

"I am well, thank you. I am adjusting to everything, making sure I have everything as William would have." I lower my eyes to the desk in front of me, a neat pile of papers stacked to one side, papers he never had an opportunity to read.

Sir Francis takes a seat on the other side of the desk. "It was a beautiful funeral, my lady. Saint Martin's is a wonderful resting place beside your parents, such a peaceful place for such an incredible man. He will be missed dearly."

I nod in reply.

My brother's body was brought back from France. Part

of me wanted to see him for one final time, to look upon his face to make sure that he is finally at peace. I didn't. I couldn't. I wanted to remember William when he was alive, his smile, the way his eyes sparkled in the afternoon sun, the way the room lit up at the sound of his laughter. All gone.

Sir Francis opens his mouth as if to speak, but only closes it again, his brow furrowed in deep thought. After gazing around the room, his hands fidgeting on the chair's armrests, he says, "I am so glad King Edward and his youngest brother, Richard Duke of Gloucester, made a special visit. I saw that you thanked the king for his kindness and for all that he has shown your family. I know that could not have been easy for you, my lady, after… well. I can understand how you, deep down, blame him for what led to your brother's death."

"The king should have fought his own battles," I reply, regretting the slight hatred in my voice straight away. "I apologise, Sir Francis. I just never thought myself to be in this position. This chair in which I now sit was never meant for me."

He sighs, his shoulders relaxing as he edges closer towards the desk. "You are the last in your family's line, my lady, and as there are no male heirs, it is you who inherits the title of Countess of Leicester. Unfortunately, or fortunately as some might see it, that is attached with responsibilities, lands and wealth."

I squeeze my eyes shut for a brief moment as I try not to allow Sir Francis's words engulf me. Ever since I was given my brother's ring, I have known what it symbolises, what I am expected to continue now he is gone. It is unusual as, ordinarily, a woman like me would only inherit if I was married, then my husband would take everything and I would fade into his shadow. King Edward has granted everything to me instead of hunting for a long-lost male relative. To say I was unprepared is an understatement. I had just lost the most precious and dearest person to me in the whole kingdom, and now I am forced to take his place as if he was never here. Will those at court accept me? Listen to what I have to say?

Why did you have to leave me, Brother?

I am not allowed to simply shut myself away, pace the well-worn floor, wipe away tears that sting my eyes. One comfort I do have is the fact that the Leicester estate was once a gift to my mother upon her marriage to my father, one of the first women in all of written English history to be given the same powers as her male noble equals. It caused quite the stir once this news had danced upon the lips of all the king's gossiping nobles. Just like my mother, I will continue the family's legacy, no matter how daunting it is. In the past, I would have shied away from such attention, happy that my brother was there to shield me, but there is nowhere to hide now. I know that I am not alone; I have my aunt, my uncle and Sir Francis to guide me, but I long for a close friend now that William is gone.

I open my eyes and shake my head gently. I am glad Sir Francis has happened upon me this morning, as now the bleak coldness begins to melt away, I have a proposition for him.

"Sir Francis, I know that your niece, my brother's betrothed, lost her father the same day I lost William." At the funeral I remember seeing a tall, slim blonde lady, only a couple of years older than me, silently weeping. "Lady Warrington is currently under your guardianship and care. I know that William would have liked to see the two of us become friends. So… I wondered if Lady Warrington would like to stay here, with me? I feel it is my duty to look after her as my brother would have wished me to do so."

Sir Francis, with a small smile upon his face, nods his head in agreement. "That is a spectacular and generous offer, my lady. Would you like me to inform Isabelle on your behalf?"

"No," I reply lifting my head a little higher, a thin smile on my lips. "I will do so myself."

***

"I can't believe they made me feel so small," I mutter to myself as I make my way to my bedchamber. "I may as well have sent my uncle in my place! No, no, I am Countess now, I will carry out my duty as my brother would have."

I have not long been home from my attendance at Westminster Palace, and the whole journey back all I could think about was the faces of the men there, and how they rolled their eyes and whispered to each other as I spoke. King Edward gave me his blessing to discuss funding for a well-needed women's hospital in Leicester, but without the backing of his councillors, there was not much he could do. When I was met with a wall of scoffs and tuts, I almost shrank back into my own shadow. It was only when the king added his support did everyone else suddenly agree that it was a good idea too.

This will get easier, won't it?

"If I had stood up straighter, spoken more loudly, more clearly, would they have..." My ramblings are interrupted by hushed tones slipping through the crack in Isabelle's bedchamber door, left slightly ajar.

"It wasn't her fault."

"Lady Warrington, please do not lie to me."

I pause just outside the door.

"I wouldn't lie to you, my lady. You, your husband and the Countess have been nothing but kind to me, allowing me to live here in this beautiful castle; why would I be anything but truthful?" Isabelle says.

"Now I know you're lying," my aunt scoffs.

I lean in towards the door so that I can overhear the rest of their conversation.

"I wouldn't lie to you. It was the Earl who overstepped his mark."

"A man with such good breeding and family would never do such a thing," my aunt states.

"An Earl is perfectly capable of acting like an ass, as much as any other man, title or no title."

I try my best not to laugh at her accurate observation.

"I hardly think—" my aunt begins.

"If I hadn't stumbled upon them, I dread to think what would have happened. You should not have left him alone with her!"

"Oh, yes, it's my fault. Katherine isn't the issue here." My aunt sounds exasperated.

"Correct."

"Do you really think that I would not have known if the Earl was untrustworthy? I am a good judge of character."

I muffle an amused laugh behind my hand, hoping that they don't hear me.

"I know a bad egg when I see one."

"Clearly not!" Isabelle raises her voice, something that I haven't heard her do before.

I lean in a little closer.

"The Earl of Rotherham is nothing more than a scoundrel and a liar. He thinks that because of his status, wealth and power, he can bully women into doing whatever he wants. Well, he was wrong the moment that thought crept into his disgusting pea-sized mind."

Of course, the Earl of Rotherham. Only a few weeks ago was he very keen to get me alone. I tried my best to avoid such a situation, but my aunt's insistence on seeing me betrothed to the next man through the castle gates is making it more difficult to avoid the barrage of possible suitors.

"Lady—"

"I haven't finished." She stomps her foot, silencing my aunt, something not many people have dared to do before. "I thank God that Katherine is not as stupid as he thought she is. If she hadn't pushed him into the lake, I dread to think what he would have done to her. The way he spoke to her like she was a plaything or a piece of meat you can buy at a market. He is disgusting. How Katherine remained calm, I don't know."

"Calm? She was hardly calm, Isabelle! The poor man was soaked to the bone! She knows how this will look to those outside of these four walls. Her reputation is at stake. Katherine knows that she cannot go around and do whatever she likes!" My aunt's voice increases in volume.

"You mean protect herself? He bruised her arm, that is how forceful he was."

I hold my breath, placing my hand over the bruise hidden underneath my sleeve.

"Katherine doesn't need a man to take all of this away from her. It's time you started to give her the credit she deserves. She is your own niece! You are the only mother figure she has. Your husband knows she is perfectly able to step out of her brother's shadow; why can't you?"

"You forget your place. What do you know of our family history? She's too young, too stubborn. She needs to be married off as soon as possible. A woman is only seen as powerful if she has a husband beside her. That or we send her to a nunnery."

Isabelle lowers her voice, a hint of pity behind her words. "Why is it that when a woman comes across as strong, beautiful and confident, other women are less eager to support her and would rather throw her to the wolves? We need to support one another if we are to survive in a man's world. I thought you of all people would understand."

Isabelle's footsteps fade away as she exits through the door on the opposite side of the room, which leads to another staircase. I have not heard her speak so passionately before.

I silently leave my post, a small smile creeping across my face, remembering how I felt when Isabelle first arrived only a few months ago. I was so nervous, worrying about whether we would get along, almost convincing myself that I would not have time for friends. She was very quiet. I thought perhaps it was because she was still in mourning, as she had lost both her father and her betrothed in one day. However, she has been the only one I can truly confide in. She is kind, loving, beautiful, and one whom I can call my sister. It is truly remarkable how grief can tear people apart, but also bring them together, a shining star in the deep dark sky.

Three

Several years later…

I gaze wearily out of my bedchamber window into the sunlit courtyard below. The cockerel has only just sounded his morning greetings as the servants run around preparing for Sir Francis's arrival. I have not seen him in a little over two months, the last being when we were looking over new plans for repairs to the old Roman walls that hug the town just over the other side of the River Soar. I make my way to the Great Hall, my stomach rumbling at the prospect of a hearty breakfast.

"Good morning!" It is not too long after I have sat down that Sir Francis strides into the Great Hall where I, Isabelle, my aunt and uncle are quietly eating breakfast. He bows his head to everyone and smiles broadly at me. "Lady Turner, how beautiful you look today." He bows once more as I smile back at him being his usual charming self.

"Thank you, Sir Francis, but I do not look half as

beautiful as your niece." I incline my head towards Isabelle, who sits there shaking her head in amusement. "To what pleasure do we owe your company?"

"Do I have to have a reason to visit my favourite family?" He gestures to all of us, including my aunt, who just sits there with an expressionless smile on her tired face. "I wish to speak to my niece if you can spare her?"

Isabelle lifts her head, looks at me then her uncle.

Sir Francis presses, "I have a promising adventure for you, my dear, as I am sure you are excited to hear."

Straight away there's a slight panic in Isabelle's eyes, but no one else seems to notice.

"If you wish, Uncle." Isabelle keeps her voice steady and follows Sir Francis out of the room.

The remainder of us sit in silence. Outside in the courtyard, the clattering of hooves and muffled voices sound as various people arrive through our castle gates.

I sip from the goblet in front of me and start to play with my empty plate until my aunt looks at me with narrowed eyes, summoning one of the servant girls to take it away. I sigh and fiddle with the long sleeves of my gown instead, picking at a loose thread; I am not one for sitting still for too long. I hope that Isabelle is alright. I am not certain, but the last time Sir Francis visited he mentioned that he was in talks with a few suitors for his niece. After speaking to Isabelle about it, she confirmed that he had spoken to her in regard to the prospect of marriage, something she remains tight-lipped about.

I walk around the grand table and start to wander about the echoing room. The room is decorated with white and red banners, the colours of Leicester and my family.

The Leicester crest sits high above the grand fireplace, in which no fire has been lit as the summer heat has arrived early. The tall windows at the end of the room welcome a beautiful array of light.

I remember when William and I used to sneak in here after lights out and he would tell me spooky tales of ghosts and goblins that haunt this old place. Even though he was tired after attending meeting, after meeting, after meeting, with local lords and landowners, he would always have time for me. I never truly understood why he poured so much of his time into the county and its people, but of course, now I do.

"Katherine, would you sit down, you're giving me a headache." My aunt scowls, her sighs loud enough for the whole castle to hear her. "If you're concerned about Isabelle, I wager it will be a very strong match. She is well educated, talented, beautiful and gracious, as well as coming from a fine family..." She grins, adding, "All the things you should be displaying more openly, truth be told."

"I have been too busy, Aunt, with pleasing King Richard. I have to support him where I can. I do not want to be seen as going against him. He replaced the majority of those who helped rule the south whilst his brother was on the throne; I do not want that to happen to me." I sigh, trying to push down any anxious thoughts about the slight unease our new king has brought about since his coronation.

I have only been to court a few times since William passed and, every time, I felt like a child lost at sea amongst all the colour and experience of those who held similar titles to me. I was the only woman there who dared to speak out amongst her male peers. Although, the amount of disapproving looks I received only spurned me on further to make my voice heard.

Aunt Golding rests her hands on the table and looks up at me, her brow furrowed. "Katherine, you have inherited this grand estate. You need to find a husband soon or—"

"Yes, I know!" I snap.

She stands up, slamming her hands on the table. "This country is not at peace, not since the death of King Edward and his brother's sudden taking of the crown. You will need the support of a wealthy and powerful husband if another civil war breaks out." She lifts her hands, looking around with a deep frown at the castle, which has been my home for over twenty years. "You must be wed soon. You want power and true status? Women only receive that through marriage," she says, folding her arms.

"Do I get a say in this matter? I want to marry someone who is my equal, someone who loves me and whom I love."

My aunt scoffs.

"These lands will not be managed by whoever pays the largest amount. No matter whom I marry, everything will still be in my name and under my power. I will not be duped or made a fool of. I am experienced enough to spot a thief or liar."

"You do not know men, Katherine. You might think you do, but I am not talking about those who seek you out for a business deal. Men with evil ambition will do whatever they can to take what they want from you. They have their ways…"

The door to the Great Hall swings open and in strides Sir Francis with a pale-looking Isabelle closely behind.

I run up to her and take her arm. I scan her face with concern. "Isabelle, what is it? Is everything alright?" I guide her to her seat and sit beside her, brushing all other thoughts out of my mind.

"Lady Katherine. What do you think to the proposal?" Sir Francis asks.

I gaze up at him, having no idea what to say in reply.

His bushy eyebrows turn downwards at me. "About the betrothal for our beautiful Isabelle?" he asks again.

I don't not know what to say. To whom? When? How? Where? Why? All of these questions swirl around in my head. "I…" My mind freezes.

"She's very happy, of course," my aunt steps in. "But she is speechless on account of thinking of her own marriage prospects, which will take place before long, I am sure."

I ignore my aunt and turn all my attention to Isabelle; she is fiddling with her fingers in her lap, eyes puffy from crying. I take hold of her hands and smile, squeezing them. She gazes up at me and returns a sad grin.

Isabelle looks towards her uncle and swallows whatever upset is in her heart. "Uncle, I thank you and I look forward to seeing him soon."

Sir Francis strides up to his niece and takes hold of her hands, ripping them from mine. "Excellent, I am happy to hear you say so. Sadly, I must leave you all. I am sorry that my visit is so short, but I have an important letter to reply to. I shall return soon for dinner." He bids farewell and leaves the room as quickly as he entered it.

Isabelle turns to me. "Shall we go for a walk?"

I nod, eager to find out who the lucky man is.

As we step out into the late spring air, I link my arm through Isabelle's. "Who has your uncle promised you to? How about Sir Daniel Harrow, so you can be his fifth wife? Maybe… Lord Martin Visor, who looks like he should have died twenty years ago? Oh! How about Sir Robert Carlisle, the dashing gentleman with little hair and even less brain?" I laugh, trying to lighten the mood.

Isabelle takes a prolonged look behind her as Sir Francis mounts his horse and leaves through the castle's gates. Slowly, she turns to me. "Let's walk further into the grounds."

We turn the corner and walk alongside the North Tower, which leads down a small path, snaking its way amongst the bushes and trees, eventually leading to the wider grassland. The sun is high in the sky and casts long shadows from behind the trees of the deep forest in the distance. Thomas Moore is hard at work with his youngest son, digging over flower beds of freshly planted blooms.

We walk silently side by side; I find it best to let her speak first in order to steady her mind. She gestures to a small, wooden bench that looks out onto the sparkling lake below. Isabelle's eyes glaze over, and when she finally speaks, her voice is unsteady. "I'm scared, Katherine."

I know exactly what she is going to say, but I ask anyway. "What about?"

"I don't even know him. I told my uncle, 'no', but he wasn't having any of it! I've only met him a couple of times." Her voice is slightly panicked. "All I said was hello and goodbye! How am I supposed to form a relationship on that?"

"Who has your uncle promised?" I ask, my voice soft.

Isabelle shuffles in her seat and plays nervously with her fingers again, then pulls at her beautiful green dress. "Sir Henry Percival, soon to be Earl of Wiltshire."

I look at her in amazement. Sir Henry Percival is now one of the richest men in the south of England. Sir Percival's family were richly rewarded with titles, lands and money, nearly three times as much as my parents were when the late King Edward fought against the Earl of Warwick.

"What is there to be worried about? He is one of the wealthiest and most handsome young men in all of the country. I say bravo to your uncle!" I try to sound excited, even though inside I am deflated for my friend at the possibility of a loveless marriage.

Isabelle shakes her head. "I have no choice. I don't love him."

There is that word: love. There is no escaping the fact that marriage and love are two entirely separate things. Without trying to sound like my aunt, I glance at Isabelle. "You may grow to love him. You just need to give it time, that is all. You were betrothed to my brother once, without even having the chance to get to know him that well."

"You're saying to me that I should marry him, even though I do not love him?" she sighs. Isabelle stands up and starts to pace, back and forth. "You have told me so many times, Katherine, that you will settle for nothing less than you deserve: love and equality. How come I am not allowed the same dream? He may not even like me. I've heard that he is *very* close to his mother… I also heard that he loves his clothes more than he would ever love a wife." She slumps back onto the bench with a heavy sigh.

"Isabelle. Do you know how many rumours were circulated about me when my brother died?"

She shakes her head.

"The best one I heard was that I was actually a man who wore women's clothing and that is why I am yet to find a husband. It is also why I am still the head of my house, because of course, a woman in power must actually be a man, as women's minds are too fragile for anything other than smiling and braiding our hair."

"But I'm not like you, Katherine. What if he was told something that is utterly untrue about me and he believes it? Something like that would kill me."

"You are one of the most beautiful girls in England. You *are* a strong woman, Isabelle. You don't take no for an answer, you are kind and always thinking of others. He will be a fool if he does not fall instantly in love with you."

She breathes a heavy sigh. "There is no other way now: my uncle has made a deal with him and his mother and I have agreed to it all. Besides, I have no choice. I cannot be a burden on you until I die. If my uncle passes and I am still unwed, I will be left destitute. We are to be officially betrothed in the coming months. I shall be married by the end of the summer. Is it all happening too fast?"

I place my hand gently on her arm, trying my best to be reassuring, unsure as to what else I can do. "You are lucky that your uncle has chosen someone suitable for you. I have heard that Sir Henry Percival is a good man, he is kind-hearted. I am sure you two will be happy. It will take time… that is all."

The clouds begin to close in on the sun's rays, and the wind chills my skin. "We had best go in."

Isabelle takes my arm and guides me back towards the path that leads to the courtyard. Once we arrive inside the comfort of the solid stone walls, we are greeted by my aunt.

"Katherine, Isabelle, where have you been?"

"We went for a walk, Aunt, down by the lake."

"Well, the seamstress is here for your fitting, or had you forgotten?" She places her hands on her hips and sighs.

"I have not forgotten, Aunt. I merely had more important matters to attend to," I reply, not completely a lie.

"You need a new dress for the jousting tournament that your uncle and I are hosting with you! You can't go looking like that." She waves a hand at my pale-blue dress, one of my favourites and one I have had for a long time. "Also, you'll need something to wear for your archery tournament, no?" She raises an eyebrow at me.

I sigh. She has me there.

We have decided to host a few events at Leicester Castle for a celebration and, to be honest, to display my wealth and power. After a trip to Westminster Palace a couple of months ago, I've been able to ascertain a select few nobles I can rely on, and so I have invited them to my jousting tournament. Of course, I know all too well that you cannot fully trust anyone at court, especially those who express an overly keen interest in your land and wealth. Hosting the tournament should, however, be a good way for me to demonstrate my openness to those whom I trust, and also show me if they return the favour.

Silently, I start to walk towards the staircase, but am

stopped in my tracks when my aunt adds, "Moreover, you will need to look your finest tomorrow."

I pause to think back to all of the meetings I have scheduled in, but nothing special comes to mind.

"You will have an important visitor."

"Who?" I ask, laughing as we hardly receive anyone of high status anymore. "I have not been informed of anyone important visiting."

"Lord Henry Tyrell, the Earl of Dornton."

My eyes widen at this name. Earl of Dornton… Lord Tyrell… no, it cannot be. I whirl around and face her, anger filling my veins. "I hope that that is a joke, Aunt. You know that the Tyrells are *not* our allies," I state.

"We don't have enemies anymore, Katherine. We are all at peace now. Lord Tyrell will be visiting us. He is arriving tomorrow morning and you will have the honour of entertaining him."

"Why wasn't *I* consulted on this matter? Did he write to me, the sole owner of this estate?"

"No, in fact he wrote to your uncle. It is him you can thank for this meeting." She smiles triumphantly, knowing that she has finally cornered me into a meeting with someone she believes to be a serious suitor, but I have other plans.

"He should have written to *me*. I am Countess here and it will do him well to remember that." I sneer, already agitated at being ignored by the earl.

"It doesn't matter now, Katherine. Lord Tyrell is arriving tomorrow whether you agree or not."

"Very well, seeing as I cannot turn away a man such as the Earl of Dornton," I reply.

"Oh, on another note, there is someone I would like you to meet," my aunt adds.

"Who now?" I ask, throwing up my arms in defeat. "Another enemy of mine? Perhaps Prince John has come back from the grave to rob me of all my land and taxes, horrified that a woman sits upon the Leicester throne?" I reply.

My aunt just stands there, hands folded against her chest, void of emotion as she purses her lips. "No, Katherine. If you come with me, you will see for yourself. I believe that they will be an excellent addition to the household."

"If it is not a puppy, I will be furious," I mumble to myself.

Isabelle giggles, making her way in the opposite direction towards the Great Hall.

When we arrive in the small parlour room, a young woman greets us. She has pale skin, dark brown hair and dark eyes to match. She is dressed in plain but beautiful clothing, her hands neatly crossed in front of her. I gesture for us all to sit, as I try to hide my confusion as to who this lady is. Silence fills the air, something that makes me feel uncomfortable, but just as I open my mouth to speak, my aunt leans forward.

"Katherine, I would like you to meet Lady Bess Hargreaves, the late Duke Hargreaves'... *other* child."

"*Other?* I thought he only had a son? The new Duke Hargreaves?"

"Yes, well, Lady Hargreaves was an... *extra*... late addition to the family," my aunt replies as she avoids eye contact with either of us.

It suddenly dawns on me what she is implying.

"Indeed, it is true, my lady. I am my father's bastard child," Lady Hargreaves announces – not proudly, but matter-of-factly.

My aunt inhales sharply at the word, but I find it quite refreshing to hear the truth spoken so plainly.

"Hmmm. Katherine, I thought this would be a good opportunity for you to take Lady Hargreaves under your wing, so to speak. In exchange, she will be given accommodation, education in the running of a grand estate and a true purpose in life."

"I had a purpose when I was living with my father!" the young woman barks, taking me by surprise.

"I suggest that you don't speak to me or anyone else like that around here, do you understand?" I state, amazed at the anger contained inside this innocent-looking woman in front of me.

"Yes, Countess." She takes a deep breath.

"I may be quite relaxed when it comes to those who serve under me, but I am a Countess and head of this house, so you will speak to me and my family with respect."

"Yes, my lady, I apologise." Lady Hargreaves sinks into the chair, gazing down upon the floor. "My father mentioned on several occasions how marvellous Leicester is – not that I had heard of it myself – but when I heard that a woman was in charge instead of a man, an unmarried woman especially, I agreed to come. It was also my late father's wish that my lady finds a suitable match for me."

"A match?" I ask in surprise.

"Ah, yes, your brother mentioned that to me, and I am sure that we can find the perfect man for you. Title or no…" Aunt Golding adds, leaning further back into her chair.

"Of course, I am sure we can help with that," I reply, still confused as to why my aunt is keen for me to take her on, especially if she is going to be more trouble than I deserve.

I have never taken a lady into my household before, preferring not to trust anyone outside my close circle of family and friends. I know that a woman in my position should have taken a lady-in-waiting years ago; I suppose it would reflect badly on me if I rejected her now that she is here.

I look over at Lady Hargreaves again, who has a small, impatient frown upon her face. "Very well, I accept." I stand up before that frown increases. "Welcome, Lady Hargreaves. I look forward to getting to know you better."

"Yes, my lady. I have no other choice…" she mumbles, apparently less quietly than she had hoped.

"I understand that it will take some getting used to, but if you earn respect from me and the other members of this household, both nobility and common, then I promise you that I will help find a suitable match, if that is what you truly desire."

"Yes, it is," Lady Hargreaves replies.

"Very well, go and find Elanor who will help show you around and get you started."

Without another word, she turns on her heel and heads down the steps that lead towards the bustling kitchens.

Without missing a beat, my aunt claps her hands together, a huge grin upon her lips. "Now that unpleasantness is out of the way, maybe you could think more upon making yourself presentable for the Earl of Dornton."

"How could I forget, Aunt?" I reply with as little enthusiasm as possible.

Four

The next day, I wake early with the sun as it stretches into my room. Outside, the birds begin to chirp and sing, exchanging greetings with their neighbours. I open my eyes and adjust to the golden glow of the morning.

It is not long until Lady Hargreaves arrives and I sit patiently in front of the mirror, watching her comb my hair. I begin to think about the day ahead. I do not want this meeting today. What will we talk about? I have nothing to say to Lord Tyrell. I could be doing one hundred other things, anything but another lacklustre meeting with a new earl. What does he want anyway? Why has he suddenly taken an interest?

After I am dressed and ready, I push a pile of old letters to the side and take a golden chain from my wooden box, which sits on my bedside table, pausing for a brief moment. My eyes stare at it as if William will walk through the door and reclaim it. Of course, he doesn't. I use the cuff of my sleeve to rub a smear off it; William would hate for me to get it dirty. I fasten the necklace around my neck.

"There. Now I am ready." I smile a smile I don't feel inside.

I make my way down to the Great Hall slowly. Whilst my uncle greets me with a beaming grin, my aunt receives me with a fixed expression. "Ah." She holds out her arms towards me. "Katherine, you look wonderful."

She herds me into a chair at the top of the hall and commands that I eat the bread and preserves that are offered to me by the kitchen maids. The bread sticks in my throat, so dry that all the liquid in the world wouldn't wash it away. The jam only makes it a tiny bit more manageable as the pips are now caught in my teeth. I discreetly use my reflection in the window as a mirror to make sure that my teeth are free from any unwanted food.

I look up as a figure stands in the doorway, my heart beating a little quicker as they come into focus, but then it only slows down again since it is just one of the servants replenishing one of the bread baskets.

I gaze at the empty plate in front of me.

"Lord Tyrell is a well-respected man. Please do not play any of your games today," my aunt says.

Trying my best not to sigh too heavily, I reply, "You have nothing to fear on my part. I cannot speak for the gentleman himself, however."

"Katherine, that is enough. What happened between your family and Lord Tyrell's is in the past. Please leave it there."

I remember once when Lord Tyrell's father, Lord John Tyrell, came to Leicester Castle unannounced. It wasn't the first time this had happened, throwing accusations at my family, shouting and spluttering for the whole castle to overhear; his last final desperate attempt at ruining my family's reputation. I can't remember too much; my brother never spoke to me about it and I can only remember being escorted away by my aunt from all of the commotion as Lord Tyrell ranted like a madman. My brother was never one to worry, or at least show people that he did, but that day something in him changed, and I saw a new vulnerability in him.

"Am I that desperate for allies, Aunt?"

"Lord Tyrell is a wealthy and powerful man. He has long since distanced himself from his father's exploits. Even the king thinks highly of him. Do you really think we would allow for a dishonourable gentleman to enter through your gates?"

I don't reply.

"No, we wouldn't. Please trust our judgement, Katherine."

Someone in the doorway catches my attention and we both look over to it. Lady Hargreaves enters the room, an expressionless smile upon her face. She curtsies. "Lady Katherine, I have been instructed to tell you that the Earl of Dornton has arrived."

I speak as evenly as I can, ignoring the quickening pace of my heart, "Where is he?"

"He is just settling his horse, then he will wait for you in the Council Chamber."

"The Council Chamber?"

"Well, you can't expect him to just sit around waiting outside, Katherine," my uncle jokes.

"Please ask Johnson and Giles to escort him, I don't want him getting lost," I order. "He won't be here for too long, I am sure."

My uncle squeezes my shoulder, before following me and my aunt out of the Great Hall towards the Council Chamber.

I am not usually nervous in these situations; I meet with different lords and noblemen on a daily basis, but this feels different. If only the late king had listened to my father and banished the Tyrells from the country like he had done to others in the past. I wouldn't then have the burden of meeting the remaining son.

My palms begin to sweat. My mouth is dry and my throat burns. We approach the Council Chamber door, which is guarded by two of my men.

My aunt scans them from head to toe, but without allowing her to utter a single word, I state, "They are here at my request, Aunt. One can never be too careful. You taught me that."

With my head held high, I enter the room like I have done on countless occasions. I barely give him a second glance, curtsying politely. As I stand there with my hands clasped in front of me, my aunt and uncle step into the chamber, closing the door behind them.

Seeing as he wrote to my uncle and not myself, I see it as only fitting that my uncle greets him first.

"Lord Tyrell." My uncle takes a small step towards our visitor.

"My Lord Golding. It is a great honour to meet you." Lord Tyrell steps forward and kisses my aunt's hand. "My lady, it is a pleasure."

There is a pause as his gaze lands on me.

"Lady Katherine Turner, the Countess of Leicester, a pleasure."

As my aunt and uncle move to one side, Lord Tyrell steps into focus, and I cannot seem to look away. Though dark, his eyes are surprisingly warm and welcoming. He holds me in his gaze for a few long seconds before I remember to offer my hand; his lips are soft. He is tall, broad-shouldered, with hair as dark as the midnight sky curling loosely around his head. The puffed sleeves of his cream shirt are secured in place by his black tunic, which fades into the darkness of the rest of his outfit. He stands with a surprising, illuminating presence, filling every dark corner of the room. I notice a bandage on his wrist slightly obscured by his sleeve – perhaps from a hunting accident – and a small thin scar that runs across his jawline.

"Lord Tyrell." I clear my throat, remembering where I am and who this man in front of me truly is.

"It is an honour to finally meet you, Lady Turner." He twists and picks up something from the windowsill – a single blood-red rose. "This is for you." He hands it to me.

I breathe in its beautiful scent. "Thank you." I lift my eyes to meet his, smiling.

"A beautiful flower for a beautiful woman."

Twirling the flower in my hand, I caress the sharp thorns that protrude from the stem. "My father once said, when a beautiful flower smells so sweet, sometimes you forget to look out for the thorns." I place the rose on the table in front of me. I feel my aunt bristle beside me.

"I would never assume a great woman such as yourself to be so easily pleased, but I thought I could at least try."

Lord Tyrell's smile catches me off guard, putting me at ease as he holds my gaze steadily.

"I thank you for your visit, my lord," my aunt chimes, seemingly bringing us both back into the room.

He looks only at me as he answers her, and my cheeks heat. "The pleasure is all mine. I have admired this castle greatly since I was a boy."

I exhale through my nose, though luckily it appears to go unnoticed as my aunt asks about his travels. Of *course*, he admires this castle. His father *also* admired this castle – so much so that he marched here with a small band of men and commanded that my father give it up. I was young at the time, but I remember this was when the country was not at ease; power battles raged as ownership of the throne was fought over. I was scared, scared for what war could mean for my family.

"Have you visited Leicester before, my lord?" I interrupt the conversation bubbling around me.

He looks at me, his eyes wide. "Yes, I have, my lady. I knew your brother."

I stare at him. Before I was born and my mother was still alive, the late Earl of Dornton used to visit often, so I was told, but his visits were never about business; he was there as an old friend. I recall my brother informing me that our parents and the late Lord Tyrell were at court together, so I assumed that they must have been old friends, but after what happened when my father died, there must have been more to it than that.

"We used to run around the grounds together, playing pretend swordfights, chasing the chickens in the yard… we had great fun together, William and I. It is a great loss to us all that he is no longer here."

I study him curiously. Either side of me, there is a

slight shift in my aunt and uncle, who know that the mention of my brother can trigger something in me, a fierce protection over his reputation. "I do not remember you at all. Only that—"

"You were just a baby when I last saw you," he interrupts. "My father wanted to keep me away from here, so I lost contact with the old place."

"Our fathers never saw eye to eye." I test to see if what he is saying is true. "My brother had the same opinion."

"Katherine..." my uncle warns.

I ignore him. "Therefore, I doubt what you have said is true."

My bluntness does not make his expression waiver. "I would never forget a beautiful county such as this. Whatever my father did, I can safely say that I had no part in it. Just like you, I was not even alive when our fathers fought over their differences. I am not proud of his past, but that doesn't mean that we have to be enemies." He looks at me with sadness in his eyes. Something in them forces me to lower my gaze.

"I did not mean to offend you," I say. "I just... my father..."

"It is alright, my lady." His eyes soften, alongside my own defences.

Stillness fills the room, and I begin to wonder if all that I have been told about the Tyrell family is true. The man that stands before me is not rude or overconfident, nor full of rage or anger, as was his father. Maybe I misjudged him? Maybe the little our father told us when we were young was born from a misunderstanding, something that William continued to believe and pass on when he was in power? But our father would never have lied to fuel such hatred between our houses for no reason.

My uncle clears his throat. "Are you staying in town, my lord?"

"I have property in Nottingham, so I will be staying there tonight."

"The Earl of Nottingham is a great friend of ours," my aunt adds, never missing an occasion to mention a few of our closest friends. "Such a jovial character."

"Indeed. I don't know anyone who has a bad word to say about him."

"That's probably because you can't get a word in edgeways," my uncle chuckles.

"Ah yes, he certainly knows how to captivate his audience. I have been to his castle up on the hill a few times; beautiful views of the river and surrounding countryside."

"We haven't been to the castle in such a long time, have we, Katherine?" My uncle tries his best to involve me in the conversation.

"Sorry, no, erm, I have been rather busy, Uncle. Anyhow, Nottingham Castle does not compare to mine, does it?" I bumble, pretending that I was listening intently.

"It has been a very long time since I have seen the wonders of Leicester Castle, my lady. Would you be so kind as to show me around perhaps?" Lord Tyrell asks in earnest.

"By all means, Lord Tyrell," I reply, still trying to untangle fact from fiction, my mind in conflict.

"Please. Call me Henry."

All four of us exit the room and head towards the courtyard. My aunt and uncle leave me and Lord Tyrell to explore the grounds on our own. I spy Isabelle at the top of the gatehouse steps, keeping a watchful eye on us both, not forgetting what happened last time a nobleman tried to get me alone.

As we walk, the sun glistens behind the protective walls, casting long, dark shadows across the courtyard. I keep trying to iron out any creases on my new gown. On our way around, Lord Tyrell tells me a little bit about himself: where he grew up, his education, likes, dislikes and of his family home in East Anglia. He asks me a few questions, too, mirroring the information he gave me. I keep my answers short and to the point, trying not to overthink everything. He does not mention his father, not even once.

"Your accent is not what I thought it would be," I muse as we walk about the castle grounds, side by side.

"Ah, yes, I was educated in Winchester, so I'm 'fraid that me accent is no' wha' ye might think it migh' be." He attempts a native East Anglian accent with a grin, failing miserably, to which I cannot help but laugh.

"Please don't do that again!" I chuckle. "You're a long way from home. Do you have any brothers or sisters?" I ask, already knowing the answer.

"No. I do not have any siblings, so it is just me when I am at home. I don't often stay too long because of that. It can get lonely. I have friends and staff of course, but… listen to me, sounding miserable!"

"No, I completely understand," I reply. "Sometimes you can be surrounded by everything you could ever need or want, but without being with those you love, it can feel… empty."

He sighs, as if relieved to have finally found someone who understands his frustrations. "Sometimes it's easier that way, though, having to only look after yourself."

"Then who tends to your tenants and lands?" I ask, curious how someone can manage and maintain a good reputation and wealth without having to oversee everything.

"I have a few trusted men who take care of that for me. Of course, they leave all of the big decisions to me."

"Like what colour the cushions should be and what tunics your guards will wear?" I tease, my laugh catching me off guard.

"Those are very important things to consider, my lady," he chuckles in return.

We head further away from the stone walls and deeper into the gardens. I sneak a glance his way and catch a secret smile on his lips, which makes me blush.

"Have you ventured much outside of your castle walls?" he asks, plucking a leaf from a nearby tree and shredding it between his fingers.

"I only go to court when I have to… I prefer to be here with my aunt and uncle as much as I can. I can't allow for everything to fall onto them. It is my responsibility as Countess to carry on the hard work and dedication my brother and parents achieved in their short lifetimes. And I never had the chance to travel abroad as a child. My mother died when I was born, and my father never took me with him when he left home."

"Do you have many visitors? Your castle is in a great location by the river, on the old Fosse road."

"Sadly, no. We don't," I sigh. "It's just me, my aunt, my uncle and Lady Warrington."

He frowns, and I quickly explain, "She came to stay with me when her father died. She is like a sister to me."

"I'm glad to hear it. As I said, our roles can be very isolating. I hear that our new king has visited a couple of times. It is not often that royalty visits their loyal subjects," Lord Tyrell suggests with wide eyes, an eagerness for my answer behind his voice.

"Yes, he has… though less so than his brother did when my brother was alive."

He steps in front of me, so I can't move further. I am about to protest when he adds, "I am sorry about your father, and your brother. I truly am. I know that I cannot easily mend my father's past actions, but I hope you can see that I am not like him. The sins of the father are not that of the son."

I look at him – really look at him. He is no longer smiling. In fact, his mouth is closed in a thin frown and his eyes are burning. He takes a step closer, this time just a short breath away. "I know that you must think that I am here purely to finish off what my father started, but I can assure you that I am not."

"I never thought that you were," I lie. "So, tell me, what are you doing here? As I have just told you, we don't receive many guests here at Leicester, only ill-suited suitors or those looking for trouble."

"I am on my way back to Nottingham and I longed to see if the rumours were true."

"Rumours?"

"The rumour about how one of the most powerful and beautiful noble ladies in the whole kingdom lives here, left to fight for herself. Ruling on her own without any man to take it all from her."

He is not what I expected at all. Tall, dark and handsome is a description written in the many romance poems that take up space on the top shelves of my dusty library. I expected Lord Tyrell to be arrogant, cruel and selfish. He may be a little cocky and sure of himself, using that heart-stopping smile of his to catch me off guard, but he has surprised me.

His deep voice captures my attention once more as we head back towards the entrance of the castle. "I would like to thank you again for allowing me the time to visit you today. However short it may be."

"You're most welcome. It is always good to meet new people."

"You have my allegiance, my lady, if you wish it."

"Thank you," I reply, captivated by his smooth voice.

"I can see why people are curious. It is a beautiful county, run by a beautiful woman. All I'm saying is that I can see why men from near and far would want to come and see for themselves."

I try not to blush again by changing the subject, not being used to this intense feeling of heat between us. "Have you been informed of the jousting tournament I am hosting?"

"Of course!" he replies. "Even better: I shall be competing."

"A serious contender! I like your courage."

"Who will be representing your house?"

"Sir Francis Grey. My uncle is too old and I don't currently have a horse to call my own…"

"No horse of your own?" he questions, a small frown upon his brow.

“Sadly, my grey mare had to be put down… she was old… my brother purchased her for me…” My voice trails off at the memory of that horrible day when she could no longer stand on her own. I couldn’t watch when my uncle had to close her eyes for the final time. She is buried in the grounds.

“We’ll have to fix that,” he says as we climb the steps to the entrance doors.

“Are you staying for some refreshment?” I ask, surprising myself at not wanting our short time together to end.

“Only if my lady permits me to.”

As we enter through the large oak entrance doors, I spot my uncle and aunt making their way into the Great Hall together. As we follow them to our own seats, my aunt studies me, her eyes questioning, but I just give her a small encouraging smile as Lord Tyrell offers his arm and we enter the hall together. I am informed that Isabelle has retired to her bed with a bad headache, and I find I am disappointed that she won’t be meeting Lord Tyrell. I value her opinion.

The afternoon flies by as we spend it chatting and laughing, and I begin to enjoy his company, as I hope he enjoys mine. He is very easy to talk to and is very attentive to my aunt and uncle, giving them all of his attention when they talk to him. When I show him one of my favourite rooms in the whole castle, my beloved library, his enthusiasm for literature and books is almost infectious. My father was never one for reading; he preferred to collect books because they made our family look wealthier and well-educated; it was William who introduced me to the love of reading.

As I show Lord Tyrell the different tomes that sit heavily on the middle shelf, his arm brushes against mine, sending a small jolt up my arm. I step away from him, caught off guard again and pretend to be interested in something on the opposite side of the room.

"This is, erm, one of my favourites."

"Chaucer? I have to say that your taste is impeccable, my lady."

"Yes, well, I've spent a lot of time in here. It's nice to be able to shut the door on the rest of the world from time to time."

"If you're ever in East Anglia, I would be delighted to show you my library. I have books from all over Europe I am eager for you to see."

"I rarely leave the Midlands these days, but if I ever find myself that way in the future, I will of course take you up on your offer. I find libraries hard to resist for some reason," I muse.

He caresses the spines as he walks slowly across the room. "You don't chain your books to the shelves either, my lady. That is unusual."

"I trust those who reside under my roof. Besides, not everyone has the luxury of being able to read, my lord, and I do not let just anyone in here." I try not to blush as I catch his eye. If I am, he doesn't mention anything about it.

Well into the early evening, we relax by the Great Hall fireplace. Lady Hargreaves loiters at the side of the room, pretending to tidy the table from dinner. Her eyes linger on Lord Tyrell as she makes her way over to me. "Is there anything I can do to help you, my lady? Or your guest perhaps?"

Lord Tyrell glances at her, but I make sure I am the one to reply, "I don't think so, but my guest can answer for himself. Lord Tyrell?"

"No, thank you." He studies her for a short while, a slight frown on his face.

I decide to help him out. "This is Lady Hargreaves, my lady-in-waiting."

"Ah, now I remember, the late Duke Hargreaves' unnatural daughter?"

Her cheeks turn a deep shade of red. "Unfortunately, yes."

"Do not be ashamed of who you are! I am sorry for your loss," he states, leaning closer towards her.

"Thank you, my lord," she breathes.

I clear my throat. "You will retire for the evening with the others after you are finished here." I gesture over to the last few remaining plates and goblets on the table.

She bows her head with a small scowl and makes her way over to the doorway on the other side of the room, collecting the remaining items from the table as she passes. I catch her looking over her shoulder one more time before exiting the room.

As the moon rises in the sky, taking over the night watch from the fading sun, Lord Tyrell sighs and states that he must leave soon if he is to reach Nottingham before the day is over. I slowly escort him to the Entrance Hall, and a servant hands him his riding gloves and hat. When he places his hat on his head, it's at a slight angle, and I can't stop myself reaching out to correct it before I snap my hand back again.

"Thank you, my lady, that is much better." He winks. "I

am glad to have stopped by when I did." He looks up at the old armour, swords and shields that adorn the walls, each with their own tale to tell. "I should have visited sooner. I should have been here when..." he pauses, "... when your brother was still alive. Been there as a friend."

I cast my eyes down, trying to hide my sorrow. I look up at him again. "I just wish that William had told me about the two of you..." I cannot shake off this strange feeling whenever he mentions my brother.

Lord Tyrell takes half a step backwards, no longer able to look at me. "He wouldn't, though, would he?" He shakes his head. The creases in his youthful face crumple slightly.

Before I can stop myself, I place my hand on his arm. "I am sorry, Henry... I didn't mean to upset you."

"It's fine, Kath... my lady. I am the son of your father's enemy, why would William admit to being friends?"

"It wasn't like William to keep things from me, but... when my father died, he took on full responsibility for everything as Earl. I never quite understood how such a title could change a person until he died and passed the favour onto me." I sigh.

"We are constantly judged by our predecessor's faults, are we not?" he muses. "I know that I cannot repair the past, but I can build a better future." Lord Tyrell takes a step closer. "I am sorry to see you still in pain, my lady; that was not my intention of coming here." He takes my cold hand in his and squeezes it, warming me from the outside.

"He promised that he would return..." I whisper, all the painful memories of that final day flashing through my mind, as I watched William leave through the castle gates. If I had been able to stop him, I could have saved him.

"I can protect you." His voice softens, calming and soothing.

I lift my head and check myself, annoyed at being so easily weakened by the memory of my brother. Maybe this is what my aunt warned me against, being able to see through a man's true intentions. He might have been searching for my weakness and I just gave it away so quickly. "I do not need protection, Lord Tyrell. I do not need help from any man." I raise my chin high.

He takes both my hands. "I will not harm you, Katherine."

My eyes drop to the floor; why can I not step away?

"I do not, nor would I ever, wish harm on you. I am here to heal the wounds of the past as much as I am to rectify them."

He leans in and kisses my cheek. At first, I don't know what to do, but as I lean into his touch, I begin to relax my gaze. "So, what are you really doing here?"

His features soften with a flirtatious smile. "I am here to win your heart."

He closes the gap between us and tentatively places his lips on mine. I close my eyes as he pulls me into his arms. My hands gather the loose fabric of his tunic, hungry for him, a desire I didn't know I even had. His hands tighten around my waist as we lose ourselves in one another for only a short moment. My uncle's roaring laughter drifts from the Great Hall, and we pull back from each other, breathless.

With one final smile, he forces himself out into the

fresh cool air. As the portcullis rises, Lord Henry Tyrell takes one last glance over his shoulder and I close the door, fully aware of my roaring heartbeat as his horse's hoofbeats retreat beyond the castle walls.

Five

My hands caress the spine of each leather-bound tome as I meander past one of the shelves in the library. I pause to gaze outside one of the arched windows near the little fireplace at the other end of the room. Lord Tyrell's kiss took up the majority of my night's sleep. He may not be the first man I have ever kissed, but he is definitely the most memorable to date. I can still feel the tingle of his lips, the gentle touch of his hand against my skin, the deepness of his eyes on mine…

"Yellow or green? Katherine?" Isabelle waves her hand in front of my face.

"What?" I look up, only half-registering her words. "I'm sorry… erm… green?"

"Right. How long do I have to wait until you tell me?" Isabelle snickers, crossing her arms across her chest.

It is a few days before the tournament, and Isabelle is helping me prepare the final bits and pieces for the event.

"Tell you what?" I ask, refusing to meet her eye, knowing all too well what she is referring to. I pretend to bury myself in the book I have been holding for the past thirty minutes.

"Well, I'm not talking about... the *differences between new forests and ancient ones*, am I?" She chuckles, trying to read the spine of the book in my hands.

"Why not? It's fascinating!" I joke, closing the book with a snap that sends dust particles swirling through the air. I start to sneeze uncontrollably.

"Bless you," a voice offers from the other side of the room.

"Thank you." I glance up to see the owner of the voice and find, to my surprise, that it is Lord Tyrell.

"My lord!" I nearly drop the book before I compose myself and carefully place it back onto the shelf.

"You should ask your servants to clean more thoroughly."

Out of the corner of my eye, I catch Isabelle smiling, turning her head from me to Lord Tyrell and then back to me again.

I straighten up. "Let me introduce my best friend, Lady Isabelle Warrington."

"My lady, an honour to meet you." He bows his head.

"Likewise, my lord." There is a slightly awkward silence, but luckily Isabelle pushes that aside. "I should go. I have an appointment in town, anyway." She turns to me, her eyes sparkling with glee. "I will finalise everything when I get back." She gestures towards the plan of the jousting arena that has been left scrolled up on the table in front of us.

Lord Tyrell steps out of the way, bowing as she passes. Once she is out of sight, he closes the door and makes his way towards me, taking his time to read a few of the book's spines.

"How many of these have you actually read, my lady?" he asks, stopping at a random title. "*Romans in Leicester*... well that is a given considering the whole town is surrounded by old Roman walls." He moves a few paces down the library, closer to me. "Or how about... *Kings in the Holy Land*? Now that does sound like a page-turner."

"That depends on how well you can read Latin."

"Luckily for me I know more than I care to use. *Latina est lingua morior*."

I cannot help but smile. "That depends on whom you are speaking to." I cautiously make my way over to him. "And to what do I owe the pleasure of your unexpected visit?"

"Nottingham was a delight, but it could not keep me away from you."

I try to deflect with, "I have always found Nottingham a wonderful place of vibrant people and beautiful architecture. The castle is said to have a secret network of underground caves, all interlinking with each other across the city. I even heard that a famous outlaw once hid in those caves not too long ago from the tyrant Prince John."

"Well, maybe next time you should come with me, show me all the sights that I have clearly missed. But for now, I thought I would see how the preparations are coming along for the tournament."

We mirror each other's steps towards opposite ends of the table.

"Ah, a spying mission... I should have guessed. I only get a say on where the tents go and where I want to sit."

"In that case, I will know where to find you, at least. Perhaps we could sit next to each other at the banquet?" Lord Tyrell's finger slowly caresses the parchment between us.

"You have to win in order to have that honour, and I am not so easily bribed these days."

"No?" He grins, as he bites his lower lip.

"No."

He takes my hand. "I couldn't stop thinking about you, Katherine…"

"Henry…" I lean away from him, fighting against my deepest urge to pull him in towards me and carry on from where we left off. Caution from my aunt rings in the back of my mind. She is right, I should always keep my guard up, as much as I might not want to.

"Don't say that you haven't thought about me at least once?" he whispers, kissing my hand softly.

"I…" I want to say yes, but decide against it. "My lord, please…" I try to answer, but words are replaced by blushes and I can't think of anything to say.

He takes a step back. "I apologise, my intention was never to make you feel uncomfortable in your own home. I just wanted to make my feelings for you clear."

"I am not so easily swept off my feet."

"Don't you believe in love at first sight?"

"I wish it was that simple."

"You have the world at your feet, my lady! You will have the pick of any man you desire. You can marry whomever you choose to love."

I take my hand back and step away, otherwise I might crumble under his smouldering gaze. I remind myself that I have to be cautious.

"I am sorry, my lady, I was only teasing." A broken smile forms on his lips. "I have been in your shoes myself, when my father was alive, but now I don't need to worry about that."

"I highly doubt you have had the same struggles as me," I scoff.

"Well, I guess not, Lady Katherine, but being a man does come with its own set of rules," he huffs, raising an eyebrow with amusement.

I keep a steady gaze upon him. "Like having to dress a certain way just to please those around you? Being told what you can and cannot do? Being careful as to who you talk to, smile at, stand next to? What about having to listen to slanderous and derogatory language against your own sex? Laugh it all off because it was all in jest?"

"I'm sorry that you feel that way, but you can't take out all of your frustrations on the nearest man. We're not all the same."

"But—"

"I don't make up the rules. You're right, it is a harsh world out there and I can't even imagine what it might be like for you, trying to prove yourself over and over again. But judging and treating others the way that you have been treated only makes you as bad as they are."

I feel as if I am being lectured by my aunt!

"Maybe they deserve it? Show them what it is like to follow their own rules for once?"

"Why don't you petition to the king for equal rights? As your family is so well connected, I am sure he will listen to you."

"King Richard might listen to me, but the rest of his

court would not. I have sat in a room full of those who are supposed to be my friends in arms, but none of them would ever admit to agreeing with anything *I* have to say."

"I didn't take you for a woman to back down so easily," Lord Tyrell states with certainty.

"I'm not! But without the support of those around you, being a single voice is like swimming against the tide."

When I lift my eyes to meet his after a brief moment of silence, his hand gently touches my left cheek. Desire rises deep within me again, but I resist, afraid of being just another woman who falls for a handsome stranger.

"I would be more than happy to stand with you, my lady, but even I know when I am fighting a losing battle." He kisses my hand, and my breath stops in my throat at the warmth his lips leave on my skin; his touch is all I can think about.

"When I last saw you, I couldn't get you out of my mind. No one has ever captivated me like you have, Katherine. I thought you would reject me outright, just because of my name. Why didn't you?"

"I know what it is like to be judged before you can even utter a word. Everyone just looks at me and instantly assumes that I am incapable of living up to their standards. Maybe I just like to prove everyone wrong," I reply.

"Well, I am glad that you gave me the chance." He kisses my hand once more. "Sadly, I have to go…"

"Won't you stay?" I whisper, my lips close to his ear. I try to fight every warning sign in my body.

He lifts my chin with his hand and traces my jaw.

"Henry…" I can't take the tension much longer.

Ignoring all reason, I crash my lips into his as if a fever runs through me and he's the only cure.

He grabs my waist, drawing me closer, then pushes me against the bookshelf, which creaks against our weight. I melt into his touch as his grip tightens, pushing me further away from any worries and niggling thoughts that I may have had before. It's as if nothing outside this moment matters anymore; it's just me and him.

His lips pull away first. "Katherine…" he sighs.

We part, my body suddenly cold where his body was against mine. Lord Tyrell clears his throat. "As much as I do not want to stop, I am afraid that this was supposed to be a flying visit, so I must take my leave."

My heart drops, though I do not allow it to show in my voice. "I'm sorry to see you go."

"As am I…" He kisses my cheek once more then retreats towards the door, glancing over his shoulder.

I keep my own gaze steady. "I look forward to seeing you again, Henry."

As the door closes, I shake my head, surprised at how easily he can make me lose control of my emotions – something I thought was impossible. My defences have been up for such a long time that I forgot what it felt like to lower them again. It almost feels like I could do anything, go anywhere, without the ties given to me by my birth. Perhaps my aunt is right; perhaps I should start to think seriously about taking a husband soon. If it so happens that love is a factor in my decision as to whom, then perhaps my wish will be granted too.

Six

The day of the joust has arrived and I can barely contain my excitement as I am helped to get dressed by Lady Hargreaves. My feet hurry down the stairs for a quick breakfast. The smell of cooked meats and freshly baked bread hits me as I enter the Great Hall. I don't waste time in eating everything on my plate and wait impatiently for my aunt and uncle to arrive. When they finally join me, they look at me with wide eyes. My aunt's mouth opens slightly – I suppose I am never usually awake so early, let alone already finished eating.

"Good morning, Katherine," they both chime in sync, eyebrows raised.

"Good morning, Uncle… Aunt…" I kiss them both on the cheek before heading out to the grounds.

With a spring in my step, I meet Isabelle outside, who is cautiously overseeing the remaining sections of the jousting arena. Mr Sutton, our gamekeeper, is checking over everything one last time. Two of my men, Johnson and Taylor, are also there, providing the muscle we need to be finished on time. Isabelle waves me over with a huge smile on her face and spring in her feet, as the last nail is securely hit into the post.

"Some of the contestants are getting ready in the tents," Isabelle informs me.

I shoot a look over my shoulder at the tents in the near distance; different colours light up the space around us, rich greens, vibrant yellows, dark blacks and midnight blues. The tiny little flags at the top of each tent wave merrily in the light breeze. There's a buzz of excitement in the air already.

"I should make the rounds and welcome everyone, Isabelle. I will be back soon!"

Isabelle waves goodbye for now, shielding her eyes against the rising sun, whilst the three men test the durability of the dividing fence by shaking it dramatically. As I walk towards the tents, I tell my heart to calm itself when it begins to wonder about that one face amongst the competitors today.

As I approach, music is playing, warming up the competitors as well as my own mind for the event that is due to begin shortly. I have missed holding events here at home; my father used to host them on a regular basis, but when he died, my brother didn't want to replace those memories – or that was his excuse. I have missed seeing new faces amongst familiar ones, knights bringing their whole households and families along to watch them compete, squires preparing the horses, children running around amongst them all, food being cooked on an open fire pit, songs being sung by merry spectators. Lord Tyrell was right; it can be isolating being in a high-powered position such as countess, but when you surround yourself with family, friends and laughter, it's not so bad.

The first tent I arrive at is that of the jovial Earl of Nottingham, a close ally and friend since my father fought with him in one of many campaigns abroad. "My lord, it has been too long since I have seen you!" I announce as I enter into his tent.

The Earl smiles broadly and takes both of my hands into his large hand. He hasn't aged a day since I saw him just over one year ago. His red hair and beard frame his round, chubby face. "Lady Turner! It has been too long, my lady, too long!"

"I hope you are feeling confident." I grin. "Sir Francis rides for my family's honour, today."

"Ah, well in that case then, I best make him look good for once," he laughs loudly, a roar coming from deep within his belly. "How are ya feeling with all this excitement? I can see yer father's face now… He'd be so proud of ya."

"I will feel better once this is all over. I hope no one gets hurt."

"Well, did I ever tell ya about the time I fought against the Prince of France?"

Before I can answer yes, he has already started on the rest of the tale. "He was a cocky little prick, ya know, like the French boggers are, he was looking for trouble that day, so me and yer father rounded up a few of our men – Giles was there, he'd tell ya! So, we saw him in the distance on his own and then… oh no, hold on, was he on his own?" He taps his pudgy finger on his lips for a few seconds. "Or was he with that Lord such-and-such? No hold on… he… hmm…"

I stand there for a few minutes whilst he tries to remember the rest of his story.

I have heard this tale more than once, but before he can recall his memory and start all over again, I step towards the exit. "I wish you every luck, my lord. I will see you out there shortly."

"Aye, m'lady!" he shouts as I leave, still muttering to himself about the end of his tale.

My next destination is the tent of the infamously jolly Lord Derby. A large man, whose size reflects his heart and good sense of humour, he is a long-established family friend and ally – I have known him all of my life.

"Ah, the Lady of the House, it is wonderful to see you." He flourishes his hands in a most dramatic style. His squire is squeezing the last bit of armour plating onto Lord Derby's shoulder, tightening the strap as much as it can go.

"Lord Derby, I am very happy to see you again – and competing, too! This will be a joyous occasion." I try not to smile as the poor squire struggles to get the amour in place, sweat beading on his forehead.

"My son is otherwise engaged, I'm afraid, Lady Turner," he sighs.

"How is your son? I haven't seen him since..."

"Your brother's funeral, I know, I am sorry, my lady. He hardly spends time with his own father, let alone anyone else!"

His squire finishes strapping him in, panting and nearly collapsing on the floor.

"You'll have to make do with me instead, my dear."

"I wouldn't want it any other way, my lord." I smile then quickly take my leave before parts of his armour pop off.

As I search around the loud and busy camp, it is hard to get my bearings. When I find Sir Francis outside my red-and-white tent, he is already on his horse chatting to a young man I don't recognise.

"Ah, Lady Katherine! Will I do?" He twists stiffly from side to side, careful not to fall off his horse. His heavy armour clatters, making a bit of a racket, drawing attention from those nearby.

"Very handsome." I smile. "Thank you for representing my house, Sir Francis. I didn't fancy doing it myself."

"You are far more powerful and influential by addressing the crowds than you would be sweating in armour… I'd happily swap with you!" He winks.

"I really could do with letting out some aggression to be honest!" I jest, thinking about a fresh pile of applications that scream for my attention back in the Council Chamber.

"Ha! I have no doubt, my lady!" He leans down and whispers so only I can hear, "Just tell me who I should kill, and I will make it look like an accident…"

I try to contain my laughter. "I'll slip you the list before your first joust." I wink, patting his horse on the neck. "Good luck today… don't let me down!" I point my finger at him before I take my leave, chuckling to myself.

Wandering around the tents for a bit longer, I greet various other nobles as more and more people begin to fill the jousting arena. I make my way over to the one remaining tent that I have been longing to visit this whole time, when Lady Hargreaves bumps into me.

"S-sorry!" she stammers, her cheeks flushed. "I did not see you there, my lady! I was just making my way over to the arena." Lady Hargreaves nods towards the direction of where the tournament will soon start.

"Johnson wanted me to pass on the message that we are all set for the riders to make their way into the arena and that you should make your way to the stands also," she gasps for air. "I can tell your uncle and… anyone else you were looking for if you have not yet had a chance to greet them."

"There is just one more person I need to see and then I shall be there, I promise. Please let my uncle know that I will meet him in the stalls as soon as I can."

"Of course." She nods, peering behind her at the tent I am eager to enter.

"If you could go back inside and see if anyone needs help setting up the banquet or guest rooms…"

She frowns. "I thought I could perhaps stay. I have never seen a joust before; I have heard that it is exciting and that it is a great place to meet possible suitors."

"I promised you that I would help find your future husband, and I intend to keep my promise." I try to hurry her along so that I have time to visit the one last person on my list. "For now, though, I need you to help out the rest of the staff, please. You can attend the banquet this evening." Her shoulders relax and a wide smile etches across her face at this prospect. We part ways without another word.

In the middle of the tents is a striking gold, black and white structure, and as I approach, I can hear a familiar voice inside, one that I have been thinking about all day, even if I do not want to admit it. Just before I make myself known, I am stopped in my tracks by the owner's conversation as it filters through the tent opening.

"Tighter. I can't have my armour falling off, now, can I?!" he demands. "I will have you punished for your laziness..."

Another voice intervenes, "My Lord Tyrell, most of the other competitors are making their way to the arena."

"Have you spotted Lady Turner yet?"

"No, my lord, but I believe her uncle is speaking with Lord Stanford. She can't be far away."

"Stanford... I should have guessed that he would be here... at Lord Golding's invite, no less. I cannot have any more obstacles in my way, do you hear?"

I lean is as much as I dare.

"Yes, Lord Tyrell."

"I care too much about her to have her taken from under my nose. I feel compelled to look after her, fight for her..."

Heat rises in my cheeks and I step into his tent unannounced, against my better judgement.

"Lord Tyrell."

He spins around to face me, a look of surprise – then warmth – in his eyes. "Lady Turner, the hostess herself. It is an honour to be visited by you." Lord Tyrell's voice softens as his gaze lands on mine.

His squire bows and leaves, along with a large well-armoured gentleman. As soon as they have gone, Lord Tyrell strides over to me, cupping my face in his hands, kissing me. "I have missed you. I would have visited you earlier, but it can take a while to prepare for something like this." He stretches out his arms to the side to show all of the intricate layers and pieces of armour.

"I can't stay long. I should find my uncle before everything starts."

"I haven't seen him. He's probably waiting in the arena for you." Lord Tyrell turns to face the mirror again, making sure that everything is in its right place, including his hair.

"I'm sure he probably is," I reply casually, surprised at him lying to me, when he was told not three seconds ago about my uncle's whereabouts. I watch as he smooths his hair away from his face. "I will leave you to get ready for your joust," I announce as evenly as I can.

"I will win this tournament for you. That seat next to you at the banquet will be awfully lonely otherwise."

Silently, I take my leave, passing his squire and the armoured gentleman who step into the tent again before I draw the entrance closed behind me.

I straighten my dress a little as I linger for a few seconds. The thin parting in the tent's entrance allows me to see Lord Tyrell turn away from the mirror and address the armoured man.

"She is breathtaking, Forster. A jewel that I cannot live without. I have already begun to work my charm on the young Countess… I would hate to have to start all over again. She has what I want… what I need… what should have been *mine*…"

My breath freezes in my body. What should have been *his*? Who is he talking about? Surely not…

"I can see why she is protected ferociously by those within her close circle. The Countess herself, though… I must say that she makes my part in all of this a lot easier than I had planned… She thinks that she is the cleverest person alive; once she is mine, that will soon change."

"What?" I breathe involuntarily.

Was everything he told me, everything he did a… lie?

Am I really that pathetic? How could I have let my guard down so easily? I retreat back towards the arena, anger building in my chest. I can still feel his lips on mine, his hands around my waist… I am so stupid! I thought that maybe… Tears begin to sting my eyes, but no tears shall be shed over so small a man as the Earl of Dornton.

"He has no idea what underestimating me can do. He wants me to be his, does he? I will make sure he never lays eyes on me nor any other woman ever again," I promise to myself as I weave in and out of the crowds.

Seven

More and more people are beginning to flood into the stands; a mixture of nobles from around the kingdom, local lower nobilities and townspeople, take their places, ready for the main event. My hands ball into fists at my side, my teeth grind against one another, anger filling all my senses. The sounds of the bustling crowds as they make their way to the arena fade, their bleary figures brushing past me, some even bumping into me, but I do not stop for their apology. I try my best to hold my head high, ignoring the panicked drumming of my own heart. Everything around me begins to blur as hot, angry tears threaten to spill onto my cheeks. I need to have Lord Tyrell removed from my grounds immediately, and without fuss.

At last, the happy, unmistakable laughter of my uncle comes from a midnight-blue-and-white tent near the far side of the grassland. As I reach the entrance of the tent, I take a few seconds to compose myself, breathing more evenly and making sure that my emotions do not betray me.

"Yes, lad, I do remember that moment! The look on your mother's face, well, I thought she was going to throw you out for good!" He laughs.

"Is this something I am better off not knowing?" I question, as a young squire parts the tent's entrance and allows me entry.

"Ah, Katherine! Please allow me to introduce you to Lord James Stanford." My uncle stands aside to reveal a tall, blond-haired man, finely dressed in plain but beautiful armour. His eyes are a piercing blue, which crease slightly at the corner as he smiles. He towers over me as he takes my offered hand in his. I would guess him to be around my brother's age, if he were still alive. A few scars, now faded, highlight the handsome features on his face.

"It is an honour to meet ya, Lady Turner." His accent is remarkably strong; Yorkshire, if I am not mistaken.

"Lord Stanford and I go way back," my uncle explains. "I served with his father many years ago and used to stay with his family before you and your brother invited us to stay at Leicester."

"We 'aven't seen one another for a long time." Lord Stanford glances at me but averts his gaze when my eyes meet his.

"You'll have to tell me of the trouble my uncle used to cause. My aunt mentions it a few times. She is very good at not letting go of the past." She is not the only one.

"That is not necessarily a bad thing, m'lady. Ya can never be too cautious when it comes to choosing those ya want to be yer close friends and allies."

"Yes…" I reply, as I try my best to suppress the stabbing feeling in my chest.

My mind is once more consumed by the haunting coldness that I overheard from Lord Tyrell's tent not five minutes prior.

"M'lady? Lady Turner? Is everything alright?"

"Yes. Sorry, my mind was elsewhere."

I take a quick look around his tent: his squire is busy tidying up something in the corner, and next to him is an old-looking mirror in a gold frame, about six foot in height – it must still struggle to fit all of Lord Stanford's height in at one time. A small table and two simple chairs sit in the middle of the small tent, a few random papers litter the desk, and there is a trunk next to me, beautifully carved with swirls and leaves, an impressive heavy iron lock guarding whatever is inside. But where is my uncle?

Wordlessly, I step outside, hoping to find my uncle waiting for me, Lord Stanford not too far behind me.

"Good luck, my lad!" My uncle slaps him hard on the shoulder, almost knocking him off balance, then begins to walk towards the arena.

"Uncle, can I just—" I begin to ask for a private moment, but he has already left my side.

I try to catch up before I lose him to the heavy crowd around us. Perhaps I can ask for his assistance in ridding my lands of the Earl of Dornton.

"Uncle, I need to speak with you urgently!" I shout, aware of drawing unwanted attention from those around me, but he has already disappeared further into the crowd.

"Lady Turner, do ya need me to escort ya to the arena?" His deep voice startles me a little.

"No, Lord Stanford, I am perfectly capable of walking on my own."

"I'm sure ya are, m'lady. I will look out for ya in the stands," he replies with a grin.

"You and every other man out there apparently."

Without a second glance, I make my way over towards the arena. I just need to round up my men and command that they remove the earl at once. No one is allowed to make me feel like a fool. No one. Time, however, is not on my side and I am pushed further and further towards the stands.

Johnson captures my attention by waving his hand in the air and calling my name. Perfect timing; he will help me remove Lord Tyrell at once and without anyone else knowing. "My lady!" he breathes heavily. "Your uncle and aunt are looking for you. Everyone is waiting for you in the arena."

"Where is Lord Tyrell?" I ask, trying my utmost to keep a level tone.

"He is in the arena already, my lady, along with the other contestants."

No! I am too late. I should have just barged in on Lord Tyrell and confronted him there and then. I was too weak to do so myself, and now I cannot remove him as planned, not without the whole county watching.

"Very well," I sigh, closing my eyes to recentre myself.

The sound of trumpets roar, and riders, on their well-armoured horses, make their way into the jousting arena, applause ringing out, bouncing off the castle walls. It is a good distraction from my heaving chest and clenched jaw.

With encouragement from my uncle and Isabelle, who are seated beside me, I swallow at the small lump that has formed in my throat as I step forward a few paces in front of my seat, pushing everything else aside. "Thank you to my lords, ladies and everyone who has been kind enough to make it here today for Leicester's first jousting tournament of the year. Today, we have the finest knights throughout the kingdom competing against one another."

Lord Tyrell catches my eye, but I look away instantly, anywhere else, and find that my eyes land on Lord Stanford, who sits on his decorated grey horse comfortably, his eyes following me.

"There will be several rounds in which riders compete against one another, knocking out their opponents until only two riders are left. It is between these two lucky gentlemen that the winner will be decided. Knights, take your places. The Earl of Nottingham and Lord Derby are the first to go head to head."

Every inch of the stands is geared up for today's excitement whilst each rider showcases their horse around the arena, nodding their heads in respect towards me, just like they used to when I was a little girl (though of course, it was my father who was the host of the joust). When it is Lord Tyrell's turn, he pauses just in front of me and lowers his voice so that only I can hear. "Lady Katherine, I will honour this tournament by winning it in your name." His voice is just like when we first met, a twinkle behind his eyes and a warm smile on his lips.

It takes every restraint that I have not to either fall for his honey-soaked words or punch him in his perfectly chiselled jaw. Instead, I too lower my voice so that only he can hear me, leaning over the barrier slightly. "Well, let's see if you can remove any more obstacles in the way, shall we?"

He flashes a confused smile.

Behind him, I spy Sir Francis imitate stabbing Lord Tyrell in the back jokingly to which I shake my head, trying hard not to laugh at his attempt to cheer me up, something he never fails to do. I look away from him as my eyes fall onto Lord Stanford, who simply nods his head, muttering, "Lady Turner," before riding off towards the entrance of the arena.

Before the flag falls for the first joust, the tension is tight in the air; the horses grunt with anticipation, scraping their hooves on the ground, ready to canter towards their opponent. Young children stand on the tips of their toes, eager to see their favourites battle it out.

I wince as the Earl of Nottingham strikes Lord Derby's shield with a clear hit, nearly knocking his opponent off his horse. Pockets of the crowd gasp as both lances hit their opponents in the chest, but unfortunately, Lord Derby is the one who loses his balance and falls off his horse with a heavy thud. One win for the Earl of Nottingham.

"Let's be honest, he wasn't going to win being in *that* shape," my aunt scoffs, to which my uncle frowns and Isabelle tries not to laugh.

With a taste of what is yet to come, the crowd begin to bang in rhythm with their fists on the side of the stalls opposite me, drumming up the atmosphere whilst we wait for the next contenders: Sir Michael Eaton and Sir Edward DeLise. As the flag is lowered, Sir Michael's horse loses interest in the charge by trotting off to the other side of the arena, sniffing at an apple a little girl is eating in the crowd. I cannot help but feel embarrassed on his behalf as the crowd roars with laughter. He tries his best to steer his horse back into the competition, but to no avail. One win for Sir Edward by default.

"Well, I didn't expect that!" my uncle laughs.

"Neither did he," my aunt replies, clapping her hands together with a joyous smile upon her face.

I sit up a little taller as Lord Tyrell and Lord John McNally ready their horses on either side of the arena.

My uncle leans towards me. "I have heard Lord McNally's steed is the best in Scotland, Katherine. I hope Lord Tyrell will do well against him."

I only nod in reply as I recall the first time I met Lord McNally – we were both at court. He and his former kitchen maid then mistress had just married, a scandal in any court. Even without that, many do not see him as their equal, even though he owns twice as much land and is three times as wealthy. Being originally from Scotland, they never really gave him a chance from the outset, despite King Richard's recently signed truce with Scotland.

The cheers from the crowd bring me back to the present moment as the flag is lowered and both horses whinny at the sharp kick from their masters. On the final charge, Lord Tyrell raises his lance at the last second, knocking Lord McNally clean off his horse, which bolts for the crowd, securing Lord Tyrell his victory, much to my disappointment.

So much for Scotland's best steed.

This round decides on the last competitor going forth into the next round. Sir Francis Grey, representing my house, is joined by Lord James Stanford, his armour shining in the midday light. All four of us (Isabelle, my aunt, my uncle and myself) sit on the edges of our seats.

Isabelle mutters a small prayer. The flag is raised and both men kick their horses fiercely towards each other at full speed. The Yorkshireman is the first to get a clean hit on Sir Francis, who nearly topples from his opponent's blow, but remains seated.

Lord Stanford takes a hit from Sir Francis, dropping his lance.

"Damn it," he curses under his breath. As he trots his horse to the other end to retrieve it, he lifts up his visor and quickly glances up at me before kicking his horse to the end of the arena, ready for the next charge.

"Come on, Sir Francis!" Isabelle bellows. "You can do this!"

The next charge is over in a blur. Sir Francis topples from his horse and lands with a thud on his back, amour clanking painfully as he does so. I cannot help but groan as my family's chance of becoming jousting champions is snuffed out in an instant.

It is hard not to laugh, however, as I spy Sir Francis flailing his arms and legs in the air like a fat dog stuck on its back, but he is helped by Lord Stanford, who quickly dismounts and heaves him up off the ground.

"Thank you, my lord! Most sporting of you!" Sir Francis pants. He looks towards me and shouts above the cheers of the crowd, "I'm sorry, my lady." He turns to Lord Stanford. "It's up to you now to win for my lady, seeing as you knocked me off!" He tries to laugh, but only winces in pain.

"If the lady will 'ave me to represent 'er, I will do as she wishes."

I find myself studying Lord Stanford for a brief moment, his smile entirely captivating. He catches me watching him and my thoughts are snapped back into reality, my cheeks burning.

I summon them both whilst Mr Sutton and Johnson are repairing the arena ready for the next round. "It seems that you have taken out my rider, Lord Stanford."

He blushes, rubbing the back of his neck.

"My house's honour now relies on you."

"It would be *my* honour, m'lady."

"Do not fill me with false hope, my lord," I reply, trying my best to remain in control of my rapid heartbeat.

Lord Stanford tries to hide a grin as he and Sir Francis make their way to the tented area and out of sight.

After a short break, it is not long until the next rounds commence, starting with the Earl of Nottingham and Lord Tyrell. This is not as easily won as I thought it would be, both riders going through five charges until Lord Tyrell unseats his opponent, who rolls around in the earth as his horse bolts out of the arena.

The next match must be one of the shortest in English jousting history: Lord Stanford and Sir Edward DeLise. As quickly as they mount their horses, it is over. Lord Stanford knocks Sir Edward off his horse, splintering his lance in the process. My cheers must have captured Lord Stanford's attention as he makes his way over to me, collecting his shattered lance off the ground on the way.

I cannot help but lean over the barrier so that he can hear me amongst the roar of the crowd. "I hope you can keep your lance in one piece for the final round, my lord. I am counting on you more than you know."

"Maybe I just wanted an excuse to come and talk to ya." He grins before leading his horse out of the arena.

At last it is time for the finale!

"My lords and ladies, I am pleased to announce our two finalists! From Yorkshire we have Lord James Stanford," I announce, my voice a little hoarse from the dirt and dust that whips itself around the arena.

Applause and a few cheers echo around me, my uncle amongst them as Lord Stanford bows and waves to the crowd.

"And the Earl of Dornton, Lord Henry Tyrell."

Equal amounts of applause and cheers erupt from the crowd, though he does not react, focusing purely on my words.

"Both men will valiantly joust until one unseats the other."

They both dismount and walk over towards me.

"I wish you both good luck."

Isabelle taps me on the shoulder and hands me a small silk handkerchief; I am supposed to choose my champion, the one who will fight for me in the final joust. I look from one to the other and weigh up my choices, but I know exactly whom I will be giving my token to. "Lord Stanford, as you unseated my representative, it is now your responsibility and honour to take his place as my champion."

"Thank you, m'lady."

I can feel Lord Tyrell's eyes burn into the back of my hand as my left cheek grazes Lord Stanford's slightly whilst tying the knot securely in place. I breathe in his scent: earth, leather and sweat. I am surprised by how rough his stubble is.

I step back. "My lords," – I look towards Lord Tyrell – "play *fairly*."

With that, they both turn and mount their horses again, Lord Tyrell digging his heels into the side of his horse and racing to the entrance side of the arena. Lord Stanford nods his head and trots his horse over to the opposite side.

Isabelle leans into me. "I thought you would have given your token to Lord Tyrell?"

"Lord Stanford is our representative. It makes more sense to give it to him," I say, attempting to reassure both Isabelle and myself.

"Well, I'm sure Lord Tyrell would understand," Isabelle whispers.

The tension builds as both riders are handed their final lances. The flag is hoisted high in the air, waiting for both men to announce that they are ready. As soon as their visors are down and their lances are gripped strongly in their hands, the flag is lowered, and they canter their horses straight towards one another. My heart beats faster and faster as the two men collide, Lord Stanford gaining a clear hit on Lord Tyrell's shield.

"Yes!" I cheer aloud. He will surely never show his face here again if he is defeated!

This setback doesn't seem to faze Lord Tyrell for the second charge, as he composes his horse and aims his lance directly at Lord Stanford's exposed chest. Luckily, the Yorkshireman is too quick and blocks his lance with his shield, much to the crowd's excitement. The third charge goes in Lord Stanford's favour as he is able to nearly knock his opponent free off his horse by aiming at his chest; a successful hit. He can do this! He can make my house proud!

"Come on!" Lord Tyrell shouts as he regroups at the end of the arena, ready for the next round.

Lord Tyrell charges at his opponent and lifts his lance high as if to strike Lord Stanford's helmet. Lord Stanford raises his shield to block this high challenge, but just at the last moment, Lord Tyrell lowers his lance and forces it into Lord Stanford's chest, knocking him clean off his horse.

"No..." I breathe, jumping onto my feet.

The crowd goes silent. I too stand in silence, staring out towards Lord Stanford's motionless body on the other side of the arena. I want to sprint down there and make sure that he is unharmed, but all I can do is watch on.

The crowd cheers at Lord Tyrell's victory, who is happily trotting around the arena, soaking up all of the glory his win has given him. Eventually, Lord Tyrell takes off his helmet, and stares down upon his defeated opponent. I cannot hear what he is saying, but he is smiling victoriously. Lord Stanford, now able to move, seems to laugh, but whether or not it is in good humour is unclear.

At the realisation of what Lord Tyrell's victory entails, my heart drops as my plan to remove him from my grounds after the tournament is shattered. The prize is not just a magnificent trophy, it is to appear by my side as my guest of honour at the banquet. With so many eyes on me, it will not be viewed well if I refuse the champion his prize. I could tell everyone the truth of what I heard, but it is my word against his, and who are people likely to believe: a well-respected powerful earl or just me?

"Earl of Dornton, congratulations on winning the final joust and the tournament."

Cheers fill the arena.

"To the knight who came in second place, my own champion..." I turn to face Lord Stanford, who looks winded but smiles through his pain, "... I thank you for representing my house with honour."

I turn to Lord Tyrell again. "My lord, it is my... pleasure to award you the victor's trophy."

Isabelle hands me a golden statue of a knight on his horse with a delicate lance in his hands.

"Congratulations!" I muster as much enthusiasm as I can; I can blame it on the loss my house has suffered today.

I lean in and kiss both of his cheeks, but before I can pull away, he whispers, "I said I would win this for you and I have."

I do not allow my anger to resurface as I take a small step back. Before I have the opportunity to reply, the trumpets sound, marking the closing of the tournament, but the beginning of a long evening.

Eight

Isabelle watches Lady Hargreaves as she tries to pin my last remaining sections of hair into an elegant headdress that Isabelle has loaned me. I stare out of the window to watch the sun setting in the sky, tinging my room with a pink haze that lingers in the distance, whilst sleepy birds make their way to their nests and leave space for their night-time cousins to rise with the darkness.

"Thank you again for allowing me to attend the banquet this evening, my lady." Lady Hargreaves smiles sweetly, anticipation in her voice.

"Do you have an evening dress to wear, Lady Hargreaves?" Isabelle asks.

"You may both call me Bess, Lady Warrington, and yes, I have."

Once Bess has finished making sure everything is in place, she steps back to admire her work. I turn my head from side to side and look at Isabelle as she nods with approval in the mirror.

"Thank you, Bess, you have improved so much since you started here."

"Thank you, Lady Katherine. I have been practising on a few of the servant girls once they have finished for the day."

"It shows. That will be all, Bess. You'd better get changed for this evening, too."

"Oh, I will do, my lady, I will! Thank you." She leaves the room, a skip in her step.

Isabelle waits for me to dress, but I do not move. I stare at my own reflection, almost expecting to see the future appear before my eyes in the mirror itself. Twenty-four hours ago, I would have never thought that I would be feeling this way. Less than four hours ago, I thought that anger would propel me through the evening, but now I just feel… empty.

Just after the competition ended, I informed Isabelle of what I'd heard outside of Lord Tyrell's tent. She was shocked to say the least and tried, at first, to come up with a reason why he would say such things. But it didn't take her long to realise that I had been duped by him. I have been blinded before, but it's never hurt as much as this, and I cannot quite place my finger on why.

"Katherine, please don't worry about this evening, I'm sure it will go smoothly."

"Yes, but how am I supposed to smile and laugh and pretend that everything is as it was before? I can hardly make it known to everyone what I have overheard. Besides, not many noblemen will believe me over the famous Earl of Dornton, if he was ever to deny it, which he would."

"Did you talk to your uncle? I am sure he would want to know."

"No. By time the tournament was over, he was already halfway down the arena to talk to the Earl of Nottingham. I didn't think it was an appropriate time to tell him. I haven't seen him since."

"Perhaps tonight you could get him alone?"

"I will try, but you know how these banquets stretch out for hours and hours, and how all eyes are trained on the hostess to see when she will mess up." I sigh, feeling deflated about it all.

Isabelle moves across the room and runs her fingers over the delicate fabric. "Well, come on then! You can't go to the banquet in your undergarments, Katherine."

After Isabelle has helped me into the beautiful gown, she holds out the chain with my brother's signet ring attached. "Don't forget this. Now, stand back so I can see you."

"Satisfied, my lady?" I chuckle, twirling around on the spot for good measure. The fabric whirls around with me, the detailed, golden thread picking up the remaining light outside.

"Perfect. Let's show these so-called men to never cross you again."

When we reach the Entrance Hall, my aunt and uncle are already waiting for us.

"Katherine, my dear, you look wonderful." My uncle holds me at arm's length, smiling like he always does.

My aunt nods with her own seal of approval. "Isabelle, we will find our seats whilst Katherine greets the remaining guests." Taking Isabelle by the arm, my aunt whisks her away into the Great Hall before either of us utters another word.

I take my place by the doorway, waiting for the next couple to be brought forward by one of the servants who stands at the entrance. "My Lord and Lady Winchester, how wonderful to see you again," I greet both of them with a warm smile. "Please do take a seat, I will be in shortly."

As they make their way into the Entrance Hall, a few more guests file in one by one. The Earl of Nottingham strides in confidently.

"Ah, my lord!"

"My dear, dear, Countess." He takes my offered hand and kisses it. "Thank you for inviting me to this wonderful event today." He beams from ear to ear, glancing around at the old shields and armour that decorate the walls. "It's been such a long time since I have cast my eyes over your impressive collection."

"I'm so pleased you are with us this evening, my old friend!" My uncle steps forward and cups both of the earl's strong hands into his own. "I'm sorry you didn't win the joust…"

They step aside and carry on their conversation, leaving me to greet the stragglers.

As the last few guests arrive, my eyes are drawn towards a refreshed and handsome-looking Lord Stanford as he enters through the doors.

"Lady Turner." He takes my hand and kisses it. His hands are rough, calluses showing his fair share of hard work and toil, along with several old wounds to match.

I ignore the rising heat upon my cheeks. "Thank you for coming. I would have thought that being my champion would have given you a slight edge."

"It was an honour to represent yer house, m'lady, if

only for a little while. It gave me comfort as I flew through the air and 'ad the wind knocked out of me."

"I'm sure you have faced much worse than that, my lord," I chuckle.

"Aye, I have. It was more my pride that was dented."

Out of the corner of my eye, I catch my final guest appear in the doorway. I try not to look at him directly, concentrating all my anger and upset into balling up my fists; I remember my father doing so on many occasions when he had to deal with those he despised.

Lord Stanford shifts a little closer towards me but stops as Lord Tyrell approaches.

"Countess of Leicester!" Lord Tyrell steps in between me and Lord Stanford. "You look beautiful."

I count to three in my head before replying. "Lord Tyrell. Well done again on your victory. I didn't think you were going to be able to beat my chosen champion."

"I was up against a fierce opponent indeed." He glances over at Lord Stanford who has taken a respectful step back to allow me to greet the guest of honour. "Just not quite fierce enough this time."

Lord Stanford's eyes narrow as they linger on Lord Tyrell, slight tension in the air.

Before we head into the noisy Great Hall, my uncle joins us, patting Lord Stanford on the shoulder heavily. Lord Stanford winces but tries to hide his injuries.

"Well, my lad! I must say, hard luck, but well done, Lord Tyrell. That was truly one of the best jousting tournaments I have attended in a long time."

"Thank you, Uncle," I reply before either of the men steal the credit of such a fine tournament.

"Now, shall we take our seats, Lord Stanford, before Katherine and her guest of honour make their grand entrance?"

"Aye, of course." Lord Stanford nods before turning away.

"Shall we?" Lord Tyrell offers his arm.

I hesitate before accepting it.

It takes every ounce of restraint to not hit this man in the jaw and add another scar to his near-perfect, smug face. Perhaps now is a good opportunity for me to tell him what I overheard. But just as I am about to muster up the courage to do so, Lord Tyrell stops walking and turns to me.

"Lady Katherine, I have been meaning to get a moment alone with you."

"Me too."

"I am glad to hear it!" He leans in to kiss me, but I turn my face away just in time. "I thought that was what you wanted?" He flinches as if my actions physically hurt him.

"Because you care a great deal about what *I* want, correct?"

"You know that I care a great deal for you, my lady." Lord Tyrell's voice intensifies at my sudden harshness. "Have I not proved this many times since our first meeting? If I may, you seemed out of sorts at the tournament today. I hope that there is not a misunderstanding between us."

I need to choose my next words carefully in case anyone overhears me. "Lord Tyrell, please understand that I am not as stupid as some people make me out to be. I have not worked hard all of my life to kneel to any man, no matter how *charming* they think they are. You are not the first to attempt to seduce me against my better judgement. I have my own mind and I will not be so easily taken in or fooled by anyone."

Something flashes in his eyes, so quickly that I almost miss it; perhaps shock or even anger being pushed deep down inside. He takes a small step back, his gaze lowering to the floor.

"My lady, I apologise for any offence caused. Though I am not sure what I have done to offend you." His voice is well controlled. "I would never do anything to harm you."

"I wish I could believe you." I truly do. I take a deep breath, pushing down the slight wobble in my voice.

"Why would I lie to you? Have I not shown that I am your loyal servant? That I would do anything to make sure that you are happy?"

My happiness? I have heard all this before. I was captivated by Lord Tyrell, a refreshing change to my grey existence, but he was yet another pretender, another idiot trying to get what he wants by manipulating others. How foolish was I to allow him to do so? No, this is not my fault, it is his.

Suddenly, Johnson appears in front of us, a light relief from the tension building between Lord Tyrell and me. "My lady, your aunt has sent me. She wondered if you were planning on keeping your guests waiting for much longer?"

With a degree of difficulty, I plaster a warm smile on my face "Of course, thank you." I decide to pause our conversation for now.

The crowd settles and silence fills the Great Hall as we walk in together. Bess catches my eye from further down the room, dressed in a beautiful red dress. She is seated next to Isabelle, who frowns at the man who is glued to my side. As I make my way to the head of the table, my eye is caught by the blueness of Lord Stanford's eyes as he watches myself and Lord Tyrell.

I gesture to everyone in the room to sit, signalling for the feast to begin.

Plates full of fish, meats, cheeses, breads, fruits, vegetables, and sweet treats flood the Great Hall, excitement and delight bouncing around the room; the amazing smells putting me at ease. Surveying the room, I make a mental note of those who I need to talk to in order to gain their trust and support; one of many tasks for me this evening. Those who I am more familiar with smile back at me, and I feel a rush of comfort from them, swirling and churning with all of the emotions building up inside me. I have never felt this overwhelmed before in my own home. I distract myself by surveying the room again.

Isabelle is in deep conversation with my aunt, probably gossiping about the noblemen's much younger wives and how they seem to be replaced every season. My uncle is still talking to the Earl of Nottingham, more than likely discussing the same topic that the Earl began when he first arrived this evening. Bess is happily chatting away to one of the noblewoman's wives; I am pleased to see her finally smile.

The light tapping of Lord Tyrell's foot against my own and the brush of his shoulder against mine pulls me back into the realisation of the man sitting next to me. I jerk away sharply at his touch as if his skin was red hot, burning me.

"Lady Katherine, you have outdone yourself this evening; this food is perfect."

"Thank you, Lord Tyrell, but I didn't cook the food myself. Perhaps you would like to thank my kitchen staff?" I reply as I tuck into the food on my plate.

"I don't normally make a point of thanking every woman who had a hand in making the food that I eat," he snorts, surprised that I have even mentioned the idea.

"You assume my kitchen is packed with only women?"

"Well, where else would they be? Is that not the role that God has liberated the female lower class for?"

"*Liberated*? You think that freedom, in the minds of my female staff, is simply cooking and cleaning?" I ask, my disgust for this man magnifying.

"Like I said, my lady, what else is there? We don't want them to rise above their station."

I stamp my wine goblet on the table. "Imagine a woman who thinks herself equal to men! Whatever will we do if that happens?" I reply before picking up the goblet again and taking a sip of its contents. Annoyingly, he just carries on as if I had not spoken against his words.

Why didn't he show this version of himself when we first met?

I try to drown out the rest of my guest's commentary on the lower classes and how female workers should either be at home raising their children or cleaning and cooking for their husbands. I can only make out the odd few words that flow around me, anything but Earl Dornton's idiotic voice, Lord Stanford being one of them: "Aye, it was 'bout time my mother rested after the hardship she 'as been through. Luckily, we 'ave a few well-trusted and loyal servants to keep 'er company when I'm away from 'ome."

I wonder if his mother's eyes are as blue as her son's?

The room is abuzz with noise as our plates and the last scraps of food are taken away. Music begins to play in the background, which brings me a new sensation of dread: the first dance. It is customary for the head of house to dance with their spouse or guest of honour, which means only one thing.

"My lady, would you do me the honour?" Lord Tyrell offers me his hand, his figure towering over me as I remain seated.

A space has been cleared on the opposite side of the room to allow for dancing. Lord Tyrell leads me out onto the dance space, and the guests watch on with anticipation as we take our starting positions. I try not to lean into his touch as he leads me across the floor, dipping me low when the song demands it. His hands are warm against my waist, pulling at the fabric as he feels the curve of my hips underneath. I shift uncomfortably, stepping away from him when the music instructs me to.

Not too soon into the dance, Lord Tyrell lowers his voice. "When it comes to you, a few seconds apart is too long."

"You've been with me all evening, my lord, that is more than most guests can boast tonight." We separate as we circle one another in time to the music. As much as I want to carry on dancing to the other side of the room, I cannot.

"One evening is never enough." His hands travel up my arm, his thumb drawing little circles on my wrist as he finds my hand and continues to spin me around on the spot. The heat from his body is overwhelming.

I have danced to this tune many times before, each partner following the music perfectly, each wanting the same thing, however. Thankfully, I don't have to endure Lord Tyrell's intense gaze for much longer – the song ends, with a loud applause bringing us back into the room.

"Thank you, my lady." He finishes our dance with a soft kiss to my hand. "I have promised myself to another for the next dance, but I do need to talk to you in private about something before the night has ended, so I will come and find you when I can."

"That is only if *I* have time for *you*."

He bows without another word and heads towards his next victim. To my surprise he approaches Bess, who shyly accepts his hand. What does he want with a lowly lady-in-waiting? Curiosity takes hold as I stand on the edge of the room, watching them carefully. If my gut instinct is right and Lord Tyrell is not to be trusted, then it is my duty to make sure he does not taint some other clueless woman. This is easier said than done, however. Hands grasp mine and meaningless flatteries are exchanged with lords and ladies as I make my way around the edge of the dance space, and I give up trying to watch them both.

As the second song finishes, Sir Francis finds me and drags me away for the next dance, one that is a lot livelier than my first. As much as he tries to smile, I can tell that he is trying to push through the pain gained from his fall earlier today. "It is good to see you smiling again."

"I always smile, Sir Francis," I beam.

He glances over at Lord Tyrell who is captivating

all of Bess's attention for the third dance of the evening. "What happened earlier today? One minute you can't stop smiling whenever Lord Tyrell is nearby, then the next…" – we weave in and out of the other dancers in time with the melody playing loudly on the other side of the room –"… you can't bear to look at him."

"He's just another disappointment. Perhaps I should go it alone. Reject all men before they have the chance to double-cross me."

"That's a bit extreme, Katherine. As much as I want to agree with you, you know that you need strong support to survive the harsh times we live in."

"By 'strong' you mean 'male', I presume?"

"Come now, you know that I do not make up the rules. I know that you are far superior to any man who would dare challenge you over what is rightfully yours. You can never be too careful, though, Katherine. Trust your instincts. I will support you no matter your decision."

We continue the dance in silence as Sir Francis grimaces his way through the steps. However, a few seconds later, we have to stop as he can no longer stand due to the injuries he sustained in the joust. I escort him over to the seated area, trying not to collide with the other dancers, and sit him on the wooden bench pushed aside from the banquet.

"How do you feel now?" I ask, making sure that he is as comfortable as possible, asking a passing servant for a fresh goblet of honey mead.

"Ah, just fine, my lady, thank you." He winces, trying to move into a more comfortable position.

"If you insist." I take a seat next to him.

"Don't let me stop you from all the fun!"

"I would much rather sit with you all evening than parade myself with the others." I wave a hand at the dancers on the other side of the room.

A few minutes later, a long shadow falls over us, extending its hand. "Would ya like to finish this dance, Lady Turner?"

"Stealing my dance partner too?" Sir Francis jokes, wincing as pain appears to shoot into his side.

I stare at Lord Stanford for a split second, not sure if I should take his offer or not. I had sworn off getting to know men for the rest of the evening, so why do I hesitate now?

"Katherine" – Sir Francis nudges me with his elbow – "don't judge everyone with the same thoughts."

Lord Stanford raises one eyebrow, before I reply, "Fine. Thank you, Lord Stanford. I accept."

The music slows down to a less lively tune as Lord Stanford draws me in closer by the waist, his hand placed above my hip. The feeling of his body close to mine is strangely comforting, like a warm fire on a cold day. I find myself leaning in closer, my head in line with his shoulder.

"Thanks for inviting me to today's tournament, m'lady."

"I've hardly done anything."

"You don't take compliments very well, do ya?" he muses.

I tilt my head back to look at him. "Maybe I'm just tired of hearing the same old thing."

"Then ya must get tired very easily, m'lady, as I'm sure I'm not the only one who has said such things tonight.

Lord Tyrell, for example, seems to only hold ya in high regard."

I follow his line of sight to Lord Tyrell, who is chatting merrily to a man I do not recognise.

"Why is everyone obsessed with that man?" I mutter, just wanting this feeling of betrayal and anguish to leave me.

"He's not as popular as he makes out. He's made a few enemies 'ere and there."

"Are you saying he's not to be trusted?"

"Aye, but it is not for me to press my opinion on ya. I'm sure yer more than capable of working that out for yer self."

I ponder his words. It's been a long time since an outsider has asked me to decide and think for myself; it's almost refreshing. We glide across the room and his hand tightens around my own as if anchoring me to this moment, like nothing else exists beyond it. My eyes find their way to his, gaining courage as the song continues. The more I am aware of his hand that is neatly placed at my waist, the other hand closely wrapped around my own, the more I notice the intensity of his blue eyes and his hair, golden and radiant as the sun. His eyes don't leave mine.

Almost without realising, the dance finishes, and we propel ourselves into the next. As the song continues, I relax further into his touch, forgetting everything that came before this one pure moment.

I laugh at the happy memory of watching William learn all of the new dances for the season, my aunt being a regular dancing partner.

"Did yer brother ever marry?" Lord Stanford asks.

"No." I shake my head. "He was betrothed to my best friend, Lady Warrington, before he died." I nod in her direction where she is now laughing with my uncle. "They hardly knew each other. If only he was here, he would see how much she now means to me."

"I can tell ya brother means everything to ya."

"He did… he *does*. I wouldn't be me without him, no matter the small amount of time we had together." My smile fades as I remember dancing with him for the last time in this very room, only two days before he left for the coast.

"I'm sorry, m'lady, I didn't mean to bring up the past." He pulls me in a little closer, as if trying to shield me from the ache in my heart that the memory of my brother always leaves.

I try to change the subject. "That must have been one hell of a blow that Lord Tyrell's lance gave you earlier."

"It was, but I'm made of much tougher stuff than that."

"What did he say to you? It didn't look too friendly." I quickly scan around the room, making sure that we are out of earshot of Lord Tyrell, who I spy dancing with a lady on the other side of the Great Hall.

Lord Stanford releases a small laugh. "Aye, he did say somethin'." He frowns as he stares into the distance for a fleeting moment. "How long have ya known 'im?"

His question catches me off guard. "Not that long, in fact. He turned up one day out of the blue. I do not know as much as I'd like. His family and mine were never friends. I have been trying my best not to judge him by his father's actions, but he is making it increasingly difficult."

"Restraint is a rare talent, Lady Turner. I don't know many people in your position who would do the same."

We twirl around the room again, weaving in and out of the many dancers who now fill the space.

"How do you know him?" I ask in return.

"I've met 'im a couple of times in the past. Can't say we're best of friends. I've 'eard that ever since his father died, he is looking for a way to gain even more wealth."

My eyes follow Lord Stanford's over to the opposite side of the room.

"… and it looks like he has found 'is way to achieve just that."

The music fades as the man in question approaches. Lord Stanford releases my waist, the coolness of where his hand was sends a chill through me; he is more hesitant to let go of my hand. It is only when Lord Tyrell is standing two metres away that he does so, slowly. Before I have a chance to question what exactly Lord Stanford meant, Lord Tyrell speaks.

"My Lady, I believe that it is our turn for the next dance."

"Perhaps I shouldn't be monopolising all your dances, Lord Tyrell."

"I insist." It is clear that he won't take no for an answer.

I reluctantly accept, stepping away from the comfort of Lord Stanford, but before the next song begins, he clears his throat. "Lady Turner, I 'ave to take my leave."

I turn to face him in disbelief, forgetting about Lord Tyrell for a moment, who huffs in irritation beside me. "I hope I haven't bored you, my lord."

He chuckles. "No, yer the opposite of boring, m'lady. I simply want to arrive back in town before it is dark. I don't know this land too well."

"Where are you staying?"

"At the White Boar Inn. Then I must make my way back 'ome."

"Oh." I'm surprised at the disappointment in my voice. "You're leaving so soon? Will you be back in time for the archery tournament I'm hosting? My uncle must have sent you an invitation on my behalf?"

"I am sorry, but I am not sure if I will be back in yer beautiful county any time soon."

His answer silences me for a few seconds before I raise my chin and put on my best smile, something that I have perfected on many occasions when hope is replaced by disappointment. "Of course. I understand. York is very far from Leicester. I wish you safe travels, my lord."

Lord Tyrell guides me away from Lord Stanford. I don't look back as the Yorkshireman exits the Great Hall, taking all of the air and light of the evening with him.

Nine

Sir Robert Hartford is already waiting for me in the Council Chamber, tapping his foot and drumming his fingers against the oak chair as he stands opposite me. The bald patch that is highly visible at the back of his head seems to shine in the morning light.

"Sir Robert, it is a pleasure as always to see you." I plaster on my best smile as I shut the door behind me.

"My lady," he replies, taking my hand gingerly, before I motion him to a take seat.

"I am sorry for keeping you waiting, my lord. How may I be of service?"

He looks around the room, frowning, eyeing up the growing pile of papers waiting on my desk. "I would like to discuss my personal finances." He glances around the room again, small beads of sweat appearing on his brow. "Erm… isn't your uncle going to join us? I would prefer to discuss this matter with him."

I inhale and hitch a smile on my face before I answer. "My lord. You may or may not have realised, but I am actually the sole heir and head of house for the Leicester estate, so it is me who you will be dealing with."

"Yes, I am perfectly aware, my lady, but this just isn't *natural*." He laughs, waving his hand around in front of him as if to make me magically disappear. "Women don't have the capacity to discuss finances; it's just not in your nature."

Scraping my chair even closer to the desk between us, I grasp my hands together, mimicking what I would actually prefer to do to his neck if I had the chance. "I understand that having someone of my *appearance* is not common practice."

"Being a woman, you mean?" he scoffs.

I breathe deeply through my nose and sit up even straighter in my chair. Sir Robert is not one to mince his words, but even this level of disrespect is beyond his regular insolence.

I sigh. "Let me remind you of something. When my mother died, my father took over the estate. When my dear father died, he passed on the estate to his eldest child, my brother, William. When William died, he passed it onto me. His only heir and blood relative. The *king* agreed to this. I am the Countess of Leicester. I am the one who looks after these lands and my people. I am the one who decides how many acres each individual receives. I am the one who decides how the taxpayer's hard-earned coin is spent within the county. I am the one who approves and rejects petitions with the stroke of my pen and the wax of my seal."

"Y-yes, well, erm, monetary matters should not take up a lady's time," he splutters, his face turning an amusing shade of pink. "You see, I think that…"

"As *I* was saying, I understand that you are here today to ask for a loan, to help with the costs that both you and your wife have carelessly accumulated. Your grand country manor in Ashby-de-la-Zouch has just received an extensive refurbishment, has it not?" I don't allow him to answer. "Now you want to ask me for money so that you can pay your servants and tailor's bills, after throwing what little money you had on your grand furnishings and gold-painted ceilings." I ignore his spluttering protests and grab a piece of parchment from the drawer next to me, dipping my quill into the ink bottle, as I begin to write down his name. "I have read your letter, even though you addressed it to my uncle instead of me."

"My lady! I was only…" He has the sense to stop talking altogether when he meets my eye.

"Only making another mistake, my lord? Yes, you were." I begin to scribble down the summary of his request in silence, allowing him to borrow a tidy sum. "You will pay the money owed to those who have had the misfortune to serve you," I conclude. With a stern look – one that I have learnt from my aunt over the years – Sir Robert shrinks in his seat. "You will pay me the full amount owed in January of next year with ten per cent interest added on top of what I have loaned you. If you do not pay this full amount back, I will have no choice but to take it from you one way or another." I sit back in my seat, watching him, unflinching as he tries to think of something to say. "Do you understand that, Sir Robert, or would you like to wait for my uncle, who I know will think that ten per cent is a ridiculously low amount of interest on a loan this size?"

"M-my lady, that is most kind!" he replies, sweat blotting his brow.

Without a word, I sign the document and press my seal into the hot, red wax blob next to it. "Here." I thrust it into his hand then abruptly stand, pushing my chair back with a resounding screech.

He quickly follows suit, hardly being able to look at me as he heads for the door.

"Oh… and, Sir Robert?"

He turns to face me, wringing his hat in his hands.

"Bring your wife with you next time. I would love to ask her a few questions."

The twist of his lips and the blank expression on his face before he rushes out of the door amuses me.

"Then I can ask her how she puts up with you," I mutter to myself, slumping back into my chair again.

Searching one of the drawers for the ledger, I scribble down what is owed to me by Sir Robert and, most importantly, his due date. My whole body slumps further into the chair as I rest my chin on my hand, a headache threatening to take hold.

"How did it go?" My uncle pops his head around the door before entering the room. "I just saw Sir Robert in the corridor. He said that you granted him his loan?"

"Yes, I did. If I hadn't, then the only ones who would suffer would be those he owes the money to. They are the ones who cannot afford to lose out on payment because the oaf in the big manor house can't keep his finances in check." I nearly break the quill as I shove it into the ink pot.

"If word of your generosity reaches the whole county,

you'll have everyone lined up outside this door asking for a loan." He laughs. "I hope you added interest."

"Ten per cent."

"Ten per cent! That's steep, isn't it?" Raising his eyebrows, he picks up the ledger and casually reads my new entry.

"I was simply doing the right thing. If he doesn't pay me back then I will take what is owed."

My uncle passes me the ledger, which I slide into its drawer before sitting back and closing my eyes. "Sir Robert told me that having a woman dealing with finances is *unnatural*. How can a man such as he dare to insult me in such a manner?"

"It takes more than some old knight to get under your skin." My uncle pulls up the chair that Sir Robert vacated, leans over the desk and takes my hands.

I slowly open my eyes and look at him.

"You've dealt with far worse in the past."

"I know, but it still doesn't make it just, Uncle. My brother never received this much grief when he was in power."

My mind thinks back to one of my first visits to Westminster Palace after William died. Even though I have the same rank, most of the nobility only looked down on me: a woman amongst men. I am proud of how I have now found my own voice, no longer allowing others to speak over me or dismiss anything I have to say before I can even utter a single word. Perhaps I should be kinder to myself.

"William never had it easy either, Katherine. No one ever does. You can't please everyone."

I sigh, knowing that my uncle speaks the truth. "I know, I just feel like everything and everyone is against me. I don't know who to trust."

"Is this to do with Lord Tyrell?" he asks, leaning forwards.

"Not just him, Uncle. I can't trust anyone outside these stone walls."

"You can only go with your instincts. Everyone under your roof adores you. What happened between you and Lord Tyrell? I thought you held him in high regard?" He lets go of my hands and sits more comfortably into the chair.

"I have been meaning to tell you of this since it happened, Uncle, but there was always something else in the way; besides, he is gone now." I take a deep breath before telling him what I overheard on the morning of the jousting tournament. The pain and anger I felt that day still bubbles up within every time I revisit it.

When I have finished, my uncle sits back in his chair and shakes his head with disappointment. "I am sorry, Katherine, I understand how that must have felt like a dagger in your side."

"So, you believe me?" I ask, doubt rising inside me when I think about how powerful Lord Tyrell is.

"Of course I do, Katherine. I would never doubt your word!"

The tension in my body releases. "Anger is all I felt. I will never allow myself to feel anything like that again."

"I understand your anger, my dear. Unfortunately, the kingdom is rife with men like him and always will be until the day this world ends. You just have to learn to live with them."

"How? How can I do that, Uncle?" A headache begins to stretch across my forehead.

"Well, the first thing you need to accept is that you can't ignore him or hope that he will suddenly disappear, Katherine. Men like that, once they have their sights set on something they desire, they find it difficult to let go."

My uncle's reply is somewhat disappointing. I'm not sure what I expected, maybe a little anger, but I know that my uncle is not one to act recklessly at every man who has upset his niece, as much as I would like that sometimes.

"I want him barred from my lands," I state.

"I'm not sure that is a good idea, my dear, though it is justified. You can't turn your back on him, Katherine, it would only make you more vulnerable. He is a powerful man with a network of connections."

"This is ridiculous! *I* am a powerful woman! I hold the same seat of power as he, just here in Leicester, not East Anglia. He may come from a longer line of nobility than myself, but I deserve every inch of respect that he holds!" I announce, agitated at the thought of everyone, even my own uncle, ranking me below that horrible man. "If I was a man, I would not have to deal with this. I would have every right to banish him from my lands, but of course, it's not that simple, is it?"

I know that my uncle is only trying to be helpful, but I just feel as if everything is stacked against me sometimes.

"No, it's not. I can only imagine how you must be feeling right now. Anger, betrayal, disappointment. All you want to do is to push him over the castle walls into the river below, correct?"

I nod with a hint of a small smile.

“Well, unfortunately, you can’t get rid of your problems that easily. You have to be smart about these things.”

“I don’t want him anywhere near me, Uncle. I just have this feeling that he won’t leave me be, like I am his prey and he is the predator. He enjoys the thrill.” I shiver.

“It’s not like you to allow for just one small narrow-minded man to bring you down. Is there anything else that is bothering you?”

Everything. Lord Stanford’s sudden exit. Isabelle’s betrothal to a stranger. Sir Robert and his idiotic bald patch.

“Nothing I can’t handle,” I lie.

“Well, I might have something to cheer you up, my dear. Come with me.”

I glance down at the pile of paperwork that somehow never seems to end, knowing if I go with him, I’ll be even further behind.

“It’s a damned better sight than that lot, I promise you. Come with me.”

Leaving the dimness of the Council Chamber behind us, I follow my uncle outside and towards the stables. As we descend the entrance steps, I pause for a second and look around at the old castle walls around me. When I was a child, I used to find the tall stone walls suffocating, blocking out the light and warmth from the world outside. I used to beg my father or brother to take me on their travels, away from here; I wanted to feel free from this place. That was a different time, but now? Now, the walls keep me safe, keep my family and friends safe, safe from those outside who would do us harm.

We’re greeted by one of my men, who has a mischievous smile dancing on his lips. “My lady, my lord.”

I am immediately suspicious. "What's going on? What has my uncle made you do?"

"Nothing that I did not want to be a part of. If you will follow me, my lady."

Intrigued, I follow both men into the stables. The smell of straw on the floor mixes with the rich aroma of leather. Both men suddenly pause. I nearly plough into them but stop just in time as my uncle gestures towards a beautiful horse standing before us.

"This is a gift from Sir Francis, Katherine," my uncle beams.

"What? Is this because he still feels guilty for losing the joust? I told him to stop blaming himself!" I reply, feeling a pang of guilt at how my words could have been received so harshly.

"No, Katherine. He wanted to cheer you up and we both thought that this big fellow here would do the job nicely. He's a couple of years old, broken in by Sir Francis and his Master of Horse in Northampton. I know you had your heart set on a grey mare from the Earl of Oxford, but he informed me a few weeks ago that the king has actually had his eye on the same mare and... well, you understand."

I take a small step towards the handsome creature, barely hearing my uncle's words. My hand is steady when I reach out, but still, my breath catches in my throat when he turns to greet me. His eyes shine a brilliant shade of brown; his matching coat is glossy with a midnight black mane and tail. He sniffs and snorts at my extended hand, judging to see if I am trustworthy or not, then lowers his head, allowing me to stroke his soft white nose and pat his neck.

"He is magnificent," I breathe, all my worries and anxieties washed away in an instant.

It has been a few months since I've had a horse of my own, only being able to borrow my uncle's or Isabelle's whenever I wanted to ride to town. I did have my heart set on the beautiful grey horse when I visited the Earl of Oxford, not long after King Richard's coronation, but I can see now that I was always destined for this horse. The way he leans into my touch, the softness of his coat, the strength in his legs: he is perfect.

My uncle brushes him with his bare hand, smiling to himself. "What will you call him, Katherine?"

I think this over carefully. "He deserves a strong powerful name, like Richard or Edward, or one from Greek mythology like Zeus or Heracles."

"Zeus?" my uncle sniggers.

"Hmm. Perhaps instead I should call him…" Searching into the horse's deep brown eyes, I am reminded of one person in particular and it is the perfect name for the perfect horse. "William." I smile.

John Gamble, one of my most trusted stable hands, stands beside me and admires the magnificent horse in front of us. "He is a beauty, my lady. Give him time to settle and you will be able to ride him through the woodland."

A small rumble of thunder shakes the sky outside, startling William slightly as well as me.

"I think you might want to rush inside, my lady, I will stay with William here to calm him until the storm subsides."

I open my mouth to protest, but a clap of lightning splits the heavens above, closely followed by another rumble of thunder. I gasp in shock at the loud noise, thunder being something I have always hated since I was a small child. I nod and quickly follow my uncle outside. The rain pelts down. As I rush towards the entrance steps, my hair is soon soaked, along with everything else that is not protected from the rain. It is as if I have jumped into the lake! Soaked to the bone, I push open the castle's oak doors and slip inside.

"Katherine! You're soaking wet! Whatever made you want to go out in this weather?" My aunt's voice startles me more than the storm outside, her frown not too dissimilar to the darkened clouds. She wrinkles her nose at my drenched appearance, only suddenly realising my uncle too is soaked to the bone, wringing out his hat as water cascades to the floor. Bess appears next to me, her head flicking from me to my aunt and back.

My aunt shakes her head again. "Perhaps a bath is in order, Katherine. If any guests happened by, what would they think?"

For once she is right. "Bess, would you please run me a warm bath and lay out some dry clothes?" I ask, trying my best not to shiver.

"Yes, my lady, right away."

Without another word to my aunt, and leaving my uncle to his wife's wrath, I follow Bess up the spiral staircase and into a cosy room with a ready-lit fire. It is not long until the tub is filled with water.

Just as Bess is about to leave, she turns to face me once more. "My lady, thank you again for allowing me to dance amongst your guests at the joust's banquet. I have not had that much fun since… well, I don't know."

"Of course, Bess, you are a part of my household now, it is only fitting that you enjoy banquets as much as my friends and family. How did you find last night? I saw you dancing happily with a few young men." Lord Tyrell being one of them, but I decide not to mention his name in particular.

"It was magical!" she replies, a wistful look upon her rosy face.

"I am happy to see you settling well here at Leicester. I know that change can be a daunting thing to a young woman. I am here any time you need me." I smile, the heat of the fire relaxing every muscle in my body.

"Thank you, Lady Turner. I will leave you be." She shuts the door firmly behind her.

The water is nice and warm after the cold of the rain outside. I empty a cup of water over my head, allowing it to cascade down my body. I lose myself to the quietness around me, with just the soothing sound of the rain hitting the window outside. I glance towards the blue lake and the blackened sky. In the distance, the town's lights are being lit. I can't help but wonder if, wherever Lord Stanford is right now, he is gazing at the night sky too… but then again, why would he?

Ten

For the next few days, the weather remains bleak. Working through the mountain of paperwork and application letters piled in front of me is beginning to drain my soul. Only one letter grabs my interest: a brief account from the Earl of Nottingham, who has written me an essay on the time he got lost in his own city caves.

Once I have finished, I write to Sir Francis about something that has been on my mind for some time. I fold the parchment carefully and seal it with hot, red wax. I peer into the hallway, hoping that I can catch one of the servants to courier my letter for me, but sadly, it's quiet and no one is there.

The courtyard is empty also, so I wander around to the stable block whilst there is a break in the rain, where I am met by John Gamble. When I ask after his father, Charles Gamble, who regularly delivers my correspondence to Sir Francis, he points me towards the stable door on the far right. I push open the door, hoping to find Charles, but when I look upwards, it is not the farrier Charles is talking to, but someone else entirely. I try to hide the shock on my face, replacing it with irritation then annoyance, the letter crumpling slightly in my clenched fist.

"Lady Katherine. I had hoped to see you." Lord Tyrell turns to face me.

"Have you come to shoe the horses, my lord?" I ask, though I already know the answer.

He laughs in good humour. "Not today, Lady Turner, though if it meant spending more time with you, I would gladly do so." Handing over his horse's reins to Charles, Lord Tyrell walks towards me with a smile dancing on his lips. He lowers his voice. "I could not stay away for any longer. I have been longing to see you, Katherine."

It takes all my strength to stand this close to him and not push him away from me or stamp on his foot.

Before I can say a word to him, Charles Gamble approaches, eyeing up Lord Tyrell. "My lady, my son informed me that you wanted to see me?"

I step around my unwanted guest and produce the letter from my pocket, handing it directly to him. "This must go immediately to Sir Francis Grey. I believe that he is at home in Northampton. Please make sure that you are the one to give it to him."

He accepts the parchment with a deep bow. "I shall leave straight away, my lady."

"Thank you. You may take provisions from the kitchen for your journey."

Charles nods and leaves me alone with Lord Tyrell.

"A letter?" he chimes, clearly thinking that he can be so familiar with me.

"Yes, a letter. I am well educated for a woman in my

position." I stroke his horse's mane, looking anywhere but at him.

He lets out a small, amused laugh. "I was not suggesting anything less. I was only curious." He edges towards me again, brushing his hand against my own. His persistence is admirable – I just wish it wasn't in pursuit of me. I wonder if I can accidently make his own horse squash him?

I sense Lord Tyrell study me for a minute or two, following my hand as I stroke the horse's soft nose. He leans against one of the posts, arms folded. "Are we not friends anymore, my lady? I feel like you are trying to avoid me." He reaches out towards my face, but I jerk away from him. "You're not as warm, not as… *eager* to see me. The first day I met you, you were completely different to how you are now. I tried to talk to you, but there has always been something or *someone* in the way." His eyes darken over for a split second; I wonder who he is referring to.

The walls of the stable begin to close in around me, so I edge towards the entrance, but Lord Tyrell blocks my path. His weight shifts slightly onto his right leg and his hand moves to his belt where a small knife sits. He studies me.

"Are you upset with me because I danced with your lady's maid? What was her name?"

"Lady Hargreaves? No. It's not that." I grit my teeth.

"Is that jealousy I hear in your voice, my lady?" His lips curl.

"Why would I care whom you dance with? That is your business and your business alone."

"Then what is it, Katherine? Please tell me. I don't like

to see you so upset. If I am the cause, then perhaps I can be the cure."

I take a deep breath before facing him. I should have confronted him about what I overheard sooner, but I've just not been able to find the right opportunity, wanting him to fade away. I guess now is better than never.

"I overheard you."

"Overheard me? When? Overheard what exactly?" he asks, shifting from his right foot to his left.

"The morning of the joust, outside of your tent. You probably thought that I had walked away, unable to hear you, but something made me stay and I am glad I did."

"I don't understand, Katherine," he laughs.

"Do not toy with me. You gloated that you only showed interest in me because you want me for my fortune and title. You're not the first man to try to seduce me under false pretences, but you are the first who nearly duped me."

Lord Tyrell stands there for a moment. He opens his mouth to answer, only to close it again.

I continue, "It was very stupid of you to speak so openly about your own selfish intentions towards me. You should feel lucky that it was me who overheard you, rather than Lady Warrington or Sir Francis."

"I-I don't know what you are talking about," he huffs, a smile plastered onto his lips.

Of course he would deny it. I didn't expect anything less.

Maybe these words will jog his memory.

"'I have already begun to work my charm on the young Countess… I would hate to start all over again. She has what I want… what I need… what should have been mine… I must say that she makes my part in all of this a lot easier than I had planned.' Do those words sound familiar to you?" I recite the words that bludgeoned me so that day outside his tent; I will never forget those words.

A small silence sits between us – there is no need for words – until Lord Tyrell replies, "I don't think you understand, you make it sound so cruel. I would never have meant for you to…"

"Overhear you? Of course you didn't!" My arms fly in the air, exasperated. Why can't he just admit it? I would have more respect for him. He should be honoured that I am still here talking to him!

"I would never mean you any harm! You must have been mistaken, my lady. I have fallen for you, body and soul."

"*I'm* the one who is mistaken!?" I laugh bitterly. "Please, don't deny it. I know what I heard and it did hurt me, I'll be honest." I take a step back, gathering myself, before I say something that I might regret, or that someone might overhear.

If I had been told not that long ago that I would be upset over hearing such lies from a Tyrell, I would have laughed. How is it that he was able to nearly break me? No man should ever be able to do that, to me, Countess of Leicester.

"Fine. You are right, Katherine. At first, I was enticed by your… reputation of wealth and status."

My eyes grow wide and my heart stops for a spilt second. I knew it was true, but hearing him admit it is entirely something else.

"However, once I saw you, once I kissed you… I swear

that all I wanted was you. Your wealth doesn't matter to me. It is you I want."

I shake my head, almost disbelieving what I am hearing. I suppose he wants me to forgive him, go back to where we left off in the library before the joust, but I can't. "What has been said cannot be unsaid. The damage has already been caused. I suggest that you leave here and don't bother me or my people ever again. You are no longer welcome here."

His eyebrows rise and his eyes widen in horror. "Please, how can I make it up to you?" He steps forward, reaching for my hand, but stops himself. "I never meant to cause you pain, my lady. I will try my best to make it up to you. Is there anything I can do to prove myself to you?"

"No. I am not a woman to be messed about with. I rarely give second chances, Lord Tyrell," I reply, tired of his grovelling.

Lord Tyrell nods, his eyes downcast. Silence settles between us for a quiet moment.

"Now, if you don't mind, my lord, I need to be elsewhere."

"Of course, my lady. I-I will see myself out."

I walk ahead of Lord Tyrell, keen to see him gone once and for all. Before he mounts his horse, he clears his throat. "Good day, Lady Turner. I apologise again that my words stung you so. I will make sure that I am worthy of your respect again."

And with the gentle echo of his horse's hooves on the cobbled floor, he is gone. I breathe a big sigh of relief, though I cannot help but ponder upon his parting words.

Eleven

The day of the archery tournament has finally arrived. Isabelle and I have gathered in the library for last-minute planning.

"You will be at the head of the table, here." Isabelle marks my initials on the beautifully drawn table plan. "Of course. I'll sit myself down here." Isabelle marks her initials on a seat further down from my own.

"Absolutely not. You know that the lower down the table you are, the less important you are."

"Fine, but who will I be sitting next to?" Isabelle asks, her delicate finger hovering over the name beside her own. "Oh!" she exclaims. "I didn't realise it would be today."

The sorrow in her voice captures my immediate attention. My eyes gaze upon the name that lies beneath her finger's shadow: *Sir Henry Percival.* She hasn't quite been herself since the day she agreed to marry Sir Henry.

"I'm sorry, Isabelle, I should have warned you." I place my hand upon her shoulder, which slumps forwards. "I can only hope that today will go smoothly for the both of you." I am met with silence. "Look, how about I… shoot an arrow into the crowd and you can pretend to be injured?" I laugh, attempting to cheer her up, but when I duck my head to level with her own, I see that she has begun to cry. "No, no, Isabelle, please don't cry. I promise I won't really maim you."

Isabelle sniffles at my feeble attempt to cheer her up. "I will soon be married, Katherine. I don't know when, but once I am, everything will change." She pauses for a moment, chewing the side of her lip. "Please don't think that I am being ungrateful, but I don't want change. I can't imagine living my life anywhere else! I'll have to live in Wiltshire or wherever my husband demands me to go. I don't want to live away from here, away from *you*! When my father died and you so kindly allowed me to stay with you, I finally found my place! A sister! I thought that I would marry a local lord and live down the road in one of your fancy houses and we would be near each other forever. But now? Now my time is running out and… and I don't want to be dragged into the unknown."

My heart swells with affection for Isabelle. I thought that having her marriage already sealed would be a blessing; it is much better than having to navigate her way through false courting and betrayals like I have had to endure.

"Whilst I cannot guarantee a future without its hurdles and trials, I *can* guarantee that I will be there for you no matter where you are, no matter what happens. We can never be sure of the future, that's what makes life so exciting, but I can guarantee that you will never be alone."

Isabelle finally looks up at me, her eyes glistening with

fresh tears. "Thank you, Katherine. I know that you always will be, I just... I don't know. I've never truly felt in control of my life until I met you. You're so sure of what you want and where you are going. I wish I could be the same."

"Isabelle, you know that is not completely true. I just adapt." I flash a smile, and she can't help but mirror me. "Anyway, you are in control – well, you certainly will be once you are married. Behind every powerful man, or in front of, there is an even more powerful woman. Remember that."

After wiping away Isabelle's tears and what feels like the world's longest hug, I make my way outside to the newly erected archery range where the tournament is to be held. We kept the main stands erected from the jousting tournament, positioning them just behind where the competitors will stand so they will have a wonderful view of the arena. Mr Sutton is instructing a few of my men as to where the targets should be and there is the determined noise of men hard at work bustling all around me.

"Mr Sutton, if it is alright with you, I would like to practise before the other competitors arrive. Would it be possible for me to set myself up over here?"

"Yes, my lady, of course. We only have the two remaining targets to set up and then we have finished."

It is perfect weather for the tournament: no rain, just the odd burst of wind. The sun shines directly on my back, which adds comfort to my shaking hands. The first arrow hits the outer circle, with the second missing completely. After muttering a quick curse, I observe the space around me, but luckily, no one witnessed my misses. As I pull the arrows out of the target, making sure they're not damaged, my mind is taken back to the day that Sir Francis informed me of my brother's death. I was standing right here. It was just an ordinary day for me, practising without a care in the world. Everything changed that day... nothing is the same anymore.

I start again, pulling back my first arrow.

"Hello, my lady!" Sir Francis greets me with such excitement and happiness as he bounces towards me with a huge smile, it is almost too overwhelming.

"Sir Francis! How wonderful it is to see you." I peek behind him at two unfamiliar faces.

"Lady Turner, may I present Sir Henry Percival, Earl of Wiltshire, and his mother, Lady Anne Percival."

My eyes widen at finally being introduced to the one man I have been keen to meet ever since I heard his name. He is a tall man, rather round, with reddish hair and clean-shaven. His eyes almost disappear when he smiles, eclipsed by his own rosy cheeks. My eyes wander over the richly coloured, gold-embroidered fabric that adorns his large frame; he couldn't be missed in a crowd.

I offer him my hand.

"It is an honour to meet you, my dear Countess of Leicester."

"The pleasure is all mine."

His mother steps forward and curtsies. "Lady Turner, an honour."

"I hope that you are both excited for the little tournament I have put on today."

"We are very excited, aren't we, Mother?"

His mother silently observes the arena. Her thin nose, cold grey eyes and pale skin are completely the opposite to her son. I just hope that they love Isabelle as much as I do; they would be fools not to.

"It is great news on your betrothal, my lord. I congratulate you both," I say, keen to see Sir Henry Percival's own view on the matter.

"I have been informed that she should be here any moment now." Sir Francis scans the stands frantically as people begin to take their seats.

All four of us watch as Isabelle walks towards us, accompanied by my aunt and uncle. She looks pale, wringing her hands tighter and tighter, so they appear almost stark white, the closer she approaches. She looks everywhere but at Sir Henry; I can see her heavy breathing from here.

Their eyes meet.

"My dear Lady Isabelle Warrington." Sir Henry takes her hand and kisses it, as if she is the most precious thing on earth.

"My lord," Isabelle replies, looking down to the ground.

He releases her hand, his eyes lingering on her face.

Tension eases from Isabelle's shoulders as he addresses my aunt and uncle, "My Lord and Lady Golding, an honour to meet you."

"The honour is all ours, my lord." My aunt smiles.

I am acutely aware of the sudden volume of noise from behind us as the stands begin to fill and the other competitors begin to take their places on the range.

"Well then, I must take my leave. I have reserved you all the best seats in the main stand." I bow my head as my uncle and Sir Francis wish me good luck.

My aunt nods, still clearly annoyed at me competing

in my own event. She would never say anything in front of honoured guests, however. She leads Lady Percival to the main seating area in the centre of the stand, Isabelle and her betrothed not too far behind.

I do pray that he is the right man for her. I suppose neither of us have a choice; the union is official and will take place very soon. I don't want to lose her, see her shipped away to the south; a prospect I once thought was my fate. I haven't been very good at keeping friends, and have only ever really had my brother, then Isabelle, to confide in. I will miss her terribly.

Mr Sutton informs me that everything is ready as I make my way over to him on the other side of the arena. Everything is perfect. I stroke my hand over a round straw target, which sits at the end of one of the courses, a thin white rope pegged into the soft ground to indicate where an archer must stand when it is their turn to shoot. I wish my father and brother were here to see this; they would be proud of what I have achieved.

Soon the stands are full as the rest of the competitors have finally joined me on the field. I look around at the competition. I recognise the majority of them, but Lord John McNally is the first to greet me, his warming smile a comfort as always.

"My Lady Katherine. It's an honour to stand with ya in this grand tournament."

"Thank you, my lord, I am honoured to stand next to you," I reply.

Nine out of ten slots have been filled. My eyes linger on the empty target not too far away from me, wondering who is running rudely behind. If someone had thought to insult me by not attending, then they chose the wrong woman to insult.

I lean over to Lord McNally. "Do you know who we are waiting for?"

"No, I'm afraid not, my lady. I'm guessing yer uncle didn't give ya the list of names?"

"No, you know him as well as I do! He would never allow for me to have an advantage over the other competitors."

"Aye, he's a stickler for the rules that one."

As I begin to grumble and curse at the empty spot, I am startled by the sound of the trumpets that signal the beginning of the tournament. The crowds quieten. My uncle takes his place as announcer in the main stand where I stood not that long ago for the jousting tournament, and it looks like he has prepared a welcoming speech.

"Lords, ladies, gentlemen, on behalf of my niece, the Countess of Leicester, I welcome you all to today's archery tournament here at the great Leicester Castle."

Polite applause echoes around the stands.

"You are all in for a treat today as each competitor shall be pitted against one another, with only the two archers who score the highest number of points going through to the final round! There they will compete under the pressure of time in order to score as many points as possible." My uncle's enthusiasm and salesmanship are inspiring! I should ask him to write my next speech. He turns his head towards the competitors. "Now, my lords and lady, if you could take up your positions. After your name has been announced, you will then aim and fire your arrow into the target in front of you. Don't miss..."

Each one of us lines up in order. I am the first.

I breathe deeply and close my eyes for a few seconds, sensing hundreds of eyes staring at my back. I step forward. The sun is beating down on me. I breathe in and then, as I breathe out, I release the arrow, which spins through the air and plummets into the centre of the target, a perfect shot. The sound of applause from the crowd brings a small smile to my face.

"A perfect shot by the Countess!" my uncle announces.

Before each competitor takes their shot, my uncle announces their names in the following order: "Lord William Basildon… Lord John McNally… Sir Rupert of Loughborough… Sir Oliver Coalville… Lord James Barrow… Sir Robert Turnby… Lord Lewis Redford… Sir Francis Harrison…" and then, "Lord James Stanford."

My heart beats harder as my head snaps round to look for the man in question. How did I not know he was here? Searching the line of contestants, my eyes land on him. A small smile forms on his lips as he tries to avoid my gaze. I replay the last I saw of him – his leaving into the night, not knowing when I would see him again. I felt surprisingly forlorn as if a piece of me was taken with him.

He releases his arrow, which slices through the air into the centre of the target: a perfect shot.

His hair has been recently cut, and the stubble on his face hides a few old scars. The moment he informed me that he wasn't able to attend today, I told myself that I would never see him again. My mind wanders back to that night and how I felt in the warmth of his body, which was closely pressed against mine as we danced… The way my heart beat quicker as I caught him watching me from across the room… How a small part of me missed him… How I hardly know him.

It is only when Mr Sutton hands me more arrows that I realise it is my turn to go again as the next round begins. My mind is all over the place. I find it difficult to concentrate, too busy sensing his gaze upon me. I shake my head to clear my thoughts, his piercing blue eyes like a fire upon my skin.

"Concentrate, Katherine," I whisper to myself.

I close my left eye this time in order to zone in on the target at the end of the field, and miraculously my arrow finds the edge of the centre of the target again. Sir Francis and my uncle cheer as I step away from the standing line, pleased with my second attempt. I can breathe again.

Eventually, my uncle proclaims the start of the final. "I am pleased to announce that we have our finalists! Lord James Stanford and Countess of Leicester, you now compete for the tournament's grand prize."

I have no idea what the prize is. Isabelle joked that it would be my hand in marriage, and if I won then I got to marry myself; it's not a bad idea. I would normally oversee this sort of thing, but my uncle insisted that he took care of it, seeing as I was to compete as well.

"In this final round, each competitor will have until the hourglass runs out, in which time you must score the greatest number of points to win."

I didn't even know we owned an hourglass that small.

"Are you ready? Our Countess will go first with her practice shot."

I try to clear my mind again, releasing all of my thoughts into the sky above me so that I can concentrate.

I can do this. I have to! I do not know how I will look to the crowd if I lose on my own soil. This was my idea in the first place, to get my name onto the lips of those who dare misjudge my gender as my weakness.

This, however, is broken by a voice next to me. "Good luck, m'lady."

I look for the owner of that deep voice. Lord Stanford grins at me and nods towards the line where I must stand. My hands start to shake: the target is further away than before and I have to pull the bow with more force in hope that it will make the distance. Luckily, my bow is still as strong as the day that William gave it to me. His final gift.

Out of the corner of my eye, I catch Lord Stanford's mouth turn into a grin as he whispers so that only I can hear, "Take yer time, m'lady."

If this was an attempt at putting me off my aim, then he was successful, as my arrow slices through the air and hits the blue outer ring. "I blame that on you, my lord," I growl, annoyed at being distracted so easily, being made to look foolish.

"Ya were unlucky. At least it was only yer practice shot."

Lord Stanford takes his aim slowly, as if to prolong the strain of the bow, and when he lets go, the arrow buries itself neatly into the centre of the target. A perfect hit. I stand in amazement as the sound of admiration for the Yorkshireman echoes around us.

I try to find comfort in the stands where my family and friends are sitting. As I scan their happy little faces, I catch sight of Lord Henry Tyrell perched at the end of the main stand. My blood runs cold and my fist clenches at my side, nearly snapping my bow in half. How dare he defy my wishes and walk upon my land! Were my words not clear enough? Would he dare do this to another member of nobility? He is clever, I will give him that. He knows that I can do nothing about him being here, not with so many people watching. I must have been staring at him for far too long as Lord Tyrell does a mock salute before frowning.

"Looks like I still have an everlasting effect on 'im," Lord Stanford chuckles, his blond hair bouncing across his face as it is caught in the breeze.

"You're not the only one," I reply without thinking. I quickly change the subject. "I will not make this contest as easy for you, just because you thought you would surprise me after you said that you couldn't attend."

"I never said definitively that I wouldn't be able to. I didn't want ya to lose all 'ope from winning."

"Because you're so well known for your archery skills, Lord Stanford."

He lets out a small, amused laugh. "I'm known for better things than that, Lady Turner." He leans into me, the heat from his body intoxicating as I find myself tilting towards him.

"My Lady Turner, it is your turn." Mr Sutton's voice jolts me into reality.

Lord Stanford and I clear our throats and draw our attention back towards the competition.

I shake my head once, twice, three times to try to clear my mind. I line up my shot. It takes me two attempts to get my focus back, my aim a little off target. However, on my third, I hit the centre with a satisfying thud into the straw target. The hourglass for my final round has stopped and all I can do is breathe again.

As my rival takes up his position, I suddenly have an idea on how to distract Lord Stanford from winning.

"Take your time, Lord Stanford," I whisper just as he is about to release his bow, putting him off his aim as the arrow sinks into the outer circle.

"Now who's tryin' t'sabotage who?" he asks, a small grin on his lips.

"Oh, I'm known for more than that, Lord Stanford."

He looks at me with a smile and a light laugh, but nothing seems to faze him as I try to whisper unhelpful thoughts, as his second, third and even fourth slice satisfyingly into the centre circle. I stand there for a second counting his score in my head, but Lord Stanford's smile all but tells me that I have lost.

"Congratulations, my lord," I say as the crowd applauses and cheers behind us. "Is it nice to finally win something?"

Lord Stanford runs his hand through his hair and laughs. "Maybe the competition wasn't as fierce this time."

"Fierce?" I take a small step towards him. "If you want to see how fierce I can be—"

The booming voice of my uncle interrupts me as he says, "Lords and ladies, I present to you your champion: Lord James Stanford!"

The applause from the crowd springs us apart. Lord Stanford collects his prize, a golden arrow, too heavy to actually fire. I admire it from a distance as it glints in the midday sun above us; it would have looked wonderful in my library.

As both competitors and the spectators make their way back up the hill and into the castle courtyard, I turn to collect my arrows from Mr Sutton.

"Bad luck, my lady. You'll get them next time." He smiles.

"I certainly will, Mr Sutton! Thank you for helping today."

Just as I am about to turn around to leave, I nearly knock into the victor himself.

"Careful, m'lady."

My hands press against his chest to balance myself as he holds me tight. We stay like that for a fleeting moment. I can feel the steady rhythm of his heart beating. Before either of us can say anything, my aunt and uncle arrive to congratulate us both. We step away from one another, dusting ourselves down.

"Well done, my girl." My uncle beams, crushing me against his chest.

Even my aunt gives me a warm hug. "Well done, Katherine. You impressed me out there today."

"You tried your best, Lady Turner." Another voice joins us, one that pins me to the spot.

"Lord Tyrell." I place a tight smile on my face as he makes his way towards us. "I thought you were on the other side of the kingdom, far, far away from here?" I ask, insinuating my distaste for his trespass upon my land.

"It is expected for the champion of the joust to attend the next event, even if they do not take part themselves. Also, I said that I wouldn't miss it for the world and I always keep my promises." Lord Tyrell grins a hungry grin I have seen before, that day outside of the tent, his words laced with ill-intent. He diverts his attention to the Yorkshireman close beside me. "Lord Stanford. I did not know that you were so good with an arrow. I thought you didn't have time for these sorts of things with your estate in the way that it is," he remarks through a slanted grin.

"I'd rather put my skill to good use, Lord 'enry, and show what I can do. There are those of us who can do as we say and those who can only dream."

"*I* have no need to prove anything. I already won the joust… if not something else."

I try to remain calm at Lord Tyrell's attempt at insinuating something stronger between us. "I need to make sure that all my guests are making their way in the right direction before retiring to the castle." I begin to back away from the small crowd forming around me, feeling too many eyes on me, and my keen desire to be away from Lord Tyrell before I do something *very* unladylike. "I will see you all at the feast this evening."

"I'm looking forward to it," Lord Tyrell replies.

Something inside me churns at his words. His voice irritates me, his presence is an insult to my authority. Before I take another step, I say to Lord Stanford, making sure that Lord Tyrell can overhear, "As you are the winner, Lord Stanford, you have the honour of sitting next to me at the head of the table. I am most looking forward to getting to know you better."

I don't wait for his reply or Lord Tyrell's reaction, as they both watch me walk away.

Twelve

Bess quickly tidies up my hair, pinning it in place with the same headpiece that I wore for the joust's banquet. She soon leaves me to myself as she too needs to get ready, and I want to be alone in the comforting peace before the heavy evening ahead.

In the silence of my bedchamber, I close my eyes and count to ten. I take a deep breath in, then exhale, trying to steady my nerves. I have never been this anxious before an event in my own castle. I thought that after I exiled Lord Tyrell from my castle grounds, it would be enough for me to feel free of him. Why didn't my uncle throw him out for me? I suppose it is because he is keen not to make an enemy out of him.

I also thought that I wouldn't see Lord Stanford again. I had tried to erase him from my mind, but he has always been there, lingering in the distance whether I acknowledged him or not. As I fidget with the hem of my sleeve, it becomes clearer as to why I am feeling a little more nervous than usual. There is something about Lord Stanford that makes my pulse quicken every time I see him. I try to push him out of my mind, but then I think about his smile and those beautiful blue eyes.

"This is ridiculous," I grunt, grabbing William's ring and securing it around my neck.

I shut my bedchamber door firmly behind me, putting one foot in front of the other, trying to ignore my rapid heartbeat in my chest.

There is a cacophony of noise in the Great Hall as benches and chairs are scraped back and everyone gets to their feet. I feel every pair of eyes follow us as Lord Stanford and I sit at the top table.

"Please be seated," I call.

Once everyone has settled, the servants present the main dishes and the fine-looking wild boar that I shot yesterday, which has been freshly decorated with a plump, red apple in its mouth.

Lord Stanford's gaze drifts to the creature, perfectly roasted. "Yer uncle told me that I should thank ya for our main dish tonight."

"It was a team effort. My uncle flushed him out, I shot it and Isabelle supervised." I laugh, remembering how Isabelle stood way back from everything and everyone else whilst it all happened.

"Ya made the fatal kill?"

I prickle. "You sound surprised, my lord. If I was a man, would you have asked the same question?"

"Ah, yer putting words into my mouth, Lady Turner. I didn't mean to cause offence. It's just that I am intrigued by yer more *adventurous* side."

His foot casually grazes my own and it is everything for me not to lean into his touch.

Wine is poured into our goblets as music soon starts to fill the room and the lively beat washes away my worries. I take a few gulps from my goblet, nearly finishing it before I have a chance to eat anything.

This soon catches the attention of Lord Stanford who only laughs at me with amusement. “Ya want to be careful, m’lady, powerful stuff that.” He nods towards the wine in my hand.

“I think I can handle my own wine. I’ll have you know that my father has wonderful taste. Excuse me… *had* wonderful taste.”

“I don’t doubt it.” He too takes a sip from the cup in front of him. “How does it feel to be the head of house, to ’ave everyone stare whenever ya walk into a room as grand as this?”

“Would you prefer everyone to look at you instead of me?” I say.

“I can see why any man’s attention would be distracted whilst yer in the room.”

I pretend to take another sip from my goblet, but in fact I am trying to hide the redness of my cheeks.

“I do not care for such attention. To answer your original question, it is something that I did not know would fall to me, but I am proud to carry on my family’s legacy. If I may be frank, it seems it is easier for men to do business with other men. Sometimes I wonder if I should just ask my uncle to step in. I find it hard to be taken seriously when it comes to more crucial matters.”

“I’m sure that yer doing just as well, if not better, than

yer uncle. I have only ever heard him and others praise ya."

His words warm me a little, rarely hearing such positive words from a new acquaintance. I hide my smile behind yet another sip from my goblet, for the first time in a long while not knowing what to say in reply.

More food arrives and we pile up our plates again – it is as if we haven't eaten in days! As I finish mopping up the last puddles of sauce from my bowl, I glance over at Isabelle as she laughs at something her uncle says, her future husband gazing admirably at her as she does. I was so worried for her, remembering her spilt tears soon after she agreed to marry Sir Henry, but looking at them now, as she tilts her head closer towards his, I hope that will be the final time she will ever need to cry.

Lord Stanford rises from his seat, drawing my attention away from the rest of the room, and extends a hand, asking for a dance. I accept. As soon as we face one another, he pulls me closer towards him, gently caressing the back of my hand with his thumb. The lute begins to play and we move in time to the steady rhythm, and I am unable to take my gaze away from him. It is as if it is just us in the room.

"I… I 'ave been thinking about dancing with ya ever since I saw ya last," he murmurs, his gaze falling away from my own.

I try my best not to allow my heart to take control over my head at hearing these words, but the closer we move together, the harder it is.

"Well, if you stayed longer last time, perhaps you could have danced with me again."

"I didn't want to go, but…" He pauses.

"But what?"

"It doesn't matter, I'm 'ere now." He pushes a rogue hair away from my face, his fingers lightly brushing my cheek, ignoring the staring faces around the room.

"James," I whisper, leaning into his touch, warmth radiating from his body, comforting me.

"Katherine, I…"

"Yes?" I ask, barely being able to breathe, as if doing so would mean I couldn't hear his voice.

He stands up a little straighter, pulling away slightly. "I'm just so 'appy I beat ya today."

I smile and tighten my grip on his hand, digging my nails in lightly.

"Ouch!" he laughs. "Otherwise, I wouldn't be so lucky as to be this close to ya."

"You didn't have to win to do that," I whisper, my heart-filled thoughts spilling from my lips.

As the song continues, he pulls me in tighter. My hands fit perfectly in his. The rhythm picks up and so do our steps as we make our way around the room, not breaking away from each other for even a second. I let out an exhilarated laugh as I spin around and back into his arms once more, feeling a little lightheaded. As the music fades and we find our finishing positions, we stand there, looking at one another. His eyes sparkle in the candlelight as his handsome face lights up when he smiles.

I wet my bottom lip with my tongue slowly; his eyes immediately follow. "James, would you like to—"

Before I can finish my request, I am cut off by a light tap on my shoulder.

I whip around to face the person who dares interrupt

us, only to find Lord Tyrell extending his hand towards me. "May I have this next dance, Lady Turner?"

I prickle at his boldness, staring at his open hand so alien to me. "Actually, I was just about to..."

"You don't want to look like you have favourites in a room full of friends, do you?" Lord Tyrell grins.

"You are correct, Lord Tyrell. Hence why I have other matters to attend to rather than just dance. Thank you for reminding me."

I step away from both men – the warmth of Lord Stanford and the coldness of Lord Tyrell – and make my way to the other side of the room, hoping to get lost amongst the crowd whilst trying not to lose my cool and steady my heart. As I observe the room, I see many of my guests spending their time chatting amongst themselves: old friends reunited, new friendships beginning, lovers meeting in secret; the Great Hall is filled with laughter and life. As I make my way amongst the crowd, I spot Lord Winchester and his wife, a perfect opportunity to make closer acquaintances.

"My Lord and Lady Winchester, it is wonderful to see you both again."

Lord Winchester, a rather round man, turns to me without a smile. "Lady Turner."

Heavy silence lingers.

I have been meaning to forge stronger alliances with Lord Winchester, who is the earl of the city which he is named after. I believe that we can be valuable allies to one another, especially as my county is regularly supplying the wool his people need in order to make his wife's fine clothes. Winchester is still a powerful stronghold of the south.

"How are you enjoying the wine, my lord? It is a fine vintage from when my father was the earl here." I gesture to the goblet in his hand.

His face doesn't display any emotion when he replies, "It is adequate."

I purse my lips together, otherwise I might tell him something he would find utmost *in*adequate.

"Not as fine as the wine we have in *our* cellar is it, my dear husband?" Lady Winchester speaks up, looking down her pointy nose at me.

"Indeed," her husband replies. He looks down at her, his eyes narrow as he huffs through his nose, behaviour I have seen in many men who hate a confident wife.

"Perhaps next time I am in the south of England we could discuss this at further length. I am interested in talking to you about—" I begin.

"When do you ever leave this quaint little town, my lady?" Lord Winchester's curt tone cuts me off. "Besides, it is not becoming for one to invite oneself to another's property without a formal invitation. I will, however, let you know when we are available to receive you, Lady Turner. Now, if you would excuse us." He shakes his head a little and turns his back away from me, leaving me staring, teeth gritted with unspoken anger.

His words and tone are nothing new to me, especially from such powerful members of court. I used to ball my hands into fists and grit my teeth, almost ready for a fight, but then I would remember that being aggressive would only cause more harm. It is best to smile politely and walk away.

"Very well, my lord. Thank you for accepting *my* gracious invitation for today's festivities. Please do enjoy my father's *adequate* wine. Don't forget to leave before it becomes too dark. I'd hate for you to lose your way." I don't wait to see if they have a response before I walk away.

I find myself sitting on the edge of the crowd again. I catch my aunt throwing various unprepared men upon Bess to dance with her. Sir Francis and Lord Derby are deep in conversation about one thing or another near the far side of the room. Isabelle has been by her future husband's side for all of the evening. My uncle and Lord Stanford have tucked themselves away near a magnificent display of sweet treats, fresh from our kitchen below. I pluck a strawberry off the top of one of the tarts, popping it into my mouth, savouring all of the sweetness that tingles on my tongue.

"I remember when your father started the renovation on that house! It was just after he had repaired your family's monastery. It's good to see it in a capable man's hands once more." My uncle pats Lord Stanford on the back. "Ah, Katherine, Lord Stanford was telling me about his plans for his estate back home."

"Oh, really? And what do you have planned, my lord?" I ask, keen to learn more about him.

"I want to extend the Grand Hall and place a beautiful stained-glass window at the bottom, so when ya sit facing it, ya can see all of the beautiful colours shine through."

"I'd love to see it when you have finished," I offer, before realising how improper it might have sounded.

"I couldn't think of a better person to ask for their honest opinion. Other than my sister of course." He laughs, side-eyeing my uncle.

"Ah yes, your sister has an opinion about everything!" he chuckles.

Before I can protest their insinuation that I like to give my opinion on everything, Sir Francis joins us and asks to speak to my uncle in private, leaving me and Lord Stanford alone. I feel his soft gaze upon me, but when I steal a chance to look at him, he looks away.

"Are you staying at the White Boar Inn again tonight?" I ask, afraid of this night, and his company, ending too soon.

"I 'ave been invited to stay 'ere in yer castle, if that is alright with the lady of the house?" he asks, a small smile curved upon his lips.

I sharply intake an involuntary breath. I knew quite a few of my guests were staying here tonight, but I never realised Lord Stanford was one of them.

"Good. I mean, that's… suitable, so you don't have to travel in the dark." I try to rescue myself. "I think a few other guests are staying here also."

"Not in the same room, I 'ope."

We both laugh, a slight nervousness in the air between us, or is it excitement?

"Well in that case, I hope you enjoy your stay. If you ever need anything, I'm sure one of my servants will help you, or me if I am available… just in case anything happens." My cheeks soften into a light blush; it must be the heat around the room.

"I would like that, m'lady."

Our fingers brush one another's as I lean closer towards him. Slowly, as if he's waiting to see if I will pull away first, his hand takes mine and doesn't let go. His warmth is so enticing. The longing I feel whenever he is not with me is something I have never felt before, like a thirst that can never truly be quenched.

He reaches for a strand of hair that has fallen over my eyes. "Katherine." His hand lingers on my cheek. "I truly think that yer the most beautiful woman I 'ave ever seen. Ever since I saw ya in my tent that day, I can't get ya out of my mind."

I search his eyes, trying to see if what he said is the truth. I kept attempting to convince myself that he felt nothing for me, that he was just too polite to turn away my invitation. Perhaps he is only after that which Lord Tyrell is after too. Lord Stanford is not like other men that I have met before, though. He hasn't tried to impress me with grand gestures of triumph or by putting others down to make him seem superior. Whenever he is around me, I feel like I can be myself, rather than having to be cautious or noble all the time. He is kind and courteous, as well as being respected by those around him.

"James, I... I..." I pause, thinking of what I want to say. I want to reply with: *I cannot seem to be able to get you out of my mind. Whenever you are away from me, you are all I can think about. When you are with me, when your hand takes mine, you are all I want.* But I can't seem to say those words just yet; that would be foolish.

"Have I made the great Countess speechless?" he chuckles, to which I can only laugh in reply, settling my thoughts again. "I would never pressure ya into anything ya didn't want to say. I wanted ya to know how I felt before the evening ends."

My reply is wordless as I take his hand in my own.

Before we are able to join the other dancers who are eagerly waiting for the next song to begin, our path is blocked by Lord Tyrell, who has clearly drunk too much wine as his eyes glaze over when he speaks.

"I hope that I am not intruding on anything," he asks as if he is my lord and saviour, spying on me from afar.

"Yes, you are, Lord Tyrell, you are intruding on a delightful evening, not only with your presence, but your lack of self-control with my wine cellar," I reply, my impatience bubbling to the surface for the first time this evening.

Lord Stanford also takes a small step towards Lord Tyrell, towering over him. "Please move aside. It doesn't look too good on ya to be standing in the Countess's way."

"Huh." Lord Tyrell blinks at Lord Stanford then me and then back again. "Well, it looks like your country charms are finally working well on my lady, but then again…" he slurs, his breath so pungent I recoil.

"Let's not start something ya can't finish, Tyrell." Lord Stanford places his hand on his belt, perhaps where his dagger ordinarily sits.

"I think the lady can speak for herself," Lord Tyrell replies, swaying on his feet.

"That is enough." I lower my voice, hoping that the rest of the room is oblivious as to what is happening over here. "You have overstepped your mark for the final time, Lord Tyrell. Leave my home and my guests quietly before you do yourself any more harm."

I try my hardest not to shout and push this disgusting lord away from me. My eyes scan the hall for my uncle and Sir Francis, but they are nowhere to be seen.

Gaining confidence from somewhere deep inside his blackened soul, Lord Tyrell lets out a small dark laugh, devoid of humour. "Katherine is not one you can have your way with and then leave, like you have done with so many women in the past, Stanford."

His words take me aback. What could he mean by that? What does he know that I don't? Surely, he is speaking out of pure jealousy. I know that my uncle would never want me near Lord Stanford if such rumours were true. My uncle is a longstanding close friend of the Stanfords. No, I don't believe Lord Tyrell at all.

"I don't care what ya say about me, Tyrell, I know the truth and yer clearly do not."

His words hang in the air between us. If we were alone, I would ask him to repeat it, but instead I am reminded of exactly where I am by Lord Tyrell's smirk as he lets out a small, drunken laugh. "Ha! How scandalous. I see that maybe you have already been at work, Stanford."

How dare he? After he tried to seduce me, what tiny speck of moral ground does this man have left to stand on? Perhaps I should have been more careful with Lord Stanford, not allowed my heart to rule over my head again. But he is different. I feel different! This is more than lust, more than desire, something for which I have secretly longed for some time, and I will make sure Lord Tyrell will not stand in my way!

"That is enough! I am the lady of this house and neither I, nor my guests, will be spoken to in such an insulting way, Lord Tyrell. Has anything I said resonated with you? You state that you want to be friends. Well, if this is how you treat your friends, I do not want to be yours! You have overstayed your welcome here for the final time!" My hands ball into fists at my side, my voice rising with each syllable, gaining more interest from those around us.

The rest of the room turns silent. I can feel the heads of everyone turn to look over at us from all corners of the room. Even the music seems to have stopped. Lord Tyrell senses this too, standing up straight. His face begins to turn a lighter shade of red, either out of embarrassment or shock.

"My lady, I-I do not mean you any harm. I apologise. Please forgive me." Lord Tyrell turns on his heels and heads for the other side of the room without another word to anybody.

My heart slams against my ribcage and my blood pumps in my ears. I catch my uncle and Sir Francis glance over at us, eyebrows raised, but I choose to ignore their attentive looks with a shake of my head; I can handle myself.

"Please, continue your evening," I raise my voice so that everyone in the room can hear. I nod at the musicians who play a merrier tune as if nothing has happened. I just hope this doesn't reflect badly on me and my house.

After a brief moment to collect myself, I turn to Lord Stanford who has been patiently waiting by my side whilst I gather my thoughts. "I am sorry about that. No guest of mine should ever be insulted in my home."

"There is nothing for ya to apologise for." He pauses, looking towards the path Lord Tyrell took before exiting the room. "Please be careful of that one."

"I think I can handle myself," I bite back, a little harsher than I intended.

He looks at me with bated breath. "I am very sure that ya can. I did not mean that ya can't, I just don't want ya to be in harm's way."

"I appreciate your concerns, James, but I do not need a knight in shining armour anymore."

As everyone retires for the evening, I follow Lord Stanford up the winding staircase and to the end of the corridor, which separates our rooms from one another.

"Goodnight. It was a wonderful evening," I breathe, drops of disappointment at having to end it here lacing my words.

Lord Stanford remains quiet, taking a small step towards me. "Does it have to end 'ere?"

"Yes, I'm very tired," I reply, uncertain, staring towards my bedchamber door.

"In that case, goodnight, Lady Katherine."

I face away from him, but something makes me pause. Do I really want the night to end here? Can I walk away now when he is just a few feet away? Will he leave early in the morning so that I never see him again? I close my eyes, thinking back to what my uncle said about listening to my heart, rather than my head. When I open them again, I spin around, my mind made up.

Lord Stanford has not moved an inch.

Without thinking, I close the gap between us, our breath taking up the short space between our lips. I close my eyes, plunging into the kiss, wrapping my arms around the back of his neck. Lord Stanford mirrors my hunger as I melt into him. His hands move to my waist, pulling me impossibly closer with a gentle tug.

I steer him to the other side of the corridor, stopping just before the door to his room, not daring to let go or alert those sleeping in the rooms around us. I push the doorhandle upwards and we throw ourselves inside. As soon as the door is closed, he pulls away from me for a second, staring deeply into my eyes, hand against my cheek. I press my lips against his again, hungry for his touch.

I was sure that I could resist him. I was sure that I could just push him out of my mind and forget that he ever existed, but I can't. I don't want to. I vowed to never let another man near me after I learnt the truth about Lord Tyrell, but Lord Stanford is all I can think about. I don't want to play games, wait for him to approach me. I am a woman who knows her own mind, who takes bold action, asking for forgiveness instead of permission.

As his lips touch mine, his arms wrap around my waist, unable to let go. I didn't want this night to end and I will make sure it doesn't so easily.

To my disappointment, he pulls away. "I would never want to put ya in a situation yer uncomfortable in, nor one that would cause ya harm."

"I am in control of my own actions, James. I choose this. I choose you."

Soundlessly, he wraps his arms around me in reply and kisses my lips, then my neck, then behind my ear, nibbling my earlobe. We make our way over to the bed in the middle of the room, stumbling blindly.

I lie down next to him. He studies me, smiling when I ask, "What? What is it?"

"Nothin'. Yer just so beautiful."

"You're just saying that so I stay."

"Is it workin'?" he smirks.

"Maybe," I tease, before taking a more serious tone. "I feel safe with you, James. I don't often say that to many people. Now kiss me before I change my mind."

The night gives way to the early hours of the morning.

With an overwhelming feeling of joy and happiness, my eyes begin to feel heavy, finally catching up with the rest of me as we fall into a deep and peaceful sleep. I lay my head on his chest and smile when he wraps his strong arms around me. I have never felt this safe, this happy. He seems to shine light into every shadow, life into everything he sees, love into every smile.

***

Just as daylight hits the window in his room, I wake up to the sound of the birds chirping outside. I know that I must go before the rest of the castle awakens for the long day ahead. It wouldn't be worth even thinking about the consequences of someone finding us together like this, but the movement of James beside me melts some of that anxiety away.

"Morning, James." I close my eyes as he kisses my forehead. "I don't want to, but I have to go."

The smile on his handsome face fades. "I don't want ya to go, but I understand ya have to."

I rise and straighten my dress, pinning back my hair, just in case anyone spots me out in the corridor. Before I reach the door, I turn and find him looking up at me from the other side of the room. He walks over as I lift the latch, taking my hand in his and leaning in to brush his lips against mine.

"I will see you soon, James."

"Not soon enough," he sighs, kissing me once more before I open the door and sneak my way back to my own room, hopefully unnoticed.

Thirteen

I shut my door silently and let out a small breath. The sun has only just risen, stretching across the sky in a pinkish haze. It makes my room glow with a red intensity, which is strengthened by the crimson and gold drapes hanging from my four-poster bed.

I change out of my evening clothes and sit on the edge of the bed. There isn't much point trying to get back to sleep – how can I? I trace my finger across my lips where Lord Stanford's lips met mine, where his hand trailed down my side, how I shivered with delight as he whispered into my ear. He is everywhere.

I am bought back into the present by a knock at the door, after which Bess enters with a bowlful of fresh water.

"My lady." She curtseys before placing the ceramic bowl near the window.

Bess looks at me with narrowed eyes and slowed movements – my hair is still in the same style in which she left it, though a little rumpled, and I am not normally this awake at this time of the morning, let alone sitting on the edge of the bed. If she notices any of these things, she doesn't mention it.

I splash my face, using lavender soap to scrub at my skin. I inhale the floral aroma whirling around the murky water in the bowl in front of me and feel myself waking up, my focus sharpening. We move over to the vanity unit and Bess begins to restyle my hair for the day ahead.

"I didn't see you retire to bed last night. Is everything alright?" Bess asks quietly whilst she brushes my hair, and I stare out of the window absent-mindedly.

"Fine, just fine. I… went to bed early but didn't get much sleep. Too many things to think about," I say, hoping that Bess doesn't think any more of it.

After I am fully dressed, I make my way downstairs and find myself bumping into Lord Stanford.

Our eyes meet, and my cheeks grow hot. I so desperately want to reach out to him, feel his touch against my skin again, the eagerness of his lips against mine, soak in the warmth that radiates all around him. However, I take a small step back, as though shaking myself awake from a daydream.

"I hope your accommodations were to your liking," I say. On the one hand, I am aching to know whether he has any regrets about what we did last night. But on the other, I'm not sure I want to know.

"Aye, m'lady, the room is lovely." His eyes linger on mine then drop to my lips.

Everything is silent around us, but before I can think of anything else to say, he closes the gap and takes my face in his hands, planting a long and lingering kiss on my lips. All doubt is blown away in an instant. I can't think of anything but him; all other thoughts are pushed out of my mind completely.

Reluctantly, I pull away, half in consciousness of being seen by anyone who could pass us in the corridor.

"I ain't been able to think about doing anything else since I last saw ya," he whispers, his voice like a siren's song to me.

As noises further down the corridor become louder, we step back from one another.

I straighten myself and clear my throat. "Everyone will be in the Great Hall; we'd best make ourselves known. Plus, I am starving."

Isabelle, Sir Francis and my uncle are already seated. There are a few guests dotted about the room enjoying a fresh selection of fruits, breads and preserves for breakfast. Lord Stanford and I sit with my uncle and Sir Francis just as Isabelle stands up to leave.

"I have that effect on people, Lord Stanford. Isabelle especially," I tease.

Isabelle turns to face me, a small grin playing on her lips in amusement. "That's not the only effect you have on people." She grins, quickly darting her eyes towards the Yorkshireman next to me. "I promised to visit Sir Henry and his mother in town today and so thought I would get ready to ride out soon." She looks down at the empty plate in front of her, then adds, "You are welcome to come with me if you wish? It would be nice to ride with you."

"I'd love to, if you can wait a little longer?" I gesture towards the fresh plate of food in front of me.

Isabelle nods. I turn towards Lord Stanford, who is carefully pouring a refreshing beverage into my cup. "Lord

Stanford, you are also welcome to join us, if that is alright with Isabelle?"

"Of course, more than welcome!"

"I do 'ave business in town, so I would be delighted to accompany ya both. Besides, who else will make sure ya don't get into any trouble?" He grins, taking a bite out of a piece of freshly baked bread.

"That is settled then. Katherine, Lord Stanford, I will meet you outside when you are ready." Isabelle sneaks a quick glance at me with a wide-eyed expression before she leaves the room.

I roll my eyes and shake my head as she shuts the door behind her. I hope no one else noticed her lack of subtlety.

I go back to finishing my breakfast, but soon we are interrupted by my uncle.

"How did you find yesterday's festivities, Katherine? I thought it went very well," he asks as he grabs a bread roll from the basket next to him.

"It was great to see everyone enjoying themselves, Uncle."

"Yes, it is so nice to see everyone having fun for a change, don't you think?" Sir Francis adds, now engrossed in a letter in front of him.

"Did you enjoy the food?" my uncle asks, slathering his bread roll in jam.

"Yes, I dare to say that we have the most talented cooks in all of England, Uncle." I shove a honey-covered bread roll in my mouth to stop myself from having to answer any more questions about last night. Underneath the table, Lord Stanford's fingers stroke my hand; it takes everything I have to not react openly.

"And, Lord Stanford, how did you find yesterday? I trust you slept well?"

Lord Stanford nods at my uncle and takes a gulp from the goblet in front of him.

"I trust Katherine didn't keep you up too long? I saw you two chatting away before leaving for the evening," my uncle asks.

Lord Stanford tries his best not to choke on his drink, coughing a few times. I reach for a napkin to disguise my red cheeks. "Not at all! After all the food and dancing, I fell asleep straight away."

"A lucky escape for you then! I know that sometimes she can talk for hours!" My uncle chuckles, not seeming to notice anything out of the ordinary. "Don't tell the other guests but..." he leans in and whispers, "we made sure that *you* had our best room, lad." He laughs joyfully. "I trust you are staying for a few more days? I would love to take you out hunting."

"I intend to stay a little while longer." His eyes flit towards mine. "If Lady Turner allows me to?"

"Of course she doesn't mind," my uncle replies before I can say a word. Luckily, my uncle is correct.

Lord Stanford nods at my uncle, but then turns towards me, eyebrow raised, waiting for my answer.

"I'm sure I can put up with you for a few more days."

My pulse quickens at the thought of stealing more moments with Lord Stanford like last night. Now he is under my roof, will I be able to control my true desires? I will have to be careful. I don't want others to see the effect he has on me.

His hand finds mine under the table again, gently twinning my fingers with his.

"Where's my aunt?" I ask, trying to steer the conversation away from yesterday's activities.

"Oh, she's in her quarters I believe – embroidering or something, I don't know." My uncle leans back in his chair, coughing heavily.

I sit up alarmed. "I hope you're feeling well, Uncle."

My uncle is a strong man for his age, having lived through many bleak wars like my father. I've never seen him ill before and I hope I never will.

"I'm fine, my girl, I'm just tired… getting old," he jokes before taking a sip from his goblet. "Besides, I must be off. Sir Francis and I have a few errands to run."

Once my uncle and Sir Francis have left the room, chatting to one another, Lord Stanford lets out a small, relieved laugh, running his fingers through his golden hair.

I twist to face him. "So how did you sleep, my lord?"

"Like I was next to an angel, m'lady," he laughs.

***

Isabelle is already on her horse and waiting to leave when we step outside. She strokes her mare's neck softly. It is a fresh, sunny day with only a few fluffy clouds in the sky and a scattering of birds chirping happily in the nearby tree. John leads William out of the stable and then helps me into my saddle. As I take the reins from him, Lord Stanford appears and saddles up beside me on his beautiful grey horse.

Lord Stanford's eyes find my own, and I cannot help but feel happier with him around. I instantly feel safer, stronger, like we could achieve anything together. I know that it would seem that we barely know each other – and in many ways we don't – but there is a secret understanding between us, something that I can't quite explain yet.

We trot through the castle's woodland, the light of the morning shining brightly through the trees, highlighting the green veins of the leaves in the canopy above us. I enjoy the peaceful sounds of the birds, the smell of fresh earth beneath our horses' hooves and the chance to escape the stifling walls of the castle. This was my father's favourite trail to take me on when I was just beginning to learn how to ride. He would always be by my side to make sure that I didn't fall off or wander somewhere deep into the trees.

"A gold coin for yer thoughts, Lady Katherine."

"Oh!"

Lord James catches me off guard as he slows down next to me, Isabelle just a few paces ahead of us.

"I was just thinking back to when I rode through here with my father when I was young and just learning to master a horse of my own. I remember this one time my father took me and my brother hunting. My horse got spooked by something in the trees and *bolted*. It was all I could do to hold on.

"You know, my father was a strong and powerful man – he faced death countless times on his marches for the king and saw things I can never imagine – but in that moment all I saw in him was panic. He looked… vulnerable, somehow. Luckily, he caught up with me and took hold of my reins, managed to calm the mare. It's barely a story worth remembering, really. But I will never forget how scared he looked." I pause for a moment. For some reason, I can't bring myself to look at Lord Stanford. I clear my throat. "He, um, he never let me ride out alone after that."

"That sounds scary for any rider, let alone a child," he says.

"Oh, and William was *beside* himself. He blamed himself for some reason, fretting about letting me out of his sight, but there was nothing he could have done. Anyway, it's not like I fell off or anything. I've always been a tough girl, after all."

A comfortable silence passes between us.

"I do admire yer strength, Katherine. I 'ave seen what this world can do to innocent people, especially those who aren't prepared for the outside world."

I raise my eyebrow in amusement. "I can assure you that I am not as innocent as you might think I am." I blush, realising how that might have sounded. "W-what I mean is, that I have life experience and can handle anything that is in my way."

A small smile curls onto his lips at my innocent faux pas, before he continues with, "I know that now, and I can see that yer father and brother educated ya well, teaching ya about the harsh realities of the outside world. It's something I wished my sister had been taught when she was young. She's learnt the 'ard way." His gaze grows hard and distant.

"What do you mean?" I ask. Most men want rid of their siblings so they can rule alone, regardless of what is best for that person. It just goes to show how much Lord Stanford is not like other men.

"Let's just say that her choice of husband wasn't the best decision."

"Is he really that bad? I know you told me last night that he is hardly at home, but is that truly a bad thing? I have heard of many married couples who live more happily apart than they ever could together."

"Aye, I just wish that I had been there to warn her," he sighs.

I'm intrigued to find out more but sense that now is not the moment to question him.

"Anyway, she loves him more than anything else in this world and I wouldn't come between that."

Isabelle shouts over her shoulder, "You know how important it is that I am not late. It doesn't look good for a woman to make her future family wait in a town they don't even know."

"Maybe you should focus more on your future *husband* than what his mother thinks," I comment, not really thinking to filter my thoughts before I speak them out loud.

"One day you will find out that it's not that simple, Katherine," Isabelle sighs with annoyance.

"I'm only telling you what I would do in your shoes. You are marrying *him*, not his mother. As soon as you are his wife, you have the power to kick her out of your marital home and you can release Sir Henry from his chains once and for all."

She only grumbles in reply, staying quiet for the remainder of the ride.

It does not take long to reach town. We enter through the old Roman walls at Southgate then turn onto Friar Lane towards the market. The streets of Leicester are already a bustling hive of women buying food from the market, men trying to sell at the highest price and children running through the lanes, their shouts of laughter bouncing off the walls. Smells of herbs, leather, wool, warm baked goods and fresh flowers permeate the air, which is quickly followed by the stench of horse manure, rotting fish and other unpleasant smells. I greet a few of the townspeople who smile and bow politely as I pass.

Eventually, we turn onto St Francis Lane and stop outside of the Guild Hall – a small but beautiful building – and tie up our horses who happily drink up the water in the trough in front of them. Whilst waiting for Isabelle to unhook her cloak from her saddle bag, I look up at Saint Martin's Church, standing tall in the centre of the town. It towers above us as the bells begin to ring out, signalling the end of morning prayers. Memories of my father's and William's funeral are all that I see when I look at the building. Despite having attended various baptisms, Easter celebrations and Christmas masses, all I see is sorrow. Perhaps one day, I will be able to look at it in a happier light, but that will take time.

Eventually, the three of us make our way towards Greyfriars on the other side of Saint Martin's where Isabelle agreed to meet Sir Henry and his mother. Both are patiently waiting outside.

"Lady Warrington, Lady Turner *and* Lord Stanford, it is wonderful to see you again." Sir Henry takes Isabelle's hand and kisses it softly. "Thank you for being our guide in this beautiful town of yours, my lady, and my Countess Turner."

"It is no chore, my lord, I want you to enjoy all that my county can offer, and there is no better place to start than Greyfriars." I turn to speak to Lord Stanford, who is looking up at the impressive building, admiring the beautiful glass windows that sparkle in the sunlight with a plethora of colours. "Lord Stanford, you won't be disappointed either."

He turns to me with a tight smile. "I regret that I must leave ya. I 'ave to meet a gentleman in town who I 'ave been avoiding since I arrived."

"Oh." I try my best not to sound too disappointed. "Do you require company?"

"It's alright, thank you, m'lady. Please excuse me, I will meet ya here as soon as I am done."

"Of course." I stand still, a little reluctant to let him go.

"Well, Katherine, shall we?" Isabelle touches my arm, breaking my gaze from the tall, blond Yorkshireman walking away from us. I wonder if I should follow him to see who this mysterious gentleman could possibly be, but before I have the chance, Sir Henry calls my name and I join them inside.

We are greeted by one of the monks, who is dressed plainly in a dark-brown smock neatly tied in the middle with a white belt. He welcomes us inside, blessing us with holy water as we enter. Greyfriars is not as elaborate as Saint Martin's; the stained-glass windows depict Christ and his virgin mother Mary in the different stages of his short life, from his birth to his death and resurrection at Easter. During the twelve days of Christmas, it is a tradition that the Countess or Earl of Leicester and family visit the different places of worship and pay their respects to our Lord and God, giving the monks a purse of gold as a donation.

Looking down at my feet, I pick out the intricate flooring of the church, the terracotta-coloured tiles, painted with symmetrical designs, perfectly set in a spiralling rhythm throughout the building. When I look up, to my surprise, Sir Henry and his mother have drifted to one end, leaving Isabelle and me at the other.

I lean in towards her and whisper, "I thought you were here to spend time with your future husband?"

"I was. I *am*. It's just that they wanted a tour of the whole building and I didn't want to leave you alone."

"Isabelle, please, I don't believe you. You need to put your foot down. These first few months will cement your standing in their family. Don't let his mother take anything away from you."

"Katherine, please, let me handle this in my own way," she bristles, a warning for me to back off.

We kneel and pray silently for a little while. I pray for my parents' and brother's souls so that they are blessed in God's keeping. I pray that the people of Leicester are safe from disaster and disease. I pray for strength for the days to come. After a moment's quiet reflection, I stand up again and bow my head towards the altar in respect before leaving Isabelle deep in her own prayers.

My footsteps echo around the high ceiling and bounce off the stone walls. I try to lighten my steps so as not to disturb those around me. I know every inch of this place. I hope that this building stands strong for hundreds of generations to come and is not left to rot and ruin like a few I have seen outside the county.

A stained-glass window catches my attention as the light dances around the room in an array of beautiful colours. The greens, blues, yellows, oranges and whites almost sing. I soak in the dappled light. I am lost in my own thoughts for a peaceful moment, until I feel a familiar presence behind me.

"Which scene is your favourite?" I ask, without looking behind me.

"Hmm… it's less about which image I prefer, but who I'm seeing it with." There's a smile in his voice.

I keep my eyes trained on the window in front of us. "She must be a lucky lady."

"Does she think so?"

"You mean me? Well, I couldn't possibly tell you that."

"And why not, m'lady?"

I finally turn to face him. I try not to smile, but it is impossible. "Because that is for him to find out."

As I lean in closer, a monk floats past us, so we quickly turn to face the stained-glass window again. I dart my eyes to the high altar, praying that God forgives me for my lustful thoughts. Lord Stanford rests his left hand on his dagger and the other pushes back his hair. All I want is to be held in his arms again. He consumes me. I try to think of something else to distract me from such thoughts.

"I am sure that this window is not as beautiful as that in your monastery in the north. I would love to see it one day."

"And I would be more than 'appy to take ya."

I long for him to kiss me again.

"Lord Stanford, welcome back." Isabelle meets us alongside Sir Henry and his mother. "I hope you were able to do everything you needed in town?"

"Aye, I did, thank you."

"Beautiful place, Lady Turner," Sir Henry comments as he gazes about the room, his smile the widest I have ever seen.

"This is my favourite place to come and collect myself. Perhaps even receive divine intervention on… certain matters," I add.

"Indeed," his mother replies. I had almost forgotten what her voice sounded like; it has been that long since I heard her speak.

"Well, shall we go, if everyone is ready?" Sir Henry only looks at Isabelle when he asks this.

She nods in reply.

"Please lead the way, Sir Henry and Isabelle," I reply, forcing his mother to step behind them for once.

As we step out of the cool building, the sun is shining above us in the perfect blue sky. I shield my eyes, adjusting to the bright light.

"What a beautiful day." Isabelle breathes in deeply.

"It is." Lord Stanford smiles, gazing at me, the weight of his heated gaze too much for me to hold.

"So, what would you like to do next? Perhaps I could show you inside the Guild Hall, look at a few prisoners or two in our brand-new cells?" I jest, but no one laughs. "Or I could take you to the White Boar Inn. The landlord is a personal favourite of mine; it is a wonderful place to sit and hear about what is happening in the town."

"Oh yes, that's a wonderful idea! The landlord is such a character, you'd really like him." Isabelle turns to her future husband with delight.

He beams, looking like he would go anywhere with her. "That sounds wonderful," Sir Henry replies.

"Ahem," his mother clears her throat and raises one eyebrow up at her son. "I'm not so sure."

His smile soon dissolves as he looks down at his feet. "Ah yes, regrettably, my mother and I must leave you here. We will be back soon, I promise. I said that I would walk around the Roman walls with her."

"Of course, it is a remarkable sight," Isabelle replies, her voice falling flat at his sudden change of plans.

I stand there a little dumbfounded for a split second, wondering why and how his mother has such an effect on him.

"Why don't you go with them?" I whisper to Isabelle.

She shakes her head with downcast eyes. "I need to get back home anyway," she says to me. "I hope you have a lovely time, my lord – my lady." Isabelle leaves as Sir Henry and his mother separate from us.

Lord Stanford and I exchange a small glance to one another, his eyes widened to match my own, and I quickly follow Isabelle.

"Isabelle!"

She ignores me.

"Isabelle, wait."

She stops and spins to face me. "I'm *fine*, Katherine! I wanted to head home anyway." Isabelle mounts her horse and trots off in the direction of home without hearing another word.

Lord Stanford's face scrunches up. "Should we follow her?"

"We'd best. I don't want anything to happen to her."

He helps me up onto my horse before mounting his own, and we quickly follow Isabelle towards Eastgate, then Humberstone Gate. It is not too long by the time we catch up with her. I nearly reach out, but decide against it, knowing all too well that she wants to be left alone, at least for now.

William pulls back next to Lord Stanford's horse as we walk through the canopy of trees once more. Silently, Lord Stanford plucks a nearby flower and presents it to me. A beautiful yellow-petalled flower; it smells sweet. He leans over and tucks it behind my ear, brushing my cheek with his hand as he does so.

"Is Lady Isabelle all righ'?" Lord Stanford asks, nodding in her direction.

"She will be. I mean, I think she handled that pretty well. I don't think I would be able to keep my true opinion to myself."

"I don't doubt that. Sir Henry seemed excited to spend the rest of the day with her. I don't know what changed his mind."

"I do. His mother," I grumble. Even picturing her thin, grey face agitates me. "Having an only son means she seems to have glued herself to his side no matter what. Perhaps afraid of her precious son seeing sense," I spit.

Before I can say anything else, Isabelle shouts, "Come on, you two! Before it rains!" releasing me from my irritated thoughts.

"After you," Lord Stanford gestures, only to cut in front of me as I try to nudge William on a bit faster.

I trot around him. "I'll race you!" I canter at full speed before he has the chance to get ahead of me.

"You'll need that head start!" he shouts, but I am too far ahead to reply.

"Catch up!" he yells as he darts by in a blur.

By the time I do catch up with him, he is already a few paces away from Isabelle, who only shakes her head as if we are two badly behaved children.

Finally, when we're back home, Lord Stanford helps me dismount as soon as we reach the stable block. I make my way over to Isabelle, her arms folded across her chest. I wrap my arms around her shoulders. "Are you sure you're alright?"

"Yes, I'm fine, honestly. I just have a few things on my mind." Her gaze is cast down towards the stone floor. "Please, Katherine, I love you, but I just need a little space. Please don't think ill of me."

I take a respectful step back. "Of course, I understand. You know where I am if you need me."

"I'll come and find you soon. My uncle wished to speak with me this afternoon anyway." And with that she disappears into the castle.

After a little pause, worrying about Isabelle and how her sudden demeanour has changed since last night, I turn to face Lord Stanford. "I'll give her the space she desires. In the meantime, would you like to walk through the gardens?"

"If ya want to, then we shall."

He offers me his arm, and I willingly take it. I lead him past the neatly shaped shrubbery and into my mother's rose garden, the one place in this entire world I can never grow tired of. It is peaceful, such a respite from the crowds of town. We stand there in comfortable silence for a few minutes, soaking in the beauty around us. The sun has hidden itself behind the clouds in the sky above and I shiver. Lord Stanford turns me towards him as he wraps his arms around me, adjusting my cloak in order to shelter me from the chill in the air. He kisses my forehead, which makes all my worries and pain melt away.

Footsteps on the path leading towards us break the peace, making us spring apart from one another.

"My lady." Thomas Moore bows, his hat wringing in his hands. "You have a visitor, my lady."

I clear my throat. "Thank you, Thomas, may I ask who?"

We are soon disturbed by the crunching of footsteps on the gravel path. My heart sinks as a man dressed all in black appears, a small smile on his face.

"I thought I'd find you here, Lady Katherine." Lord Tyrell. He looks at me and grins, but then his eyes land on Lord Stanford as if seeing him for the first time. "Your aunt mentioned that you had a visitor, but she didn't say *who*," he adds through gritted teeth.

I brush past Lord Stanford, replaying last night's rift over in my head; I cannot afford another disagreement between us. "Lord Stanford is here as *my* guest. You will treat him with the same respect as you should me."

"I wasn't aware that he was still here," Lord Tyrell replies, a tight, controlled smile on his face.

"Neither I nor anyone on my estate need to inform you about whom I allow to stay in *my* castle. I do not need to seek counsel from anyone, especially you."

Lord Tyrell recoils ever so slightly. "Well, I know you well enough to know that you do not take anyone's advice. You are your own person and free spirit… something I have always admired. I have actually come here to apologise again for my rude behaviour towards you and your *temporary* guest."

I ball my hands into fists at my side again. How many times does this oaf have to be told that he is not welcome here?

"Lord Tyrell, why do I have to keep repeating myself? The words you have spoken about me have been unforgivable. I have told you that you are not welcome here at Leicester Castle. If you wanted to apologise for your ill behaviour, then you should have written it in a letter."

I would have burnt it straight away.

"I know, but I truly am sorry for upsetting you like I did." There is a slight hurt in his voice and his eyes can no longer look at me. "I can only apologise in person. I know the words you overheard were distasteful to you, and I have apologised so often, but you cannot shut me out forever, my lady."

I take a furious step towards him. How dare he believe that my word is not final.

"I will do what I please, Lord Tyrell, whether you agree with it or not. I was gracious enough not to expel you from my archery tournament there and then. Please do not mistake this kindness as a weakness. Now leave, before I ask my men to throw you out."

Lord Stanford takes a step towards Lord Tyrell. "I suggest ya leave now, Lord Tyrell, before yer embarrassed further."

"I can handle this, James," I hiss.

The sudden change in Lord Tyrell's demeanour is quick. He clears his throat. "Ah! The valiant Lord James

Stanford. *Just* Lord Stanford, no dukedom or true title to call your own."

Lord Stanford shifts his weight onto his right leg and his fingers twitch as if they want to furl into a fist, but they remain by his side. "My estate in Yorkshire is plenty enough for me and my family. King Richard is 'appy enough for me to help strengthen the north. I'm not like ya, trying to seize every bit of land ya fancy. Failing miserably, as I recall." He takes a step closer and narrows his eyes at Lord Tyrell, who seems to stand his ground just as fiercely. "Is that why yer really 'ere? To try and conquer Lady Turner's lands and take over the estate and steal 'er title? How are ya going to do that, Lord 'enry? Kidnap her and force 'er into marriage?"

I step between them again. "That is enough!"

Only Lord Stanford seems to notice, his attention fully on me. I lower my voice so that only he shall hear. "James, you are not helping."

My attention is drawn towards the black-clad earl in front of me.

"I would choose wisely, Lady Katherine Turner of Leicester. You do not want to be caught *in bed* with the wrong people," Lord Tyrell smirks.

I stare at him, my heart pounding. Did he see me and Lord Stanford together last night? Did anyone hear us? Did someone tell him? No, we were careful enough to make sure no one was around to see us. Besides, even if he knew, there is nothing he can do to prove it, nothing he can do to turn others against me.

Lord Tyrell shakes his head and turns his focus solely to me. "Be careful, my lady. Eyes and ears are everywhere, and you do not want to be caught doing something that would jeopardise your position as head of house. Reputation is everything in this little game of King and Queen."

I stand firm, unwilling to be shaken by his empty threats. "What I do is of no consequence to you. I will not be spoken to in that manner. You will leave us now, Lord Tyrell. I do not wish to see you today, nor tomorrow, nor the next day. Do not plague my castle grounds again. Do you understand me? For if you ignore my words again, I will make sure you are escorted from my grounds without a second glance from me."

Lord Tyrell hesitates for a moment as if to protest this dismissal, but instead leaves in silence, through the garden and back towards the castle courtyard without uttering another word.

Fourteen

One evening, as night falls over the county, I try to locate my uncle, keen to get his advice on an issue I was presented with the other day about the rebellions in the south and the high probability of a rise in taxes. It is something I try to avoid, stubborn about figuring out my own solutions, but I have finally relented. After searching the empty castle for a few minutes, I find myself at the door of the Council Chamber, which is uncharacteristically shut. I reach for the door handle and freeze at the hushed voices coming from within.

"It is not that easy," a voice – that of my uncle – is saying. "It is the other nobles. I can see them. Looking down their noses at her because she is a woman in *power*. With King Richard's uneasy reign, it has become difficult to keep the peace with those who do not respect her. I try my best, but I am not the Earl of Leicester so my influence can only extend so far."

"That is not true, my lord, the Earl of Nottingham

and Lord Derby, for example, adore her. They are very powerful and well-respected men."

I balk. It's Lord Tyrell! Why is he in there with my uncle and without me? I grip the handle, but something within me tells me to hesitate. He is still speaking.

"If she is to gain support and trust from the lords around her, especially King Richard's new set of nobility in the south, then she will need the support of a husband."

My uncle scoffs. "Really? What makes you think that is true? My niece is a powerful woman, Lord Tyrell, one who does not suffer fools lightly. If she were to marry, it would not be for power or fortune; she already has those things. Are you insinuating that *you* can provide her with what you believe she needs?" he asks.

"My lord, I have grown fond of Lady Turner. I wish the best for her, but I fear others nearby only want her for her fortune."

My fortune? Now this does sound familiar. Does Lord Tyrell really think that I wouldn't have informed my uncle about his true nature? My uncle won't stand for his lies. I'm surprised he even allowed an audience with the man, and without informing me too. I cannot help but feel disappointed at this; I thought we told each other everything. There must be a reason why he kept this meeting from me – perhaps Lord Tyrell cornered him; perhaps this meeting was disguised as something else at first. Yes, that must be it.

"You?" Another male voice joins in the conversation. Why is Sir Francis in there too?

My hand curls into a fist at my side; do they not respect my position of Countess and head of this house? Am I to find out *after* everyone else?

The floor creaks on the other side of the door but I remain firm, eager to hear their true thoughts. I press my ear against the door.

"I promise you that I am not after her fortune," Lord Tyrell says.

My uncle interjects, "Ha! I know that is not true; my niece informed me she overheard you, speaking as if she was a common prize to be won, someone *you* can control and bend to your will! Do you really think she would not have discussed this with me? You are lucky that I do not turf you out myself!"

The sputtering of anguish spills from my uncle's mouth. I am relieved to hear him put Lord Tyrell in his place bluntly.

Lord Tyrell replies, "It is true, my lord, I cannot deny that I was curious about her fortune and status, having heard only rumours at court of her unmatched beauty and power. But as soon as I got to know her, that all changed, I promise."

"So, you say," Sir Francis chips in, clearly unamused.

Lord Tyrell counters, "With another war looming, you will be called up once again, leaving her alone. Those left who are loyal to her will soon forget their promise of protection to the house of Leicester and will only be thinking about their own. As loyal as we all are to King Richard, the south of the country has never been happy with his attention to the north."

"What does that have to do with anything?" My uncle sounds agitated. I can picture him rubbing a hand across his brow.

"Let me be the one to offer my hand in marriage to

Lady Katherine and I will protect her. I will make sure her legacy is protected."

My heart suddenly stops, and my mouth opens to protest, but I decide to keep quiet. Marriage to Lord Tyrell? That must have been his true purpose of cornering me in the stables the other afternoon, seeking out my uncle to ask him for a private audience. He knows that I would refuse him, perhaps even laugh in his face. I can see it now. He would propose marriage in front of everyone, difficult for me to refuse, but I would refuse. Gladly. And without my consent, he has nothing.

"She will not marry you, my lord."

I smile at my uncle's words.

"She will. She has to. If not by her own will then by the agreement made—"

"The agreement was null and void, my lord, you already know that as well as I do," my uncle interrupts.

What does he mean? An agreement? What agreement? I hear footsteps move around the small room, becoming restless with each step.

"She will have no choice. No other suitor will touch her when they know. Soon she will be an old maid and no man will have her."

Old maid? How dare he! I grit my teeth forcefully. I reach for the door handle again, keen to show him what an *old maid* can really do.

"Watch your tongue!" Sir Francis demands, stamping his foot hard on the floor below our feet. "You speak about her as if she is nothing but a common milkmaid! How dare you!"

"I mean no disrespect, my lord." Lord Tyrell lowers his voice, clearly unprepared for the strong defence against his proposal. "She must marry soon; you know she must. Even a man equal to her station would be expected to marry eventually, provide an heir and so on."

A small pause hangs in the air between the three men, a pause that I do not like. Why has no one mentioned the fact that *I* have a choice in all this? My future is my own and I refuse for anyone else to make it for me. If I want to marry, I will, but it will be for love and mutual respect, that much I have made clear.

"Who else has proposed marriage to your niece? Who else is there but I?" Lord Tyrell asks, his voice almost desperate.

There is pause until my uncle speaks up. "There is another."

Without realising, I have ceased to breathe. There is not an inch of space between me and the door that separates me from the three men on the other side.

"Who?" Lord Tyrell sneers. "Surely not that Yorkist bastard? What does he have to offer?"

I jump back, startled at the sudden sound of a fist slamming against either the desk or the wall.

"I will not have you slander Lord James Stanford!" my uncle growls, almost losing control of his anger. "He is a fine gentleman with as much strength as you and twice as much respect from those around him, including my niece. I knew his father well – loyal to his king, his country and his family until the day he died. His son is just as loyal and just as *brave*, Lord Tyrell. You will not speak untruths about him in my presence."

My mind flashes back to that night we spent together. I cannot get Lord Stanford from my mind. The feeling of his lips on mine, his gentle hands upon my skin... the way he smiles and laughs... his kindness and respect for me and my family. If he were to propose a betrothal, would I accept straight away? I cannot help but smile at the thought, and there within lies my answer.

"I apologise for my passionate words, my lord, I mean no offence. I can assure you, Lord Golding, that I have Lady Katherine in my heart. I will prove this to you if I have to."

My breathing becomes heavy with anger, and it takes all my strength not to march in there. Ordinarily, I would, but something tells me that if I barge in now, I will never hear the truth; all words would dry up.

Sir Francis's voice has faded slightly as he moves away from the door, but it ripples no less with undercurrents of warning. "*Prove* to us? I remember a time *your* father thought he could bully and manipulate his way through nobility to finally get his hand on more land. Luckily, King Edward gave my great friend, *Katherine's mother*, the titles, land and wealth she deserved. Isn't it strange to think that your father could have been the one to stand by Lady Sophia's side instead of Lady Katherine's late father? Is that what this is all about? Revenge for your father, who lived the bulk of his life sour about the rejection from a woman?"

What does Sir Francis mean by this? It is true that the late king gave the Leicester lands and all that came with it to my *mother*, not my father, upon their marriage. It has not been clear to me exactly why the king himself favoured a woman, not even of his own blood, over a man; it is a question that I have never needed answering. I have heard ripples in the past that my mother was engaged to another, only to end that agreement to marry my father. If this other man was the late Lord Tyrell, Lord Henry Tyrell's father, surely *he* can't be bitter about choices neither of us were involved with? I know breaking an engagement can cause a scandal, but my mother must have had the king's support, or my family would not be where it is today.

"If Lady Katherine's parents hated my father so, then why did they sign the agreement?" His breathing becomes laboured with anger, and he stops himself, as if recognising his loss of control.

"If it is my niece's hand in marriage you are truly after, it is she whom you have to convince." My uncle sighs, clearly tired from this evening's events. "Though, I doubt you will earn her trust ever again. And can you blame her? I cannot force her to do anything. She ranks above all of us here and I will not disrespect that."

Sir Francis's voice too grows louder as he heads towards the door. "Once her mind is made up, there is no persuading her otherwise. You are fighting a losing battle. You cannot bend her to your will."

The door creaks open, and, without thinking, I jump back and hide in the darkness behind a nearby tapestry. Flattening myself against the stone wall, I hold my breath for fear of being caught. One set of footsteps makes their way down the corridor and into the distance.

All is quiet.

I am about to emerge from my hiding place when I hear my uncle and Sir Francis stand in the doorway. "I do not like him, Golding. I cannot help but think that he will bring nothing but trouble."

"Agreed. Luckily, our Katherine is a strong and level-headed woman with more experience under her belt than that rat of a man." My uncle sighs again.

"I'm surprised you allowed an audience with him at all! I admit that I would not have done the same. Does Lady Katherine even know about this secret meeting? It does make me feel uncomfortable talking to him behind her back, you know."

"I know, I know... as much as Katherine would disagree with me, we cannot all turn our backs on a man like Lord Tyrell. I want to keep the peace, as much as I do not like him myself. I hope that she will forgive me when she learns about this meeting. I just can't help but think that ignoring him and belittling the man will only cause more harm than good. Power is the currency at court, and that man is wealthy beyond our comprehension, though I have never understood how."

The footsteps pause; they are inches from me, on the other side of the tapestry.

"I just hope he doesn't do anything rash, my friend."

The two men resume their walk down the corridor, their voices fading. I slip out from behind the tapestry, finally able to breathe again, and place my hand on my heart to steady it.

Everything I have heard tonight is a lot for me to digest in one go. Lord Tyrell must think the more he tries to weave himself into my life, the quicker I will just give into him. Rejection only seems to spur him on, as if 'no' is not something he can comprehend. I have never been so grateful for being given the power to decide my own fate! I could easily have been swept aside, forced to marry Lord Tyrell and fade into the shadows.

I remember once that my uncle told me I was going to change the world, set a new path for this country one way or another. At the time I wasn't sure what he meant, but now I understand. If the late King Edward himself saw strength in my mother, regardless of her gender, then I will prove to his brother, King Richard, and to the rest of the kingdom, that he was right in making that choice. I will show that women, when given equal opportunities, contribute more to this world than just children, fancy clothes and demure little smiles. We will set this world anew, showing that, together, men and women are stronger than they ever were under the rule of just men.

As I pass the Council Chamber door, my attention is caught by a single blood-red rose, sitting on the edge of the desk. It looks remarkably fresh, reminding me of the exact same rose Lord Tyrell gave me the first time we met. He must have left it there on purpose like some sort of token, hoping I would find it and think of him. I quickly march into the room, grab the rose, open the small window on the other side, and throw it into the wind.

My chest is heaving, my jaw firmly shut. If Lord Tyrell was the only man in the world whom I could marry, I would rather join that rose and leave my fate to the wind. How dare he go behind my back and ask for an audience with my uncle, too scared to face me with his true intentions! But what of this agreement he mentioned? I wonder what he could be referring to. A small twist in my stomach begins to unsettle me. To what lengths will he go to obtain what he believes to be his?

Fifteen

"No!" I shout, sweat sticking to me as I jolt awake, my chest heavy and breathless.

I dart my eyes around the room, a veil of thin light peeking through the curtains. *It was just a dream.* My breathing steadies as I try to grasp onto flashing images from my restless night's sleep. I remember little of this dream, only the overwhelming feelings of horror, quickly followed by loneliness and emptiness. Flickering images come to me of a dark figure looming above my body, cold blank walls, the puff of a candle extinguishing… but the images slip away from me before I can make much sense of them.

Thankfully, Bess enters my room after a short knock at the door and prepares me for the day ahead. In the Great Hall, I settle myself opposite Isabelle and next to Lord Stanford, who greets me with a quick kiss across my knuckles, instantly calming my reckless thoughts. I quickly scan the room and wait for the servant to pour a fresh cup of ale. I am keen not to be overheard. My uncle and Sir Francis are eating their breakfast at another table, engrossed in their own conversation.

"Katherine," Isabelle asks, a thin crease across her brow, "is something the matter?"

With another quick glance towards my uncle and Sir Francis, I make sure only Isabelle and Lord Stanford can hear me. "Last night, I wanted to discuss a trivial matter with my uncle, but as I passed by the Council Chamber, I overheard three male voices…"

I inform them both about what I overheard. Isabelle's goblet lowers in her hand, eventually landing on the table as if it suddenly bears too much weight for her to hold aloft. Lord Stanford sits silently, waiting patiently for me to finish. He locks eyes with my own, reaches for the goblet next to him, but never takes a sip. When I have finished, both Isabelle and Lord Stanford look towards one another, a small understanding passing between them both as if they have agreed upon the same opinion. It is Isabelle who speaks first.

"I cannot believe he would set up a private audience with your uncle and mine without your knowledge! I must say I am a little saddened to learn that my uncle had a part in this, Katherine, keeping it all a secret," she huffs, her eyes sliding over to an oblivious Sir Francis.

"He wasn't comfortable with keeping me in the dark, but I am not too happy about it either. Anyway, that is a minor detail." I sigh, poking the remaining crumbs of bread around my plate.

Lord Stanford adjusts in his chair, remaining silent. I notice the way he clasps his hands together then releases them again, something I have learned he does whenever he is agitated. Last night, whilst I struggled to fall asleep, I wondered if I should inform Lord Stanford or not. Why should I burden him with such facts? Would it be something that he has an opinion on, or would he rather not be involved? Would the thought of another trying to stake their claim on me ignite insatiable jealously? Perhaps it might spurn him on to make his own move towards securing my hand. It is the latter thought that won over my quandary.

Isabelle frowns. "Well, he can ask your uncle for permission as much as he wants; Lord Golding is not your guardian or your keeper; he has no power over you. If he truly thinks that he can persuade your uncle and mine to change your mind about him, then he really is deluded."

I only nod in agreement, happy at hearing such words: it is I who decides my marital fate, not those around me.

After a small pause of silence, Lord Stanford clears his throat, drawing my full attention to him. "I am sorry that ya had to overhear that. For a man like Tyrell to go behind yer back and try to negotiate for yer hand in marriage only amplifies the type of man he truly is. Perhaps he thought that by doing so he would get the answers he is seeking, but I am glad to hear that was not the case." He sounds genuinely relieved that I am disgusted with Lord Tyrell's attempts, rather than considering them seriously; he should know that I would never accept his hand.

I want to ask him: *What would you do to make sure you are the one I choose to marry?* but decide against it. I have asked myself a few times lately, what would I do if Lord Stanford was the one pursuing me, what if he was the one I overheard last night asking my uncle for my hand in marriage? My heart flutters at the thought, but is that what Lord Stanford wants? Does he want to spend the rest of his life with me? Doubts have haunted my dreams at night, and it takes all my strength not to ask such questions to the man by my side, for the fear of hearing something that would break me.

Isabelle asks, "I wonder what his true motivations are, though. He will be greatly disappointed to learn that, upon marriage, the titles and wealth still belong to you." She smiles wickedly, as if enjoying a mental image of a disappointed Lord Tyrell.

"You're right, Isabelle. My mother was one of the first women in English history to be given the same powers, title and land as the men before her. I will not be the one to lose the Leicester estate to Lord Tyrell or to anyone. In marriage, everything I own is still mine in name, though, in the wrong hands, I can see how I could easily be pushed aside."

"You and I both know that ya wouldn't allow that to happen. Besides, what ya should be focusing on is what *you* want, nobody else," Lord Stanford offers, his fingers caressing mine under the table.

"I want to marry for love, just like my parents," I splutter, unable to control my words, encouraged by his touch. "I am determined. Although, between my aunt and the expectations of the world we live in, I sometimes feel like I will be married off to the highest bidder."

The corners of Lord Stanford's lips turn upwards. He lowers his voice so that only I can hear, and with a smirk he adds, "I had better start saving my money then."

I smile and push my shoulder into him with a sudden flutter in my stomach.

Just then, Isabelle is called over by her uncle. She excuses herself and leaves Lord Stanford and me in comfortable silence. I have a question for Lord Stanford that I have wanted to know the answer to for some time, but never had the opportunity to ask.

I take a small intake of breath. "What about you, James? Surely you are freer than me when it comes to matrimony?" My heartbeat quickens, no matter his reply.

"Yer right. Thankfully, as a man I can choose whoever I fancy." He smiles, not meeting my gaze. "I'm lucky in that sense, but I want to marry for love too."

"And have you found that special someone yet?" I ask in almost a whisper.

He interlaces his fingers with my own. "Katherine… I…" He fumbles for the right words to say, and every second I wait is agony. Eventually, his eyes soften as he stares into mine. "I find that I am falling for ya more with each day that passes."

"James…" I can hardly speak.

I am now impossibly close by his side. The rest of the Great Hall has faded away and there is no one else besides the two of us. Until this point, I didn't want to admit out loud how I felt. Perhaps I was waiting to see if his intentions matched my own before I revealed them so openly. We have known each other for such a short amount of time. I kept telling myself that we are still strangers, despite the excited, warm feeling in my heart whenever I am near him. Am I in love with Lord James Stanford? I am not sure I can open myself to that question so soon.

I move my other hand onto his thigh. His voice hitches ever so slightly as I squeeze his tensed muscles with my fingers. "I never want to let ya go, Katherine. I want to protect ya from all of those who try to darken yer door. I know ya can look after yerself, but it doesn't mean I couldn't forgive myself if anything ever happened to ya."

"I couldn't ask for anyone more worthy." I pause as I prepare myself for the next few words – words I don't want to say, but which must be spoken. "As much as I don't want you to go, I can't keep you here, away from your home, from your family. You have an estate to run; your duties bind you to Yorkshire."

He laughs and shakes his head as if what I said was ridiculous. "What happens if I take ya with me?"

"Visit you in Yorkshire?" I pull back so that I can see if he is serious. For a fleeting moment I indulge in that fantasy, but reality begins to flood my senses. "I would like that, James, but I have so much to do here. I can't just leave whenever I feel like it."

James kisses my hand. "Well, good job I plan on staying 'ere for a little bit longer then. At least until I have seen Tyrell off for good."

He laughs, but I do not join him. Lord Tyrell's outburst in the Council Chamber, his odd choice of words when I overheard him in his tent at the joust about making sure no one else is in the way… these bring a small terror to my heart.

"Please, James, be careful," I warn, my voice a little sharper than before.

"Why?"

"I just have a feeling that Lord Tyrell has something planned for you… for us. Something sinister. Something that we will never see coming."

Sixteen

As I look out onto the town in the distance, I can see the various candles being lit for the evening, tiny sparks of yellow light flickering through the trees, mirroring the starry night sky above. Tonight is Isabelle's betrothal celebration banquet, one in which the date will be announced for when she will become Sir Henry's wife. I thought we had more time together, as sisters. I can already hear the guests arriving as I open my window. I inhale deeply, as if I am to hold my breath for the rest of the evening. My hand touches where William's ring hangs protectively against my chest before I close the window again and head downstairs into the throng of people.

The Great Hall is lavishly decorated in bright reds and deep blues and, as I enter the room, the majority of people are already standing by their places, waiting for the main event to begin. I am not seated in my usual place at the head of the table, but just a few seats down, as the seats of honour have been reserved for Sir Henry

Percival of Wiltshire, his mother, Sir Francis and the bride-to-be.

My mind distracts me from sombre thoughts by looking around the room at various familiar faces: the humble Lord Derby, the stern-looking Earl of Worcester, a sleepy Sir Michael Eaton, and the forever jovial Earl of Nottingham. My eyes wander over to the opposite side of the hall, where a mixture of familiar and not-so-familiar faces are scattered amongst the many seats. It is not long until I find a man all dressed in midnight blue, golden flecks in his hair catching the light from the candles that shine brightly about the room. He winks at me and it takes all of my strength to not show the rest of the Great Hall my ever-growing feelings for Lord Stanford, who is just out of reach.

Our gazes break when the doors are opened wide to reveal Sir Francis and Sir Henry Percival's mother, who are closely followed by Isabelle and her betrothed. Everyone applauds at their entrance, and I am in admiration at Isabelle's ease and gracious manner as she floats her way down the Great Hall and stands in front of her seat at the high table. It is as if a king and queen have entered the room, dressed in beautiful rich clothing. Isabelle's gaze flickers to mine, and I smile warmly. She smiles back. I hope that my presence on this most important evening will allow her to feel more relaxed.

We all sit down except for Sir Henry.

"My lords and ladies, I thank you for attending tonight's celebrations."

A small, polite applause echoes around the room.

"I would like to announce that a date has been set

for our union to be made in the sight of God when the summer is replaced by autumn, and when the leaves begin to fall." He gestures leaves falling with the turning of his hand, which is both very amusing and very theatrical.

Lord Stanford catches me smiling behind my hand and mirrors my amusement.

"This may signal the end to hot days and warm summer nights, but it will be the beginning of a life filled with love and admiration as Lady Isabelle will be my wife."

Everyone claps and cheers as Sir Francis pipes up with a "Huzzah!" which echoes around the room as we all join in.

This is the first betrothal celebration Leicester has held since my mother was gifted the estate all those years ago. It is strange that Isabelle is at the centre of this one, as she was once betrothed to my late brother, William. I do wonder what life would have been like if he was here today and Isabelle had married him instead. Where would I be? Would I have been carted off to marry some Earl of Somewhere, or was I always destined to remain here and oversee the running of the estate and lands? Were Lord Stanford and I destined to meet? Fall in love, perhaps? I shake my head to rid it of such trivial thoughts.

Music starts to play merrily in the background as the feast begins. There are many plates set before us: pheasant, wild boar, poultry, and a selection of delicate fruits. Across the room, Lord Stanford is talking to a gentleman I don't know of, laughing and grinning; how I so wanted to be seated next to him this evening. I also spy my aunt as she pushes some meat around her plate, checking to see if it is perfectly cooked. The Earl of Nottingham, I notice, has captivated at least half a dozen others with one of his heroic tales.

My uncle captures my attention by pouring more red wine into my goblet. "So, is this evening satisfactory for my Countess?" My uncle chuckles, nearly overfilling my goblet in the process.

"Yes, Uncle, everything seems to be going well," I reply, still scanning the room, making sure everyone is happy.

"You don't have to be on ceremony all the time, Katherine – enjoy yourself! Try not to get bogged down with the talk of politics or attempt to impress people. We do not need to worry about paperwork or neighbourhood quarrels tonight. Just enjoy the fine food, rich wine and handsome company." He nods not too subtly over towards Lord Stanford, who is blissfully unaware of the attention.

"Uncle, you are as subtle as a cow in a green field." I shake my head and laugh.

My uncle leans in closer so that no one may overhear him. "How about this? I want you to forget about being the head of our house tonight, Katherine. Pretend that you are attending a celebration in someone else's castle; let yourself be a guest, dance with whomever you want, whenever you want. As long as you save a dance for me, my dear!" He takes my hand in his, warm and comforting. "I just want you to be happy. You know that I will never choose your path for you; you have worked too hard for your future to be dictated by an old man like me."

I quickly ask myself if this is a good time to bring up the fact that I overheard him and Lord Tyrell that evening. No. I can't; that would only look ill on my part. I must allow him to tell me himself. Though, I am curious as to why he has not informed me yet.

I keep my thoughts to myself for now and reply, "I thank you for that, Uncle, I truly do. I know that not every woman has the same opportunities as I, so I know that I must do my best with what I am given."

My uncle waves a dismissive hand. "Do not think about politics tonight, Katherine."

"It's hardly politics, Uncle, you know how I try my hardest to fight for others who are not as lucky as me. It is not fair that other women—"

"Katherine." My uncle stops me from launching into another rousing speech. "Your food is getting cold."

I laugh aloud. "Is that your way of telling me to be quiet, Uncle?"

"I wouldn't dare tell a Countess when she should or should not speak, but today…"

Taking my uncle's advice, I saviour every morsel of food that touches my tongue. I relax a little more into my chair and refill my goblet without a care as to who is watching. He is right. Tonight is about my best friend and her future husband; I do not need to work the room. I am a mere spectator, fading into the crowd, getting lost in infectious laughter and love.

It seems like everyone else has finished eating too as Sir Francis commands the band to play a more upbeat tune, and many of the guests get up from their seats and make their way to the space that has opened up in the centre of the room.

I take this opportunity to let my stomach rest as I blend into the crowd, watching on from a distance as Isabelle and Sir Henry dance with one another in beautiful synchrony. He has eyes for none other than his wife-to-be, who appears to be enraptured by him in turn as he gently leads her around the room. When I look at them both, it makes me realise that true love does exist and that my own prospects are not as bleak as I first thought they were destined to be. I convinced myself for many years that I would only be able to marry for power or status, protecting my family's legacy and to protect the people of Leicester. Nevertheless, as I look upon the happiest couple in the room, their love inspires me to listen to my heart and grab hold of the love I have been seeking for so long.

I am drawn to the other side of the room, and Lord Stanford meets me in the middle of my path.

"M'lady." He takes my hand and presses his lips against my bare skin, turning over my wrist and planting another sweet kiss, which sends tingles around my body. "Why aren't ya dancing?" he questions with a smile, looking around the room. "Has the great Countess of Leicester not found a suitable partner?"

"I'm waiting for him to show up. Have you seen him at all? Tall, blond hair… looks devilishly handsome in a blue tunic." I bite my lip, almost surprised at myself for flirting so obviously in such a crowded place; perhaps my uncle knew what he was doing when he kept refilling my goblet.

"He sounds like a fine man. Well, while ya wait around for yer Prince Charming, may I have this dance?"

We make our way through the crowd and towards the other dancers who are waiting for the next song to begin. As the music commences, we raise our arms so that our hands faintly touch one another's above our heads. As the music changes to a livelier beat, he then takes my hand down to my side and puts his other hand on my waist; it takes all my control not to melt into his touch. I spin away, circling around him as his eyes follow me. It is as if there is no one else in the room with us. The music changes to a softer rhythm. He pulls me in closer, and I slowly lean my hand against his chest, closing my eyes. All I can feel is his steady heartbeat, his hand on mine, his cheek against my forehead. It is everything to be in this moment, to be here right now. I never want this to end, but of course, only too soon does the music fade and we break apart with obvious effort. Our hands fall by our side as the rest of the world draws in around us. It is like waking from a dream.

As other dancers leave to seek their next partner, only Lord Stanford and I remain. He takes a step towards me again, but before either of us can utter another word, Sir Francis taps me on my shoulder.

"I must insist on having the next dance with you, Lady Katherine."

Annoyed at being interrupted so abruptly, I nearly decline, but when I see how happy Sir Francis is, thinking back to all that he has done for me, I cannot say no. "Very well, Sir Francis. I do owe you a dance considering last time you had to retire early." I turn to face Lord Stanford. "Thank you for the dance, Lord Stanford, if you will excuse me."

"Find me afterwards," he whispers in reply. I reluctantly lose him to the crowd again.

Sir Francis and I line up with the other dancers and

the music begins. As we fling ourselves around the room, out of the corner of my eye, I see a man I do not recognise talking to Bess. He leans in close to her ear. I can only make out a few words…

"…tomorrow… I look forward to seeing…"

Bess looks either confused or deep in thought at what he is saying – whatever the truth, it doesn't look to be good news. As I draw closer, the man flits his eyes towards me, forcing me to quickly look away, hoping that he didn't notice me staring at them both. When I look up again, they are both gone. Who was he and what does he want with Bess?

I leave the dance area as soon as the song is finished to seek her out, but I cannot find her in the crowded room, nor the stranger she was talking to. Perhaps I am overreacting; maybe it was an innocent exchange between two strangers, but her reaction was not one of joy or excitement. If he is harassing her for not wanting to dance with him, then I will personally make sure he is thrown out!

Finally, I spot her on the opposite side of the room, speaking with the Earl of Nottingham. As I make my way towards her, I soon realise that she is stuck listening to one of his great monologues. I quickly divert my path away from them both, keen not to be sucked in too, and head towards the refreshments table instead; she will be safe with the earl for some time, I think!

As I pour myself a glass of mead, Lord Stanford approaches. Leaning towards me he whispers, "What do ya say to us sneaking out of 'ere?"

The feel of his hand on mine, his fingers entwining with my own, makes my pulse quicken. The heaviness of his voice and his hooded eyes make an unappeasable ache begin to bloom deep within my stomach.

"What would everyone say if they saw us sneak off alone together?" I tease, lowering my voice.

"They would just be jealous that they don't get to spend the evening with the most beautiful woman 'ere."

My stomach flips at the raw hunger in his eye, a primal tension between us, one that I am itching to explore.

Without another word, I grab his hand, checking that we are out of sight from wandering eyes, and sneak through the door at the back of the room that opens to a small storage room. Luckily, I know every inch of this castle and know that no one will disturb us in here. I tilt my head towards his, my lips hovering above his own, and reach up for a deep kiss.

He moans as he captures my lips again and again, each kiss stoking something deep inside him as he wraps his arms tightly around my waist. I forget about every feeling I have as Lord Stanford's kiss is all that I need to satisfy me. I pull him down onto an old bench. His lips move to my jawline then to my neck; it is difficult not to cry out. I lean my head back so that he can capture as much of my skin as possible. I find him intoxicating. All of the air has been taken out of the room and he is the only thing I need to breathe again.

"I 'ave longed to taste yer lips. It's all I can think about, night and day."

"James, I want… I need you," I gasp as his hands make their way down my side and linger on my thigh, squeezing gently as his mouth makes its way to my own, silencing all words.

I find a deep desire within me like nothing I have felt before, as my own hand wanders down his chest and lingers just above his belt, venturing lower still, resting on his inner thigh.

He inhales sharply. "Katherine, ya've no idea what ya do to me."

"What do you think about as you lie in your bed at night, only a few feet away from my own?" I whisper, lightly touching his inner thigh again.

He moans my name. "Katherine."

As his hands make their way towards my breasts, I arch my back at his touch. I cannot think of anything or anyone else. He consumes me. In one swift motion, I move from his side and straddle his hips, a small look of intrigue on his face as I do so.

"Is this a better view, my lord?"

"Aye, it is." Lord Stanford wastes no time in pulling me towards him again, his lips capturing my own with feverish haste.

I bite my bottom lip and lean in for another kiss, but gaudy laughter from just outside the door freezes us both on the spot. The laughter grows louder so I quickly dismount from his lap and untangle myself. I smooth my hair back into place as Lord Stanford pulls down his shirt sleeves and runs his hand through his golden hair. The thought of being seen in here like this snaps me back to reality; how did I lose control so easily?

"How about we continue this somewhere more private?" he asks, standing up and offering his hand out to me.

I hesitate, not because I don't want to, but because I know that once I say yes, I will lose what little control I have left. I have spent so much of my life making sure that I am in control of everything I do, scared of my freedom being taken away by the next man who walks through the castle gates. Then I met Lord James Stanford and I slowly felt myself letting go, and without even realising it, here I am. Whenever I am near him, whenever I hear his voice, his laughter, see him smile, I would happily trust everything I have, everything I am to him.

I silently slip my hand into his as we sneak our way out of the room and back into the crowd that is still gathered around the centre, watching the newest set of dancers merrily leap about the room. I nod towards the small door on the other side of the Great Hall, the one normally used for servants, one that will allow us to escape unseen.

As we make our way over, a hand taps me on the shoulder, which startles me more than usual. "Ah!"

Lord Stanford's hand tightens on my own and then swiftly releases as we both turn around and I see who has stopped us, mere inches from our night of freedom.

"I am sorry, Katherine, I did not mean to scare you!" Luckily it is only Isabelle. She glances down at the non-existent space between me and Lord Stanford, then raises an eyebrow at my hair. "Was I disturbing something?" she asks with a playful hint in her eyes.

Whilst my heart recovers, I try my best to brush off Isabelle's suspicions. "You just startled us is all. I'm sorry I have not been able to speak to you this evening. I didn't want to steal all your attention tonight. It is about you and Sir Henry Percival, after all."

If she does suspect anything, she is very good at hiding it. "Thank you, Katherine, the evening is going by so quickly! I'm so sorry to ask, but" – she glances over at Lord Stanford, so fast I almost miss it – "can I talk to you *privately* for a moment?"

"Of course." I turn to Lord Stanford, trying my best to disguise my disappointment at being disturbed. "I will meet you back here so we can carry on... our conversation."

"I will await yer answer when yer ready, m'lady," he replies with a polite bow before leaving me and Isabelle alone, joining my uncle and aunt near the fireplace as if nothing happened.

"Let's go in here – no one ever uses it." Innocently, Isabelle leads us to the storage room that my Yorkshire guest and I were busy occupying not two minutes ago. I try my best to act naturally and not enjoy the flashbacks of sitting on Lord Stanford's lap as his lips made their way down to my neck.

"I will miss all of this when I am married." Isabelle breaks my wandering mind. She gazes down at her twisting hands.

"Isabelle." I tilt my head. "You know that you are always welcome here. Even though it won't be the same without you" – I bump my shoulder into hers with a smile – "I will always be here, my uncle, aunt... even Johnson and Giles will still be here for you whenever you return."

She looks at me with only sadness in her eyes, a look that I did not expect to see today. "I do not want to live so far away from here, from *you*."

I take her hand and squeeze it. "Don't be silly. Anyway, you will be far too busy to be thinking of me or this old place." I cannot burden Isabelle with my own anxiety of her leaving Leicester so soon.

Tears begin to well up in her eyes, but instead of allowing them to fall, she sniffs and attempts a smile. "I hope you are right, Katherine."

"I am," I laugh and give her the tightest hug I could possibly give to anyone.

Inside, my heart breaks a little. I understand completely what change is like, having to adapt to new circumstances that are beyond your control. I do not want Isabelle to leave, but I know that she must, just like I would have had to if my brother had survived and I was the one to marry someone far away from here. I have to remain strong for her. If I show even an ounce of sadness, it could set a small seed of doubt in her own mind and, knowing Isabelle as well as I do, that will only set her on a path that will not do her any good.

I push open the door fully and step out so as to view the rest of the room; Isabelle joins me, her face creasing into a small scowl.

"Look at Sir Henry; he hasn't been able to take his eyes off you since the day you met as betrothed. It is going to be scary at first, but with someone who loves you as much as he does, there will be nothing to worry about. You two are the happiest and most loving couple I have seen; it is almost sickening."

Isabelle glances at Sir Henry, who smiles back from across the other side of the room. "I guess you're right, Katherine. I just… no, it doesn't matter."

I squeeze her hand again so that she looks towards me. "You can tell me anything. You know that."

After a short pause, she swallows and looks at me with what I can only describe as guilt in her eyes. "Do you ever think… what if your brother had never perished that day? If we had become true sisters? Do you think that he would mind… that William, your brother, is looking down on me and is angry that I am engaged to another?"

I try not to think about my brother and Isabelle too much; their betrothal was agreed long before my father died, let alone when I was old enough to understand what that all meant. Sadly, my brother died before they could even plan a date. Did he love Isabelle? I don't know. I never wanted to ask him, scared at being pushed aside by another woman in William's life, a woman that I barely knew. How silly that all seems now.

"He would be proud that you have been blessed with such a perfect match, Isabelle. William was not a jealous man." I smile, trying to fight back tears. "I know that he would only want the best for you."

"I just feel like we never got the chance to…"

"Isabelle, look at me." I stand up straighter. "You are free to marry Sir Henry Percival without any judgement or guilt from the Turner family."

She laughs happily, wiping a rogue tear that falls onto her cheek. "Thank you, Katherine. You truly are the best woman I know." She hugs me again, sniffling back tears. "Anyway, enough about me! What about you and Lord James Stanford?"

"What about him?" I ask, trying not to blush as the images of his lips hungry against mine flash in my mind again.

"The way he looks at you… he can't take his eyes off you." Her eyes roam across the room to where the man himself is standing, talking to my aunt who laughs at something he's said. "You're not the only one who can see into a man's heart." She squeezes my hand, gesturing over towards Lord Stanford again. "You'd have to be blind to not notice."

She doesn't give me time to protest as she leaves me alone to join her future husband.

Seventeen

The light from the library's window fades as the clouds shield the sun from my view. The book feels heavier and heavier in my hands, my thoughts anywhere but on the pages in front of me. Lord Stanford left for Nottingham only a few hours ago, promising to be back by nightfall. He told me that he needed to visit a friend – I didn't question who. The longer he is a guest in my home, the harder it is to think that one day he will have to return to Yorkshire. I want to keep him close. I want to feel his hand in mine, hear his voice and his laughter. I have wondered if he is close to asking me to marry him, for surely that would be the next step in our relationship. I just don't want to admit such things aloud, afraid that I will shatter this fragile possibility.

"Katherine, I need to speak with you."

My aunt's voice pulls me from my thoughts and I sit up a little, startled.

"Of course. You can speak to me whenever you want to, Aunt," I reply.

"I'll cut to the chase. I think it is time for you to begin to look for a future husband."

I inhale, my breath freezing in my throat before I compose myself again and calmly place my book on the arm of the chair. It is not the first time, and shall not be the last, in which my aunt suddenly declares I am in need of a husband.

"And do you have anyone in mind?" I ask, not really caring for her answer.

"Your uncle and Sir Francis had an audience with Lord Henry Tyrell a few nights ago and he is offering you his hand in marriage."

And there it is. My uncle and Sir Francis still do not know that I was there that night, listening to everything they said behind closed doors. I have wondered how long it would take before my aunt or uncle approached me with his offer and what exactly their true thoughts were upon the matter. Though, my uncle stated clearly it is for me to decide.

"Is that so?"

"Yes, Katherine, and I think you should accept." She folds her arms across her chest.

"And what do my uncle and Sir Francis think?"

"They… want you to marry soon." She chooses her words carefully.

I narrow my eyes and sigh at her vague answer. "I am referring to Lord Tyrell's proposal in particular, Aunt. What do they think I should do? Accept him? Not that it matters, neither rule above me."

My aunt moves the book I have balanced on the arm of my chair to the vacant seat opposite. She sits beside me, making sure not to trap her heavy dress underneath her. She takes my hand.

"They want you to be happy, Katherine. As do I. Lord Tyrell is a great match for you. He is well respected. I have heard many powerful and influential people say that you two are suited for each other. He has a good fortune, and he is handsome… I'm not sure what else you need, Katherine." She laughs, perplexed, as if I had asked a stupid question.

"Love? Affection? Someone who will not disregard my own thoughts? Someone *I* choose."

A small silence fills the room.

"Katherine, love should *not* be the number one reason you choose a husband! You have to marry advantageously. If you want your bloodline to continue, you need to marry in order to have an heir. A woman in your position needs to choose wisely!"

I stand up abruptly, annoyed at being made to consider marriage proposals from the highest bidder, no matter how I *feel*.

"Why can't I have both, Aunt? Lord Tyrell is a self-entitled pig and you know that he does not have my best interests at heart. How can you believe anything he says? He doesn't care about me, about you, about this place! All he cares about is himself and his pride. He is an annoying fly buzzing around me all the time, thinking that he can force himself upon me. He is not to be trusted."

"Katherine." Her voice is surprisingly calm. "Please sit back down. Neither a man nor a woman in your position has much choice in the matter. Lord Tyrell is a respectable man. He cares for you, that much I can see…"

I don't sit down. "How? How does he truly show that he cares for me? Are my words and my opinion not enough for you?"

"Of course I care for your opinion, Katherine! It's just that sometimes your head is so engaged elsewhere, worrying too much about what strangers outside these four walls think of you, that you only notice others' true intentions once they no longer revolve their lives around you."

My body freezes in shock at her sudden accusation. It is as if she does not understand how I have battled with the anxieties my position costs me. It is as if every minute of my day, my life is constantly on show for all of those who are watching me, waiting for me to fail so they can sweep in and say that they told me so. What sort of Countess would I be if I allowed my uncle to run the estate, allowed him to make all the decisions for me, whilst I sat back and watched with no control over my own life? What sort of role model would I be to those around me, to my servants, to the people of Leicester if I allowed the next man in line to claim me as his wife and take everything me and my family have worked so hard to protect?

"Did you not just hear what I said about the man? I couldn't care less about Lord Tyrell! You know as well as I do: he is only interested in adding my lands and titles to his own. I overheard him, Aunt, at the joust. He just wants to expand his pathetic empire! The more I say no, the harder he tries to win me over. I banned him from my grounds and he openly defies me!" I pace around the room again, enraged with even the thought of having to marry that man. Why can't my aunt see how much I am against this? "He only smiles for you and my uncle to appear as the kind gentlemen many blind people profess he is. He is arrogant, rude, misogynistic… is that the type of man you want for me? Would he make an excellent husband? A great father? Is that the type of man you would happily see ruin your own sister's legacy?"

"Do not bring up my sister in all of this, Katherine Turner!"

I shrink a little at the authority in her voice, lowering my eyes to the floor to avoid her piercing stare. I remember too many times when she would raise her voice like this – usually after I had done something unladylike or spoken out of turn.

"Of course I don't want you to marry a man you despise. I am not that cruel, Katherine. I know what the world is like out there. You have these walls to protect you, your uncle, Sir Francis, your servants, me… we're all here to protect *you*. Do not ever think that we do not have your best interests at heart."

The anger that has built up slowly deflates; it has been such a long time since we have been so honest with each other, I had almost forgotten what it was like.

"I apologise, Aunt. I never meant to cause you offence. But there will be another option, for I will not marry Lord Tyrell."

I sit next to her again, our emotions simmering down to a more controlled level.

"Well, who else is there? No one else has come forward."

I gaze across to the opposite wall and out of the window.

"Lord Stanford?" she questions with a sigh before I can even utter his name.

I do not look at her, which only cements my answer.

"I know what you are thinking, Katherine."

"Do you?" I scoff. If she truly does, why is she forcing Lord Tyrell on me?

"He is a fine man. Your uncle respects him… but he is not as wealthy or as powerful as Lord Tyrell. He doesn't even have an earldom. I can't see how he would improve your situation."

My gaze drops to the floor; the thought of Lord Stanford being rejected by my family because of his wealth and influence is something that I have never thought would go against him. I have plenty of wealth for the both of us, and I do not care for titles.

"Katherine?"

I turn my chin upwards to face her again.

"You may think that you two have been secretive of your… *affection*… for one other, but eyes are always on you and always will be. He may be a fine, good-looking man, hard-working, strong, level-headed, but I fear that he will not always be by your side. Yorkshire is over one hundred miles away; he will surely want to live in Yorkshire and not here. You can't expect him to give up his life, his friends, his family."

I have not put too much thought into the logistics if Lord Stanford and I were to marry. If I were not the sole heir to my estate or cared too much about the people here, perhaps I would be happy to live in Yorkshire, far away from here… but why should I be the one to give everything up?

"I will not abandon my life here, Aunt, not for any man. Besides, Lord Stanford is such a kind, honest, noble man that I wouldn't be surprised if he wanted to live here instead of York. He does not have the same position as I, therefore he can afford to live away from home."

My aunt frowns slightly at my optimistic suggestion. "I doubt any man would be happy to do so, Katherine. Leicester is not exactly the jewel in the crown. As much as you might deny it, he is a man, Katherine; they're all alike, one way or another."

"You don't know him like I do, Aunt. I can sense that he is… that he is… that I…" The words I want to say do not make it out of my mouth, as though something is holding them back.

"I know that you *think* you know everything. It's exciting when you fall in love with someone and they with you in return." Her eyes glaze over in a happy memory. "I remember when I was around your age; I was sent to court with your mother to be one of the queen's ladies-in-waiting. It was a huge honour! When I was there, I fell in love with an earl. He was handsome, just like your Lord Stanford – tall, strong, beautiful smile – we fell for each other instantly." She has such a warm look in her eyes, as if she is back there at court with this mysterious earl.

"But the queen had already chosen a suitor for me and my parents also approved of the match. I was the eldest daughter and had very little choice, so I was shipped off to France, and within the next few weeks, I was married to a man I hardly knew."

Her eyes are closed and her lips are downturned as she rises from the chair. "I was heartbroken when I was told that I couldn't marry the man I loved, but it was my duty and an honour to marry well for my own sake and that of my family. I had to leave any thoughts of a happy, love-filled marriage behind me, and so must you." She opens her eyes; her expression turns to one of resolve, as if she has already made up her mind for me, ignoring everything we'd just spoken about.

"But what about the love of your life? Why couldn't you have married him instead, told the queen and your parents that you had already chosen a suitor yourself?"

My aunt raises her eyebrows. "Don't be naïve, girl! I had no choice. It was either live in France or be exiled from court and disowned by my family. You do not go against the Queen of England."

"Tell me then, Aunt, if you had a second chance, wouldn't you have damned it all and run away with him?" I question, desperate for her to see things my way for once.

"No." Her voice shakes slightly. "I never saw him again and that was that."

A heavy silence fills the air as she heads for the door. Before opening it, she turns to look at me. "My first husband died only a few years after we were married. We had no heirs. By the time I was sent back to England, the 'love of my life', as you so beautifully put it, was also dead."

My heart sinks at her words. "I am so sorry."

"Don't be." She dismisses my concerns, patting my hand gently.

There is a moment's silence and I chew my lip. "What if Lord Stanford is my 'earl'?"

My question hangs in the air before my aunt clears her throat. "I did what I had to do and I would do it all over again, Katherine. Love is only a small part of any strong and successful marriage." My aunt's posture changes from one that is drawn and heavy to one of resolve and self-duty.

"You can't mean that."

"I do. Anyway, I met your uncle soon after arriving back home from France and look where that took me!" She attempts a small smile. "All I ask, Katherine, is that you think it over. You only get one chance at this in life. This is not a decision to be made quickly, or lightly. I know you are likely to follow your heart over your head – you have your mother to thank for that – but promise me that you will think this over seriously."

"I will, Aunt. I promise you." Though my mind is already made up.

"Answer me this: if Lord Stanford had never returned your feelings, would you reject Lord Tyrell so coldly?"

I try not to dwell too much on that horrible thought. A life without James is something that I can no longer imagine.

"Yes, after what I overheard him say at the tournament. I am just grateful that I did not fall too deeply before then."

After taking my hand and squeezing it gently, she leaves the room without another word.

I pause for a short while, turning my aunt's words over in my head. *Why won't she just let me decide my own fate? I need to get out of here, I need space to breathe.*

My feet take me through the winding corridors and finally outside. I take a seat on the entrance steps, lifting my face to meet the sun. It is warm in the rays of the afternoon, only a few clouds in the sky as birds sing happily around me. I am startled by how far the sun's shadows have moved across the steps – a good amount of time has passed since I first sat here. I do not want to lose all that my parents and brother have fought and died over. I cannot let their hard work be for nothing. But the thought of marrying Lord Tyrell angers me. A few months' ago, I would have thought about this more carefully. He is a powerful man, but instead of keeping the wolves at bay, I would be living with one. Regardless of whether I overheard him at the joust or not, I do not love him, I cannot love someone such as he, and I refuse to settle for less.

As I sit here contemplating my future, a shadow forms over me. Without looking up, I already know who it is. I reach my hand up as she pats me on the shoulder.

"Katherine, what are you doing out here all alone?" The tall, slim figure stands beside me and squeezes my shoulder. "Have you seen your aunt yet? She was looking for you this morning."

"Yes, I have." My voice sounds harsher than I wanted, but I cannot hide my true feelings from Isabelle.

She takes a seat beside me.

"She wants me to consider Lord Tyrell's proposal."

"I'm guessing you told her no." Isabelle frowns. She knows my aunt as well as I do; she is not an easy character to persuade.

"That and many other words," I sigh, hugging my knees to my chest and resting my chin upon them. I value my aunt's opinion very highly, but she is wrong with this. She would see me marry the next man to enter this courtyard if she could, as long as they had money and status. "Anyway," I say, smoothing my hands down my dress, "how is Sir Henry and his delightful mother?"

Isabelle's jaw twitches. "He has ridden to Rutland today. He's taken her with him." Her tone is short with a hint of bitterness.

"How unlike him," I reply, my eyebrows raised.

"Well…" Something catches Isabelle's eye in the distance. "Who is that?"

"If it is my aunt then tell her that I am not here."

I stand up and start to make my way inside, but Isabelle holds her hand against my arm, forcing me to look in the same direction. I shield my eyes against the sun with my hand, spotting the gatekeeper sprinting down the steps towards us. The clouds move across the sun and the world is still.

Blood pounds in my ears in time with the hammering of hooves. The person riding the horse looks heavy and unevenly balanced, slouched forwards.

The gatekeeper's cries are now ringing in the air as I sprint down the entrance steps.

I know that man. I know that shape. I know the feeling of his soft grey tunic against my cheek.

"James?" I steady his horse and shout to Isabelle. She grabs the horse's reins, soothing the startled creature as best as she can whilst crying for help.

I reach up to touch his hand that is clutching his tunic, only to see it drenched in thick red blood, strangely warm as it drips onto my own. I stare at it in horror. What looks like a broken arrow shaft is lodged in his side, acting like a plug in a barrel.

I have never seen this amount of blood before. I don't know what to do… I attempt to speak but no words come out as my eyes take in this horrific sight in front of me. It is a nightmare. All of the horrors and darkness in the world have swallowed me whole, and I do not know how to get out. The blood dripping from his wound is an endless, oozing river.

I reach for his hand again, which is now dangling by his side. "Lord Stanford? Lord Stanford? James?"

He weakly opens his eyes and looks towards me. I gasp and fight the sting of tears in my eyes. His face is also bloody; new cuts have joined old wounds. What happened to him?

My shouts have drawn the attention from those nearby, Johnson and Giles being the first to arrive.

"My lady! What has happened?" Giles asks, his breaths laboured and sharp, taking in the bloody scene before us.

"We need to get him off his horse now!" I shout, my hands shaking uncontrollably.

The two men step towards us, but I am already taking Lord Stanford's feet out of the stirrups. Without thinking, I use all of my strength and help him dismount, nearly buckling under his weight, before he collapses only a few steps away from where I was sitting peacefully just minutes before.

"My lady, be careful!" Johnson shouts, as more and more people gather around us; it is suffocating.

Kneeling beside him, I clasp his face between my palms and tap his cheeks gently, but he does not stir or open his eyes again. I hover my cheek above his lips, trying to feel his breath against my skin, but I cannot and panic. Isabelle grasps my arm and points to his chest, which is rising and falling so slowly I almost missed it. My hands continue to shake as I push his hair out of his eyes.

My gatekeeper looks on in despair as my whirling thoughts finally make it out through my lips, "Who did this? Wh-who was it? How did this happen? Who did this to you?" I shout as Lord Stanford's eyes open but then begin to close again. "No! Stay with me. James, stay with me, look at me."

He tries to speak. A small spark of hope.

"It's me. It's Katherine." I cup his cheek in my right hand as I hold his cold hand against my own, ignoring the fact that I am now covered in blood, his blood.

"Katherine?" His voice is barely a whisper, a former shadow of his bold, northern self. Above the commotion around me, it is difficult to hear him speak as Johnson barks orders at those gathered around us. I do not hear their words exactly as I concentrate on Lord Stanford in front of me.

"Shush," I try to reassure him, "You are safe now. I'm here."

I desperately scan the splintered shaft of the arrow, to see if there is anything that can be done. I carefully place one hand onto Lord Stanford's chest as I grip the shaft of the arrow.

"No, don't take it out! It could kill him! We need to fetch a doctor. Now," Isabelle screams, her voice startling me as I remove my hands, leaving the arrow still buried deep.

Isabelle turns to my gatekeeper. "Go and find Lord Golding immediately!"

"Yes, my lady; I will send for a doctor too." He runs off up the entrance steps and out of sight.

Lord Stanford begins to lose consciousness again. "No,

no, please, James, look at me. Look at me! Help is on its way! You will be fine." My eyes cloud over with tears that I refuse to let fall.

He is getting weaker with every moment that passes. I do not understand. What happened? I press my hand harder against his seeping wound, desperate to try to stop the bleeding. Why won't it stop?

"We need to find whoever did this to him!" I shout, tears pouring down my face.

"K-Katherine," Lord Stanford calls, consuming my attention. "O-out in t'woods…" He inhales as much air as he can take. "They…"

"What happened? Where in the woods? Who did this?"

My voice is frantic. I have so many questions rushing through my head. Who? What? Why? Where? How? I can't make sense of anything! For the first time in a very long time, I do not know what to do. I look up into the fading sunlight as I hear my uncle, Sir Francis and John Gamble push their way through the crowd around us.

I look up at Sir Francis who is only able to ask, "What happened?"

"The woods… he said that something happened in the woods," is all I can manage, tears welling up.

"Johnson! Giles! Taylor! Go out into the woodland and search for whoever or whatever did this! They could still be at large," my uncle commands; I am thankful for him taking swift action when I can only stare in disbelief.

The three men rush past us towards the stable, grabbing whichever horses are available and cantering through the portcullis towards the path that Lord Stanford travelled.

"We must take him inside, Katherine." Sir Francis kneels next to me, careful not to put his knee in the pool of blood that has begun to collect at the side of us. Sir Francis looks at me with a knitted brow and held breath. "Katherine, we must move him inside."

Memories of that day when Sir Francis broke the news that my brother was dead flash through my mind. I sit there still paralysed, unable to move; is it happening all over again? Am I about to lose another?

I dare not release my hand from Lord Stanford's, but I know that I cannot hold on forever. I shake my head. "Yes." I stand up, Lord Stanford's grip becoming weaker and weaker, eventually slipping from mine. "You are right. W-we must take him inside."

The barriers I have learnt so often to build within myself rise once again. I compose myself, preparing for what is yet to come. I have to be strong, not only for myself, but for him. It will not do having the head of this house acting hysterically, unable to make clear decisions when those who look up to her require it the most. We will catch whoever did this, but right now, Lord Stanford needs medical attention, he needs care, he needs me to be strong.

"Take him inside," I command.

My aunt rushes towards us, short of breath as if she has run from the North Tower. "What is happening? I heard the commotion."

"We don't know how or why, Lady Golding, but Lord Stanford is… he's badly injured," Isabelle steps in and informs my aunt.

Isabelle ushers her back inside as the men lift Lord Stanford inside. I don't leave him as he is carried through the entrance doors and into the Great Hall. They place his body on the cold stone floor.

"He cannot stay here. Take him upstairs!" I shout, agitated at the thought of him being dumped on the cold floor like a peasant.

"Where exactly, my lady?" John Gamble asks.

"Anywhere. His room, my room." I stop to think, he cannot be carried too far in this condition. "William's old room is the closest, just at the top of the staircase." My mind is running at a thousand miles per hour; I cannot think straight. I turn to Bess who has joined to watch the commotion. "Bess, please go and fill several jugs of water. I also need bandages and whatever you can find to ease the pain."

"W-what happened to him? Did he…? Surely not." Shock drains her face of all colour as she takes in the devastation in front of her. Her eyes do not leave the blood staining his tunic.

"I need you to help. Water and bandages."

She nods and rushes off in the direction of the kitchens.

I follow the men into the room that was once my brother's. They lay him gently onto the bed and peel off his clothes, ripping the shirt that clings to his chest. All I do is stand there and watch. I am helpless as the doctor finally arrives and ushers everyone out of the way to examine his new patient. It is only by his voice I realise that it is the same doctor who has tended to my family throughout my life: Doctor Bell. The doctor studies the man lying neatly on the four-poster bed and, with care, moves the arrow slightly with a metal object, I assume to determine how deep it has cut.

"I will have to pull it out of his side now, or it will get infected," he states. "I do not think it has splintered inside him… it should be a clean removal. He might have internal bleeding, however."

"You must do what is needed, Bell." Sir Francis comes to stand beside me and cups his arms around my shoulders. I do not say anything.

I lose track of the conversation happening around me. I stand there frozen, watching this horror playing out before me. It is as if the Devil himself has put on a play and is forcing me to watch. The smell of blood tinges the air, a metallic hint on my lips. I gaze down upon my hands, now red and sticky, the terror almost swallowing me whole. Thankfully, my attention is drawn away from this nightmare as Bess with two more maids enter, placing two jugs of water and a bundle of cloths onto the side table. They leave promptly after catching sight of the poor man on the bed in front of us. I almost wish I could do the same, but I need to be here.

I watch on as Doctor Bell pours water around the arrow to clear away the blood. He dabs a piece of linen around the wound.

"I need to analyse the best way possible to remove the object from his chest and without leaving any splinters inside the body too," the doctor murmurs.

Doctor Bell turns to face John Gamble. "Take this." The doctor hands him the soiled cloths which were once white, now red. "Right, now the tricky part," Doctor Bell mumbles to himself. "I need to pull this out as quickly as possible, then patch up the wound before he bleeds out. On the count of three. One… two… three!"

He pulls the arrow clean from Lord Stanford's side who cries out at the pain, only to slip into a sleep-like state moments after the arrow's removal. I stare at his chest, checking for signs of breathing. I think I see it rise and fall, or perhaps my mind is tricking me.

Blood trickles from where the arrow left a small wound in Lord Stanford's chest. After cleaning the wounded area several times, the doctor dresses the affected area with the bandages, making sure to stop the flow of blood. It feels like hours have gone by when, I presume, only minutes have passed.

Once the doctor has finally finished, I take a step closer to the bed and then another until I am perched on the edge. His skin is very pale and the colour of his lips has faded. I touch his hand just to feel a pulse or a sign of life.

Doctor Bell moves away from his patient as Sir Francis offers him a clean towel to dab the blood off his hands. "Well, this man is very lucky, the amount of blood he has lost..." He shakes his head in disbelief. "The next few days will be the most important. I am sorry to say that he might not survive."

I stop breathing, air caught in my throat. He might not survive. He might not survive? What will happen if he does not survive? My hand curls around Lord Stanford's tighter, never wanting to let go. I am his anchor to this world. If I let go, how can he find his way back to me?

"Thank you." My uncle and Sir Francis shake Doctor Bell by the hand.

"I will need to check on him regularly."

"You must stay here with us, Bell." My uncle claps the doctor on the back, offering a thin smile.

"That would be most kind of you. That way I will be able to make sure he has the best care possible."

"Of course. We shall send a boy to fetch your things." My uncle steps out of the room leaving me, Sir Francis and the doctor alone with Lord Stanford.

"Lord Stanford must rest, my lady."

Sir Francis steps towards the doctor again. "Yes, thank you, Doctor Bell. He is in good hands now..."

Sir Francis leads the doctor out of the room so that it is just me alone with Lord Stanford. I still cling to his hand as losing him is not even worth thinking about. As soon as the sound of various voices outside fade away, a few tears begin to flow down my cheek. I begin to wipe away the tears that fall, but all I can feel is dried blood, his blood, staining my cheek. The taste of salt and metal mix upon my lips.

It starts with the shaking of my shoulders, and then my hands, followed by the lowering of my head towards his chest. It doesn't take long for built-up grief and shock to take over, tears pouring down my cheeks as I gasp for breath. I try to muffle the sobs that escape me, but I can no longer pretend that I am strong, that I can deal with this tragedy, that I can face the thought of being without him. I am grieving for a future that hangs in the balance.

Eventually, I have no more tears left in me to shed. I gaze upon the man in front of me, but how long can he go on fighting?

Eighteen

I can't sleep. I pace from one end of my room to the other, only to sit on my bed, drumming my fingers against the mattress and then retrace my steps again. The images of Lord Stanford's blood staining my hands flash in my mind on a continuous loop. I shake my head from side to side, trying to banish these nightmares, but as soon as I sit down again, the scene replays itself on repeat.

Not long after I left my brother's old bedchamber, my uncle informed me that Johnson, Giles and Taylor couldn't find anything out in the woods. No animal tracks, no footprints, no misfired arrows. Nothing. Only a trail of blood leading from the edge of the woodland into my castle courtyard. It's as if whoever attacked him has disappeared.

My mind turns to his family. Do they know yet what has happened to their son, brother, uncle? In all the commotion, I never thought to let them know. Do they even know that he is here? I light the candle next to my bed and grab a sheet of paper to scribble a note to Lady

Stanford as to what happened. As I put ink to paper, I wonder if his family know I exist at all. What happens if he doesn't pull through? My quill hesitates above the paper, ink splashing slowly onto the parchment, drip, drip, drip, until I put the pen down and stop writing altogether.

The air is still.

What will people think once they know what happened here? Will they start to point the blame at me and my family, labelling us as unable to keep those who stay with us safe? My mind begins to wonder about who could have done this and why? I'm not aware of Lord Stanford having any adversaries around here, though I know that I have a few. Perhaps it was an accident, but surely someone would have come forward by now? Maybe they are too scared to do so? I'm not even sure what the punishment would be. No, this was no accident; the hit was too deliberate, too accurate.

I cannot sit here any longer. Listening at the door for any sign of movement, I slowly open it and peek round to see if there is anyone lurking in the shadows. Breathing a sigh of relief at the empty corridors, I make my way towards the top of the stone staircase and to William's room. When inside the door, I close it shut behind me and shift my gaze towards the bed. Shielding the room from my burning candle, I look upon Lord Stanford as he lies there motionless.

There are so many questions I want answered. I place my candle on the small wooden chest next to the empty chair by his side and sit, watching his chest rise and fall; it comforts me. "Please don't leave me."

A few tears cascade down my cheek. I loosen my grip of his hand.

"Katherine..."

"James! I am here! I am here," I whisper, startled but relieved to hear his voice amongst the darkness.

His eyes flicker open but all of the sparkle and strength is no longer there, as if it was drained out of him along with his blood. Even his hair seems to have turned a shade darker. He looks into my eyes, but winces as he tries to move closer.

I jump forward, resting a hand on his chest. "Please don't move. You must rest." I touch my hand on his forehead. "You're burning up, James."

I feel like I am in limbo. I should leave him to rest, but I can't bear the thought of leaving him all alone in the dark, especially here. My brother's room was once a place I avoided, not being able to bear spending more than a minute alone in here. Now, I don't want to leave. I can't.

With care, I move around to the other side of the bed and tuck myself next to him. Lying on my side, I brush away a few strands of hair that have swept across his eyes, then place a gentle kiss on his lips.

"I thought that I was going to lose you, James."

Without a reply, he drifts off to sleep again. I lie there, looking at him for a few moments, but my eyes become heavier and heavier until finally, I fall into a dreamless sleep.

The next thing I see is the morning light streaming through the window and I hear the faint twitter of the blackbirds outside. Lord Stanford is still asleep in the same position that I found him. His body is covered in a thin layer of sweat, even though he feels cold. I leave the bed to open the window even wider for the fresh air to whip around the room, hoping that it takes away his sudden fever with it. It is not long until the door creaks open to reveal Elanor with a bowl of water and a white bundle of linen tucked tight under her arm.

"Oh! My lady, I am sorry, I didn't mean to disturb you. Your uncle asked me to bring these for the doctor when he is ready."

"Thank you, Elanor." I take the bowl and fresh linen, resting them next to the extinguished candle, hoping she thinks I have only just arrived to check in on our unexpected patient. "When will Doctor Bell arrive?"

"He spent the night here, my lady, as requested. I believe that he is currently in the Great Hall eating his breakfast and will be along any minute now."

"Thank you, Elanor," I smile, as she curtsies and leaves.

With a small, relieved breath at being left alone again, I turn my attention to Lord Stanford resting on the bed before me. With a light touch, I pat a clean, wet cloth across his forehead to cool him down, but as soon as I remove it, even more beads gather again as if they had never been disturbed. His breathing is heavy, a painful expression twisted upon his face. I speak his name several times in order to coax him back to me, but he does not answer. It is as if he is lost in a nightmare and I cannot reach him.

"Lady Turner, how lovely to see you. How is he?"

I didn't even notice that someone else had joined me until Doctor Bell is at my side.

"His temperature won't cool down."

"Let me see…" Doctor Bell examines his patient's face and chest. He leans in closer and looks at the wound by peeling off the bloody layers of linen that need changing.

Stepping away from the bed, I can only watch in silence as he redresses him with the new bandages, hoping that they help to stop the bleeding.

"He may have an infection, which is causing this sudden fever. This can often happen with wounds such as this."

Before I can press him for further details, the door opens behind us and in steps my aunt, her lips pursed tight as she picks at the hem of her sleeve. "How is he?" she asks, her hands now clasped in front of her as she keeps a small distance from the bed.

"He might have an infection," I reply without looking at her. I keep my gaze purely on the Yorkshireman, my Yorkshireman.

"I am sorry to hear it." She stands there silently for a short moment, before adding, "Katherine, I need to speak with you."

"Not now, Aunt," I dismiss her. Anything outside this room is not worth my time.

"Please."

"There is not much else we can do, Lady Turner," Doctor Bell says with his hand on his chin in thought. "We can only wait for the fever to break."

"How long will that take?"

"I cannot answer that with certainty, I am afraid. However, once the fever is broken, he will be marching back to his full strength, I am sure." He attempts a smile, but I can sense the doubt behind his words. "He will need full-time observation and I am sure that he will get the proper attention he deserves whilst he is under your care. I will of course stay within these walls until the fever has passed, but it could be days, even weeks before we see improvement."

I step closer to Lord Stanford as Doctor Bell moves away to confer with my aunt. I do not pay their words any attention as I reach for the damp cloth and press it against Lord Stanford's forehead once again. It pains me to see him in such a way, a contrast against the tall, strong man I first met. Instead of wanting to shrink away, dislocate myself from it all, I only want to watch over him, attending to his wounds, making sure that he recovers.

I also want to make sure that the culprit for this pays for what they did to him. What they did to *me*. Could it have been a hunting accident? Did he spot something on his way back from Nottingham? Are thieves and poachers back hunting in the woodland? Or did someone hide and wait for his return, knowing that he would take the route that leads to and from the castle? But why? That is the question that I keep turning over in my head: why?

"Can I speak to you for a moment please, Katherine?"

It is clear from her tone that she is not going to retreat and so, reluctantly, I leave Lord Stanford's side and allow Doctor Bell to take over my watch.

We reach the library in silence.

"Katherine, I am sorry about what has happened to Lord Stanford. I truly am." She gently places her hand on my shoulder as we sit near the fireplace.

I try not to catch her eye for fear of bursting into tears.

"Doctor Bell has informed me that the arrow only just missed his vital organs and he has lost a lot of blood. He is worried that this has weakened him to the point of Lord Stanford not being able to survive… If he does, then he will not be as strong as he used to be."

I sit there in silence, trying to take in what she is saying.

"Katherine, please, don't get yourself too attached, I don't want your heart to be broken by death once more."

I keep my eyes straight ahead, hardly blinking. "He will pull through, Aunt, I know he will. It is only a fever, and we have seen worse in others before and yet they survived." I try to convince myself as I say these words, thinking about Leicester's outbreak of disease not that long ago. "Instead of wondering whether his life hangs in the balance, we should be wondering who did this to him. *Why* would they do this? What are they hoping to gain?"

"You are right, Katherine, but we cannot go accusing people. You know that poachers lurk in the woodland and forests; it could have been anyone. It could have been an accident."

"I thought so too, but to misfire an arrow that high into the air and to land it that accurately into James's side…" I stand up and pace between the fireplace and the window. "I just can't see why or how that is possible, unless someone was aiming at him deliberately. Maybe they wanted to make it look like an accident. If no one had been out there on the steps then he could have died, and we would not have known—" my voice breaks.

"I understand how you are feeling, Katherine. I lost my first husband before his time. My sister, brother-in-law and nephew have all been taken from me. I know what he means to you; I can see that now. I can see how you think that you cannot live without him."

"I have known too much loss, Aunt, and I cannot bear to lose him. Not now."

Silence falls on us as we sit near the window, similar to how we did yesterday.

"I know you love him."

Tears begin to flow down my face. My aunt takes a handkerchief from her sleeve and dabs them away, gathering me up in her arms. "I just don't want you to get hurt. If he dies…"

"Aunt, don't… please."

"But then if he lives…"

She doesn't say anything further on the subject as I curl up on the chair and lift my heavy eyes up to hers. Just before I drift off to sleep, she perches on the arm of the chair and kisses my forehead as I lose myself to dreams of a darkened future.

Nineteen

I have never known time to slow as much as it has over these past few days and weeks. If it wasn't for watching the sun set in the morning and the moon rise in the evening, I would think that I was stuck in limbo. Helplessly, I would watch over Lord Stanford, one day bleeding into the next.

You would think that I would be used to such destruction. My father regularly marched back from battles with more than one scar or chunk of flesh missing. If he came back without such a trophy, I would wonder if he had been on the battlefield at all. There was an occasion when I thought he was going to die, a gash the size of my fist cut deep across his thigh. It took the best healers and doctors in the county to save his leg, and I thank God that they were able to. My father was lucky as all that remained of that battle was a thick scar and a new limp whenever he walked. Initially, I thought it was a blessing, thinking perhaps he would stay at home with me and William more often, stay away from another fight that was never his to lead in the first place. I was wrong. If anything, it spurred him on as he desperately tried to prove to those around him, including the late king, that there was no need to send him into retirement just yet. My brother would call him a stubborn fool, arguing that he was not fit to mount his horse anymore, let alone canter into battle. He was right. After such a quarrel, my father marched out of our castle gate for the final time after receiving an order from King Edward, never to return alive. I have always wondered if William regretted parting with our father on such bitter terms. I just remember the sombre look upon his face in the weeks that followed our father's death; I didn't need to ask him.

Perhaps that is why I cannot stay away from Lord Stanford for too long, no matter how hard I try to fill my day with empty tasks. If he succumbs to his injuries, I know that I would regret being away from him. I was never able to be there for my mother, my father or my brother, but I can be here for him. I will protect him from those who tried to end his life, shield him from any rumour that dared dance on the lips of gossiping nobles and townsfolk alike, keep him safe.

I have forbidden anyone in our household to speak of what has happened. The last thing I need is for those I do not trust to march here demanding an investigation, spreading lies across the rest of the kingdom. It has been done before. Our country may not be at war currently, but it does not take a lot for someone to stoke the fire and set ablaze relationships that are already fragile.

I scrapped then rewrote the letter to Lord Stanford's family several times. I didn't know what to write! Should I lie to her, pretend that his injuries are only minor, or should I tell her in great detail what happened? Should I write at all? Eventually, I wrote, sealed and sent the letter off all the way north to Yorkshire. My uncle offered to travel with the letter himself, but I need him here to support me, as much as I pretend that I can handle all of this alone.

Dear Lady Stanford

I hope that this letter finds you well.

I am sorry to inform you that your son, Lord James Stanford, has suffered life-threatening injuries and is recovering at my home at Leicester Castle. He was riding out in the woodland when the incident occurred. Luckily, I was there to help him and made sure that he received the medical attention he needed. The full extent of his injuries is not known, but I can assure you that he is receiving the best care he requires. I sit with him every day, ensuring that he is as comfortable as he can be.

If you wish to visit your son, I will welcome you with open arms. We can prepare one of the guest rooms ready for your arrival if you wish. I would also like to extend this invitation to your daughter and her family.

I am sorry that our first correspondence is not about something of a happier nature.

I will send you a report on your son's progress as soon as I can.

Yours truly,

Countess Katherine Turner of Leicester

I couldn't risk my letter being intercepted and so decided to omit the details of what actually happened that day out in the courtyard. As soon as her son has fully recovered, I will be able to inform her of the truth. Details are still unknown as to what really happened. I pray that Lord Stanford will be able to fill in the missing pieces. I just hope his family do not blame me, as I have started to blame myself…

Not too soon after my message was sent, I received a reply:

Dear Countess Turner,

It is an honour to hear from you.

You were careful not to disclose any details as to my son's injuries or how he came to get them. That is very wise, given that messages such as this can be diverted so carelessly. I am sure that, if this was no accident, your uncle, one of my late husband's oldest friends, will help you find the culprit and bring them to justice. We will aid you as much as we can, but there is not much we can do.

Strangely enough, my son had written to me not too long ago stating that he is to stay in Leicester for an unforeseeable amount of time and will return home when he can. I won't reveal the full extent of my son's letter, but I can tell that he is in very capable hands and I cannot imagine a more suitable hostess.

On another note, thank you for your kind invitation, but I must decline. My health is not what it used to be, perhaps my son informed you, but the long journey to your home is not possible at the moment. I am also engaged helping my daughter look after her three little boys, seeing as her husband is engaged elsewhere. I apologise that this might not be the news you wanted to receive from me. I do look forward to meeting you one day, my dear Countess Turner.

Please do send updates when you are able.

Wishing you and your family well.

Lady Stanford

I have reread this letter more than three times, trying to read between the lines. It's hard not to. She does suspect that her son's injuries are more than I had revealed in my initial letter. Should I have been more direct? No, if someone intercepted my note and I revealed all that I know about what happened, it would be bad for both of our families.

My heart beats a little quicker at the mystery behind her words about Lord Stanford's correspondence. What has he told his family about me? About us? That will have to wait for the time being, but it brings me comfort to know that I am no longer a stranger to his family, even though we are yet to meet.

I filed Lady Stanford's letter away in a drawer for the time being, focusing on her son for now. Over the past few days, he has been in and out of consciousness, hardly being able to exchange a few words before needing to rest again. Isabelle has given me the idea that I should read aloud to him. She remembers her own mother reading to her when she was ill and it gave her comfort to hear her voice, soothing the pain away.

I have spent the last hour trying to find a suitable book, my mind wandering from one thought to the next. I finally settle on a volume of poetry tucked away on a high shelf, long forgotten against the newer, more modern tomes that Sir Francis gifted to me in the past few years. I stroke the book's cover, opening the cracking pages to see beautifully written letters decorate the page.

I hold it tight against my chest. It is strange to feel nervous reading aloud to him. I have not read aloud to others for such a long time; what if I mess up and have to start all over again? This is silly. I meet with hundreds of different people each year, host banquets and attend gatherings in London for our king, having to speak at each event with no trouble. So, why do I have butterflies in my stomach at the thought of reading to Lord Stanford?

As I push his door open and step inside, I take a small breath before composing myself and sitting in the empty chair next to his bed. I look over him, checking to see if he is awake – of course he is not – and then open the book to a dog-eared page that I remember being one of my brother's favourites.

I stumble a little on the first verse, but soon get into the rhythm, enjoying reading out loud for pleasure once again. As I finish the first stanza, I steal another brief glance towards my audience who sleeps soundly beside me. The bedchamber soon heats up as the sun stretches into the room, so, whilst still reading, I walk over towards the window and push it open slightly, stumbling as I do so. The cool breeze is refreshing as it rustles through the trees in the distance, whipping a few fallen leaves off the ground as it makes its way through the castle grounds below.

I lose my way on a verse and have to start again, but then a voice on the other side of the room pulls me towards the bed.

"Do ya 'ave any Chaucer instead?"

I almost freeze on the spot, book limp in my hand as the voice comes into focus again.

"Not that I mind poetry," he chuckles, half laughing, half choking.

"James?" I rush over to see him. It has felt like forever since I have heard his voice this clear.

He reaches up to cup my face. I close my eyes and place my hand on his, soaking in his familiar warmth that I have longed for. The sense of relief is overpowering. I truly thought he might never recover, but for once, I am so very glad that I was wrong.

"Katherine," he sighs, his voice faint. The sound of my name on his lips again overwhelms me.

Before I think of anything else, I throw my arms around his neck, holding him so tight, savouring the feeling of him in my arms. "James, I have been so worried, I-I thought…" The sentence dies on my lips, not daring to enter down the dark path I would often visit whenever I thought about our future together.

"Ah! Careful!" He shifts as he tries to get comfortable again. I leap away as fast as I can, afraid of causing more damage.

"Sorry! Perhaps I should fetch Doctor Bell?"

"No, there's no need. I have everything I want right 'ere." He attempts to sit up but doesn't make it that far.

"Lucky for you, you didn't hear too much of my poetry reading."

A small smile appears on his face, a little sheepish. "Well, actually, I've been awake for a while; I just didn't want to disturb ya."

My cheeks heat as I remember the numerous times I stumbled over various words or had to reread a line. Perhaps my aunt was right; I should have focused more on ladylike pursuits when I was younger, not that I regret running around with a fake sword in my hand instead of a poetry book.

"Why didn't you say anything earlier?"

"It was far more amusing to hear ya stumble then swear under yer breath whenever ya misread a line." He chuckles. "It made poetry more entertaining."

"So, not only was I rubbish at reading aloud, but I also chose a rubbish subject too?" I laugh, swatting his arm, immensely happy at the thought of being with him again.

"Ya could have read one of yer uncle's manuscripts on different types of soil and I would have enjoyed it." He takes my hand and raises it to his lips, which are a little rough and cracked.

I begin to reach for the jug on the table next to me.

"Please, may I have a little bit of that ale, Katherine? It's like I've not drunk in days."

I wish it were only days that he'd lain here.

I place the poetry book on the edge of the bed so I can pour ale into a large goblet, careful not to spill any. "Let me sit you up." I help ease Lord Stanford to sit upright in the bed. I notice dark purple shadows under his eyes. "Here." I offer him the goblet of fresh ale, from which he takes a deep drink and then another until the goblet is empty.

He leans his head against the old oak headboard; it is

as if he's just run a mile, out of breath and sweaty. I take a seat on the bed, careful to not sit on him or trap my dress underneath me.

"I feel like I could sleep for another week," he sighs, barely able to keep his eyes open. "How long have I been like this? Just lying 'ere?"

"At least three weeks now."

"Three weeks?" he replies. "H-How can it be? I can hardly remember anything."

His face twists from what looks like annoyance to confusion as he presumably tries to piece together what happened and how he came to be here like this. Up until this moment, I have not really thought about what would happen once he was fully awake and moving. He is bound to have questions, but I fear that I do not have the answers he deserves. We have heard nothing from outside these walls and the searches my men have carried out were fruitless. Perhaps part of me just wanted all of this to go away.

"What do you remember, James?" I ask, hoping to gain insight into what happened that day, but I know what his answer will be.

"I-I can't remember. Only riding out to Nottingham, was it? I'm not even sure if I made it that far. I just remember the woodland and the trees, the birds singing above me… then… darkness. What happened, Katherine?" His expression twists into a deep frown then relaxes, only for his brow to contort into a frown again.

I wish I could take all his pain away with one kiss. I swallow a lump in my throat before I answer. "Well, I'm not sure exactly."

He looks away from me for a second, eyes unable to meet my own, his breaths shallow. "What do ya mean?"

"I'm sorry, James. I can only tell you what I witnessed. Otherwise, I was hoping you could tell *me*."

"I can't help ya. I'm sorry." His eyes lower to his hands in his lap, which pull at the soft bedding. "I hate being like this. Useless and a burden on yer house. I would understand if ya no longer wanted me 'ere."

How can he think such thoughts? I take his hands in mine. "You can never be a burden on me and my house, James. Never." I stare deeply into his eyes until he looks away. He must know that I would never reject him for something that was not his fault in the first place. The thought of losing him was too much. I will fight every man in the kingdom before he is taken away from me. But that is the issue… me. "You have nothing to be sorry for, James. If it wasn't for me, you probably wouldn't be in this mess in the first place."

He looks at me with such disbelief, it almost makes me feel selfish for saying my dark thoughts out loud. "Why'd ya say that? None of this is yer fault."

"It's difficult to think that when you nearly died on my castle steps." I swallow a small lump that has formed in my throat.

He weakly squeezes my hand. "I won't allow ya to say such things. If this is what has brought us closer together, then perhaps it was worth it."

"That's very sweet of you, James, I suppose, but until I find out what truly happened to you and why, I don't think my guilt will melt away so easily."

"Then I will help ya. If I remember anything, I'll let

ya know, but…" He scowls in deep concentration. "I can't remember right now."

I lean over and kiss his forehead, thankfully no longer sticky or hot, the fever long forgotten. "Don't worry, James. I'm just so happy to see that you are well."

A happy silence rests between us as his thumb gently stokes my hand. I have missed him so much. After a short while, he stops and looks up at me, a small smile on his lips, but then he quickly drops his gaze.

"Katherine… ya mean more to me than ya know. What y'ave done for me, how ya make me feel… if I don't tell ya now then I will regret it forever."

I lean in towards him, hooked onto his unspoken words. "What, James? Tell me what?"

"That I-I love ya."

My breath catches in my throat and time stands still. To hear him say those words out loud to me now is something I never expected. With my reply I can finally feel free and no longer need to keep my secret from him. "James, I love you too."

I lean into him as he closes the gap between us, pressing his lips against mine. Tender, it is as if our lips are touching for the first time, time freezing for this one perfect moment. He cups my cheek with his hand, pressing us impossibly closer together. I steady myself by placing my hand on his chest, but our moment is fractured as he yelps in pain and I suddenly break away from him, my heart racing at the hurtful sound in his voice.

"I'm so sorry, James! Are you alright? Do you need to rest?" My heart hammers in my chest with fright.

"No, no, I'm fine… honestly." He grins, but then

inhales sharply as pain clearly shoots through him again. "On second thoughts, I'll lie back down… but only if ya join me?"

"You really know how to get a woman into bed, don't you, my lord?" I chuckle, unable to resist him.

Once he is lying down again, I join him, kicking off my shoes in the process. I so badly want to carry on where we left off. My eyes keep glancing at his parted lips as I lean in closer, my thigh resting against his. He gathers me into his arms. Without hesitating, I drift my hands over his exposed torso, pausing at the sight of the many different bruises and scars tattooed on his skin.

"Did these hurt?" I ask, mesmerised, tracing each one with my finger. "What about this one." I lightly trace a thin, dark line that travels across his right pec. "What's the story behind this?"

As he answers, his eyes roam over my body. "France. About fifteen years ago. If it wasn't for my father, I would've been left for dead."

"What happened?"

"I was sent out on a scouting mission to see where the French army were and found myself in the middle of an ambush instead. One of the Frenchmen's arrows skinned the top of my chest. I had stupidly not worn my breastplate that day as it was damaged in an earlier battle. I thought I was invincible back then."

One by one, I take my time to kiss every purple mark and every scar.

"Yer touch could heal any man," he whispers.

Twenty

I make my way to the Great Hall, hunting down whatever is left of breakfast. Just as I am about to grab an apple from a basket of fruit, Isabelle stops me in my tracks, placing her hand on my arm, a concerned look upon her face.

"Katherine, I wondered if I could talk to you for a moment?" She looks around the room. "Shall we take a turn about the gardens? It's so stuffy in here."

I nod and we make our way outside and into the gardens.

The birds are singing beautifully, flitting from one tree to the other as the sun shines down upon us; it's warm enough to not need a cloak. The gravel underneath our feet crunches as we weave in and out of the trees, sticking to the well-laid path that Thomas Moore carefully maintains every day. As we reach my mother's rose garden, Isabelle pauses and gestures for us to sit on the seat we always occupy whenever we are together in this beautiful and peaceful space.

After a small pause, Isabelle clears her throat. "Katherine, I have to go to Northampton with my uncle tomorrow. I am so sorry, I know that it is not great timing, what with Lord Stanford and everything, but it's only for a few days, just whilst I prepare for my wedding. I only just found out this morning."

With everything that has happened over the past weeks, I had totally forgotten that Isabelle's wedding to Sir Henry Percival is only in a couple of months' time. I thought we had more time together.

"I can't believe that the wedding is so soon! Is there anything I can do to help?" I ask, but in all honesty, I am not sure what I can offer right now.

She looks at me, her left eyebrow raised. "You have more than enough on your plate here, Katherine. As long as you are there with me on the day, everything will be alright… everything will be fine."

Sensing that there is clearly something else, I try to coax the truth behind her words. "There is nothing to be nervous about, Isabelle. Sir Henry loves you, that is clear to see! The ceremony will be just a blip in comparison to the rest of your lives."

"It is true; he has told me that he loves me." Her smile fades and a small shadow flits across her face. "But it is not the ceremony that I am worried about."

The graveness in her voice alarms me. "What is it that worries you?"

Everything around her is changing; sometimes I forget that. Her life has been dictated to her by the men in her life. First her father, who united my brother and Isabelle in a betrothal, and now her uncle, who has set up this one.

Traditionally, it will then be her husband who controls the remainder of her life, but the way he dotes on her, he is like a flower leaning towards the sun, always in want of her love and warmth.

"What happens if… if I can't give him an heir? His mother *implied* that if I fail to provide a male heir then I will bring shame upon the house of Percival and shame to my husband. She only had one son, but that was enough. Everyone loved and accepted her after that. All we need is one son." Her voice quietens as if the mere thought of disappointing her mother-in-law is more important than her husband.

Women who marry rich and powerful men are looked upon to give their husband a male heir. That is our sole duty, the one purpose of being on this earth, so I am told. As we are the ones who carry the baby for several months, we are given one hundred per cent of the blame if the first born is not a boy. Of course, it is all ridiculous. Women are more valuable than men; it's just a shame the majority of society disagrees with me.

I exhale loudly, angered that someone of little importance has upset my best friend so. "Don't let that old bore dictate your own happiness. You are marrying Sir Henry, not his mother! It's about time we take our own future into our hands. We are more than mere baby incubators."

"What if—"

"No ifs, Isabelle," I say before she can set herself down a wallowing path of misery. "What will be, will be. Let God decide, if that makes you feel any better. I am proof that a male heir is not necessary, am I not?"

Isabelle rests her weary head against my shoulder and I hug her close. My heart breaks for her sorrow. "Being a woman has its advantages, remember; some men will do anything a pretty girl asks of them. You put far too much pressure on yourself. You need to stop worrying about what others think and focus on what you want: your own happiness. I will always be here for you, Isabelle. You can rely on me. We have each other, no matter what. If everything else goes wrong or if we end up with nothing else in this world, we will always have each other."

I hold Isabelle even tighter to my chest whilst she sniffs quietly to herself, as if this act alone will shelter her from all harm.

We sit here in peaceful silence. The birds chirp happily in the sky above us. The breeze is a refreshing change to the coolness inside the castle walls. I will miss this when Isabelle is married; I must make the most out of the little time we have together. I wish she could stay with me always, but I cannot lock her away with me forever; she must forge her own path, even though it might seem like she has very little control along the way.

We continue to sit in silence, enjoying the sounds of nature around us and the sound of hooves clip-clopping around the courtyard in the near distance. The sun is so warm and inviting, like a blanket has been wrapped around us both. My eyelids become heavier with each minute that goes by, but the possibility of falling asleep is disturbed when we hear heavy footsteps on the gravel path behind us.

"Hello, my fine ladies!"

We both sit up at the sudden intrusion. When my mind realises who it is that has disturbed our peace, I stand up as fast as possible.

"I am pleased to have found you."

The Earl of Dornton, Lord Henry Tyrell, strides towards us. He is dressed in his usual dark attire, a pretty feather sitting proudly in his hat, catching the rays of light as it sways in the light breeze. Slight stubble peppers his jawline, purple lines underneath his eyes, a contrast to his sudden cheery demeanour.

"Do you enjoy defiling my wish, Lord Tyrell? Or did you trespass on my land to see how much you could get away with?" I ask, not wanting a reply.

"I know that you no longer wish to be in my company, Lady Katherine, but I heard the news about Lord Stanford. How awful that you had to witness it. I would not wish that on you for the world. And you, Lady Warrington, having too seen the devastation."

My mind, foggy from our time resting in the sun, takes a little longer to digest his words. Did I hear him correctly? How did he find out about what happened here, or is he merely speculating, hoping to get a bite of the truth?

"You have wasted your journey again. Your concern is not needed." I fold my arms across my chest, trying to steady myself.

"Yes, well, he will get himself in difficult situations. Does he not know how dangerous it is in these woods with many poachers and outlaws?"

"Outlaws? Hardly. Poachers and thieves are not known to shoot down passing nobles," I mock.

"Not common outlaws maybe, but there are many men who pass through here. It could have been anyone with a keen eye and a good aim."

I narrow my eyes at his words. Lord Tyrell is very good

at being vague, almost like he is trying to gauge if what he has found out is true before revealing anything. The fact that he has mentioned the woods and poachers indicates that he already knows much more than I wanted. As much as I cannot stand him to be this close to me, I am curious as to what information he has.

"Well, whoever is guilty did not do a very good job," Isabelle states, standing a little taller, her head high.

I almost elbow her in the ribs to keep quiet, but Lord Tyrell replies too quickly before I can interject.

"He is making a fast recovery? That is good news," he replies, but his voice lacks relief.

I stand up a little straighter and lower my voice. "You seem to think you know all about it. You didn't happen to be in the area that day, did you?"

A shocked smile etches across his face. "Me? No, my lady. I was in Nottingham at the time. You may ask anyone at the castle if you need a witness as to my whereabouts. Perhaps ask King Richard himself."

"What a coincidence. Lord Stanford was also in Nottingham that day."

His smile falters a little, but he quickly recovers, almost laughing. "I would be careful going round accusing others, Lady Turner. It would not be good for you to cast your finger of judgement at the wrong man. Especially if he has more power and influence than you can handle."

His threat is obvious, but it will take more than that to scare me.

"I'm merely asking if you saw anything. It wouldn't do you any favours to incorrectly judge my question."

Isabelle shifts next to me but doesn't leave my side.

"Well, at his age, Lord Stanford is not as reactive as he once was, I'm sure," Lord Tyrell grins.

I laugh. Lord Stanford's age is not something I have truly thought much about. Yes, he is older than some of my other suitors, but many women have married men over twice their age.

"I will settle your inquisitive mind." He takes a small step towards me before I can say anything else. "I heard that he was shot fatally with an arrow, possibly barbed so that it was impossible to get out. I, sadly, do not possess such armoury nor do I have the time or skill to waste hunting for nobles in your enchanting forests."

Some of his details are inaccurate, but how does he know this much?

"Who told you this?" I ask, not being able to help hooking onto his bait.

"It doesn't matter. Did you really think something as shocking as this could stay within your castle walls so easily? You are not a naïve woman, so I will answer for you: No! I, of course, will make sure no one else learns about what happened here that day. A dark mark like this upon your house is not worth thinking about. You are lucky he did not die."

My hands form into fists at my side, agitated at his arrogance, trying to goad me into an uncivilised response. "He is recovering well. If you are so concerned, why don't you visit him yourself?"

He takes a step backwards. "I must decline, my lady, for my visit is only to see if the rumours were true and if so, to offer my good wishes to you all."

Isabelle interjects, clearly trying to defuse the tension

between us, “Thank you for your good wishes. We shall pass them onto Lord Stanford on your behalf.” She turns towards me. “Katherine, we need to get going, the doctor should probably be relieved from watching over his patient.” She lays a hand on my arm, coaxing me away from Lords Tyrell’s blatant goading.

“Lady Warrington is right. Go and see to your injured patient. You don’t want anything else to happen to him. I, for one, would hate to learn that he perished whilst under your care. I know the rest of the kingdom would too.”

Anger takes over me at the mere thought of Lord Tyrell meddling with things that he should not. I take a step towards him, speaking through gritted teeth, “What do you know about it? If you had anything to do with what happened to him, I swear I will…”

“Will what? Have me hanged? Humiliate me? Have me exiled?” A strained laugh leaves his lips. “I’m curious as to what a woman thinks she can do with very little power outside her four crumbling walls. If it wasn’t for your uncle and Sir Francis Grey, you would have been conquered a long time ago. The day your brother died was the day that this place started to fall apart, the day a woman thought she could play with the men.” He leans in closer to me, lowering his voice so only I can hear. “It goes against the laws of man. The walls are closing in, Katherine… I am just trying to help you. The other nobles who come from a long line of wealth and power are beginning to feel that the king has paid too much attention to you and not them.

“Jealous nobles are known to act on impulse, and I would *hate* for you to be their new target. Do not be surprised if those you consider to be allies and friends suddenly fall away from you. If you keep pushing me away, you'll have no one to blame but yourself. I have tried to be civil, Katherine, but every time you *reject me*… Let's just say, no one will come to rescue you this time."

Several words, thoughts and actions ring through my mind. I want to punch him in the nose so it bleeds, but what would that achieve?

"Do not threaten me on my own land! It is *you* who should be careful around *me*."

He takes a step back again, clearing his throat so that Isabelle may hear. "Whoever did try to murder your precious Lord Stanford, it was not me."

My eyes do not leave his. His voice rings true, no slight wobble or shaky breath, but surely he knows something about what happened; he must do. If what he says about the other nobles pointing their envious eyes towards me and my family is true, perhaps I should be warier, but why should I believe him? I regain my composure, trying my utmost to make sure that he doesn't see the way in which he can so easily get under my skin.

"I was hoping you could see how strong Lord Stanford is and how the perpetrator failed. Perhaps another time? It won't be long until he is completely healed and we can put all of this behind us, and Lord Stanford and I can move on with our lives together."

Lord Tyrell's eyes never leave mine, his jaw set tight, almost like he is restraining himself from saying anything in reply. Eventually, he adds, "Another time. I bid you both a good day."

He spins on his heel and walks up the path whence he

came. Before he reaches the end of the path towards the castle courtyard, I quickly add, “Oh, Lord Tyrell?”

He pauses and turns to face me one more time.

“Be careful out there in the woodland.”

Twenty-one

"Write to me as soon as you arrive, Isabelle," I demand, hugging her tighter.

"I promise," she replies, her voice muffled as she burrows her head into my shoulder.

With reluctance, I let go. I chew the inside of my lip, a small distraction from the heaviness in my heart as she climbs into her carriage. She will only be gone a month, but already I feel as if she has been away for more than a year. With James's recovery and Lord Tyrell's secret proposal, I cannot help but feel overwhelmed. With Isabelle gone, I know that I have James to confide in, but I do not want to burden him with such matters, for fear of driving him away.

As the carriage pulls away, I watch it disappear, and Isabelle with it. I take a deep breath and blink back the threat of tears that have begun to sting my eyes. Walking back inside the castle, I hug my arms as a light chill runs through me, though it is not cold outside. The castle already feels empty as I wander towards the Council

Chamber, already counting down until we see each other again.

***

My uncle has finally persuaded me to leave the stone walls of the castle and ride out to the centre of Leicester, through the streets of the town I love so dearly. On our return, we trot our horses through the lush green woodland that leads towards the castle gates. Clearly something has been on my uncle's mind all afternoon, as when we reach deeper into the woodland, his horse matches the easy pace of William.

"Your aunt told me a while ago that she informed you about Lord Tyrell's proposal."

This sentence takes me by surprise, but I allow him to continue.

"She said that you rejected this idea and perhaps would prefer another suitor."

I do not look at my uncle, instead keeping my gaze straight ahead, thinking about the heated discussion I had with my aunt over the same topic.

"She did," I reply before adding, "though I am surprised you did not tell me about it yourself."

"I am sorry for keeping this information from you, my dear," he replies with a deep sigh. "The reason I didn't tell you was that I was surprised at the meeting as much as you were. I thought you would have been in the Council Chamber with us, but when I arrived, Lord Tyrell stated that it must remain between us."

I huff. "And you didn't think that was odd?" My hands

grip onto the reins, the leather of my gloves rubbing against the leather of the reins.

"I was curious as to what he wanted to say, yes. But when I caught onto what his true purpose was, I was firm in telling him that I am not the one to say yes or no; that decision is yours alone," he adds.

"You should have told me sooner, Uncle. It undermines my position as head of the house of Leicester," I state, my voice a little heavy with disappointment more than anger. "So, what do you think I should do if he were to offer his hand in marriage? Accept?" I tilt my head to the side, eyebrows raised. My question is more to test his sanity rather than take his advice.

"It doesn't matter what I think! I admit that I probably do not show it enough, but I do care about your opinion, your views, your life. You are the decision maker of your own fate, my dear. This is your land, your people, your future."

I breathe out a heavy sigh. Since my brother's death, I have felt like I've been thrust onto a large empty stage, eyes from everyone around the kingdom staring at me, watching and waiting to see what I will do next. I have questioned myself and thought: *Perhaps it would be easier if I give up and marry the highest bidder, fade into their shadows*, but then I think about my mother. Even though I never knew her, I can feel her strength push me forwards, the wind carrying her voice, whispering to me to never doubt myself and to continue to be strong when others only want to see me fall.

My uncle leans in a little closer and drops his voice, breaking my train of thought. "If you want my advice, I wouldn't want to marry Lord Tyrell either." He pulls away with a slither of a smile, followed by a small snigger.

"I don't think you're quite what he is looking for, Uncle," I chuckle.

***

Night has fallen, and I rush around trying to neaten my hair after taking a nap on my bed after the ride out to town this afternoon. Why didn't anyone wake me? I am never allowed to sleep in, let alone when it is near time to eat in the Great Hall! I take a very quick look in the mirror and neaten the creases in my dress that have ironed themselves into the fabric. This will have to do!

Lord Stanford has been able to spend more time out of his room, walking about the castle and grounds. I have never felt so relieved in my entire life. He still winces as he walks, though he tries to hide his pain by coughing or breathing heavily. Tonight is the first night since the incident that he is well enough to dine with me; ordinarily he is too tired or in pain to sit in the Great Hall for too long. My feet carry me as quickly as they can, nearly tripping on the worn stones as I leap down them in pairs. The thought of my aunt's scowling face greeting me alongside Lord Stanford and my uncle is not something I wish to endure today.

I surprise myself by being out of breath as I push open the doors and find that I am alone.

"Where is everyone?" I ask aloud to nobody.

Movement of a shadow catches my eye near the fireplace, but to my relief it is Lord Stanford. I rush towards him, a wide smile across my face.

"James! I am so happy to see you here this evening. How are you feeling? Do you hurt anywhere?" I ask, as I scan every inch of his face and body for any signs of a fever or bleeding; there is none.

He clears his throat, his eyes darting around the room. Without a word or a reply, the Yorkshireman, a little unsteady, offers me his hand.

"James? Is everything alright?" I ask with hesitation, taking his hand, trying my best to settle the butterflies in my stomach. The way the candlelight flickers in his deep blue eyes reminds me of the midnight starry sky outside; it is hard not to get lost in them.

"M'lady, let me show ya something."

I follow him, half expecting to step into his arms as if nothing has passed since we last danced together, but instead he bends down on one knee.

"James?" I question, my mind blank.

My heart is racing. I am utterly speechless as he holds my hand, focusing on his lips as they form a shy smile. It is so quiet, as if the world outside has paused to watch the two of us in this very moment. The moon peeks from behind the clouds to see what will happen next.

"Lady Turner… Katherine, ya have been the constant light in m'life when all else had gone dark. Without ya I am lost. I wouldn't be 'ere today if it wasn't for you." He pauses, his voice wobbling.

My eyes watch, as he reaches behind him and produces a beautiful golden ring. The metal shines, catching the light from the nearby candles. I stand there staring, hardly knowing what to do, what to say. The way he holds it with so much care between his strong fingers,

I can tell this means more to him than anything in the whole world.

"I love ya with every ounce of strength I 'ave in m'body. Yer my life. I cannot imagine my existence without ya."

A single tear rolls down my face. He catches it gently with his thumb, grazing my cheek. "Lady Katherine Turner, Countess of Leicester, will ya do me the honour of becoming my wife?"

"My lord… I…" Words dry in my throat, for I know what I want to say, but do not know how.

All time has stopped. I want to remember this moment, this feeling for the rest of my life. I want to remember the beating of my heart. I want to remember the sparkle in his eyes. I want to remember the warmth radiating from his hand as it clutches mine in anticipation, my smile that won't fade for an eternity, and the never-ending love I have for this man.

Before he allows me to answer, with haste, he states, "I wanted to ask ya sooner, but something or another was in the way." With an inhaled breath, he touches the area in which the arrow struck him; he was so close to death. "If ya say no, I will not blame ya, I will not hate ya, I will…"

"Shh." I quieten his ramblings with the touch of my finger pressed upon his lips. "I love you, more than anyone I have ever loved in my life."

He replies with a relieved smile.

"So, yes, of course I will marry you!"

Tears now flow freely as he slips the ring onto my finger. He scoops me up in his arms and spins me around, sealing his lips with mine in a feverous kiss. I feel like all the darkness in the world has disappeared. My head is spinning, my heart is filled with utter joy. I hug him even tighter, never wanting to let go, almost afraid that this is a dream. I open my eyes for a second to check, but when I do, he is there, and I know that it is not.

"I love ya, Katherine. I promise that I will only fill yer life with happiness and love."

"That is all I ask, James, you are all I ask for."

"Congratulations, Katherine! I could not be happier for you!" My uncle bellows as he enters the room, jolting me out of our peaceful moment.

Where did he even come from?

"My lad, your father would be proud, and I am proud to call you family." He embraces James in a strong hug, patting him on the back.

I laugh. "How did you even… never mind that; I might not have said yes!"

As my uncle steps away, I realise my aunt has been standing behind him all this time. She greets me with a tight, warm embrace.

"Oh hush, Katherine. There could only be one outcome. Congratulations." She lets go and takes a step back. "I am so very happy that you are able to marry for love. Your mother would not have wanted anything else for you, my dear." Her voice breaks as she pulls out a handkerchief from her sleeve and dabs her eyes gently with the corner of the white cloth.

Before I can even fathom what is happening, my uncle booms, "This calls for a celebration!" He darts around us like an excited child at Christmas. "I must write to Sir Francis straight away, and Lord Derby… oh everyone must know!"

"Leave that for another day," my aunt sighs, rolling her eyes. "For now, we must celebrate the happy couple and prepare for the most celebrated wedding of this century!"

Nothing is kept a secret for long in this place. Soon, Bess enters the room, rumours already no doubt flitting amongst the household.

"Is it true?" she asks, grasping her hands in front of her, an excited grin upon her lips. "Are you betrothed to Lord Stanford, my lady?"

"Bess! Yes, yes, it is true, though I am surprised at how quickly news spreads through these old walls," I laugh.

"Well," – her cheeks turn a shade of pink – "your uncle's voice carries a fair distance. Besides, I saw Lord Stanford mutter to himself earlier, a beautiful ring in his hand. It could have only meant one thing, my lady."

I can only laugh and shake my head in amusement.

"But, regardless, this calls for our finest wine, my lady!" she delights, though her smile falters for a split second.

With a beaming smile from my uncle, Bess runs off to grab a bottle or two of my father's finest vintage. She returns shortly, placing them carefully on the table in front of us. My uncle is the first to grab a bottle and shakes it slightly so that the contents within crash from side to side.

"Your father had great taste, Katherine. Though, I don't remember this particular one." He studies the dark bottle, the cork held tightly by thick black wax, sealing its contents.

"It was hidden behind another," Bess answers. "Why don't you open it, Lord Golding?"

My uncle opens the bottle with haste, pulling the cork with all his strength. He sniffs at the contents as his eyes widen with a slight cough. He offers it to me.

"Oh." I almost choke on the strong scent. "That is… fragrant." I pass it over to my aunt.

"Smells divine, if not a little pungent." She picks up an empty goblet, pouring it to the brim with the red, shimmering liquid. "Hmm… very sweet indeed."

My uncle laughs as my aunt swallows a large gulp only to start coughing. My uncle tries to grab it as she waves the bottle in the air, but it slips through his fingers and it smashes onto the floor with an almighty crash.

I can only look onwards with sadness as the red liquid oozes across the floor, pooling near our feet. Shards of glass are scattered everywhere. Ordinarily, I would have been annoyed at my father's reserves going to waste, but there is no room for such emotions tonight. I gaze over at my fiancé, who only has eyes for me.

Twenty-two

It began with light-headedness, followed by heavy coughing.

"Take it steady, Aunt," I say. "Here, sip this."

I pass her a small goblet of mead, hoping the honey essence will drive the cough away, but it only seems to make it worse. I grab a handkerchief from her bedside table only to find it covered in blood splatters. All I can do is stand here and just stare at it. How can this be? She took to her bed the day after James proposed to me. Was it something in the food? Was it the ale or wine? Or was she ill before this and she never told us?

The door creaks open, and in walks Doctor Bell. I turn to him with a thin smile. "Doctor, thank you for coming. Her cough has worsened and she can no longer stand."

My attention drifts back to my aunt whose breath is strained and ragged, her eyes shut. I move out of the way to allow him to examine her.

"Her temperature is high, and I can see that she has been coughing up a little blood."

A little? If that is a little, I would hate to see what he thinks is a lot.

Doctor Bell continues, "I will sit with her for a while, observe her, make sure I am not missing anything. Rest is likely the best cure for now, my lady."

It is strange. I would have thought Doctor Bell's presence would have had a calming effect on me, but I still shudder at the memories of his last visit and how he pulled the arrow from James's chest.

"Thank you, I shall leave you in peace. If you need anything at all, call for one of my servants if I am not around."

I pull the door shut behind me and I release a shaky breath, but my aunt's health is not the only thing I am troubled by today. Lord Stanford received a letter from his sister this morning stating that she urgently needs him back home due to the ill health of his mother. I selfishly want him here with me, and why not, we are newly betrothed! I know I cannot keep him from his family; it has been too long since he has been home. I am sure they will be relieved to see him well after recovering from his injuries.

My knuckles tap against the door to his room.

"Come in," he replies, and I push the door open just wide enough for me to fit through.

"How are you getting on?" I ask.

"Nearly there," he replies, his voice a little quieter than usual.

I sit on the end of the bed as he packs a small saddlebag for the long journey to Yorkshire. My eyes watch every movement as he neatly folds a spare tunic into his nearly full bag.

"I'm sorry, Katherine, I know going home right now isn't ideal." His jaw tightens.

"Let me go with you, James," I reply, looking up at him through my eyelashes.

He sighs, as if the weight of my offer is too much to carry. "As much as I would love ya to, yer uncle needs ya here. So too does yer aunt."

I hang my head, knowing that he speaks the truth. If I was away from home and something happened to her, I know that neither of us would forgive ourselves.

We walk out into the courtyard where his horse is standing, already saddled up with supplies for his journey. After James mounts his horse, he leans down and kisses me slowly almost like he is trying to savour every last second. I can hardly bear to see him go so soon after the announcement of our betrothal; I feel like we should be celebrating together, not apart.

My breath catches in my throat with each fading sound of his horse's hooves. Then, he is gone.

***

My aunt's room is at the top of the North Tower. Once a place full of light and warmth, now the curtains are closed shut and the fire has been lit. My uncle frequently spends all waking hours of the day sitting next to his wife, watching over her. I cannot help but think how, not that long ago, I did the same thing for James. I try to take my uncle away from the castle, away from the sorrow that has begun to seep into his heart, but he will not leave her side.

As I lock myself away in the Council Chamber, looking through a pile of recent applications, my heart leaps out of my skin as Bess rushes in unannounced and out of breath. The look of distress on her face is enough for me to rise from my chair at once.

"My lady… please… you're needed in your aunt's room immediately," she puffs, her hand clutching her chest.

Without a word, I rush past her, down the spiralling staircase and up another to the North Tower. I don't think about what could be awaiting me on the other side as I reach for the door to my aunt's room. After my eyes adjust to the dim light, I notice my uncle hunched over a small stool next to her, holding onto her weak hand. Her face is pale, whiter than I have ever seen before, her hair flowing freely by her side instead of in her usual neat bun. The smell of sickness hangs thickly in the air like a sticky mist. It takes all of my strength not to choke on it.

My uncle rises. "Your aunt's health has worsened. She can hardly breathe… I-I fear that she will not make it through the night," he chokes.

"Where is Doctor Bell?" I question, trying to find a remedy to all of this. I want it to just go back to how it used to be when we were all so happy.

"Doctor Bell has been taken away to the town to attend to another patient's ill health."

I crease my eyebrows in confusion and frustration. "But he promised to stay here and look after her, like he did for James."

"Bess relayed the message this afternoon, an urgent plea. A small boy and his mother have taken seriously ill, Katherine, we couldn't keep him here."

"Yes, of course, Uncle, I am sorry. I didn't mean to sound so selfish."

A small silence sits between us. The rasping of my aunt's voice fills the air with every heartbeat.

"We need to fetch another doctor then, before it is too late," I declare, hardly able to look upon my aunt as she struggles to breathe.

"There is no one else. Doctor Bell will be back soon, I am sure," my uncle replies, fidgeting with the ring on his finger.

I pace the room from one side to the other, repeating my steps each time. I wish James was here with me; he would know how to calm my mind, say the right words of comfort.

I look upon my aunt's thin and fragile body; it looks as if it is made of glass, delicate to the touch. A wave of slow anger washes over me as the long minutes tick by with no word from Doctor Bell, no word from anyone. My chest rises and falls in rapid succession, my fist clenching at my side. How can I leave her like this? Would she allow the same to happen to me, if it was me lying on my bed as I took my last breaths? No, she would do whatever was in her power to see that the kingdom's best healers were brought to the castle. She would fight. She would never stop.

"I cannot stand here and wait for her to die!" I shout into the air above me, my uncle jolting in surprise. "I must go and fetch Doctor Bell. He saved James's life. I know that he can do the same for my aunt. I am certain I know where he lives; his wife must know which house he is at with his new patient. I can ride there quickly and be back with the doctor before it is too late."

My uncle turns his head towards his wife, slowly nodding at the fact that there is clearly no other option, nor does he have the strength to argue. "Yes. He must be sent for, but there is no need for you to go. Send John."

I want to go. I want to escape from this room. The walls are closing in, the air is thick and heavy. I need to leave for the fresh air and clear skies outside. I wasn't able to help my father nor my brother, but I can help my aunt.

"I will go, Uncle. William is the fastest horse we have, even faster when he is with me." I can tell he doesn't like my plan by the way he purses his lips tightly, but I do not need his approval. "I will be back soon. I promise."

"You cannot go alone, Katherine. Johnson and Taylor will ride beside you, make sure you get there safely," he commands, though with little force.

He is right. The woodlands are known for wild animals and the odd bandit. I can handle both, but it will be safer with another rider by my side.

"I will, Uncle. Don't worry about me. Everything will be fine." I smile thinly, folding him into a long hug, which we no doubt both need so desperately.

I race downstairs, collecting my riding cloak and gloves along the way, planning out the best route to take in my head. I wait in the courtyard for Johnson and Taylor to appear, sending Bess to look for them, but as time marches on, I begin to lose the day's final rays of light. If I am to make it in time to Doctor Bell, I have to leave now.

I mount my horse, scanning around me one more time, even calling their names, but the only reply I receive is my own echo. Sounds of running footsteps bounce off the castle steps. Hoping that they belong to one of the men, I am deflated when I see Bess catch up with me, out of breath again.

"My lady!" she shouts, capturing my attention. "My lady! Wait! I have just received word that a large tree and debris have blocked the main path from here to town. There's no way through!"

My heart sinks at her words.

Bess continues, "Perhaps you should head towards Braunstone Gate and loop around the wall to the west instead? Forge your own path through the woodland."

"Where are my men? Did you search for them?" I ask Bess, keen to be on the road.

"I-I couldn't find them, my lady. I heard that they escorted Doctor Bell back into town; perhaps they had to find an alternative route home," she suggests, her eyes darting around her as the chill whips around every corner of the stone walls.

Glancing around the old courtyard, I know that there is only one solution.

Twenty-three

The night draws in over Leicester and the darkness has arrived quicker than I anticipated. I keep telling myself the same thing: Doctor Bell's house overlooks the old Roman wall just inside the town boundary. I need to get there as soon as possible. That is *if* I can find my way; it has been some years since I have visited his house, the last time being when my father was still alive.

I fear that I may have lost my way, the path having been swallowed quickly by night's dark cape. The trees all look similar in the dimness of the evening. I am unable to clearly see the path ahead of me as the night chill begins to settle into my skin. The path is overgrown with debris, which litters the woodland floor, sharp pieces of twigs protruding from every angle and small ankle-snapping holes littering the way. I need to take it slowly in order to avoid any hazards, and I refuse to become another victim to the woodland.

Not too far away, a twig snaps, echoing amongst the

trees, forcing the flight of a nearby bird that squawks with malice as it swoops away deeper into the woodland. An animal or someone lurking in the darkness? Perhaps it was one of my men on the way to the castle gates. Going against my better instincts, I shout, "Johnson? Taylor?" but there is no reply.

I try to ignore an awful feeling of being watched from every direction and kick William on further into the darkness, with the moon's silvery light to guide me. My heart stops as I hear another snap of a twig and the rustle of crisp leaves. I open my mouth to call out, but decide against it this time.

The noise disappears and all is quiet.

Clouds begin to cover my only source of light, forcing me to blindly make my way through the last section of dense trees. *Do not panic, Katherine, we must be nearby*, I tell myself, but the slamming of my heart against my chest betrays me. In the distance comes the faint canter of hooves. Someone is riding towards us and with speed. I bring William to a halt and scan around me, but it is too dark to see. My heart flutters as a rider hurtles towards me: it must be Johnson or Taylor on their way back!

I encourage William forwards, but he stamps his hooves, unwilling to move.

"Come on, William, please! Johnson can help us!" I plead, but he does not budge; in fact he begins to back up into the small space behind us. "What has got into you?" I question, my breathing laboured with my waning strength.

The hooves of the rider ahead of us begin to slow and, as the moon emerges from its clouded prison, light finally illuminates the land around me. My attention is caught by the moon's rays bouncing off what looks like polished armour, a rider covered from head to toe in metal, something neither of my men would ever wear. It is all I can do to stand still and watch as they stop directly in front of me, steadying their horse to an elegant halt.

His voice is a little muffled behind his closed visor. "There is no need to be afraid, my lady."

I have never seen such prestigious armour before; this person must be of high importance, a knight perhaps, but what are they doing here? This knight has a domineering presence, I can imagine him being a formidable foe on the battlefield. He sits upon his horse proudly, an air of authority about him.

"Who are you? Why are you here on my land?" I ask a little defensively, unable to move my horse out of his path. My hands grip the reins tighter; my eyes dart across the woodland.

He shakes his head. "My name is of no importance, my lady. Are you lost? I can help you. You are very much off the main path."

He moves his horse towards mine again and offers out a hand as if to show that he means no harm. My mind screams for me to run.

"I am not lost," I reply with confidence, refusing his open hand. "Besides, I will not accept the help of a stranger that will not give me his name."

His horse is a little agitated as it paws at the ground.

"You do not need a name to save you. Would it make a difference if you knew my name?" he answers.

"I do not need saving," I reply, becoming more restless.

"I will be on my way now. If you excuse me." I push William forwards, but this knight blocks my path with the body of his heavy steed.

"How is it that you are alone? No guards to escort you or… your husband?"

"I do not need an escort on my own lands. Now move," I command, my voice a mixture of anger and desperation. However, that does not seem to deter him.

"I heard a rumour that someone was injured in these woods not that long ago," the stranger remarks. "A certain nobleman from Yorkshire."

My heart quickens and my palms sweat beneath the leather of my gloves. Why is this knight acting as if we are friends? I do not recognise him at all. His voice, although muffled, is unfamiliar to me. What does he know about the incident that took place not that long ago? Was he responsible, and is he here to take another victim?

"What d-do you want?"

The knight looks behind me then quickly to the side of him. "I wonder what he would do if he knew…" he mutters to himself.

Before I can ask what he is referring to, he adds, "Well, Lady Turner, I have heard so much about you."

I freeze at this stranger knowing my name, especially as I refused to give it.

"Who are you? How do you know my name?" I ask, my voice shaking from both the cold and fear.

"I am your knight in shining armour, of course," he laughs.

A sharp, intense bolt of pain grips my entire body. My vision blurs, my head spins. The world falls beneath me. My hands let go of the reins as I descend backwards towards the dark cold ground. The last thing I hear is William panicking, his hooves beating against the ground, rearing up against my attacker. I want to call his name, beg for him to get help, but I cannot focus on anything as I am plunged into darkness.

Twenty-four

I am riding through the forest, zipping past tree trunks, ducking beneath low branches, jumping over rocks and fallen trees. I can hear the air whoosh past my cheeks and through my long flowing hair, as I thunder towards an unknown destination. It has been raining. The air is muggy, and the ground is damp. The temperature has dropped significantly and my skin shivers against the sudden breeze that whistles through the canopy of trees above me. The world spins around and around and around and around…

For a while, my dream fades away and I am locked in a pit of darkness once more.

My head feels so heavy. I want to stand up, stretch my legs and arms, but nothing moves. It is as if I have been weighed down by rocks or pinned to this very spot with a hammer and nails. Muffled voices fill the air around me, though I cannot make sense of what they are saying. I try my hardest to move, stand, shout, yell, anything! But all my strength has been drained from my soul. I am tired, so very tired. I… I…

***

My eyes begin to open, but as I brace for sunlight to burn through them, I am greeted only by blackness. I raise my blurry head. No! That was a bad idea, the pain is too much. My eyes squint into the abyss. The room comes into focus… cold, stone-grey walls… a small window. Did I make it back home? The air is thick and musty.

What am I doing here? Where is my horse, William? I have to find him! He must be so frightened without me, alone in the woodland… The woodland... what was I doing there? My aunt… no, I have to get to her.

I move my head with care. Next to me is a small wooden nightstand with a weak candle that flickers, casting dark shadows around the tiny room. My attention is drawn towards a beautiful red rose that sits next to me, a beauty amongst the cold. Strange that it is here, though; it doesn't seem native to this place. Am I still dreaming? My hands touch the surface beneath me, something lumpy and hard, a bed perhaps? Above me is the only window in the room, a simple arched window with chequered bars across glass. I am only able to see the sky above; a storm is about to light up the sky.

My head slowly and painfully turns to face the other wall. My eyes make out a plain wooden table with a jug and a lump of something that was once edible – I hope it is not for me. Next to this is the door; my only means of escape. Every inch of me screams as I force myself towards it, but pushing on the handle concludes that it is locked. Bending down, I glance through the keyhole, but I am unable to see anything. Maybe the key is still in the lock?

I have to get back to my aunt, she needs me.

My vision blurs.

I stumble across the tiny space and slump onto the hard mattress, my legs giving way. I squeeze my eyes shut once more, praying that when I open them, it will all be a dream, a horrible nightmare, but when I do, it is clear that I am not dreaming at all.

Questions with no answers rattle around my head. What am I doing here? Where is here? Why can't I remember anything? Who sent me here? What will happen to me when I am found? What do they want with me?

After a long while, my head in my hands, my confusion and pain turns into anger and determination. I have to get out of here. I hurl my body over towards the door once more, each step heavy like I am pinned to the ground by lumps of wet clay, pain shooting through my skull like a blunt dagger. I bang against the old wooden door with all of my failing strength.

"Help!" I yell, my voice hoarse. "Help me! Someone please! Anyone?" I call out until all my energy is drained and the air from my lungs has evaporated. My hands are numb. "Please..." I whisper one last time.

No one answers me.

Twenty-five

The air is still and cold. My fingers feel numb and stiff. I try to bring life back into my limbs by slowly easing myself against the stone wall, rubbing my arms with my shaking hands. I tug at the sleeves of my dress as I shiver against the icy bleakness that eats away at this room.

Is that sunset or sunrise? I cannot tell as the pink haze from the sky outside seeps through the window, casting a broken arched silhouette onto the floor.

Only silence can be heard inside these four walls; I am utterly alone.

How long will I be held here? Three days? Three weeks? Three years?

"No," I tell myself, determined to fight against whatever is keeping me here. "There has to be a way out. I have to get back home."

As soon as my limbs feel strong enough, I heave myself onto my feet, using the wall for support. I try the door again, shaking the handle as hard as I can, but to no avail.

There has to be a way out. I will not stay locked up here! I sit on the edge of the bed again and think of what I can do next. Those who put me here; perhaps I can negotiate my way out. They must have the wrong person.

My thoughts are disrupted by the roar of my stomach. No one has visited me in this cell; I don't know if anyone will; perhaps my captor has left me in here to rot. The stale lump of bread is beginning to look more appetising as time slowly edges forwards. It is cold to the touch as I break into it to find that it still has some of its original softness inside. I pick at that part of the loaf and swallow down the icy water with it, as difficult as it is to do so without wanting to spit it out again.

A faint noise of scuffled footsteps echoes outside the room. I cease moving, my heartbeat the only other thing I can hear. I listen to those steps; I cease to breathe. I could just shout, hoping that the person on the other side of the wall is here to help me… but then again, what if they are here to keep me quiet for good?

The footsteps become louder and louder until they stop outside the door. Whoever it is on the other side fumbles for the keys in their pocket, cursing under their breath, agitated at trying to find the right key for the lock. I wonder if those keys sit amongst other prison cell keys.

As the door creeps open, I slide behind it so I am obscured from view. I hold my breath.

"What is going on 'ere. Hullo?" a man calls out in a thick Northern accent.

Not recognising his voice, I cease to breathe, covering my mouth and nose with my hands, making myself as invisible as possible.

"Where are ya?" the voice growls, a voice that is clearly not here to comfort me.

It's now or never.

With all my might, I barge the door with my shoulder, knocking the man to the floor, ignoring the dull ache that will surely bruise my shoulder.

"Ah!" he shouts, but I do not pause to view the face of my jailer. Instead, I run.

As I make my way down a narrow dark corridor, I can hear the man shout and curse, fumbling at the door. I don't know where I am going. I just keep telling myself to run, head for the light! Everything is a blur as I rush by. Blood pumps in my ears, my breath short and my legs weak as I reach for an open door. The light blinds me, stopping me in my tracks for a quick moment, as I throw up my arms to shield myself from the bright light. A sudden scent overwhelms me, nearly knocking me back. As my eyes begin to adjust, I find myself in what looks like a small, empty herb garden, the scent of thyme thick in the air. Where am I?

I cannot stop now.

As I head towards an arched, wooden door on the other side of the garden, I take a second to look over my shoulder to see where I have been imprisoned. Expecting a bleak ruin, I am surprised to find an old, grey-stone building instead. It is small in size, but beautifully constructed; grey slate on the roof and ivy crawling up its walls. From the outside you would never think of the darkness that lurks within, but there is no time to admire my gaol. I turn and stretch out my hand, reach for the handle and twist it.

There is not another soul in sight as I find myself

running across a muddy field, dirt splashing on my already torn dress, my boots caked in fresh sludge. My hair sticks to my face, thanks to the thin layer of moisture in the air that clings to everything it touches; it is oddly refreshing. I frantically search around for any sign of a village or town, a passer-by, or a path for me to follow, but there is nothing and nobody. Whoever is responsible for bringing me here certainly made sure I would not be stumbled upon so easily.

I do not have time to stop and digest all that is happening. My breath catches in my lungs, a burst of energy rushing through me as I blindly run through the bleak landscape. My feet nearly collapse beneath me, pulling me to the muddy ground. Gradually, I find myself surrounded by a low mist that envelops the barren land around me. There is nothing for miles, just fields and an old Roman wall, now demolished to just its foundations.

The wind begins to howl and the cold mist freezes everything in its path, like a spider's web spun across the landscape. I have to get out of the open. As I venture further, I spot a cluster of trees upon a small hill in the distance. There I can hide and shelter from the bleakness, just like William and I used to when we were children, except this time it is not a game. The mist turns into a thick fog and I lose my bearings, squinting into the distance, only just being able to make out the tops of the trees. I glance behind me. There is nothing but a wall of grey and white pushing me forwards.

My lungs are tight and my legs are heavy as I keep on walking, walking, walking, as quickly and as far as I can. I have to create as much distance between me and that place as possible. Once I am clear, I will figure the rest out. I have to. The entrance to the woodland finally bleeds into view. Surely, they cannot track me now. My throat is so dry and my stomach aches, but I refuse to give in. I mustn't give in… I mustn't.

Listening out for anything in the darkness of the trees results only in hearing the wind brushing past the leafy canopy above me. As time passes by, I begin to lose myself amongst the eerie calmness of the trees; there is a strange comfort in them, reminding me of the forests back home. Home. The woodland. Why was I out in the woodland alone? My feet stop in front of a fallen tree trunk, my legs pulling me down to sit. I pick the odd leaf out of my hair that has hitched a ride on my journey into the unknown.

The thought of my family being blissfully unaware of my situation nearly brings me to tears. As I wrap my cloak around my body to shelter me from the cold, my eyes begin to become heavier and heavier…

Snap!

I jerk awake at the sound of something in the near distance. Frantically scanning the darkness, I try to see if I can catch the movement of whatever made that sound. Surely it is not my captor? No, I will have lost them. A rabbit perhaps? A fox? I hope it is not a bear; it would be my luck to run into one of the last remaining bears left in the kingdom!

Crack!

A twig breaks under pressure, this time a lot closer. If I start to make a move now, perhaps I can slink away without it spotting me, or perhaps if I move it will try to attack me instead. *This* is why I wanted to learn survival skills, not embroidery skills! What good does embroidering a cushion do now? I couldn't even stab a bear to death with a needle if I tried.

Now is not the time, Katherine.

I don't have time to think as the sound of heavy footsteps echoes off the trees, disorientating me as to where they are coming from. I need to run, but my legs do not want to move. The sound is getting louder and louder. I have to move. Now!

Afraid, I hasten my step and head towards… I don't know where. I run down the hill, towards the unknown. However, it seems the faster I run, the faster the footsteps behind me follow, the heavier my heart pounds inside my chest, the heavier the footsteps.

Closer and closer until…

"My lady, are you alright?"

I stop dead in my tracks.

It's them. I am sure of it. My captor; who else would it be? Perhaps they will let me go, but then again, why would they? I turn towards the owner of that voice, the wind rustling around me, making it difficult for me to hear them.

They call out to me once more, "Lady Turner!"

My head spins at the chanting of my name flying at me from all angles.

"I won't hurt you, my lady!" it calls again.

My feet begin to walk in an unspecified direction, unsure as to whether I am walking towards the voice or far, far away. All I can hear is the beating of my heart as it pulses in my ears. My breath freezes on contact with the fog around me. I can sense them. I can feel them watching me, waiting.

All is quiet…

A hand reaches for me.

"Get off me!" I scream, everything within me fighting against this unwanted embrace, but as much as I fight, the tighter they grip onto my flesh.

"Quiet!" they hiss, their grip tightening the more I struggle against them. "I don't want to hurt you."

"Let go of me!" I scream, trying my best to turn to face them so that I can see my kidnapper, but they are too strong.

"Calm down!"

Their hand wraps around my mouth in an attempt to silence me, but I will not be the one who needs to remain quiet. They scream as I sink my teeth into their bare hand, making sure I leave my mark; a reminder if nothing else.

I take this distraction to break from their embrace and sprint as fast and as far away as I can.

"Wrong way, Countess," another voice, a new voice, calls to me from the fog.

"James?"

A searing pain flashes across the back of my head. I cry out in pain, touching the back of my skull. All I can feel is a sticky heat flowing down my neck, as I stumble to the ground, my vision blurring at the edges as everything begins to fade.

Twenty-six

"Come on, Katherine!" A voice calls out to me in the darkness, a voice that I had long forgotten. "Come on, or you'll miss it!"

When I open my eyes, it is still dark. A cool breeze rustles through the curtains on the far side of the room, running a small shiver across the surface of my skin. I ease myself onto my elbows and gaze about the room with bleary eyes. My head is hazy and my body feels heavy, from a deep sleep, or a nightmare. Nothing seems out of place, though I would have expected the fire to still be burning. My bedchamber door is ajar, a slither of light from the corridor outside stretches across the old wooden floor. With a little hesitation, I swing my legs over the side of the bed and touch my toes to the ground.

The voice calls once more, the same words on repeat. "Come on, Katherine!"

"Y-yes, I'm coming." I shout out in reply, almost on instinct.

I reach for the handle of the door and pull it wide open,

expecting the corridor to be lit only by a few candles, but I am surprised to see the area flooded with sunlight. I pause to glimpse towards one end of the corridor then the other. Nothing seems to be amiss.

A sudden crash turns my attention toward the bottom of the staircase. A small groan comes from the direction which my legs run towards; my confusion is soon forgotten. I race my way down the winding staircase, running my hand over the familiar worn stone as I go. The groaning becomes louder and louder with each narrow step I take, tripping on the long hem of my dress.

I fly into the Entrance Hall to find my brother in a heap in the middle of the floor surrounded by a pile of old and rusty-looking armour. For a split second, I stand there shocked, staring at my brother as if I've seen a ghost. When he looks up towards me, I shake my head and take a small step towards him, almost as if I am not in control of myself.

"Finally, she awakens!" he announces, arms out wide.

"I think you awoke the whole castle," I muse, folding my arms across my chest as I study my brother. "What are you doing on the floor? Finally remembering your place?"

"Ha!" he remarks, trying to stand up without tripping over a broken visor. "I believe it is you, my dear sister, who decided to stay in bed so late in the morning." With his foot, William pushes the visor and what looks like a gauntlet to the side. He dusts off his hands and stands up straight.

I had almost forgotten how tall he is.

"Well, now you are here, I have something to show you." William beams, a smile that warms any heart.

"And what is that exactly, my *dearest* brother?" I ask amused, wondering what else he might have planned.

"Katherine... where are ya?"

That voice... I know that voice...

"Come on, let me show you." He grabs my hand and drags me outside.

I brace myself, wanting to express how I am not dressed for the open air, but when I step through the entrance doors, we aren't in the courtyard as expected, but by the flowers in our mother's rose garden. I am wrapped in one of my favourite coats as I find myself standing beside my brother who eagerly draws me closer to the heart-shaped arrangement in the centre. I take a quick look around. Everything looks so fresh: the neatly laid gravel, the carefully trimmed bushes, even the walls look to have been mended. It is as if...

"Look, they have finally bloomed." William guides my hand towards one of the buds in the middle of the cluster of newly planted roses. "Our first bud."

I step forwards carefully, almost too scared to touch it.

"Of course, yours would be the first." He nudges me, smirking.

"Well, red roses are a classic," I chuckle.

"We will find her... I promise."

Uncle?

The distant sound of boots crunching on fresh gravel echoes around the walls of the rose garden. Both William and I search for the owner to find a tall, broad man approaching us. He is dressed in his customary dark clothing, a small stain on the front of his tunic from where the leather strap from his satchel rubs against the fabric.

The shine from his dagger at his belt captures my attention before William and I both take a small step back, allowing for him to see what all the fuss is about.

"I was told I would find you both here," he announces in a deep, matter-of-fact voice.

My father steps between us and gazes upon the heart-shaped arrangement of white, red, and purple roses that we planted not so long ago.

"Look, Father." I point towards the bud of the red rose. "Our first flower. William found it first." I shoot a small smile towards my brother who smirks at my comment; I am not usually one for giving him such credit.

Our father is quiet for a long moment. I reach out to touch his arm – it has been such a long time since I have seen him so contemplative – but I pull back, deciding against it. William catches my eye whilst we await to hear his thoughts. He comments, "Katherine's rose, Father. I should have made a wager as to whose would have flowered first."

"It was just luck, that's all… and the fact that red is a superior colour," I jest, hoping to spark some life into my father who still stands there, eyes staring just ahead of him.

Finally, he leans back, and a small smile dances on his lips, one of pride. "It's beautiful. Your mother would have been proud. She loved this garden. She loved you, loved us all." He regards William then me, his eyes glistening with unfallen tears.

William places a hand on his shoulder. "This is a fitting tribute to her and her sacrifice. We will always remember her."

I remain silent. My mother is no longer here. She is dead. All I have to remember her by are these roses, and she wasn't even here to see them bloom. I am here instead of her. I killed her. I have always wondered if my father looks upon me with sorrow instead of love. William has always berated me for thinking such a thing.

"If we all maintain and look after them, these flowers will grow year upon year upon year. When I am gone and William has taken over my position as earl, I hope that these flowers and your mother's memory will continue on," my father declares. He places a firm hand on my brother's shoulder. Turning to me, he wraps his strong arm around me, drawing me closer.

I can almost smell his familiar scent of pine and leather. I take a deep breath, wanting to savour this moment.

"You look more like your mother with each passing day, Katherine. I know that she is proud of her daughter, as am I. Look towards her when you find yourself needing strength and guidance. She will be there, as will I when I am gone. I promise you will never be alone." My father's words have a slight echo to them as I begin to feel light-headed.

"Katherine... come back to me..."

A sharp wind whips around the corner, pushing my long, dark hair across my eyes. As I push it away to see more clearly, a whisper of a voice dances on the breeze, pulling at a memory... or is it a dream?

"Katherine..."

I know that voice... it has been calling out to me as if trying to pull me away from here, but why?

My father's hand leaves my shoulder as both he and

William begin to make their way inside. I try to follow them, my feet tracing the familiar path back towards the courtyard, but when I look up, my brother and father are no longer with me. I call their names, but my voice is drowned out as a fog swallows me whole. I can hardly see my hand in front of my face. I turn to my right, then my left, with nothing but grey mist and an eerie silence surrounding me. I panic as my feet run blindly forwards, deeper into the mist.

I can just make out the castle's gatehouse in the distance, as I sprint towards it. I spread my hands out in front of me, desperately seeking purchase on something, anything. I nearly drop to the floor as my feet kick at the stone wall. I catch myself just in time, but as I cast my gaze upwards, I find myself on the ramparts of the castle's imposing walls, looking out onto the River Soar and the settlements beyond, their tiny lights twinkling in the dying light of the day.

How did I get here so quickly?

I feel something or someone press against my hand, but when I look down, no one is there. I call out into the night sky, but no one replies. Slowly, the shuffling of feet sounds behind me, shoes scuffing against the rampart's unrelenting stone. Expecting to see William or my father, I am taken by surprise when I see a beautiful woman standing in front of me. An overwhelming feeling of familiarity washes over me. I know her, but I do not recall any memories; it is as if I am staring into the face of my future self.

The wind carries her voice as if it were a whisper. "My darling Katherine." She smiles, arms wide open in greeting, the long sleeves of her dress nearly touching the floor.

I take a step closer, hypnotised. "Mother?" I question, her name dancing on my tongue as she draws closer.

Her dark hair cascades down her back and chest, her blue eyes shine brightly in the moonlight, her lips are full and red, and a golden wedding band catches the torchlight as I am pulled in towards her embrace. Her scent is familiar to me, one that almost smells ancient, powerful, of my blood.

I step back, an arm's length away from her, so that I can study her face in more detail. She is exactly as I imagined, exactly how my father and brother described her, but how can this be? Is this truly a dream? Yet, everything is so real. I can smell, I can taste, I can touch, I can feel. Where am I? I open my mouth to ask that exact question, but her face contorts into a sad frown.

"I never wanted this day to come, Katherine. You are so young." Her voice is full of sorrow, a deep frown upon her brow. "I wish I was there with you, my love."

Her voice now feels heavy, as if her words are enough to weigh me down.

"I-I don't understand, Mother… how are you… how is *this* possible?" I can barely contain my emotions: shock, love, sorrow; I don't know what to say or how to feel. "Why am I here?" I question, my voice thick with emotion, not knowing how to make sense of this.

"It is not your time. Not yet. He is waiting for you, Katherine."

"Who?" I ask, squeezing her fingers in my hand, eager to feel her soul, but I can't feel anything. "Who?"

A voice pulls at a memory, a feeling, something tries to tug me back to another moment, another time. *"Katherine, I love ya so much. I will find ya, I will come for ya. I promise."*

"James?" His voice tastes like something I have forgotten. I barely recognise his voice as it rides the air around me.

My mother smiles and nods. "He is waiting for you, my daughter. He needs you, as you need him. You are not alone, you never have to go through life alone, Katherine."

My head spins as I try to grasp at what is happening. Nothing makes sense. Why am I here? I thought we all went back inside? I remember my father retreating back into the Council Chamber, whilst William and I spent our time playing games in the library.

"Her hands are cold..." Another voice, not James's, suddenly echoes around me; the room starts to shake as if there is a disturbance in the air.

My body begins to numb... my head is h-heavy. I look around me and the world shimmers and moves, as if it is all a mirage. I meet my mother's gaze again and everything dawns on me.

"Mother. Am I? Am I...?" I can scarcely say the next word aloud.

"No," my mother replies, knowing already what I wanted to ask. "Not yet. I will not allow for you to be taken so young, when you have those who depend on you, who cannot bear to lose you, my love. I was taken from my family too soon. I will not allow you to follow the same fate as me."

With each word, the walls of the castle begin to crumble away, until we slowly find ourselves in a space amongst the stars. An endless pool of water appears at our feet, reflecting the starry sky around us. As I take a cautious step back, I do not feel the cold, nor are my feet or gown wet. The water echoes around us, as if we are in an endless cavern. Two figures appear beside my mother. To her right is my father, head held high, looking proudly down upon his wife then to me. To her left is my brother, William, who shoots one of his charismatic smiles. They look exactly how I remember them. The last time I saw them alive.

As I begin to realise the reality of it all, my eyes well up with tears. One by one, I allow them to fall on my cheeks then the pool beneath my feet, leaving ripples in their wake. Is this what the afterlife is truly like? Is this what happens to us when we die? I am not ready to pass on from the world of the living, but neither do I want to leave my family again. I have lost so much in this world; now that my mother, father and brother are with me, do I want to let them go again?

"I miss you all so much. William." I look into his eyes and squeeze his hand. "Since you were taken from me, I have mourned you every day. I don't know how to live without you."

William grins, though with sadness. "Sister. Katherine. You no longer need to mourn or cry for your losses. We are proud of what you have achieved, you have done a better job than I ever could have! You were born for the role of Countess. The people love you. The household love you. Your friends love you. We love you. You will have to face many difficulties upon your path, life will not be easy for you or the Kingdom, but you will survive and you will prevail. You will be remembered. You are the rose amongst the thorns."

He is right. My story does not finish here.

My eyes cast towards my brother, my mother then my father. All three share knowing smiles, my brother nodding in agreement with my thoughts before I even acknowledge them myself.

"You're right. I am not supposed to take my place amongst you yet. There will be a time when we will be reunited. Today is not the day, however."

"Exactly, darling daughter. Now, make haste! He is coming for you. Be ready," my mother warns.

"Who?" I ask, but everything begins to fade. "Who is?"

"Be ready, Katherine. Do not trust the dark hearts of men."

My heart races as I panic, my mother's words of warning spinning around my head. My body is being pulled backwards into another time, another space. William bids me farewell as he gradually fades into nothingness, his voice barely a whisper as it echoes amongst the stars.

Twenty-seven

"How long has she been like this?" a voice asks in the darkness.

"I do not know! I have nothing to do with this!" another voice argues.

"She is pale, her lips are dry from thirst and she is cold to the touch! I told you to keep an eye on her whilst I was gone! She hasn't improved since I last saw her only three days ago!"

"This is *your* fault! Ya didn't need to do any of this! What have ya been messing about at?"

"Securing my prize! Now, quickly! Open the door!"

Scuffling echoes around me as I feel the faint sensation of levitating, drifting off into the unknown. A fresh breeze coats my skin as the sound of a running stream, birds chirping and the sun kissing my face begin to awaken my senses.

All of that soon disappears as shadows lean over me and I am lowered onto a soft surface, my head supported by something gentle, like a fluffy cloud.

"Add more wood to the fire!" the first voice demands.

"*You* do it. This is your mess, not mine!" the second voice replies, breathing heavily.

There is a loud crack and a pop, followed by a sizzling. The numbness in my fingers dethaws as my entire body begins to relax, almost like how the earth defrosts after the bleak winter, born anew.

The welcoming sensation of cool liquid runs past my lips and down my throat. My lips are so dry and cracked like sunburnt soil in my mother's rose garden. It quickly spills down my chin and past my throat, pooling at my chest. I welcome the feeling against my skin.

"There. Thank God," the first voice breathes. "Make sure she drinks!"

Water sloshes onto the hard floor.

"No. *You* do it! This is your fault. If anyone…"

"Keep your voice down," the first voice hisses.

"I have done my part. Now give me what ya owe! I will help ya no more. I am done!" The owner of the second voice stomps further away from me.

Just as I begin to wonder if they have left the room, they add over their shoulder, "I hope ya know what yer doing, for I no longer want any part in it. God help you if ya fail."

Leather tightens against a wooden post as its owner grips it with hatred. If only I had the energy to open my eyes, I could observe this scene with my own eyes, but I cannot. It is as if I am stuck in a heavy, dreamless sleep. The owner of the first voice, now alone, curses under their breath, but it is not long until the door rattles open again.

"M'lord, ya need me?" Another new voice enters the room.

"Where have you been? Have you seen the state of her? She looks like death!" A ruffle of clothing and agitated steps shuffle around me. "You are to make sure she drinks and eats, do you understand? If she does not, then force her! Otherwise, her death will be quickly followed by your own!"

"Aye, m'lord," they agree, their voice wavering a little.

"Get her some new clothes too! I will not allow her to be left in such rags!"

I feel the warm press of someone's lips on my forehead, just like when William used to kiss me goodnight. Though, I know that it cannot be he; my time has not yet come.

I'm not sure how much times passes, but I begin to wonder if the conversation I overheard was real. Whose voices did they belong to? The first is very familiar, but escapes me… The second, however, is new.

I cannot think straight.

After an amount of time has passed, I slowly open my eyes. The light is blinding at first, but I soon adjust as the last specks of daylight dance around the room, casting the place in pink shadows. It takes me an exhausting amount of strength to heave myself into a sitting position, my arms wobbling under the strain.

After a few minutes of collecting my thoughts, I begin to realise that I am no longer in the damp, cold, grey room I was thrown into not that long ago. This room is an impressive size for a prison cell. The bed is a lot gentler and is clean, the pillows are soft and the blanket is heavy and warm, although the four-poster has been left to the mercy of neglect and age. I look upon the blanket. I have been stripped down to my chemise… I vaguely remember doing so… I must have done, for who else could have? I didn't want to wear mud-caked clothing any longer. It couldn't have been anyone else.

I shake my head to clear it of impossible thoughts, sitting here for an unknown amount of time, trying to piece together everything that has happened so far. When I try to remember, however, my mind fogs over and I find it difficult to think. Perhaps something in this room will help. To the left of me there is a small roaring fire situated in a beautiful little stone fireplace. It is neatly decorated with exquisite carvings of flowers and leaves. At the foot of the bed, I spy a worn oak chest, which looks too heavy to open as it is adorned with iron gilding. Opposite me is a small arched window; the view is difficult to make out through the misty glass as the sun begins to set.

I begin to wonder whether I am in a new building. I remember looking back and seeing an imposing building… a monastery perhaps? But who brought me here? That is still a mystery I don't understand. I shake my head as the fog descends again, a blockade to my thoughts. Perhaps I need to stand up for a while, let the blood flow to my toes.

Slowly, and using one of the bed posts as my anchor, I ease myself out of bed and begin to take in my new quarters. There is a beautiful woven tapestry hanging on the wall between the window and the door. It is a little threadbare, but it depicts a knight back from battle, and he is surrounded by what looks like a variety of different trinkets, perhaps prizes from his victories. I can just make out a few of them: books, wine, fruits, some that I have never seen before; there are even a few exotic animals peering from amongst the greenery of the background, as well as a square-type cross on his chest. Perhaps he was in the Crusades? In the knight's hand, he is carrying what I think is a flower, a white rose perhaps. The border of the tapestry reveals well-worn scripture, but as the light of day is beginning to fade from the window, I cannot make out the letters. Is it Latin? English, or perhaps French? I will have to wait until tomorrow, if I can read it at all. Perhaps it will reveal where I am and who brought me here.

***

I am woken by the jangle of keys outside of the door. It swings open and in steps a large, imposing man with a fresh jug of what I assume is water. I shrink away from this stranger, not sure whether he is friend or foe.

"Ah, yer awake. M'lord says that ya must drink. 'Ere, you can do it yer-self." He walks over to the side of the bed and puts down the jug heavy-handedly, some of it spilling onto the floor. His accent is thick, one of the North. "Also, he wants ya to wear this." He lifts up a bundle of what looks like plain women's working clothes. "Here is a bowl of water for ya to wash in." He places a large basin of fresh water onto the floor near the fireplace, along with a rag and a well-used bar of soap.

"You," I announce, "I remember you, you… you locked me in here!" I begin to recall, recognising his voice more than his face. He is the man whom I tried to escape from that day! Did he catch up with me and throw me in here instead? "What do you want with me? Why have you brought me here?" I question, trying my utmost not to sound afraid.

"Yer being 'ere has nowt to do wit' me. Ya can ask the master when he gets here," he replies in a flat monotone voice, sighing as if I am a huge inconvenience to him.

"The master?" I question. "And who would that be exactly?"

"Nothin' to do wit' me."

"What is your name?" I question. Perhaps I can get an idea of who this 'master' is by knowing the name of his henchman. But he only grunts and walks out of the room again before locking the door from the other side.

"I shall call you the Northerner then," I say aloud to the closed door. "The master," I wonder to myself, my heartrate spiking as I imagine who that could possibly be and, most importantly, why they have decided to keep me here and for how long.

Twenty-eight

He is here. I didn't think it could be possible, but it is true.

"Katherine, I am so glad you are safe!" He shuts the door firmly behind him and strides into the room, his cloak swishing behind him.

"Lord Tyrell?" I question as if he is a phantom appearing before me. "Wh-what are you doing here? How did you get here?"

"I can take you away from this, Katherine, I can make sure no more harm comes to you." His eyes gaze deeply into mine as he outstretches his hand.

I am hesitant to take it. Instead, I look away, my vision focusing on the door behind him still closed, but not locked. *If* Lord Tyrell is my key to getting out of here, then perhaps I should take my chances.

I nod my head, resolute. "Very well then, let's go, let's leave now whilst we have the chance." I try to move past him, but he doesn't budge. "Lord Tyrell, we have to leave! I do not know who is keeping me here, but they'll arrive any minute and I do not want to have to fight my way out." I attempt to keep my voice even and in control, but the more he stands and stares at me in silence, the more difficult that becomes.

"Lord Tyrell, let me pass." I drop my voice to a softer tone, hoping that it might spur something inside him. "Please, Henry, we have to go."

A thin smile forms upon his lips. "What's the rush? We won't be disturbed for some time."

"What do you mean? No, no, surely not..."

His smile fades, and as it does, he reveals the true character behind his mask. "Unfortunately, yes, but it is for your own good, my lady. I moved you from that old room into this one, the best room, just for your comfort."

It is Lord Henry Tyrell who has kept me here; it is he who is behind all of this, he who is the master of my fate. Lord Tyrell is not here to rescue me. How foolish of me to believe such a thing was possible.

My breathing is heavy and my jaw is set tight. I perch upon the chair by the fireplace for support, my eyes lowering to stare at the dancing flames as they slowly die upon the diminishing wood.

I remain tight-lipped, not wanting to waste my words.

"Katherine, I am here protecting you. We can finally be as one. Together." He reaches out his hand to touch my face, but I shrink back in my seat.

"The only thing I need protecting from is *you*."

He stares at me, studying me like one would an insect. "You will thank me one day, I promise. It will all be worth it; we just have to wait."

I reply with silence.

He takes a step towards me, though a little unsure, perhaps due to my silence and lack of gratitude. "No matter, it was decreed long ago that we are to be together."

Only a light breeze against the window and the creaking of the door fills in for my response.

"Speak to me!" he spits, his sudden burst of anger jolting me awake.

"I have nothing to say to you, Lord Tyrell."

"I never wanted to hurt you or your family, but you have made every step difficult. Everything I showed you, everything I have done for you is clearly not enough. I am not a bad person, Katherine. You hinder me at every turn! Just know that I never wanted to do this the difficult way, but you have left me no choice."

I stand, nearly knocking over the chair in the process. "No choice? No choice! Everyone always has a choice, Henry! *This* is your choice, *you* have done this, nobody else! *You* have taken me away from my home, from my family, those who truly love me! My aunt was ill, Henry, did you know that?"

He remains silent.

"You took my choice of wanting to care for her, to comfort her, away from me. I do not even know if she is still alive, thanks to you!"

Lord Tyrell takes a small step back, sucking in his breath. He begins to pull at a loose thread from his cuff. "Our fates, our choices were made a long time ago, Katherine. Long before you were born."

"What are you talking about?" I ask, becoming more and more agitated with every word he utters.

Lord Tyrell reaches into his pocket and pulls out a

well-worn parchment, neatly tied with a ribbon, and places it with care on the chest beside the bed. I can't quite read the faded lettering on the front, but the handwriting is strangely familiar to me.

"This is our fate. This is my right to your land, your estates, your wealth and most importantly… *you*."

I laugh. Surely, he is joking, but when I look at his face, he is as serious as I have ever seen him, devoid of humour or trickery. I cautiously step towards the chest and reach out towards the document, but he quickly draws it closer to him, out of reach.

"I have been patient, Katherine, I really have. I tried to make you see the man I am capable of being; you bring out the best in me, after all, but you have only pushed me away. I did not want to force myself on you. I thought we could naturally fall in love with one another, but I see that I was wrong." He curls his hand into a slight fist, but soon releases it and smiles at me instead. "The day I met you, I thought that you were the most beautiful woman I had ever seen, so graceful, hospitable, kind, even when your family had failed to tell you about *us*."

It is like we are back in my Council Chamber and he is trying to seduce me all over again with his heart-stopping smile, his dark charm, and his powerful presence that I was all-too-quickly blindsided by when we first met. I have to look away from him and the crinkled parchment for a few breaths to recentre myself.

"My father and brother told me the truth about you: you are not to be trusted."

He shakes his head as if he is tired of saying the same thing over and over again. "They thought it all was forgotten, buried, null and void, but that is no longer true. They kept secrets from you, Katherine, something I never want to do to you. They never told you about how you are bound to me by law."

He points to the parchment again. This could be a trick, a desperate move by Lord Tyrell to finally get what he wants, but the handwriting on the parchment… I recognise it as if it were my own. Gingerly, I move closer so I can read the well-worn lettering.

I read it aloud, "*The betrothal between The House of Leicester and The House of Dornton.*"

My mind is blank. Time has stopped, trapping me and Lord Tyrell together in this moment. I look away from the document, but then focus upon it, only to look away again after reading the confusing words that lie there. I look down at the writing once again, but this time something about the way in which the words have been carefully written ignite a memory: a hand, a smile, a face. I reach for it, but he snatches it away again, almost as if I am not worthy of touching it.

"Look, but do not touch. It has taken a long time and lots of persuasion for me to get my hands on this." He brushes down the parchment as if it is the most precious thing in the world. "You recognise your father's hand as much as I do. Your father allegedly destroyed this long ago, not too long after your mother died. They thought that they could just ignore it and it would all go away. I knew of its existence. I just wasn't sure how to get it. Luckily, I was able to get someone to help me."

"Give it to me. It has my father's writing on it therefore it belongs to me." I hold out my hand waiting. How stupid.

"By all means, please do."

I reach for it again, but he snatches it back once more.

"But where are my manners? I'll read it for you."

Slowly, he shows the contents of the document to me. I do not read the words; instead, my eyes are drawn to the bottom of the parchment where sits the most recognisable seal, the seal of Leicester, the seal that was pressed by the very same ring that hangs around my neck. I subconsciously press my hand against where William's ring sits next to my chest. Lord Tyrell smiles as he watches.

"Yes, Katherine, that is the Leicester seal. The very same that your mother, father, brother and you have wielded when in the seat of power." He clears his throat. "Here is what it says: *We, the first Earl and Countess of Leicester, draw up this agreement with the third Earl of Dornton, in which the first born and heir of each house will be betrothed to one another if God permits their union, and shall be wed as soon as the youngest comes of age. As agreed by His Majesty the King of England, the inheritance of any titles, land, property, and wealth shall transfer to the house that produces the male heir once marriage has taken place. God and our Majesty the King as witnesses, we hereby agree to the terms of this contract. God save the King…* blah, blah, blah, then your mother signs the document at the bottom, most beautifully, along with your father and my father." He points to the signatures at the bottom of the document alongside the Leicester and Dornton crests.

I take a step back and hold onto one of the bed posts for support. My heart is racing in my chest and so many thoughts are whirling around my head that I can hardly make sense of anything! Is this document true? Did my parents really sign away my life before I was even born? Why would they do such a thing? I thought they had truly hated the Tyrells, so why would they allow such a family to take everything they have? Unless… my father's attempt to destroy the document is what caused their feud in the first place.

Tears prick my eyes, but I will never allow them to fall, not in front of *him*. "This means nothing," I dismiss, looking anywhere but at Lord Tyrell or the document.

"Do you want me to read it again? It is very clear and witnessed by the late King of England himself. I was trying to tell you all along; you are what I need, what I am *owed*."

His words snap me out of my despair. I am not a prize to be won. I am not an object to be signed away like a piece of furniture. I am the Countess of Leicester, sole heir to my estate and lands, and I will never allow a man like Lord Henry Tyrell to take anything away from me, contract or not. My parents clearly discarded this so-called contract for a reason, and I will not allow a few words on an old tatty bit of parchment to rule the rest of my life.

A small smile etches on my lips. "You are correct."

His eyes light up.

"My parents did sign this document and everything it says is correct, but you are forgetting one vital thing: my brother was born before me. He was the first heir of Leicester, not me. You were born not too soon afterwards and as same sexes are not permitted to marry, this document is null and void. Therefore, we are free from its contractual nonsense and will never be united. My parents clearly thought the same and so did the king. This tatty parchment means nothing."

Lord Tyrell stares at the document for a few seconds, the room silent. I raise my chin in the air. There is nothing he can do about it. He has lost. I have won. But if this is the case why does the grin on his face unsettle me?

"That is true, my dear Countess, however, your brother is dead and he was unmarried without an heir. You are the heir of the estate now and according to this, you are a suitable heir, the only heir and therefore the contract still stands."

I shake my head. "No. No. This agreement was made before I was born! My brother died after I had come of age, therefore…"

"Therefore, nothing!" he shouts, banging his fist on the chest. He rolls up the contract and places it back into his tunic. "*You* are mine."

Within three steps, he is on me, pinning me against the wall, grabbing my jaw with his right hand, forcing his lips onto mine. I try to bite back, but he is too strong. His hands grab at my clothing, his fingers pressing into my thighs, chest, and breasts. I try to push him back, I try to release myself from his lust, but I am trapped, pinned under his bodyweight with no one to hear my cries.

"No! Stop it! Get off me!" I cry, but this only spurs him forwards as tears prick my eyes.

"You used to love it when I kissed you," he smirks. He breathes into my ear as he begins to hike up my skirt.

"No! No!" I scream, over and over again.

There has to be something I can use… the water jug on the hearth! As I reach for it, my fingertips graze the handle – so close. Lord Tyrell kisses my neck, and I squeeze my eyes shut, wanting nothing more than for this nightmare to end! *Come on, Katherine!* Finally, I grab onto the handle, and with my free arm, hurl it down upon his head, smashing it into several pieces, the remaining droplets of water cascading down his face.

He cries aloud, blood trickling down his cheek, a fresh cut upon his brow. Without hesitation, I pick up a piece of the broken pottery as he stomps towards me.

"You bitch! I was going to wait until our wedding day, but you have given me no choice but to take what I want now."

Before he is able to reach for me again, I scream for him to step back, pointing the shard towards him, swiping the air in front of me. "One more step and I will make sure your life is the only thing lost here today." My hands shake, but my resolve does not. It may be reckless, but I would rather take his life than mine be taken by him.

Lord Tyrell pauses, hesitating as his eyes dart to and from my face. Blood still drips, another scar for his collection, but he does not move, his eyes twitching from my hand to my eyes.

"Fine. Have it your way," he snarls. Only after a few breaths adding, "I never wanted to hurt you." His hands open towards me.

I lower my weapon, but I do not let go of it. "Now, release me from this prison," I command, my energy depleting, but I will never allow him to see how truly tired I am.

I just want to be set free, to see my family again, my aunt, James, my horse! How did I get here? Why am I here? Is God testing me, to see if I am truly worthy of the Leicester throne?

"I can't do that. Besides, you don't even know where you are. Say I did let you go; how would you make your way home? Walk? To where? How long would it take until someone kidnaps you or worse?" His eyes dart to my lips. "Can't you see? I am looking after you. I am your only saviour. Without me, you have nowhere to go, no one to look after you, love you, treat you like the queen you are. Now you see that we are united through God's will, I can provide you with everything you need and more. Look at this room, Katherine! It has a fire, clean bedding, a beautiful view… look what *I* have done for *you.*"

His presence is suffocating, his words are a jumble in my brain. If it wasn't for him, we wouldn't be in this situation. This is all of his making. Men like him are the reason women will never feel safe.

"Let me go," I repeat.

"Perhaps you should find out where you are before making such demands." He inclines his head towards the tapestry on the wall next to me. "Look a little closer. What does it say? Read it aloud for me."

"Fine. Seeing as you cannot read it yourself." I take a deep breath: "*God protect this knight on his pilgrim journey to the East. Where he will find a wealth of knowledge, beauty, and a stronger belief in the Lord Almighty. God protect his family and his honour with his everlasting love and his devotion for God, King, and his kingdom. Lord Richard Stanford…*" My voice trails off as my own words echo around me. Lord Stanford? Surely not… "It can't be…"

James told me of a monastery that his family has owned for generations. He said that it was a small monastery devoted to his ancestors who have died, fought, and lived in service of his King and Country, and it all began with his great-great-grandfather who died whilst on a campaign to the Holy Land. I never caught his name. I look closer at the figure of the knight standing proud in the middle of the tapestry. He has piercing, blue eyes and golden hair. It surely cannot be a coincidence. The Northerner has the same accent as James. Is he a worker on this estate, betraying James and turning his hands towards Lord Tyrell? Or is it something darker than that?

"Well done, Katherine." Lord Tyrell slowly claps. "I can see that you have worked it out. Yes, this is your precious Lord Stanford's family monastery."

My body freezes. "Wh-what? Why? Why here? How?" I struggle to release the words tied upon my tongue. "That's not possible, someone would have stopped you! Why would you risk James finding me here?" Each question heightens a sense of dread inside me. If Lord Tyrell is telling the truth, then how is it James has not found me? Surely, he would have been alerted to a disturbance here, or perhaps Lord Tyrell has done a good job of paying everyone to keep his secret quiet.

"I wonder what will happen when the rest of the kingdom finds out where you were being kept? His own family monastery. Was Lord Stanford jealous of the contract between us and locked you away forever? Of course, your own betrothal to that Yorkshire bastard will be void. I will make sure of it," Lord Tyrell continues.

"Your attempt to frame James will fail! No one will believe you! They will know James had nothing to do with my disappearance!" I spit. "I will never be silenced!" My hands begin to shake, betraying my words. He is wrong, the world will never believe him. James has nothing to do with this.

"When will you learn that women like you have no power? Once you are mine, you will have nothing. Well, of course you will have me, but everything you own will be mine. I won't leave you wanting, my dear Countess. I will dress you in the finest materials, bathe you in most luxurious scents and give you all that you desire, but every inch of power you once had in this kingdom will be mine. Just as it should be. Any loyalty left to you and your family will no longer exist." He takes a step back. "The story is far from over, Katherine. One way or another, I will win. I will be given what I am owed."

"I swear…" I march towards him, ill intent in every movement, but Lord Tyrell is quick to lock the door before I can reach my freedom or his neck. I pull as hard as I can on the heavy black handle in a desperate attempt to force the door open, but it is no use. I am a prisoner once again, but this time, I am running out of luck.

Twenty-nine

When James described his family's monastery, I always imagined a beautiful stone building surrounded by many gardens in the peaceful countryside. I pictured the two of us parading around the grounds, perhaps even joining the monks in prayer. I never pictured myself being trapped here as a prisoner; I never knew a house of God could contain such a secret.

Sitting on the edge of the bed, my feet resting on the old chair, I stare at the tapestry hanging on the wall. The beautiful mixture of greens and blues make Lord Richard Stanford stand out from the fading background. His eyes pierce through mine as if he is searching straight into my soul.

If I am being held in the Stanford family monastery, then why haven't I seen or heard anyone else except Lord Tyrell and the Northerner? But I remember another voice, a softer voice... Was that a member of the clergy, or a figment of my imagination? I am sure monks reside here; surely, they would have found me by now, locked in their old broom cupboard, or whatever that cold forsaken room once was.

I can't stop thinking about the document signed by my parents. *What does it all mean? Does it truly bind Lord Tyrell and me into an unbreakable betrothal?* I ask myself. So many nobles are tied into engagements without ever seeing their future spouse until they are at the altar. I just never thought my parents wanted the same fate for me. *Did my brother know about this? All I have are questions and zero answers! I have to get out of here. I have to...*

The door swings open, banging against the wall and ripping me away from my thoughts. I flinch, thinking it to be Lord Tyrell, not ready to ever feel his breath heavy against my neck again as he pushes me roughly against the wall... I release a small breath at seeing the Northerner with my morning rations of bread and pottage. My eyes follow him around the small room whilst he pours water into a well-used wooden cup.

As usual, he is silent. I cannot help but ask, "Why are you helping him? What is in it for you?"

Quietly, he pours the remaining water into a fragile bowl.

"What is your name?" I ask again.

But he remains tight-lipped.

Whilst I gingerly sip at the pottage, the taste as bland and soggy as it looks, the Northerner busies himself by staring out of the window as he waits for me to finish. Ever since Lord Tyrell's visit, he stays in the room with me, most likely making sure I don't attempt another escape.

"Why won't you help me? I could protect you. Do you even know who I am? Has he told you why he chose *me*?"

I try my best to coax a reaction out of him between each grim mouthful.

After a long pause, he looks at me with a face that I can only describe as lost, as if there is no other way back now, his eyes full of regret.

I shift myself so that I am in his direct eyeline. "I can help you. I am Lady Katherine Turner, Countess of Leicester, my father was the First Earl of Leicester, and my brother was Lord William Turner, the Second Earl of Leicester. Whatever Lord Tyrell has threatened you with, I can stop him, but I need your help. I need to get out of here before it is too late," I plead.

He doesn't move.

"Please! I know this monastery belongs to Lord James Stanford."

The mention of James's name snaps his attention to me again, as if the name itself was enough to arouse him from whatever bind Lord Tyrell has him over. He opens his mouth as if to say something, anything, but decides against it, turning away instead and reaching for the door.

As he unlocks it, I take a step forward and place my hand on his arm. He flinches, but doesn't push me away.

"Why have you betrayed Lord Stanford? He is nothing but loyal to those who serve him and his family. I'm assuming you once worked for him?"

Looking over his shoulder, he stares at me for a brief moment, chewing the inside of his cheek. "I-I…"

I hold my breath, hanging on his unspoken words, but he shuts his jaw tight again, pushing down the handle of the door in silence.

"Please!" I shout. I am so close to getting through to

him! "Lord Stanford and my uncle, Lord Golding, will have an army of men searching for me, I am sure of it, and when either finds me here, there will be no mercy for those who have played against them."

His hand lets go of the door for a split second.

"I-I'm sorry, m'lady. I can't help ya. It's too late for both of us," he replies before exhaling through his nose, his hands clenched at his side.

"What do you want? Money? Power? Freedom? I can help you!" I reach for his arm again.

But he shrugs me off. "No, ya can't! I've said it's too late! I never wished for any of this to 'appen."

Without another word he is gone.

In anger and frustration, I kick the door with my foot, screaming, "Why won't you help me! I have done nothing wrong! Coward!"

I kick at the wooden door again, hurting my foot in the process, but something is different – the door moves with ease. I carefully and silently lift the handle and my heart skips a beat as the door opens a crack to reveal the empty corridor outside.

"I did it. I finally got through to him!" I breathlessly tell myself, my head a little light. "This is my chance to get out of here."

Instead of running through the door and not turning back, I hesitate, something I thought I wouldn't do if I found myself in this situation. It would be stupid for me to go running aimlessly around this time. Lord Tyrell will find me; I am sure of it. No, I need a plan.

There must be a stable in this monastery; Lord Tyrell could not have arrived by foot. I can steal his horse and ride to the nearest town. Perhaps I can make it to York. I am bound to find someone there who can help me, send word to my uncle, James, even one of my close allies. Yes, I can do this, I am sure I can, but first I need to get out of here unseen. I need a disguise that will allow me to roam the monastery freely, but how? There has to be something in here that I can use. If this place is anything like the monasteries back home, it will be cold and dark – perhaps I can blend into the shadows somehow.

I search around the room. Maybe the bedding can help… but red is too bright a colour, even though it is faded. My eyes land on the chest at the foot of the bed. I never did find out what was in there. It is large in size and I can barely move the thing. It must be here for a reason. Perhaps it has some old clothes or blankets I can use.

I scan the heavy lock. It needs a key, a key I don't have. The lock looks old and rusty, however. I bet I can break it off. Scanning around the small space, I spy an old, crudely decorated bible. I grab it off the floor and grip it tightly with both hands. Raising it high above my head, I count down from three.

"Three… two… forgive me, Lord, for what I am about to do… one!"

With a heavy clang and a dull click, the lock falls to the ground, the bible now dented and bruised. My heart is racing with anticipation, and with a long groan, it opens as I rest the lid against the bed, peering inside the dark, musty chest. At first, it looks empty, but as I put my hand in further, I touch something soft, bed linen perhaps? I carefully pull the bundle out and lay it neatly onto the bed. It is a cloak of some kind, but what exactly?

A monk's smock! It has to be! I take a quick whiff of the material and cough uncontrollably at the stale smell. It must have been in here for a long time; there are even a few tiny moth holes. I have no other option.

I take no time to slip the dark-brown smock over my head. The material is coarse and itchy, but it will have to do. The hood is a good disguise, as it shelters my face from prying eyes. I tuck my hair as best I can so as to hide it from view. A quick look into the chest reveals a white rope belt, so I quickly tie it around my waist and head for the door. My feet pause before I leave this place. I glance over my shoulder one last time at the tapestry, before I slip out into the corridor and into the daylight.

As I pause to gather my bearings, it is almost overwhelming to be out of that room. I smile to myself. The air is refreshing, lightly dusted with the smell of a burning wick. I barely have time to register my surroundings as I make my way through endless corridors, each one looking like the other.

I am yet to see another living soul.

Am I going around in circles? My mind is spinning as I take a few minutes to breathe, holding my hand to my chest to stop my heart bursting. I exit through another door as quietly as I can, hoping it leads me out of here, but instead, I find myself in an enclosed courtyard. A path leads around the outside of a neatly cut lawn which resides in the centre. Birds cheep merrily overhead. There is no time to stop and listen to the sounds I have missed so dearly, as a man's voice echoes behind me. As I frantically search for a place to hide, my eyes land on a nondescript pillar. I will wait here for him to pass… but he's not moving; he's stopped to talk to another in hushed tones.

"Of course, my lord, I hope you have recovered."

I hold my breath for fear of being caught. Just my luck to be stuck in a place like this. If anyone turns in my direction, they will see me! My eyes dart about as I try to find another way around. I am so close to my freedom! I cannot stop now. I peer in their direction. It is difficult to see clearly, especially as this hood obscures the majority of my vision. As I glance over to the two men talking only feet away from me, my heart stops still.

No, it can't be.

Time slows. I almost cry out, but nothing leaves my lips. James… Lord Stanford, is here. I want to rush towards him, cry, scream, shout, laugh, but all I can do is stand and stare.

"That is good to see, my lord, and congratulations on your betrothal." The second man is dressed in a dark smock, not too dissimilar to mine. Although, he has an air of importance to him, perhaps he is the abbot.

"Thank you," James sighs, taking in a long breath, his hand resting at his belt. "Ya may not 'ave heard, but my future wife has… been taken… disappeared. She was last seen in the woods near Leicester. I was hoping to find her, but no luck just yet."

The man places a hand on James's arm. "I am sorry to hear this, I did not know. We do not hear of much news from outside these walls that often. Leicester is so far from here too."

James stares down at his feet and pushes his hand through his golden hair, which is a little duller and more unkempt than the last time I saw him. I want to run over, shout his name, anything to be in his arms once more, to end this nightmare! But the sudden thought of Lord Tyrell lurking in the shadows forces me to shrink back into my hiding place. What if this is a trap?

"I will of course inform you if I hear of her, my lord. Perhaps she wasn't taken, perhaps she simply ran away?" the abbot suggests, a little too casually; it wouldn't surprise me if Lord Tyrell paid him off too.

"Ran away? She's not a child! She was taken and I'll find out who took her and where! When I do, all those involved will pay the price!" James replies, his words sending a jolt through me. "I must be going. I want to reach York by nightfall." He begins to march away, clenched fists at his sides.

No! I cannot let him leave. Together they walk through the door on the opposite side. I follow them, pulling the hood further over my head and keeping a safe distance.

Just before James reaches another doorway, he turns to the man. "I wish to pray in private before I leave."

"Of course, my lord. Please take your time."

James nods and turns towards the huge wooden doors a few feet away from where I find myself; the abbot does not follow. This is my chance. I take a small step forward, only to have to spring back into the shadows as another monk floats into the room and blocks the door that keeps me separated from James. How will I get past him now? A new voice drifts past me, eager to speak to the one who denies my entry. I cannot hear what they are whispering, but they quickly and quietly leave the door unguarded and head further into the monastery, their hastened, shuffled footsteps fading into the distance.

I cease to breathe, tiptoeing my way to the chapel doors and silently closing them behind me. My eyes quickly take in the room. It is plainly decorated with only two paintings, one of the Virgin Mary and one of Christ, both framing the high altar on which sits a golden cross beautifully reflecting the light around the room. I scan the room for any sign of James. In the shadows, a figure is kneeling down on the plain, cold stone floor, his hands grasped together in silent contemplation.

"Lord, why," he sighs. "Why have ya taken 'er away from me? Is this punishment? Please, tell me that she's alive, keep 'er safe. I will find 'er… I must… I…" James pauses and opens one eye, looking towards me.

I step back a little, feeling his prickly gaze upon me.

"Can I 'elp ya?" he asks, his brows knitted like he always does when he is frustrated. "What is it?" he asks again, standing up, as he rests his hand at the hilt of his dagger that sits neatly at his waist. "Has the abbot sent ya?"

"No, my lord," I answer, my voice barely a whisper. Strange, there are so many things I want to say, yet I do not know what.

"Then what do ya want? Can't ya see that I'm busy?" It is as if he is on the verge of tears as he pushes his hair away from his face.

"J-James…" I choke, fumbling at his name.

His mouth opens in shock. "Say that again," he says. All air in the room is still.

"James…"

He takes a cautious step closer. His hand reaches towards me, all time slowing as he pushes the hood off my head; the warmth from his hands is overwhelming. Wordlessly, he takes no time to gather me up in his arms, his kisses raining down on my lips.

I sigh with relief; finally, my nightmare is over. I wrap my arms around his neck as he grabs hold of me as if to never let go ever again. My knees fail me as I collapse to the floor, dragging James down with me.

"Katherine, Katherine, Katherine," he repeats, kissing away my tears and easing my aching heart.

He clasps his hands over my cheeks. I lean into him and close my eyes, barely being able to comprehend that this is all real, he is real. It is all I can do to grip onto him, my anchor in a raging storm.

He gently turns my chin with his hand, his eyes roaming my face, the pad of his thumb tracing the scratches and the gauntness in my cheeks. "I'm so sorry I wasn't able to find ya sooner, Katherine," he chokes, as if this is all too much to comprehend.

Like a rabbit caught in a snare, soon, reality takes hold and I bolt upright, pulling away from him. We cannot be found here! I will be dragged back into my nightmare, locked up forever, never to see the light again… or worse. I have put James in danger before – it was my woodland in which he was injured – I cannot be the reason for him being hurt again.

In a panic, I turn to him and grab onto his arm, pulling him with me. "We have to get out of here! He will come for me and he will kill you! He must know that I am gone by now. He will see you and…" My breaths shorten with each word and I begin to shake.

"It's alright, I'm 'ere, no one can hurt ya." James tries

his best to soothe me, but he doesn't know the danger that we are in, or what Lord Tyrell is capable of.

"No, no, no, no… you don't understand. He won't stop at anything to get what he thinks he is owed!"

"Katherine, calm down, who is after ya? Who did this to ya?" His eyes stare into mine, searching for answers.

I don't need to reply.

"Lord 'enry Tyrell," he growls, his hands turning to iron fists at his side.

Thirty

My breath freezes in my lungs as the door creaks open. Neither of us move. The clumsy shuffling of feet echoes closer before the door shuts behind them. I want to scream, "Run!" but no words dare leave my lips. It is only when James pushes me behind him, further into the shadows, that my legs begin to move. I quickly cover my head with my hood and crouch down near a stone pillar, making myself as small as possible. James quickly arms himself with his dagger.

A man's voice rings out around the lofty chapel. "Lord Stanford? I know yer 'ere!" It's the Northerner! "I 'ave urgent news! Countess Turner, she's 'ere! Lord Tyrell has been keeping 'er captive! You must come quickly! She is missing and I fear that if he finds her before ya do…"

I nearly step out from behind the post, but hesitate; what if this is a trick?

"He's running out of patience, m'lord." His voice increases with urgency at each note. "I 'ad no choice. Ya 'ave to believe me!"

"Wait here," James whispers to me, concealing his dagger behind his back.

"No, I can help," I whisper, but he is already beyond my reach.

I steady myself behind the pillar, hand on my heart, calming my breathing. I lift my hood ever so slightly and peek towards the two men who now face each other in the middle of the room.

"Benjamin Smith?"

I hear the surprise in James's voice.

"Lord Stanford! Listen, she is 'ere, or was. The Countess, *yer* Countess. I couldn't stand it any longer and when I learnt 'er name, I knew that I had to let 'er go." His words spill from his tongue at a rapid rate, as if the past few days and weeks have been too much for him to bear.

James tenses. "*Ya* were the one to take her?"

"'Twas not me, m'lord, I swear. I 'ad no choice! He threatened to kill m'family!" Benjamin begs, his hands held up in surrender. "Please… he's posted every man he 'as all over the place. The abbot is standing outside this door now, m'Lord. We have to find her and quick. I cannot bear to think what he would do!"

If he is telling the truth, we have to leave now. I cannot cower in the shadows forever. Benjamin pauses at the sound of my heels hitting the stone floor as I step out of the shadows and push the hood away from my face. He steps back, eyes wide and mouth agape.

"M'lady, yer 'ere! I-I…" He lowers his head, backing away from me.

"I know what power Lord Tyrell has over others. I might not be able to forgive you completely, but I will look past that if you can help us now," I say, my voice firm in what needs to be done.

James shifts at my suggestion of letting Benjamin walk away without punishment, but he might be the only hope of escape; he could distract those who are after me whilst James and I sneak away. He nods slowly, though his eyes never truly meet mine.

"Aye, m'lady. After… after I left the door unlocked, I had hoped I'd given ya enough time to escape, but then he went to check in on ya and when ya weren't there, he flew into a fit o'rage! He demanded an explanation, but I pretended that ya must have stolen a key off me when I wasn't looking, so he ordered me to search the place on pain of death."

Benjamin rubs the side of his face, where there's a fresh, red mark. The thought of Lord Tyrell stalking the corridors and chambers of this place is enough to inject the feeling of utter dread, as much as I try to remain calm. It must show on my face, as James is quickly by my side, but his comforting warmth is not enough this time.

"We have to get out of here," I remark, fear threatening to take over once more. "You said that these doors are being watched by the abbot, a man who cannot be trusted. We must look for another way out."

Glancing around the room, it is clear that the windows do not open and the only entrance is being guarded on the other side. With each minute that we lose, the quicker and more laboured my breathing becomes. It is as if the walls are drawing in on us and we have nowhere else to turn.

He's going to find us… he's going to take me away again… he's going to… no! No, we will get out of here.

"I know!" Benjamin exclaims with a slap of his thigh, breaking my spiralling thoughts. "There's another way out; an old set of steps will take us to the herb garden, and from there ya can leave without bein' seen."

With no hesitation, we follow Benjamin to a small alcove in an even darker and damper corner of the chapel, where, beneath a pile of old wooden chairs and dusty tapestries, is a set of well-worn steps. Hesitantly, I descend into the darkness first, closely followed by James and then Benjamin who tries to cover our tracks by heaving the tapestries back over the entrance as if they had never moved. The small, narrow corridor is as black as if it were night. No light has ever reached these walls; they are slimy to the touch.

"Just keep goin', 'tis not far now," Benjamin encourages.

If Benjamin were to betray us, he would do it now, but what choice do we have? At least I will have more of a chance of survival with James by my side. We make our way towards a speck of light, each step carefully laid one in front of the other. Finally, and to everyone's relief, we reach the end of the darkness, to an open rusted iron gate. I can taste the sweet scent of the infant days of autumn as the fresh breeze whips across my face. I want to run out into the open, for I have missed the feeling of the air upon my skin and the sun upon my face, but I cannot let my guard down now.

"Wait 'ere," Benjamin whispers, moving past me as quietly as possible, out into the open.

The first few footsteps crunch loudly on the odd patch of poorly laid gravel as he makes his way into the fresh air. After an agonising minute, Benjamin calls out to us, marking that the coast is clear.

Just as my foot lifts off the ground, James squeezes my hand. "Katherine, before we go, I just want to say how sorry I am, that I wasn't there when ya needed me the most."

I meet his downcast eyes with surprise. "James, you have nothing to apologise about, my love. *Tyrell* did this, not you."

"But he used my monastery to entrap ya. I should've started 'ere, I should've known, I..."

I press my finger against his lips to silence his false words. "I will not have you take the blame for this. Now come on, I refuse to spend a second more in this place."

He reaches for my waist and tugs me close against him. He crushes his lips against mine as if quenching his thirst after days without water. My tongue swipes against his, savouring his taste, committing this feeling to memory. I pull away, gasping for air, resting my forehead against his.

I inhale deeply one more time. "Come on, James, the rest of our lives awaits."

I take a step into the open, but just as we do, a voice emerges in the distance.

"Get back!" Benjamin urges.

James pulls me into the dark.

"Have you seen her?" someone in the near distance asks.

"No, m'lord. I 'ave checked the secret passages and she is not 'ere. She must have run for the forest," Benjamin says.

"You wouldn't lie to me would you, Smith? You remember what I said about your wife!" The voice draws closer, full of rage and anger; there is only one person that voice belongs to. He must have been searching for some time. "She is here somewhere. I know she is."

Something flitters across my hand as I steady myself against the wall. Swallowing my scream, I take a step backwards, but as I do so, I nearly fall and cause a few loose stones to roll down into the echoing darkness.

"What was that? Someone else is here. If you have deceived me, Smith, it won't be only your family's lives in danger, your head will be first, and hand-delivered to your wife!" Lord Tyrell shouts without restraint.

The pure venom in his voice is enough to bring a feeling of pure dread into my very soul. If he catches me here, his face might be the last I see. That thought alone is enough to cement me on the spot.

"I didn't hear anything, m-m'lord," Benjamin says, though I can barely hear him above the heavy beating of my heart.

"He is here…" Lord Tyrell breathes, as if he has just caught the scent of his prey. "Stanford," he growls.

I snap my head to look at James, who stands deathly still, staring into the distance, not moving an inch.

"You are lying to me, Smith!" Each step is as angry as the next, the ground breaking beneath his feet.

"I-I can promise ya that I am not, m'lord. I 'ave kept to my word!"

James's grip on his dagger tightens, anger ebbing through his body, his hatred for Lord Tyrell reaching a new height. I want to shout, I want run into the open, but all I can do is stand still, letting the darkness hide me.

Benjamin's voice trails further away from our position.

"This door looks like it's been forced open. She must have made her way through here, m'lord," he continues.

Somehow Benjamin's plan works and Lord Tyrell's voice is now inaudible as he follows. My muscles begin to relax the quieter it becomes. I want to collapse, exhausted from it all, but I know that we are not safe yet and I do not have time to process my emotions.

I pull on James's hand and whisper, "If we don't move now, we will be trapped here and he will find us!"

"Aye, I think there is a door that leads to the small stables at the end of the garden. If Benjamin has been able to distract Tyrell, we can quickly make our way there without being seen."

I nod as he grips my hand, guiding me into the blinding light outside. I cannot remember ever enjoying the feeling of the sun on my pale skin and the breeze through my hair more. I want to stand still and forget where I am for one blissful second, but the crunch underneath our feet draws me back into the present and the moment is lost. I glance around. It seems Benjamin's trick of distraction has worked as we creep our way across the garden and to what must be the stable-yard door.

"You!" Lord Tyrell shouts, his freshly drawn blade from his belt now pointing at James. He flashes one of his cruel smirks. "Oh, Katherine, when will you ever learn that we are destined to be together?"

"Not in this life, Lord Tyrell. Not in any life."

James whips around to face my jailer. "Tyrell!" he bellows, pulling a sharp, but much smaller weapon, from his belt. "I will make sure ya never hurt a soul ever again!"

"James!" I shout, grabbing his arm before he can do

something reckless. "No, we have to go! Leave him. We have to go!" I tug at his arm as Lord Tyrell closes the gap between us. "James!"

"He cannot get away with this, Katherine! I promised to look after ya and I cannot allow him to impugn yer honour," James replies, keeping his vision set on Lord Tyrell.

"Please, James! We can figure out how to get justice for his crimes against me, but please, we have to go now!" I pull at his arm again, desperate for him to see sense.

"Fine!" James grunts through gritted teeth and, without hesitation, reaches for the door and shoves me through it.

Lord Tyrell is upon us, reaching for my arm, but not before Benjamin jumps onto his back and pushes him onto the ground.

"Go, m'lady!" he screams. "Go! Get out of 'ere!"

"Get off me, you bastard!" Lord Tyrell shouts, muffled by the earth that tries to suffocate him.

Without looking back, we sprint through the stable yard and mount James's horse as quickly as we can, my smock getting caught in the stirrups as James pulls me onto the back of the saddle.

"What about Benjamin?!" I cry, not wanting to leave him in the hands of Lord Tyrell's rage.

"We cannot go back for him now, Katherine. He has chosen his fate."

James grabs the reins and gallops us through the opened entrance gates. I cling onto his waist for dear life, the hood of my smock covering my face as tears slide down my cheeks and blur my vision. Just as we snake around the garden walls and head for the main road, a blood-curdling scream erupts from behind us. I pray that it is Lord Tyrell's blood that is spilt, but deep down I know whose silence had been purchased for the very last time.

Thirty-one

We sit in a quiet tavern, the Golden Fleece, which is not too far from York Minster in the centre of the ancient city. Being no stranger to the small, labyrinth-like streets of York, James was able to navigate our way to the inn and procure us a room without hesitation. As the skies turned to black and the rain started to pour, I dared not look up at the imposing buildings as we slowly trotted through the cobbled streets and alleyways.

All I can keep thinking about is my aunt. Is she still alive, or is she lost to me forever? I want so desperately to write to my family, tell them that I am well: I am alive! But we cannot leave a trail, allowing Lord Tyrell to follow us, for surely, he is still alive and filled with rage. I shudder at the echoing shriek from Benjamin Smith. With great sorrow, my whereabouts will be a mystery to my family for now.

Out of the cold and into the arms of a warm fire, I sit alone, trying to feel the heat through my damp clothes. I sense a few curious eyes upon me, the wet smock drowning my shaking frame, but they soon look away when the barmaid hands them their next pint of ale.

Above the hiss and pop of the fire, I catch the last words of James's conversation with the landlord, Mr Bennett.

"Well, here's yer key." Mr Bennett hands over a key to James.

"Thanks, Bennett. I knew I could trust ya."

As I look over towards them both, Mr Bennett catches my eye and gives a small nod. I look away quickly, not wanting to draw any further attention. Even though James has known Mr Bennett a long time and trusts him dearly, we thought it best that we use false names in case anyone came by and asked for any information on us, demanding to view the signed guestbook. James tried to make me smile by coming up with silly names like Lord and Lady Pettleflower or Mr and Mrs Abscond, but I couldn't smile or laugh, as if all possibility of that has been drained from me, left behind when I departed from home however many weeks ago.

"Of course, Mr Smith." Mr Bennett drops his voice a little. "I will warn ya of any *unwanted company*, but ya should be safe tonight, we're not due any other guests." He straightens up and collects a few scattered empty plates and cups whilst James makes his way towards me, taking a seat next to the fire.

My eyes are transfixed on the blaze dancing in the hearth, my mind blank. I am finally free, so why do I not feel so? How long until I feel lost again?

James reaches for my hand. "Are ya alright?" He frowns with concern, his hand squeezing tighter.

"I'm fine, James." I attempt a smile, but only manage a yawn instead.

"Our room is ready. Let's go upstairs. It's been a long day for both of us."

We leave the warmth of the fire and ascend the small, narrow wooden staircase that leads to our bed for the night. Our room is cosy, consisting of a well-used long mirror, a four-poster bed with blue drapes and bedding, framed by two nightstands. Crisscross windows look out onto the cobbled city streets below, which are eerily quiet, except for the odd drunkard staggering down the road.

As I make my way across the room, I catch my reflection in the mirror. The woman staring back at me is unrecognisable. My hair is ragged and dirty, knotted at the ends as my hair tumbles down my back and over my chest. I drop my gaze to my hands. Various cuts and bruises litter the surface; how did I get these?

"These are not the hands of an earl's daughter or a countess," I mutter to myself.

In frustration I turn my back on the mirror, heave the horrible, damp brown smock off my body and throw it across the room. I don't want to touch it ever again! I stand there staring at the lump of brown material on the floor, my arms folded across my chest, my breath heavy.

As I cast my gaze around the room, I realise that I am alone. Where is James? I flinch at the slamming of a door in the dark corridor beyond our room. The walls seem to close in on me, as I back myself away from the door and towards the windows. I try my best to open them, but they won't budge! Several candles dance as a chill enters the room. I squeeze my eyes shut, trying my best to calm myself and breathe steadily, just like my father taught me, but I can't. Every sound, every movement, every thought overwhelms me, as if I am slowly being buried alive.

Echoes in the darkness. Whispers pour into my ears. Doors open and slam shut! The sound of a key sliding into a lock and twisting until it is in place.

"No. No! I can't still be there." I don't open my eyes, I can't. "I won't! I can't…" I panic, my breath uncontrollable, my mind screaming for me to run, but I don't! What does he want from me?

A hand reaches for me and touches my shoulder. I flinch and shout, backing myself into a corner, hugging my knees so close to my chest. If I am small, he may not see me…

"Katherine, it's me! It's alright, it's James." His voice is a spark in the darkness. "Katherine, it's alright, it's alright… I promise, yer safe. I'm 'ere," he soothes, my heart beginning to slow as I melt into his embrace.

I open my eyes one at a time, expecting to be surrounded by dark, damp stone walls, but instead I only see wooden timbers and soft glowing candles, the scent of fresh linen hanging in the air. James is kneeling in front of me, his hand closed around my own.

"I-I'm so sorry, James. I thought… I couldn't… I-I-I was alone." My words stutter at every attempt of trying to make sense of everything.

I have never felt as rattled as I do now. How is that even possible? Me! The Countess of Leicester. I have faced many hardships and fought through each and every one of them, my head held high, but now…

"It's alright, Katherine. Yer safe now. I promise." He

offers me his hand, which I willingly take, gently pulling me off the floor. "I should 'ave said, but I went to ask Bennett's daughter if she 'ad any clean clothes I could buy off her. Luckily, she is yer size and has offered these."

He points to a small bundle of clothes on the bed. I pick them up, almost expecting to feel the itchy cloth scrape across my scarred hands, but to my surprise they are soft and comforting, if a little faded. I begin to unfold the plain blue dress, and as I do so, a small set of brushes tumbles out. I pick them up carefully and smile at the crude wooden handles; clearly these brushes are well used and much loved.

"Thank you," I whisper. "All I seem to wear is blue." I attempt to laugh, but only manage half a smile.

James slips his damp tunic off his shoulders and opens the fabric at his throat, releasing a deep, tired sigh.

"There's a bowl of water for ya to wash yer-self with and soap." He takes in a deep breath of the lavender-scented aroma as I join him.

My whole body is craving a soak in my tub back home, warm water cascading down my back, but for now, this tiny bowl will have to do. In fact, it is more than enough. I step closer, gathering up all the water my hands will allow and lavishly splash the cooling liquid over my face and down my neck. The lavender soap lathers up quickly in my hands as I scrub away the dirt underneath my fingernails, hands, face, and neck. I must remove all traces of the recent past, then perhaps I will be able to forget.

Silently, James helps me climb into the bed, fluffing my pillows before I sink into the deep mattress. He blows out the candle next to him, plummeting us both into darkness, the silver moon shining through the windows, casting long shadows about the room. A few unusual noises echo from the streets below, making me pause as I strain to hear them, trying my best to come up with a rational explanation for them; a drunk man talking to himself, a horse trotting down the road, a fox or a dog slinking about the dark alleyways.

James draws me into his arms and I begin to ease into his body's warmth, no longer flinching at every creak of a floorboard or squeak of a door. I try my best to close my eyes. All I want to do is drift off into a dreamless sleep; my body and mind ache for it, but I can't. My mind is in an endless cycle: happiness at being free, excitement at seeing my family and friends again… Then I think of the last time I saw them and the events that led to me being here.

"My aunt, James. I have to know: is she still alive? Did she get the help she needed?" I ask, eager to know the truth, my stomach tightening.

"When I was in Leicester only a few days ago, she was still fighting," James replies, his voice soothing in the darkness, if not a little sleepy.

A silent tear rolls down my face along with a staggered breath. "She is a fighter. I pray that I get to see her when we are home. I pray that she holds on for my sake."

A comfortable silence sits between us, both of us yawning uncontrollably. My eyes become heavy as I nestle deeper into James's arms. Just as I am about to drift off into much-needed sleep, a thought occurs to me. "How did you know where to find me, James? At the monastery, I mean."

James hasn't asked for details of what took place at the

monastery. I am sure it is not out of lack of care; he would never be so cold. Perhaps he can see the toll it has taken on my body and mind. I need time to digest everything, to heal, before I am able to make sense of anything myself.

"I didn't, Katherine. I didn't know where ya were. I had my suspicions, but I was on my way back to York when ya found me at my monastery."

"Did you suspect Lord Tyrell?" I ask.

"Looking back now, I should have known. A couple of days after yer disappearance, he turned up at the castle gates and demanded to see ya, as if you were still there... He even fooled me. He was ushered into the Council Chamber whilst I discussed with Sir Francis as to what to do with him, knowing that yer wishes are for him to never set foot on yer estates ever again. Tyrell said that he wanted to discuss trade terms with ya, not something he would normally be interested in. I just thought it was another scheme to get ya alone, so I told him ya were visiting Lady Warrington in Northampton, but that didn't turn him away. Yer uncle had a chat with him eventually, but that didn't seem to satisfy him."

"When is Lord Tyrell ever satisfied?" I stifle a yawn once more.

"I watched 'im leave the Council Chamber mutterin' to himself. Yer uncle looked exhausted when he followed soon after. I didn't see Tyrell again until today."

The thought of him wandering around *my* grounds, pretending that he wanted to see me and that he knew nothing of my disappearance, enrages me.

"William returned in one piece, I am happy to say, Katherine. I checked up on 'im when I was last at yer 'ome.

Yer uncle said his sudden appearance without his rider is what alerted them to your disappearance that night."

William, my handsome horse. I am so relieved to hear that he is unharmed.

"Who else knows about all of this? My disappearance, I mean?" I ask, hoping that this will be my final thought before I fall asleep.

"We have tried to keep the truth within the castle walls. Gossip in town is something that we're trying to avoid. Bess hasn't left the castle since ya were taken. Elanor and John might 'ave left a few times to send letters or what 'ave ya, as well as yer cook to collect food each day from the market. Yer uncle and Sir Francis trust them. The staff are loyal to ya. I don't doubt that they will keep this a secret if they can."

It will be impossible to keep this news from ever entering court and the rest of the kingdom. I do not know how people will react when they hear of the truth. Even if they do not find out about the old contract between Leicester and Dornton, they will most likely believe Lord Tyrell over me. Men have always preferred the word of another man, no matter the truth. Will people look upon me differently? Will they blame me for being careless? Say that I deserved it? That I allowed him into my home and therefore should be obliged to suffer the consequences?

It was not my fault! My aunt was in danger; I had no other option but to ride out that night! Lord Tyrell is wrong here. Not me. He is wrong, and I will make sure the world knows it.

Thirty-two

"Get away from me!" I scream, sweat dripping down my forehead and chest.

Panicked, I sit upright, searching around the room, fearful that I am still imprisoned, but I soon realise I am safe, far away from that nightmare.

We soon rise with little hesitation, grabbing what few possessions we have, bundling food given to us by Mr Bennett into a satchel along with a small bottle of mead for the journey; our hope is to resupply on the way home. The sun has barely risen in the sky as we make our way downstairs and outside into the little courtyard where James's horse rested for the night.

Leicester is a long way from here and travelling on one horse for the next couple of days will only delay us further. Luckily, Mr Bennett's son-in-law, Jack Trenchard, a young skinny man with a quick eye, has a horse spare. As I finish prepping James's horse, I catch the end of their conversation.

"I was gonna sell that 'orse at t'market on Saturday!"

Jack huffs, irritated at the prospect of having to give up his horse with little notice.

"Well, sell it to me instead," James says.

"How much? She ain't cheap." Jack leans against one of the stable doors, arms folded across his chest.

James grins and shakes his head, amused by the boldness of the young man.

Mr Bennett steps up beside his son-in-law and smacks him around the back of his head. "Don't be daft, Jack!"

"Ow, what was that for? I ain't done nothin'!" Jack rubs the back of his head.

"Ya will give 'im that horse for free!"

"Free?" Jack's voice raises so high, the horses look over their stable doors to see what's going on.

"Aye. For free." Mr Bennett stares at his son-in-law, who can only look at the dirt on his shoes.

"Why should I do that when I can get a nice amount o'coin for her on Saturday? I promised my wife, *yer daughter*, that I would buy her a new dress." His eyes narrow as he scans my clothes.

I shrink away a little, cautious of the attention Jack might be drawing.

"Don't question me, lad! If it wasn't for Lord Stanford's family 'ere we wouldn't even be 'aving this conversation! Ya know his father's the one who helped us move away from the dirt and shit to the luxury of this inn!" Mr Bennett growls, agitated at even having to explain himself to his son-in-law.

Jack's eyes widen. "S-Stanford? I thought ya were…" he chokes.

"*Lord* Stanford," James corrects, his lips curling as he tries not to laugh.

As we signed our names in the inn's guestbook under aliases, poor Jack would not have realised who he was actually speaking to. I have to say, it is amusing to see the sudden shift in his attitude towards us.

"Well, I guess that means that ya have the funds to pay for – ow!"

Mr Bennett slaps Jack around the back of his head again.

"I was just joking of course, m'lord."

"I will pay ya, Jack, don't worry. 'Ere." James throws him a small pouch of what I assume is gold coins. "That should tide ya over."

Jack scrabbles to check the pouch's contents. "Th-thank you, m'lord. She's all yours." Jack bows his head, not daring to look up at James as he scuttles off back inside the inn, a few gold coins richer.

James turns to me, taking the last satchel off my hands, and loads up our new horse. "I hope she is suitable for ya, Katherine."

I pet her gently, a beautiful tanned coat with dark brown mane and tail.

"William could do with a new friend. She will do just fine." I smile as my new companion snorts in greeting.

We push on hard southwards, dirt kicking up at our horses' hooves as we weave our way out of Yorkshire and onto the old Roman road towards Lincoln. From there we will ride west onto the Fosse, leading us home. During our ride, James glances towards me every other mile or so, checking to see if I am faring well. I don't know what to say. I am not ready to tell him of all that happened back at the Stanford family monastery. I try my best to smile warmly when he does look at me as it's the only thing I can do. The breeze passing through the trees, the birds swooping high above us, a flock of sheep bleating in the distance… it's all enough to keep me occupied on the long journey, a distraction from the ache in my unused muscles.

The city of Lincoln is where we decide to rest for the night. We find a quiet inn on the outskirts so that we can remain relatively unseen. I am not well-known to the people of this beautiful city, but the few nobles who reside here have been guests at my home before. If I was recognised and seen dressed this way alone with my fiancé, that would cause more scandal and hurt than knowing the truth behind it all.

It's bizarre, people judge one another on their appearance more than anything else in life. I was taken against my will by another, a man who is well-respected throughout the kingdom, a man who abused his station and took what he thought was rightfully his because no one would stop him. Yet I would be seen to have defiled my status by wearing such common clothing and travelling alone with a man who is not family or husband. That is enough for people to turn against me whilst my captor walks free.

Signed in under different aliases of Mr and Mrs Johnson to avoid being tracked, we remain in our room for the majority of the evening, too tired to do much else but rest our heads after dinner. Besides, I want to ride out on the old Fosse before the sun rises as I itch for the security of my own stone walls and the warmth of the Great Hall's fire.

***

James shakes me awake and, after resupplying, we're out on the road again. As I watch the cathedral fade behind me, I can breathe a little more. Although, the closer we get to Leicestershire's boundary, a feeling of unease begins to envelop me. I thought I would be more excited or even a little nervous, but there is a niggling feeling that I cannot shake. Is this how I am to feel forever? As if all the kingdom's eyes are upon me? I have done nothing wrong, so why do I feel like I have?

I turn to James, who is focused on the road ahead, constantly looking around for anything lurking in the shadows, or pausing at the sound of a twig snapping in the near distance. Sometimes I catch him placing his hand against his side where the arrow pierced through him. Is that why he is constantly on the lookout for danger, especially in wooded areas? I shake my head of old haunting thoughts and try to take my mind off it all.

"Have you travelled this road before, James? You don't seem to need to ask me for directions," I chuckle, knowing too well how much James would rather get lost before he asked for help. I used to exercise my horse here frequently before my brother died; it's a nice road to canter through. The Romans sure knew how to make straight roads.

"I used to travel on this road whenever I had to visit my brother-in-law. He used to live not too far from 'ere before he moved to Nottingham, then back to my sister in Yorkshire." James grinds his teeth in agitation, something I have noticed whenever he mentions his brother-in-law, Lord Thame.

"Why do you hate him so much? If your sister loves him, surely that is enough?" I ask, perhaps naively.

James hesitates before replying, "She does and that is why I 'ate him even more. We were best friends long ago. He was once a respectable young man, owning 'undreds of acres of land that his ancestors had worked 'ard for – it is what made my father agree to my sister marrying 'im – but as soon as he inherited his small fortune, he gambled it all away, not thinking twice about my sister or his own children. Once, he got into trouble with a local gang of outlaws. He probably owed them money from a rigged game or two. Money has changed 'im, Katherine. He 'ardly spends any time with his own family, only going back when his coin purse is empty or he is running for his life."

"I'm sorry, James, I didn't know."

James smiles sadly; it clearly still pains him having his best friend and his sister live so close to danger's edge when they could live happily and safely instead.

"My sister has a small amount of the money she inherited from our father; he left a few possessions for her too, but her husband pawned them and drank all of the earnings away."

"Why didn't your sister stop him? They are her possessions not his!"

James hesitates before answering. "Do not take this the wrong way, Katherine, but yer lucky in that yer family allows yer life to be dictated by yerself. When we are married, I will never stand in yer way. What is yours is yours, but that is not a life most men want to live nor one most women are allowed to dream of."

I shake my head in annoyance, not at James but at the

truth he speaks. It is something that I am all too familiar with, but it is something that I don't have to remain silent about.

"I know, James. I just meant that it doesn't have to be that way. Women are traded away like objects from one man to another. We are human too, we have thoughts and feelings, we love and laugh, just the same as men do. Why is it that, because I was born into this body, I automatically have less say in everything, whereas if I was born the same sex as you or my brother or father, no one would stand in my way, yet my actions are the same as they are now."

I loosen my grip on my reins, realising how tightly I have wrapped them around my hands.

James chuckles to himself, shaking his head. "Believe me, m'love, no one will ever dare stand in yer way."

The sun is beginning to set in the sky, casting long shadows onto the ground below. We stop momentarily at the edge of Leicester. I have missed this place, its people, the concoction of aromas, the safety of the old Roman walls that protect the citizens within. A few of the town's lanterns have been lit as the night sky replaces the fading sun. A cold breeze tickles my neck as the air turns still and the birds stop singing. It is as if time has paused. I search my surroundings, but as the light fades, it is impossible to make out anything in the shadows. I try my best to remain calm, but the darkness begins to squeeze the air out of my lungs. I try to speak, but it is as if someone has wrapped their hands around my throat and I struggle to make a sound.

Something catches my eye; an animal stalking us amongst the treeline, perhaps? I can feel a familiar set of eyes upon me, but when I look around, no one is there. I no longer want to linger here. I no longer feel safe. We kick our horses into a gallop and make our way through the woodland that leads to my castle's gates. It takes all my concentration to ignore the memory of where I met the mysterious knight, whom I still have no name for. James shouts to the men on the castle walls for them to open the portcullis immediately. I notice the comforting face of Giles as he barks the order to two of his men.

As soon as I am inside the familiar walls, I am overwhelmed by the sudden relief of being home again. As I dismount, the urgent sound of feet rushing on the well-worn entrance steps greets me. I cast my gaze upwards and see the round, beaming face of my uncle who is quickly followed by Sir Francis.

"Katherine!" my uncle shouts, his arms open wide.

I don't stop running until I am in his arms. I run with so much force that I nearly knock us both to the ground. I try to say something, anything, but I am drowning in my uncle's shaking frame as he hugs me so tightly. I finally take a small step back and a gulp of air so that I can see him fully, breathe in his familiar scent, see that smile, hear his laugh!

"It is good to see you, my lady," Sir Francis chokes, blinking in earnest to hold back a sob as he rubs me on the shoulder.

James steps up behind me, and I move to the side as my uncle clasps his shoulders.

"My lad. You found her. You… you found my Katherine. I cannot thank you enough. I-I…"

James places his hand on top of my uncle's. "I said

that I would go to the end of the world and tear down any city in order to find her, but Katherine was the one who rescued herself; I was just there to assist."

"He just so happened by as I was leaving," I chuckle.

Our attention is drawn towards the entrance doorway.

"Katherine? Katherine!"

"Isabelle!" I shout in shocked reply, the emotion of seeing my best friend and sister at last.

She runs down the flight of steps as quickly as I have ever seen before. Tears blur my vision as I join her halfway.

"Katherine, you're here! You're safe. I can't believe it." She holds me so closely I can barely breathe! "I was so worried. I thought you were lost to us forever."

I don't reply with words, only hug her as tightly as I have ever held her in my life. I take a small step back, shaking my head in disbelief as Johnson, Giles and Taylor have also gathered to welcome me home.

"Where is my aunt? I must see her if she is still unwell." I look past Isabelle.

Isabelle takes a step back and looks out towards my uncle and Sir Francis.

"Where is she? Is she still in her bed? I must go to her; she must see that I am alright."

I begin to make my way inside, but the stone silence stops me in my path. My uncle bows his head and throws his eyes to the floor. Sir Francis does the same. Isabelle squeezes my hand and clears her throat.

"I'm so sorry, Katherine…"

I take a step backwards, nearly falling off the step.

"No. No, no, no, no, no, no, no." I shake my head over and over again, trying to dodge the words I never wanted to hear. A wave of anger washes over me as I look at each and every one of their faces. "James, you said she was fine. You said she was alive!"

James looks at me with as much disbelief as I am feeling. "I'm sorry, I didn't know she was… I didn't… the last I knew she was alive." He struggles to find the right words.

"This is all my fault," I breathe, clutching my chest as if it will explode. "I should never have left that day. I should have been by her side. I should have been there when… It was all for nothing…"

My uncle steps forward. "Do not blame yourself, Katherine. It is nobody's fault. She is with God now. When James was last here, your aunt was still struggling against whatever it was that took her. She passed away only a few days ago. She's gone."

Thirty-three

I don't want to move. I don't want to sleep. I don't want to eat or drink. My uncle and the rest of my household left me to lie in this morning; no one was allowed to disturb me, and I am thankful for that. Even though sleep evades me, I want to just lie in my own bed under my own roof and forget about the world and what has passed. James came to visit me not that long ago to check if I was awake, but I pretended that I was asleep; I just want to be left alone.

My aunt is dead. I can barely bring myself to believe it. I keep asking myself: was there something I could have done? What would have happened if I had stayed here that night? How did she even fall ill in the first place? It was so sudden. Have I not prayed enough, given God enough attention? Why did he decide to take her from me? Even if I prayed over and over again, it wouldn't make a difference now. She is gone.

I am yet to inform anyone of my account of what transpired over the past few weeks. Isabelle escorted me to my bedchamber when I arrived, but I just couldn't bring myself to tell her about what happened. I just want to push it all away, concentrate on getting through the next few days, give my aunt a regal funeral, one that she deserves. However, I know that I cannot ignore it forever and they have a right to know, so I finally crawl out of bed and dress myself. I ask Bess to gather my uncle, James and Sir Francis to the Council Chamber as soon as they are able. Isabelle is in town tending to the last few errands for my aunt's funeral; I will talk to her when she is back.

It feels like the whole castle is watching me as I make my way to the Council Chamber. The servants in the corridor curtsy as I walk by. Some even try to smile, but I can sense the whispers and endless speculations dancing from one person to the next. Last night, I had a horrible thought about what lies Lord Tyrell could have spread about me, about us. Would news of an elopement be spread across the country, or something far worse? Regardless of the truth, scandal is more exciting for those who live for nothing but gossip and lies. People like to believe anything anyone tells them if it is juicy enough to believe.

I take a deep breath when I enter the Council Chamber and close the door behind me. I look about the room. My uncle is standing beside my usual sturdy oak chair with James and Sir Francis sitting on the opposite side. I hold my head up high and take my seat, just like I have done countless times. I can sense 101 questions that they want to ask, but all three men sit there silent, respectfully, which is greatly appreciated.

The news of my aunt's passing has made everything much harder. If she were here, she would have asked for the truth straight away, and eventually I would have given it to her. With her now gone, there is only a sense of melancholy. I look up at the door as if she is about to stride through it, demanding to know why she wasn't informed of this little gathering, but of course, she doesn't.

My uncle smiles weakly before clearing his throat, drawing my attention to him. "How are you, Katherine?" he asks tenderly.

"I am well, thank you, Uncle. Happy to be home," I reply, even though my tone doesn't quite match my words.

"I am so pleased to hear it." He pauses for a second before continuing, "My dear, I know that it must be difficult and somewhat painful to have to recall what happened that night, the night you disappeared, and I know that it is difficult with your aunt… your aunt no longer being here." My uncle takes a small breath. "It has also occurred to me that we must inform the authorities, inform King Richard of what has passed."

"I will, Uncle, after I have digested everything myself," I reply.

"Of course, but please, I only want to understand from *you* what took place. I need to know what happened following your abduction up to the moment Lord Stanford found you. He has informed me who kept you locked away and where you were being kept captive, but I want to hear everything from *you*, my dear."

I glance over at James, who looks away from me, his cheeks a little flushed. I admit that I am a little saddened by him not talking to me first, but I guess I cannot blame him. My uncle and Sir Francis must have been worried beyond all imagination, angry perhaps, so I cannot blame them either.

I pause for a long while. I chew my lip, not knowing how to begin. I place my arms on the chair's strong oak armrests, trying to draw strength from its long history of being Leicester's seat of power.

"Very well," I start. "I was disorientated as I made my way through the woodland. I know that sounds ridiculous, but I was not myself; I was worried for my aunt's health."

Sir Francis nods in recognition of my words.

"I soon met a stranger on the road, a stranger dressed in full armour. I did not recognise his voice. I thought it was so strange to see someone dressed ready for battle. What was he doing there? I can't remember too much about him, or about our conversation, but eventually I found myself locked in a dark, cold room…"

As I recall what happened, the faces of all three men distort from patience to horror. Sir Francis stares blindly in front of him, his mouth agape, my uncle drags his hand over his face with tears prickling his eyes, and James breathes heavily, only able to meet my eyes for more than a second before he curls his hands into fists, looking away again. They do not interrupt me, call out in disgust, or leave the room not wanting to hear anything further. I try my best to recollect as much detail as I can, but it is as if my mind has already begun to burn away at the truth as I find it difficult to remember each key moment.

"At the time, I didn't truly know the reason behind my imprisonment, but it all became clear the day I found out who was behind it all." I pause for a second, not knowing how to proceed from here.

I glance towards James who sits there, encouraging me with every nod and his wonderful smile. I have dreaded telling him about what I learnt. What will it mean for us? Will he be angry, upset, hurt? Will he blame me for any of this? I look over at my uncle, who has been sitting there silently, not giving away any emotion. I have wondered over and over again if he knew about this contract between the Tyrells and Turners, but perhaps I will soon find my answer.

"Lord Tyrell produced a document. It was a tattered, old-looking thing. The writing was a little faded, but perfectly legible. At first, I didn't know what it was. The writing was oddly familiar but it was only when I had a closer look that I realised it was my father's writing."

Sir Francis sits up in his chair and glances over towards my uncle, who only nods for me to continue. As I do so, I only look at James as I speak. I cannot lose him now; I cannot bear the thought of it. I want to see his true reaction; I want to be able to see that everything is well. I have heard of men who break betrothals for much less, worried about their reputation of marrying into a family who promised their daughter to another.

"It was… it was a legally binding contract signed by my parents and the late Lord Tyrell, Lord Henry Tyrell's father. It was a contract between both houses, the house of Leicester and the house of Dornton, a betrothal contract between the two families' living heirs."

James bites his lower lip, not breaking eye contact with me. My heart beats quicker, blood pounding in my ears so that it almost deafens me. I push through. I have to tell him all. "It stated that if both families produce suitable living heirs, then not only will they be betrothed to one another, but the male heir shall inherit everything upon their marriage. Both my parents and Lord Tyrell's father signed the document. It was witnessed by our late king."

"King Edward?" Sir Francis questions, his brow creasing.

I nod, swallowing a small lump that has formed in my throat.

"I refuse to accept this so-called contract. In marriage, both parties must agree to it, and I, of course, do not. And as both my parents are dead and I am my own guardian, I refuse to bend my knee to any such idea of marriage between me and Lord Tyrell," I state, my head held high.

I am met with a wall of silence, something I didn't expect, but eventually and thankfully, Sir Francis speaks up. "Well, it's simple. That contract must be void, as your brother was the eldest, a male, and therefore not suitable. I do not see what Lord Tyrell thinks will happen. Katherine has spoken and therefore we will not go through with it. Your betrothal to Lord Stanford stands," he declares, as if he has the solution already.

My eyes reach my uncle's, his lips oddly sealed. I would have expected a bigger reaction from him, but he is unmoved.

"Uncle, tell me, please. Did you know about this possible bind between Lord Tyrell and me? Is it true? Did my parents sign away their heir to a family they despise?"

The air in the room turns silent and heavy, just like when a storm is forming in the sky outside.

"I...I did," he replies slowly.

My heart sinks. Hurt and betrayal floods every part of

me. I feel like I am about to break, but I mustn't; I have to hear him out, I have to hear the truth, as much as I don't want to.

He continues, "Contract or not, Katherine, you are the one who decides your own fate. It is your right as the head of this house to do so, regardless of your gender, regardless of what tradition dictates." He looks over towards James, who is now looking towards the floor, his hands clasped together, arms resting on his thighs.

I want to reach towards him, but keep my hands to myself for now.

"It is my right to know that something as important as this exists!" I reply, frustration overwhelming me. I regret it immediately. "If I had known about it, I would have been better prepared, barred him from ever setting foot on my estate in the first place. You and my aunt told me to set old grudges aside, yet you knew about this document! Why didn't anyone tell me?"

The sadness in my uncle's eyes draws out a splash of guilt from my own.

"I am sorry. You are right, Katherine, but you and Lord Stanford have found one another and I will not allow anyone or anything, contract or not, to destroy your happiness! You have worked too hard for that." The passion in his voice is moving. I have not heard him speak with much vigour or strength in a long time. "It is true, I knew of this contract, but I was also led to believe that it was destroyed."

The Tyrells have, one way or another, tried to burrow themselves into our lives since I was born. I wonder if that is the reason why Lord Tyrell's father was so keen to remove my brother from power after my father died? Did Lord John Tyrell have the same belief as his son, that the contract would still be legally binding if I was the sole heir of Leicester?

Sir Francis breathes out a long, shaky breath. "I just cannot believe it. He would go to such lengths to... to... what exactly? What exactly did he think he was going to achieve by abducting you? Did he think that he could force you to marry him, go along with his plan?"

James remains quiet and his wall of silence is beginning to unnerve me. I glance over at my uncle, but he is now standing by the window, staring out at the clouds. Finally, James raises his head, running a hand down his face. He must sense my eyes roaming every inch of him as he looks up at me.

"I know what yer thinking, Katherine." His voice is a little shaky. "I'm not upset or angry or hurt by this so-called contract Lord Tyrell was stupid enough to pin his whole future upon. I'm only forever grateful that ya chose me, that ya love me as much as I love ya." He stands up slowly and walks around the desk, stopping at my side.

I look up at him, his tall frame towering over me as I sit silently in my chair, trying my best to keep the tears at bay.

"I made a promise to never leave ya again, to never allow anyone to put their hands on ya. If ya allow me, to this I swear: I am yours to do whatever ya want with, from now until my dying breath, I am yours, Katherine."

I allow one tear to slip down my cheek, but I am quick to wipe it away before anyone else notices.

"But what will we do?" I ask, trying my best to remain in control of my emotions.

James softly chuckles. "I will do anything to keep him away, even if it means giving him all of my gold."

"Well let's not get ahead of ourselves. I do not want a single coin going to that man!" Sir Francis huffs, tutting and shaking his head at the very thought.

"I just want it all to go away," I sigh, exhausted by it all.

As much as it pains me to admit, I want someone else to make the decisions. For once in a long time, I cannot bear the thought of the long road I have to walk in order to seek justice. King Richard will punish him for all he has done. But is that the truth? Will I ever be able to try Lord Tyrell at court, to make him face his crimes – will anyone believe me? Without my stubborn determination and James's impeccable timing, I might still be there, locked away and alone, far from home and hope.

The movements of my uncle break my train of thoughts as he leans against the wall next to me. I clear my throat as I focus again on the situation at hand. "So, what are we going to do about it all? What happens if Lord Tyrell visits King Richard to make sure that the contract is still legally binding and I am forced to honour that agreement?"

"The king just wants peace in his kingdom after everything that has happened, and he knows not to upset his most powerful countess." My uncle chuckles to lighten the mood, but I do not mirror his humour.

"Regardless of what we do, Lord Tyrell is a powerful man, as much as I hate to say it. He took me from my home, from my family and friends, and hid me all the way up north! He devised a plan to kidnap me, weaken my spirit, hoping that I give into his demands and sick fantasies. I want him to fall off the edge of the world! I want him to be hung from the nearest tree and for all to know what he did to me!" I slam my fist on the table, my voice rising with each word, unable to contain my true thoughts and wishes any longer. I take a few sharp breaths before continuing, "But how are we to do that? How am *I* to do that? I am just a silly little woman, trying to play amongst giants. What power do I truly have against him?" It feels liberating to be able to finally let my true thoughts fly into the open.

"If you want me to get rid of that man once and for all, I will do so, Katherine, but I will not do it without your permission. I do not have the same power or standing as you at court, my dear, but I am still a friend to the king and he mine," my uncle declares.

"No," I reply. "I am the one who should see this through. I am the Countess of Leicester. I will show to him what it truly means to upset a powerful woman such as me. I shall write to the king to ask for a private audience. He must be the first to learn of what took place. I have always been loyal to the Plantagenets; he will accept my request."

The room seems to relax a little at this moment, a clear direction for me to take next. I hastily, but calmly, take out a piece of parchment and write my request to speak with the king with utmost urgency, outlining basic information about the contract Lord Tyrell believes is ironclad. I should feel relieved, but when I gaze out towards the town and fields beyond my window, I know that there is something that I must do first.

Thirty-four

As I walk through the doors of Saint Martin's for the first time in over five years, I almost refuse to enter. It would mean that I have to say goodbye to my aunt for the final time, and I don't want to. It feels too soon. The last time I saw her she was in pain, barely being able to breathe, but it is a strange comfort to know that she is no longer in agony. That is what is pushing me through the doors, the fact that she is finally at peace.

The service is beautiful; Saint Martin's is richly decorated in flowers from near and far, white lilies resting peacefully on the altar. I cannot seem to concentrate or listen to any prayers or hymns; my mind is in another world entirely. I only know when to stand then sit by the gentle brush of Isabelle's shoulder against mine.

As the words of the sermon drift around me, my mind wanders to the past. There were days when my aunt and I wouldn't talk to one another, upset over something trivial, both stubborn. Other days we would sit together in the library and read silently or sew. Well, I gazed out of the window for most of the time. I never truly knew my mother, my aunt's sister, and even though I never admitted it to her aloud, my aunt is the only mother figure I have… I had… and I will always love her for it. She didn't have to leave her old life behind, live with me and my brother when my father died, but she did. Nor did she have to take on my education, turn me into the noblewoman I am today.

I have never wanted to disappoint her, even though I never showed it. She was so set against my wanting to carve out my own path, but I did so to prove her wrong. Perhaps she knew exactly what she was doing. Without her scowls or comments or agitation, I wouldn't be who I am today. We owe just as much to those who try to steer us against what we truly want in life, forcing our hand to go against their wishes, pouring ourselves deeper into our full potential.

She is now gone. At peace.

On one occasion I remember my aunt speaking about death and how she didn't want anyone to mourn her, but my uncle reminded her that it is the living who pay the price of death. Those who pass away are no longer on this earth, they are an empty vessel. It is their family, their friends, their neighbours, their community who suffer. They are the ones who grieve, shed tears, need a place to reflect and pray to God to look after the deceased's soul. It is the living who suffer.

Only when I raise my head do I realise that I am sitting all alone. The ceremony must have finished a few moments ago, everyone leaving me to my own thoughts and prayers. I am surprised that no one tapped my shoulder or whispered to acknowledge the end of the ceremony, but then again not everyone has been the same with me since I came back. It is as if they don't know what to say. The servants have been nothing but kind to me; they pretend that I have not been away from home, but I catch their stares and whispers as I walk by. Isabelle tries to carry on as if nothing happened also, but she postponed her wedding for me; how can I feel anything but guilt? As for my uncle, I have decided to keep my distance, allow him to grieve, as he allows me. Perhaps it is also best whilst I mull over the fact he knew about the contract between my parents and Lord Tyrell's father.

I wipe away a few tears that escape down my cheek, then I silently wander towards where my family now lie peacefully. It brings a small smile to my face knowing that they are together again, and a strange comfort in knowing that, when my time comes, I too will join them. As I stand and reflect, I have this overwhelming sensation that they are with me at this very moment, as if from a dream. When I look around me, no one is there, just peaceful silence.

It doesn't feel very long ago that I gazed upon my parents' grave with William by my side, but now it's just me. I shake my head to rid myself of such sorrowful thoughts, silently praying for my parents' souls, before standing next to my brother's place of rest. As I trace his carefully carved name with the tip of my finger, a strange comfort comes over me, as if William is on the other side of the stone and is too tracing the words in sync with me. I whisper, "God keep you, brother," before I leave the stillness of the church once more.

As soon as we arrive back to the safety of my castle walls, I am able to breathe again. It is as if this is the only place where I feel unscathed. It is as if I am surrounded by water, the castle walls being the only thing that keep me from drowning.

As the evening draws in, I have an almighty urge to scrub away today's events. The smell of the incense lingers in my hair and on my skin. I ask Bess to prepare a large tub of warm water for me to bathe in, a few sprigs of lavender and rose petals scenting the water beautifully. As soon as she leaves the room, I dunk my head under the water, welcoming the silence, drowning out the sounds coming from all corners of the castle. I do not want to hear anything. I want to be left alone in the watery abyss, emptying my thoughts into the water, allowing them to wash everything away.

The door opens with a faint creak, disturbing my peace. As I resurface, I want to tell whoever it is to leave me alone. But as I wipe the water away from my eyes, I see Bess standing there, looking down at the floor, picking at a few loose threads hanging from the towel in her hands.

"Bess? What's wrong?" I ask.

"I am so happy to see that you are safe, my lady," she chokes, her tone not matching her words.

"You do not *look* happy."

Bess pauses, chewing the side of her lip. "I am! I just… I-I'm so sorry about what happened to you, my lady. I do not know the details, but I can only imagine that it wasn't good." Her eyes linger towards my slimmer frame, the muscles from my arms not as obvious as they once were, the bruises and cuts on my back telling a new tale. "If I had known that evening, I would have begged for you to stay! Perhaps I should have gone in your place!"

Along with the majority of my household, when I returned, Bess was one who tried to carry on her duties as my lady-in-waiting as if nothing happened. Although, whenever our eyes met in the mirror, or we passed each other in the corridor, her gaze would never linger for long.

I soften my tone. "It was my choice. You were kind enough to tell me that the path I usually take was blocked. If I had tried to continue down that road, who knows what else could have happened. William could have thrown me off if he tried to jump it, or perhaps another tree could have fallen on top of us."

I have thought back to that night countlessly, so much so I could paint a detailed mural if I had the artistic talent to do so. It is not unusual for trees to fall in the woodland, but the odds of one falling over the path I usually take feels too coincidental. I wasn't paying too much attention to it at the time. If I had, would I have seen evidence of foul play? Did someone chop it down on purpose, rather than it falling naturally?

"But, Lady Katherine, I…" She steps towards the tub, my thoughts broken.

I reach for her hands, water spilling onto the floor. "Please, Bess, what happened to me, where I was taken and by whom… I do not wish that on anybody that I love. It has happened now and we all must move forward with our lives. Please."

"Of course, my lady." Bess smiles with sadness in her eyes, nodding in acceptance.

After drying off and changing into my nightwear, I finally fall into a deep sleep, the voice of my aunt calling out to me in the darkness, whispering my name. As her silhouette fades, her voice echoes across the increasing space between us, *"Be strong. Be ready."*

Thirty-five

The newlyweds are announced as they enter Sir Francis's Great Hall at his grand Northamptonshire estate. Isabelle looks beautiful in her golden gown, capturing everyone's attention. They only have eyes for one another, nothing but laughter and smiles, as they make their way to the top of the room and take their seats.

Today, I have pushed everything else in my life aside. My best friend's wedding is a fabulous distraction, especially after I received a curt reply from Westminster Palace. They stated that the king is currently travelling the country with his queen and will see to all matters upon his return. I am a little disappointed, but perhaps once I am home, I can find out where His Majesty is travelling to next and I can make a special visit, for what I need to inform King Richard of cannot wait much longer.

"Katherine, are ya alright? Do ya need to rest?" James asks as we wait for the feast to begin. He has been very attentive of late, understandably so I suppose. I just prefer to ignore everyone's worries and continue as normal. He touches my hand under the table, bringing me out of my thoughts. "Are ya sure yer alright? Do ya need anything? Do ya want to get some fresh air? I will come with ya if so. I know the ceremony was a little long," he asks, squeezing my fingers.

"I am fine, James! Please don't suffocate me! I am not a fragile doll who needs to be played with carefully!" I snap.

James flinches, looking away quickly. I backtrack my comments, "I'm sorry, James. I-I didn't mean to snap at you. It's just… if I need anything, I will let you know, my love. Thank you."

I cannot look at his expression for the pang of guilt I would feel if I did. I know that he is only looking out for me, and I love him more than anything else in this world. I just wish everyone would stop looking at me as if I am a victim. I am a survivor.

Luckily, the wait for food is soon over, as a gigantic roasted wild pig, surrounded by sweet fruits and delicacies from around the kingdom, is wheeled out on an elaborate cart. Everyone applauds at this glorious sight and, with a wave of the groom's hand, the musicians begin to play. The hall descends into a roar of merry voices and goblets being filled to the brim with exquisite wine.

I bite into the delicious pork that melts on my tongue. The apple sauce that accompanies the meat is a strange but refreshing complement. Soon, thoughts of anything else disappear, my mind being filled with the sweet smells that fill the room. As I sit back in contentment, I reach for the goblet of wine in front of me. James's hand hovers just over his goblet. I follow his gaze, and it seems to land on a woman I'm not familiar with on the opposite side of the room. She too gazes over in our direction, and smiles politely.

I lean in towards James. "Who is she, do you think?" I nod my head towards her, but when I look up again, she has gone.

James exhales heavily then swallows the rest of his wine in one gulp. "I 'ope ya have enough patience for this, Katherine," he mutters, standing up rather abruptly as the woman approaches.

"James! I didn't know ya would be here, but, alas, of course yer here, it's not home, is it?"

I balk at the familiarity of her tone. Who is this woman? If she was someone important, I am sure I would have been introduced before. Perhaps she is a cousin of Sir Henry's, or an old friend of Sir Francis's? Though, by the way James reacted, perhaps she used to be someone of close importance to him.

As James stands rigid, unable to move, I clear my throat and straighten my spine. "We haven't met. I am Countess Katherine Turner of Leicester. Lord Stanford is my fiancé." I hold out my hand and wait for her to take it, keen to see how she reacts; I have no patience for ill-etiquette today.

"Oh, where are my manners? My lady, it's an honour." The woman smiles sweetly. Her blonde hair is tied in a neat little bun and her dress displays beautiful embroidery. The way in which she stands with such confidence and experience makes me think she must be a woman of some importance.

"Kath – Lady Turner, may I introduce Lady Elisabeth Thame," James announces. "My sister."

His sister? I stand up a little straighter, desperately trying to hide the embarrassment on my rosy cheeks. Why didn't James say so sooner? Now I see her more clearly, I can see that her facial features are similar to her brother's. Her accent is one of Yorkshire, though weaker than James's. She is thin, similar to my build, but her eyes are brown, not blue.

"It is an honour to finally meet a member of Lord Stanford's family." I smile, perhaps a little too enthusiastically.

"The honour is all mine. I was aware that ya and the bride are very close friends, so I was hoping to bump into ya this evening, if truth be told. We were… unable to make the ceremony itself." She turns towards her brother. "Though, I would have expected my brother to introduce ya a lot sooner."

James huffs, pinching the bridge of his nose. "As I wrote in my letter, Elisabeth, Lady Turner's aunt has recently died and was ill for some time. She couldn't get up and leave because *you* wanted to meet 'er."

Lady Thame coughs a little awkwardly; clearly this is information she didn't want me to know. "Of course. I am sorry for yer loss, Countess."

"Lady Katherine is just fine. We are to be sisters are we not?" I declare, hoping not to have overstepped the mark. I wish my aunt was here to help guide me with greeting my future in-laws, a lesson we never quite got to.

"Aye, Lady Katherine, we shall. I'm very much looking forward to getting to know ya better. My brother has told me only a fraction about ya, but perhaps that is due to him spending more time with my husband than his own sister."

This is news to me. James detests his brother-in-law.

"Is your husband here?" I ask, curious to meet the infamous Lord Thame.

"He is, but I don't know where exactly." She shakes her head with a bitter twist to her smile. "I think it is best for all of us that my brother and husband spend little time in the same room together," she adds before taking a long drink from the goblet in her hand.

"Elisabeth," James growls.

"Well, ya don't exactly hide yer distaste for him do ya, brother? Ya used to be best friends once." She finishes her wine. "You were the one who introduced him to me!"

"I didn't introduce ya to 'im. He did that all on his own. Ya knew his reputation before ya 'ad even met 'im," James replies, his accent taking its full form the more agitated he becomes.

"Ya were very happy when he asked me to marry him!"

"Of course, I was 'appy, you were 'appy! What sort of brother would I 'ave been if I 'ad stood in yer way?" he cries, drawing a little too much attention to our side of the room. My touch upon his arm has little effect.

I try to interject, change the tone of the conversation. "I hear you have three sons, Lady Elisabeth, how wonderful."

"I do, Lady Katherine, but I doubt they remember their uncle due to his poor attendance at home," Lady Elisabeth replies.

I cannot help but flinch as I am probably the reason they have not seen their uncle for some time.

"I 'ave my own life! Perhaps if yer husband could be bothered to stay home for more than a day, they wouldn't need me to be the strong male figure they need in their life, sister!"

"Yer just trying to change the subject, brother!" Lady Elisabeth huffs.

James sighs. "What do ya expect me to say? I am the one who has to go and sort out his mess, settle his debts, pay whoever he's pissed off! He's lucky to have ya! I don't know many women that would put up with his arrogance, lack of morals and duty!"

"James," I try to coax him out of his rage, but my presence does very little, much to my irritation.

Lady Elisabeth leans towards her brother and grits her teeth. "Then don't! We can manage fine without ya interfering."

"Interferin'?" he questions. "I 'ave to interfere so that ya and the boys 'ave a roof over yer 'eads!"

I catch the eye of my uncle who is sitting two seats away from me. His eyes go wide as he notices the squabble happening next to me. Thankfully, the rest of the room appears none the wiser.

"I'm sorry, Katherine, this is not the way I wanted to introduce ya to m'family," James grumbles, hand tightening on the back of the chair.

"It's fine," I reply.

"No, it's not!" his sister interrupts.

I jolt at the heaviness in her voice.

"Don't bring yer fiancée into this little family tiff, James. Although ya will be a part of this ridiculous family soon, Lady Katherine, so, welcome to the family." Lady Elisabeth holds up her empty goblet in mock celebration, no cheer or smile upon her face.

The tension between the two fades, replaced with a mixture of harsh truths and unspoken anger. Thankfully, the groom announces that it is time for dancing. I have never been so relieved to watch a couple dance in my life. I excuse myself from the siblings and wedge myself next to my uncle who only raises his eyebrows in greeting.

"I see you met James's sister," he chuckles.

"Yes, it seems I have." I breathe out a long, exhausted sigh. Who knew siblings could be so draining?

James finally joins me, his eyes a little downcast and his shoulders slumped over as if in defeat. I smile sympathetically towards him, to which he replies with a long exhale of breath, no need to say anything more. As the happy couple continue their dance, I lead James towards one of the refreshment tables in hopes of filling him up with more drink in order to help lift his spirits and hopefully allow him to forget about the tiff with his sister. Grabbing two empty goblets, I fill them to the brim, then hand one over.

"Lady Turner!"

I spin around to find myself face to face with a man I don't recognise.

"Lady Katherine Turner? I am sorry that I have not introduced myself sooner. I am Lord William Thame, but please call me Bill." He takes my hand and presses his lips against my skin, rough against the stubble on his square chin. "It is an honour to meet you, my lady."

I stand still for a few seconds, until I slowly register this man's forwardness. "Oh, Lord Bill Thame, you must be Lord Stanford's infamous brother-in-law!"

I glance towards James, all too well aware of the pain and hurt this man has caused him in the past, especially since the run-in with his sister was so passionate. James's tales of warning about his character and bad habits forces me to take a small step back, making sure that there is a little more distance between us.

I have wondered what Bill looked like, considering the mess he has landed himself in on countless occasions. He is a handsome man, tall with long, dark hair, slightly olive skin, brown eyes, with a very domineering presence. His accent is nothing like how I imagined, not of the north, but more of a mixture of the south and midlands, though a hint of Yorkshire peeks through on certain words. I can see how his overbearing personality could be appealing to someone like James's sister. I can imagine passion being the glue that bound them together when they first met, though whether that is still the case is yet to be seen.

"I trust my brother-in-law has told you everything about me?" Bill grins, moving his elbow on top of James's shoulder, though he struggles greatly due to James's height.

"Of course, I 'ave, Bill! How else will she know to stay away from ya?" James shrugs Bill off, forcing him to lose his balance, though he recovers quickly.

"Ah, he has only told ya all about m'handsome personality, m'good looks, m'charm, m'wit," Bill mocks James's voice, overemphasising his Yorkshire tones. What an interesting first impression he is making.

James folds his arms across his chest shifting his weight onto both legs. "I was more thinking about yer gambling with my sister's and nephew's lives, yer never-ending debt that I, yer welcome by the way, pay off every single time," he snarls.

"I do thank ya, James. Nottingham is a very expensive

place for a man like me," Bill boasts as James sighs deeply and shakes his head. I am beginning to see why he was keen to avoid Bill this evening.

"Nottingham? Do you visit there often?" I ask, keen to keep this conversation civil.

"Not lately, but the earl and I are good friends." He grins, wine splashing down his chin.

"Why don't ya ask 'im to bail ya out then?" James enquires, which I think is asked more as a request than a thought.

If it wasn't for James's honour and love for his family, I doubt he would have kept Bill afloat all these years. I can say with certainty, after hearing the stories of Bill's exploits with his finances and his current demeanour, I will make sure not to loan him a single coin.

"We used to be best friends, ya know, Katherine. I was very much off the main path, but this one looked after me regardless." Bill leans forwards, staggering slightly.

"That is *Lady Turner* to you." James pushes Bill away from me.

Bill laughs. "Let the lady speak her own mind, *Jamesy!*"

James flinches at the nickname, clearly something he detests.

"She is the head of her own house, is she not? Out-ranking ya, I believe. A countess! The Earl of Leicester's daughter. It takes a very special kind of woman to be able to run her own estate and lands like she does, battling men off left, right and centre."

"I do not need to battle anyone off, Lord Thame," I interject, annoyed at his belittling, wanting nothing more than for this little engagement to end.

"That is enough, Bill!" James warns with a small

snarl, like a wolf warning one of their pack when they are beginning to step over the line.

"A friend of mine told me that ya could have had your pick of the litter, but ya chose old *Jamesy* here." Bill cocks his head at me as if studying a small insect, deciding on whether to let me free or to play with me a bit more.

I stand my ground though, having endured little boys like this before.

"It takes a lot of strength for a woman to do that, but is it all a façade? Are you truly as powerful as they say?"

I sigh heavily, making it known to our overbearing guest that I tire of his ill manners and wish nothing more than for him to leave us be.

"Women are all the same; they think they have control, but they have no idea…" Bill argues, his drunken words becoming unclear.

"That is enough, Bill!" James raises his voice, unable to control his frustration any longer.

Calmly, as if this tone of conversation is nothing but ordinary, I take a small step between them.

"No, James, let him continue to put his foot in his mouth. Seeing as you clearly have no control over your own finances, I will tell you this for *free*."

James huffs with amusement at my carefully chosen words, whilst Bill stares at me blankly, entertained and surprised at the same time.

"I am not an ordinary woman; you are correct. I don't need a man to protect me. I have survived long enough without one. I have faced many a man like you, who thinks that because I am woman, I therefore must be weaker and that you can baffle me with nonsense."

"Well, no, that much is clear," Bill tries to interrupt again, but I soon silence him with a wave of my hand, forcing him to shut his mouth before another syllable escapes past his lips.

"It might not have occurred to you, why would it, you don't have to worry about such things, but men, not women, decided to put unlawful barriers in our way so that we have no choice but to become dependent on *you*. In order to survive this harsh world that *you* have built selfishly for yourselves. *You* have made it so that we cannot live successful and independent lives. That is not God's will, that is the law of men. People are easier to control when they have nowhere else to turn. If only you knew an ounce of what I have been through, otherwise you wouldn't try to silence me, you would shut up and listen."

He attempts to open his mouth again. "W-what about your wedding—" But one look from me soon stops his next word in his throat.

"And before you drone on about how I am entering marriage, therefore just becoming another man's wife and property, I will tell you now, your brother-in-law is an extraordinary man. There is no one else in the world who deserves my loyalty and love. I would be a fool to settle for less. Besides, I am the head of my house and sole ruler of my county on behalf of the king, regardless of my marital status or gender. You might not be aware, but my family have the backing of the king, and no word, written or spoken, can change that."

James looks upon me with all of the love and pride in the world, until Lord Thame clears his throat and draws our attention back to him.

"Very good, Countess, very good!" Bill claps slowly. "What a lovely little speech! You must teach my wife how to capture a room as well as you do; she really could do with the same… *confidence*, you possess."

If it was just me and him here, I would show him the door with the end of my shoe.

"May I remind you we are at my dearest friend's celebration of their wedding. Do not turn this event into a northern spectacle. As annoying as you are, you are James's family and therefore also mine. You two don't have to like each other, but you can at least be civil when in front of others. The same goes with me, Lord Thame. I am not a woman you can so easily charm."

"I never wanted to upset ya, Countess. I apologise," he eventually manages to mutter, though not as sincerely as I had hoped.

James pinches the bridge of his nose and closes his eyes. He glances at Bill one more time. "Never speak to my future wife like that ever again, Bill," he says before landing his gaze on me. "Sorry, Katherine, I need some air. Come and find me once yer finished with this imbecile." He squeezes my fingers before departing for the other side of the room, leaving me alone with Bill.

I have never seen James so anxious, angry, and agitated in one go before. It pains me to see him in such distress; I know I could have been less harsh at the beginning of dinner. If we were at my home, I would happily ask for Lord Thame to be escorted out by one of my men, but I do not wish for such a scandal to happen at Isabelle's wedding. I can handle him myself.

I release the air held in my lungs into the space above

me. “You really do know how to wind him up don’t you, Lord Thame,” I exclaim now that the tension has slightly dissipated.

“It’s a talent, m’lady. Though I must say, James really is your knight in shining armour, isn’t he?”

“Knight in shining armour?” I question, an unusual choice of words.

“Come now, Countess, I know that you are proud to be a woman of wealth and status, but you must love it when James comes to your aid.”

One of Sir Francis’s men interrupts our little tête-à-tête by clearing his throat loudly; I am thankful for the disruption. “Your wife has requested your presence, my lord.”

“Very well. Until later, Countess!” Bill toasts me with his goblet, draining the last few drops before staggering away to the other side of the room and out of sight.

Thirty-six

"What is the fire telling you?" I tease James, as I bump my shoulder lightly into his.

He stares mesmerised at the dancing flames in the blackened hearth, leaning against the fireplace in deep thought.

I begin to warm myself by his side, the cold chill from our journey home defrosting in my bones.

He replies with a half-smile, barely moving from his post. "I'm just tired 'tis all."

Charles Gamble enters the room with a light knock at the door, something in his hand. "My lady, a letter has arrived for you."

I take it from him and notice the seal; it is from King Richard! Without looking up, I reply, "Thank you, Charles," and he exits the room.

"James! A letter from—"

James's sudden movement towards the window pauses my words.

“What is wrong?” I question, placing the letter on the arm of the chair near the fireplace.

The sound of thundering hooves echoes in the courtyard below. I press my forehead against the window to get a better look, and to my dismay, a small set of unrecognisable armoured men line the entrance steps, dismounting from their horses. My heart races as they unsheathe their swords. How did they make it through the portcullis? What do they want? My breathing becomes laboured, my palms sweaty. I'm completely horrified as I watch John Gamble approach the strangers, only to be met with one of the rider's boots squarely into his chest. John keels over in pain.

“No!” I pound on the window, a wave of anger washing over me.

I watch on, as John clutches his stomach. He raises his head and mouths something at the person closest to him, before being pushed by one of the others in the dirt, blood spluttering from his mouth.

“That is enough!” I shout, my nostril flaring at this insult. I turn on my heel, thinking of nothing more than how to deal with these intruders.

“No, it can't be...” James breathes. “Bill?”

I freeze.

“Bill? Lord Thame?” I question, confused as to why he would be here amongst a band of unknown, violent men. “Are you sure? What does he want?”

“I don't know, but I won't give 'im the pleasure of explainin',” he growls.

James marches out of the room after me, my head racing through a thousand thoughts; I cannot grasp at one. As we approach the Entrance Hall, a mixture of voices filters through from outside; too many for me to pick out, as they converse over one another, discord amongst them.

"Are you sure they're here? This had better not be a waste of my time, Thame," a muffled voice asks with agitation.

The doors to the castle slam shut. They are inside.

"They're 'ere. I know they are. I saw them leave Grey's estate before anyone else. Now, I have held up my side of the bargain, so you 'ave to keep yours," Lord Thame growls in reply.

Just as I am about to make myself known, an unexpected voice fills the void. "My lord, what a pleasant surprise."

Bess?

I pause at the familiarity with how she greets them, her voice fluttering with excitement. "I knew you would come back," my lady's maid replies giddily, just like how she was when she was with…

"Oh no," I whisper, dread filling my stomach, weighing me down on the spot. I shoot a quick glance at James, and without having to say another word, we both realise who heads this unwanted band of men.

"Please go and fetch your mistress," Lord Tyrell commands.

"Why are you so eager to see her? Don't you want to spend time with me?" Bess drops her voice into a sultry tone; I can picture her twirling her hair around her finger, her hand at her hip.

"I asked nicely." The sound of a sharp blade being drawn echoes off the walls.

Something changes in Bess as her voice wobbles, "Wh-who's bl-bl…"

"That is nothing for you to worry your pretty little head over," Lord Tyrell replies, before exhaling an agitated breath. "Katherine? Lady Turner?" he bellows out into the open air.

My breathing intensifies at the controlled anger behind his words.

I begin to wrestle with myself as to what to do. My body hesitates. My mind flashes back to the monastery, the cold walls, the dampness, the stale air. I close my eyes to rid myself of these thoughts. This is *my* castle, *my* lands, *my* people. He is on *my* territory and I will not settle for his arrogance any longer. I cannot allow anything to happen to Bess, not whilst I can do something about it. But something isn't right. Where is everyone? Why didn't anyone stop them from entering? I would have expected Giles to have stopped these men at the gates. My uncle and Sir Francis should be on their way here by now too, having gone hunting at Sir Francis's estate as soon as the sun rose this morning.

I gaze towards the staircase then to James and lower my voice, "I need you to meet with my uncle and Sir Francis, rally up my men whilst I distract Lord Tyrell. We will then outnumber them easily, and I will make sure they are arrested for their trespass here."

James is speechless for a second as he chews his bottom lip. "I don't want ya to be on yer own with 'im, Katherine. I promised I wouldn't let ya come to harm."

I take a desperate step towards him, placing my hands in his. "I know, James, but I wouldn't ask unless it was absolutely necessary. Please," I say, "go quickly and silently.

You will then have the element of surprise and we can rid them from my land without any bloodshed."

James hesitates.

"Please, James. When I was trapped in that godforsaken monastery, he all but showed me his true weakness."

"What?" he questions.

"Me."

James inhales, his hand gripping my arm. "No, Katherine, don't be so stupid. He will kill ya." Horror fills James's eyes.

I know this plan might seem crazy, like walking into a bear's den, but it has to be me. I am the one Lord Tyrell wants, I am the reason he is here, it must be. What else does he hope to gain? His obsession with the contract between our two families drove him into locking me away so no one else can have me.

I can do this, but I need James to see it is the only way. I need his support, to trust me with this. We are running out of time.

I shake my head. "James, please, I can distract him, keep him talking whilst you round up my men, my uncle, and Sir Francis. They will not be far behind. We don't have time to call for the authorities, they will take too long to get here. Bess is down there; I am certain of it! She can help me. I won't be alone."

He takes a small step back, holding onto the wall for balance. "No, Katherine, I beg ya. What if he is bored of ya, come to make an example. He has dangerous men with him, keen to do their master's bidding. They have entered yer grounds without honour and will not think twice to kill anyone in their way."

He is right, but what else can we do?

"I just need to lure him out of the castle somehow, isolate him from his men, gain the high ground. I will do what is necessary to rid him from my lands for the final time, James."

"No! I won't allow ya to have any blood on yer hands." His voice is firm, his jaw set tight.

"It won't lead to that. I will get him alone, make him vulnerable and we can then lock him away and call the authorities, alert King Richard, I don't care who, just let me do this!" I pull at his hand, squeezing it with all my strength. "Please, do as I say; we do not have much time."

James looks from me to the ground, then back at me again. He nods in agreement. "Alright, Katherine, I will go, but be careful, and if anything happens, run."

I kiss James with as much hunger as I did the first time our lips touched all those months ago. He pulls me closer by cupping the back on my neck, deepening the kiss; it is hard to stop. I lean back and rest my forehead against his, panting for air. Muffled voices from behind shake me back into reality and I know what I must do.

Silently, James lets go and slips out of sight. As soon as he is gone, I ready myself for what is about to happen. My hands straighten my dress and pull down the sleeves over my wrists. My brother's signet ring sits close to my chest, and with one final breath, I step out of my hiding place and directly into the serpent's lair.

"I am here, Lord Tyrell. What do you want?" I demand, as I enter the space in which he awaits.

My eyes quickly scan the room. Lord Tyrell stands in front of me, dressed in his signature black, a fresh cut across his right cheek (I wonder if Benjamin gave that to him, a permanent reminder of his death). To his left is a man I recognise as Forster, his aid from the joust, his sword slung across his shoulder. A slender, dark-bearded man stands to his right, only armed with a dagger, though the blade is not one I have ever seen before; it curves like the ocean waves into a deadly point. The one closest to Bess peers through his small, beady eyes, a crossbow slung across his shoulder, his quiver empty. There is another man standing guard by the doors that lead out into the courtyard, most of his face covered with a black hood. Soon my eyes land on a well-known face: Lord William 'Bill' Thame.

"Lord Thame. How pleasant of you to drop by unannounced with your new friends. If I had known, I would have asked for you to bring your wife and three darling boys, but I suppose they know nothing of your little adventure," I announce, looking straight into his eyes.

The weight of my words must be too heavy as he looks down upon the floor.

"Thame is here as a favour, Katherine, one of many he owes. Twice he failed me. I will make sure there is not a third," Lord Tyrell says as he too stares at Bill, who seems to have shrunk further into the walls.

My heart thuds against my ribcage and my palms begin to sweat, but I will not allow any man here to see the effect their presence has on me. I ignore Lord Tyrell for now, my eyes instead finding Bess. I start to reach out towards her, praying that she can escape unscathed, although she doesn't seem to be distressed, but actually quite calm. The way in which she stands there, hand on hip, a thin smile upon her face forces me to pull back.

Lord Tyrell approaches with his arms outstretched wide in greeting as if we are old friends, but not before I take a step back.

"Still afraid of me, I see? The last I saw you was… when was it? Ah yes, in Yorkshire. Do you ever fondly look back on our adventures, Katherine? I certainly do." A small smile forms upon his lips, not one of malice, but seemingly genuine fondness.

"Let Bess go. This is between me and you," I command, ignoring his question. "Let it be just us two, Lord Tyrell. There is no need to draw anyone else into this. We can sort this out one to one."

"You probably won't want me to do that, Katherine," he replies, folding his arms across his chest.

"And why not?"

"Maybe you should pay more attention to whom you let into your inner circle." Lord Tyrell laughs, adjusting the knife at his belt.

I watch him as he takes Bess's hand that is resting by her side.

"Don't touch her!" I snap, as Lord Tyrell twirls Bess closer to him, forcing her to face me. I jolt forwards, only to be held back by the sudden presence of Forster's sword flashing towards my throat.

"You see, without little Bess here, I would never have got to this point."

"W-what do you mean?" I stutter, frozen in place by the sudden guilt that betrays Bess's eyes, and the close proximity of Forster's sword. "Bess, what is this idiot talking about?"

"I-I…" Bess stammers, her once-confident self now crumbling.

"Tell her how you have been helping me all along." He kisses her cheek long and slow.

She melts at his touch, as if he instantly dissolves her guilt and uneasiness.

"Go on. Tell her," Lord Tyrell encourages. "Tell her how she made you feel, lied to you, selfishly pushed you aside. Tell her how it felt when her aunt treated you like dirt."

His last words ignite something within her: resentment, tightly held anger, a broken heart… manipulation. She finally meets my gaze, the beginnings of a flame glowing behind her eyes.

"You're right. I must tell her, like you asked me to."

Lord Tyrell's lip turns up at one side before he places a delicate kiss on her pale cheek again. It is as if he is trying to use Bess to make me jealous. If that is true, perhaps he really is beyond negotiating with.

"W-when I was dragged all the way over to Leicester by my idiot half-brother, I didn't truly know what was in store for me. I thought I was going to be your equal. My father, after all, was a great and powerful man, so why shouldn't his only daughter be too? But then I met your aunt. She looked down on me like I was nobody. Just another bastard child a greedy and selfish man brought into this world and threw away. Maybe she was right; maybe I was born for something as low as this." She gestures around her, scowling at the well-worn stone walls.

It pains me to hear the anger behind her voice, the disrespect in her words. I thought she was happy here. How was I so blind?

"You couldn't bear to look at me!" Bess continues. "You would have preferred anyone but a bastard's daughter," she shouts, tears stinging her eyes. "You promised to find me a suitable love match, someone who would take me far away from here so I could finally be set free."

My plan is not going to work. How has he been able to poison Bess so easily? Was James correct? Has Lord Tyrell run out of patience and is here to take everything away from me? To kill me? If I cannot save myself nor my home, then at least I can save Bess from his manipulation and deceit.

"Bess, no that is not true—" I begin.

"Tell her how it was me who saved you in the end, not her," Lord Tyrell goads, but I will allow him to control her no longer! Each word is like poison in her ear, drip, drip, drip.

"Shut up, Henry!" I shout, anger filling every fibre of my being. "Bess, why are you saying these things? I thought you finally found your home here?"

"In… in the beginning, I hated you," she states, though a little unsure, as if she has misremembered her lines. "I saw the power you, a woman, had at your fingertips, but you never used it to help anyone but yourself. I thought you were different. I thought you were on *my* side! That was before Henry entered my life." She turns to face him and smiles.

He tries to mirror her, but I can see how hollow it truly is.

"He showed me affection and love that no other person has ever done before."

"He is using you, Bess! He wanted to use you to get to me!" I shout.

Why is he doing this? Why is he so twisted? Was he always this way and I just didn't see it, or did I make him this way? Has my constant rejection blackened his already tainted heart and Bess is caught in the crossfire?

"You're wrong! He promised to look after me! To rescue me," Bess argues. "All he ever wanted was the respect he deserved. He is not an evil man! He wouldn't hurt anyone unless they deserved it! I was only helping him, helping him to help you!" Bess takes a small step towards me, her hands clasped in front of her. "He didn't force me to do anything, before you ask! I am my own person! My own woman, just like you. Henry said that you needed help that night. Hence why I helped him and his men, to make sure you were on the right path."

That night? Surely, she couldn't mean…

My vision blurs and my hands shake, thinking back to the night everything changed. It was so dark, so cold… and Bess knew all along. She pushed me into danger, into the arms of my captor.

"I was trying to help you!" Bess catches my attention again.

Our eyes meet and I can no longer hide my heartbreak. Bess pauses, shrinking a little as she opens her mouth to speak once more, but no words escape her lips.

"Help me?" I question, a small, bitter laugh escaping my lips. "Do you know what happened that night? The night I was abducted? I was hit so hard that I fell off my horse and was knocked unconscious. When I awoke hours, days later, I was held in a small, dark room, all alone. I nearly died, Bess! Why would he do that if he wanted to *help* me? Why would you allow for that to happen?"

I can barely breathe. At the back of my mind, I am praying that James has reached my men, waiting for the right moment to charge in here and end this ridiculous affair.

"It wasn't Henry who knocked you out that day, so you cannot blame him! It was Bill. So, you see, your precious Lord Stanford's own brother was the one who took you, not Henry." Bess raises her chin higher; her naivety is heartbreaking. "It was Bill's idea to bring you to Henry. Henry told me to help Bill as Henry only wanted to help *you*."

My ears block out her words as my eyes are drawn towards the only person in this room who dares not look at me: Lord Thame.

"It's true, isn't it?" I ask, just wanting to hear him deny it.

"A-aye. It… it is. I had to." His voice is barely a whisper, such a contrast to how I saw him at Isabelle's wedding celebration. "Tyrell had a debt over my head and promised to wipe it clean if I was able to get ya to Yorkshire. After I failed to…" Lord Thame bites his tongue before continuing. "I-I am sorry. I know that I should have told ya or James about how deep I was with Tyrell. I thought my part in yer capture was enough to wipe the slate clean, but then ya escaped and the debt wasn't fully repaid. I never wanted to hurt ya. I didn't know ya and James were… I promise I never meant for ya to be harmed." Tears glisten in his eyes, his long hair hiding his face. I have never seen a man look so vulnerable and defeated. "I'm sorry," he repeats, swallowed by his own conscience.

A memory from my time in the monastery flashes

across my mind where whispered, desperate voices called to me in the darkness.

"It was you, wasn't it? The second voice I heard in the monastery," I ask.

Lord Thame nods.

"But why did..."

Lord Tyrell claps his hands, drawing all the attention back towards him. "See what your actions have done, Katherine? If only you had submitted to me, we wouldn't be in this mess. Bill and his family would be debt-free and an innocent girl wouldn't be tangled into this web of deceit."

I snap my attention to Lord Tyrell and Bess once more. She stands there, wringing her hands in front of her, gaze focused purely on the floor at her feet. Lord Thame is no longer my concern, but perhaps I can reach Bess one more time, get her to see the truth.

"I can put all of this behind us, Bess, we can start again. I just need you to trust *me* and not *him*." I reach my hand out towards her. Why won't she take it?

She shakes her head from side to side, her voice softening as she says, "I-I can't now. He only wanted to know where Lord Stanford was that day... but Bill failed. He failed, so he asked me to make sure that... but I didn't want to..."

I cannot make out her words clearly, her sentences broken just like her heart.

"Blood... there was so much blood, I thought..."

"I think you have done enough damage to this poor, defenceless young woman, Katherine. Destroying her reputation. Manipulated her to your own will. Told her lies about me. About us."

I am tired of his voice, of his lies and game of deceit. "Enough!" I shout at the top of my lungs so that even God can hear me. "What do you want, Henry? You are on my lands without an invitation. I suggest you say your piece and then get out, leaving us all alone once and for all."

"Oh, Katherine, you know why I am here. I want what is owed to me. I want you to beg for forgiveness," he hisses, spittle gathering on his chin.

"I owe you nothing. I have done nothing to you to warrant this humiliation!"

"You humiliated *me*, Katherine!"

I stare at him in disbelief.

"Your little note to the King of England. I have never been his most loyal or supportive subject, but I provide the Crown with a pretty amount of coin with the amount of tax, land and goods I produce each year. That seemed to keep him on my side. I attended one of his makeshift courts in the north, ready to present the document that states you are to be wed to me, but instead, I was forced to sit alone whilst ridiculed by the Crown and the most powerful and influential noblemen in the world. Humiliated. The king informed me that he had already been alerted and decreed the document is void and that I am owed nothing. That is why I am here to simply take what I want instead; King Richard be damned!"

The letter! The letter that I was given this morning, the one I left in the library unopened, distracted by the trespassers in the courtyard. Is that the contents of the letter? Word from King Richard to inform me of Lord Tyrell's failed attempt to revive the contract between our two families? A pang of regret fills my heart. If only I had taken the time to open it, to read its contents; would I have been so bold to face Lord Tyrell alone, knowing how angry he would have been, how humiliated, as he put it. My breathing becomes heavier and my fingers begin to twitch.

I clear my throat. "I am glad of it," I declare, not wanting to show how ruffled I truly am. "You couldn't cage me, body or soul. You deserve all the mortification you received and more. You stated that you have lost everything. *I* wasn't allowed to say goodbye to my dying aunt! I nearly joined her in death!"

"I never meant for you to be harmed!" he shouts, his whole body shaking, his face twisted with a deep frown, the most truthful words he has uttered today. His breathing is heavy and his mouth is clamped shut. "I am accustomed to getting what I want, Katherine. Therefore, I will just simply take it. You shall be mine. It is what our families wanted."

He begins to march towards me, and I have nowhere left to run. He pushes Bess aside, and she hits the ground hard, a small sob escaping her lips.

"B-but, Henry, you said… you said that you will marry me." Bess's voice wavers, tears forming in her eyes, heartbreak clear upon her face as she turns to face Lord Tyrell's stone-cold eyes. He pauses to look at her.

"I am done with you, girl. You have fulfilled your purpose," he replies. How can he be so cruel?

"No!" she sobs, her heart appearing to smash into a million pieces in front of me. Bess continues to cry, but through her waterlogged eyes, she lifts her head to look at me. "I wasn't able to help you, my lady, but I can now," she continues to talk to herself, her words become more and more incoherent. "My lady! I must warn you; Henry has slaughtered—"

Lord Tyrell grabs a hold of her and wraps his hand across her mouth.

"Actually, I have one final task for you." He pulls Bess further away from me, and I am blocked from following by another of his henchmen. She tries to dig in her heels, but she is powerless against him.

"No, please, help me!" she cries.

I try to break free, but I am too slow. In one swift motion, Lord Tyrell grabs his already bloodied dagger and drags it across Bess's throat.

"No!" I scream, watching Bess's freshly cut throat drain all of her blood.

She gasps for air, holding her hands against her throat, her eyes wide in absolute fear. Slowly, she plummets to her knees as life drains from her body and blood bubbles from her lips, silenced forever.

No. No. No. No. No.

I collapse to the floor, all strength depleted from every part of me. I gasp for air, but it is as if I am drowning. Tears streak down my face, mixing with the spittle that gathers on my chin. It is as if the earth is pulling me into the depths of the castle floor, my palms outstretched in front of me. I know that I call her name, "Bess!" once, twice, three times, but I cannot hear anything, time slowing to a complete stop.

I try to reach for her, fight my way through the thick heavy air around me, but Lord Tyrell grabs my arm, dragging me onto my feet, and forces me to watch.

"Get off me, you murderous bastard!" I kick and

scream as much as I can, but my fight leaves my body and I am no longer able to stand as my knees collapse to the floor and I sob uncontrollably.

Is this what he wanted? Is this how the great and powerful Lord Henry Tyrell tries to persuade me to his side? No, he is no longer here to win me over, he is here to take everything with force, and if I do not comply, he will make sure I am silenced forever.

Thirty-seven

All I can see are her dead eyes in a sea of red.

How did we end up like this? If I could go back in time, could I stop this from happening? Lord Tyrell's voice is muffled, his movement blurred. Everything else around me is black; red is the only colour I can see. I instinctively reach my hand towards Bess, as if I need to feel that this is real, that she is no longer with me, but he even denies me that as my view of her lifeless body is blocked by her murderer.

"Where is Stanford, Katherine? What have you asked him to do?" he asks again and again, but when I do not give him the satisfaction of an answer, it is clear that he's been toying with me all along, biding time for his dramatic reveal. "Very well then."

He snaps his fingers and, as if right on cue, I hear James's voice behind me. I spin towards his voice, hope mixed with fear.

Marched in by the slender, dark-bearded man I saw earlier, James looks up at me, but then focuses on the trail of blood that slowly flows from Bess's body. He snaps his head back in my direction but is stopped from uttering a single word by a punch to his stomach. He keels over to the floor, grunting in pain.

"James!" I shout, but I cannot reach him.

I'm so sorry, James, I never meant for you to get caught up in all of this.

I have failed to protect him, to keep him from harm's way. This is all my fault. If I wasn't so headstrong, believing that I could dupe Lord Tyrell into submission, James would be safe, Bess would be alive and none of this would have happened.

"Easily caught, I see. Perhaps Bill's failed attempt on your life did go to plan after all," he laughs, a sinister sound echoing around the room.

My heart, already heavy with grief and regret, plummets even further. With Bill's debt stacked against him, he must have, on Lord Tyrell's orders, attempted to remove James from my life forever. How could he do that to his own family?

"Isn't this lovely? All of us here together. Though, Stanford, if it wasn't for you, none of this would have happened. I would have everything I ever wanted. Look what you forced me to do!" he bellows. He takes a few deep breaths then continues, "I have enough men with me to take this castle and your lands without having to shed more blood, Katherine. I suggest you take my offer before you regret it," he states, as if I there is no other choice.

All the pain, the heartache, the regret, everything I have endured over these past few months has been orchestrated by him. No longer will I allow Lord Henry Tyrell to write my narrative, to paint my future. Everything he touches turns to death and destruction. I watch the stream of Bess's blood silently as it begins to trickle through the cracks of the stone floor, like how a river flows through one land to the next. There is nothing I can do to undo all of this... but I can end it.

Slowly, I rise, no longer feeling pity or pain.

"Leave now, all of you, before you regret it," I warn, a growl deep in my throat, as I look into each and every one of their eyes. "You may think that I will bend down on my knees and beg for you to leave, Henry, but I will not. I am Countess Katherine Turner of Leicester. I am the daughter of the late Earl Richard Turner, and sister to the late Earl William Turner. I will not be silenced by you, or your men. You have trespassed upon my land, slaughtered an innocent woman, and threatened the life of the man I love most in all this world. I will give you nothing. You will leave without ever setting foot on my land ever again. Do so now, or you and your men will feel the consequences of your actions. As God is my witness, I will make sure your final breaths will be squeezed by the tightness of a rope."

Lord Tyrell blinks once, then twice before shifting on his foot. A sliver of doubt flicks across his features and that of his men too, each eyeing one another as if gauging to see who will make the next move. James, in my peripheral vision, raises his chin, watching Lord Tyrell keenly; I know that we must make it out of here alive together, no matter the cost.

"W-what a lovely speech, Katherine," Lord Tyrell replies. He shifts his weight unevenly, a hand at his hip to steady himself. "But I think I will decline."

With a curt nod towards the bearded man behind James, he raises his fist and punches my fiancé across the jaw with a bone-crunching crack. I shout James's name as he falls to the floor again, blood gushing from his mouth and nose. I reach for him, his eyes searching my own as he attempts to speak, but he is silenced by a kick to his gut.

Lord Tyrell tuts. "Look, Stanford. Look at what Katherine has done to you! Look at what you could have avoided, Katherine."

James tries to laugh as he spits an alarming amount of blood onto the floor.

"Stop it!" I scream.

"There is only one way you can stop all of this, Katherine. Though I will take everything by force if I need to, perhaps I don't even need you once this is all done," Lord Tyrell states.

I spy the dagger at his belt loosely sheathed and easily accessible if I am quick enough. I lift my head towards James, his face bloodied and bruised. Instantly he can see my thoughts and what I am about to do. He attempts to call my name, tell me that it is a bad idea, but it is the only way I can stop all of this. In a blink of an eye, I lunge forwards and seize the dagger with my right hand, holding it up against my throat. A small trickle of blood begins to flow from where the blade cuts into my skin, an odd sensation of relief and pain. As much as he pretends that he doesn't need me, I know that he wants me. At least that's what I'm praying.

The room suddenly freezes; everyone ceases to breathe or move.

"You are wrong, Henry. You can't do this without me. I

know that you want me, you always have. Tell your men to stand down, or I will end this here and now."

Nobody moves.

"Now!" I scream, pressing the blade a little deeper into my skin; the pain is nothing compared to everything that has happened leading to this moment.

After a short pause for thought, Lord Tyrell nods towards his men, and they step away from me and James. He holds his hands up in surrender and walks towards me again, hand out stretched.

"Tell your men to drop their weapons and stand back, Henry," I demand; I need them to be unarmed and unprepared.

"I cannot ask them to do that, Katherine. I know you will never harm yourself. You will…" Lord Tyrell pauses mid-sentence as a loud crash echoes from the corridor that leads to the kitchens below.

All of us stand still, and I strain to hear more clearly. Lord Tyrell's eyes dart from the direction of the noise to each of his men, the blade still grasped in my hand, blood slowly trickling down my neck.

"You lot go and check that out. Bill and I will stay here. If anything happens to us, you know what to do."

Without a word, the rest of Lord Tyrell's men quickly march down the dark corridor and out of sight, their weapons raised. Lord Thame takes his spot behind James. All is still; no one moves, no one speaks. Meanwhile, I run through multiple escape routes in my head, eventually landing on one.

I meet James's eye for a split second, and we both nod, knowing that it is now or never. Without hesitation, I spin towards Lord Tyrell, dagger raised above my head, but he blocks my attempt with his gloved hand as I slash towards him, sending the dagger flying across the room. I scramble for the blade as Lord Thame lunges forwards and stops Lord Tyrell from tackling me to the ground.

"Thame! I should have known you would betray me!" Lord Tyrell shouts, his rage uncontrollable.

"I am no longer yer lap dog, Henry! Ya must be stopped!" he replies, trying his best to tackle his old master to the ground. "No matter the amount of money I owe ya, I will never betray my family ever again!"

I have no time to thank Lord Thame for his sudden change in heart as I desperately reach for the hilt of the blade that skidded across the other side of the room. As I grab it, I turn around to see both James and his brother-in-law fight against an enraged Lord Tyrell. With one swift move, he elbows Lord Thame in the neck, making him writhe in pain, collapsing to the floor, struggling to breathe. James, bloodied and bruised, lunges for Lord Tyrell too, but is easily beaten as Lord Tyrell jumps out of the way. James lands heavily against a stone pillar and slumps unconscious.

"James! No!" I shout, but I don't have time to run to him as Lord Tyrell concentrates all of his anger onto me.

"I have been patient! I have given you more than a fair chance, but I no longer want to play by my own rules!"

He rushes for me, but he misses as I dodge at the last second and run outside into the courtyard. I don't look back. I can hear his angry footsteps pound behind me. I hesitate for a split second and look at my options; the portcullis is down and the stables are too far away. The

Guards' Quarters above the portcullis! They will be able to help me. I don't have time to second-guess my decision as I rush up the castle wall steps, tripping on a few of the chipped stones as I go. My salvation is in sight, but just as I reach the final step, to my horror, I find several of my men's bodies lying motionless, caked in their own blood.

My body turns numb as I scan the scene in front of me. Lifeless forms litter the walls, blood splattered onto the stone floor, limbs mixed with broken bows and misfired arrows and bolts. Giles is amongst them, his eyes glazed over, blood dripping from his mouth. Another has his throat slit in the same style as Bess. It takes all my strength not to cry out, scream, drop to the floor in agony. They are dead. They are all dead because of me.

In my hesitation, I am startled by Lord Tyrell's heavy footwork as he joins me on the wall looking out towards the woodland and the deep moat below. I head towards the other side of the walkway to find that the door to the Guards' Quarters is locked! Panicking, I search around me for another way out, but the only path is the way I came or over the wall and to my death.

"Do you like my little surprise?" he laughs, leaning heavily against the wall, his hair no longer sitting neatly upon his head, his eyes dark, devoid of all humanity. "There is nowhere else to go, Katherine." He sneers, stopping halfway between me and the dead bodies of my men.

All I can focus on is the cold face of Giles as his eyes stare up at the sky.

"There is only one outcome from this. What a terrible accident; all you wanted was some fresh air, but the hysteria from seeing those dead men just lying there sent you over the edge and you just had to end it all and jumped off. Lord Stanford lost his mind and went on a killing rampage! Poor Bess was his first victim. If I hadn't been here, who would have caught him in the act?" He steps closer, backing me up against the locked door. "Of course, I will bury you beside your dead aunt, your dead brother, your dead father, and your dead mother. This is the best outcome for all of us."

"I won't let you!" My voice wobbles, nearly breaking as everything overwhelms me.

"You could have had anything you wanted! I could have given you the world!" he shrieks, everything bubbling to the surface as he points his finger at me in rage. "But now, it will soon be over."

Before I can react, he rushes forwards and wraps his hands around my neck, squeezing tightly, almost lifting me off the floor. I gasp for air, using my fists to try to break free, kicking my legs desperately.

"Say hello to your dead brother for me."

I claw at his hands, but my vision blurs with every second that passes. No, surely this is not how my story ends. I have to fight back! I whisper a prayer to my family as I gather the last remaining pieces of strength and stick my thumbs into the sockets of his eyes as hard as I can. As he screams in agony, he drops me, and I gulp at the fresh air that enters my lungs, choking on it. His bloodied hands grab at my waist again, but I shove past him and grasp one of the dead men's crossbows and a couple of bolts that lie scattered on the ground; there is no use running away now.

"Come on, come on!" I call to myself, my fingers shaking as a deranged Lord Tyrell begins to make his way towards me.

I knock the arrow into place, and pull the trigger. The arrow whistles through the air, spinning towards my intended target. He looks down, baring his teeth with an almighty cry at the sunken arrow that protrudes from his tunic and tries to haul it out. With uncontrollable fury, he staggers towards me. In one swift motion, he pulls a hidden blade from his boot and raises it in the air, ready to bring it down upon me, but I have already lined up my next shot, which lands in his chest next to my first.

"I never wanted to kill you, Henry!" I scream. "You have been nothing but a thorn in my side, and I cannot let you hurt anyone else!"

He leaves me no choice as he staggers forwards, not an ounce of humanity reflecting back at me. I let fly another arrow, but I miss due to the tears that cling to my eyes.

"If you won't be mine, then no one is allowed to have you, Katherine Turner! No one!" he cries, deaf to all sense and reasoning.

I begin to frantically search around for another arrow but there are none left, just broken shafts and cracked bows. I take a small step back, not realising how close I am to the first step that descends back to the ground, nearly falling to my own death; it is a long way down. Lord Tyrell is upon me and as I hold my hands up in front of me, ready for impact, an arrow flies past my face, soaring through the air before it lands straight into Lord Tyrell's side. I quickly look behind me, ready to fight whoever wishes to stop me, but my heart stops beating, and my legs begin to give way as James hobbles towards me, a bow in his bloodied hand. He drops it as soon as he reaches me, clutching at his old wound which has begun to bleed.

"Katherine! Are ya alright? Has he hurt ya?" James asks, turning my face over in his hands, his breathing laboured.

"It's over," I breathe, as I watch Lord Tyrell slump against the wall. "You can't hurt anyone else ever again, Henry."

I take half a step closer towards him as he collapses to the floor, clutching at the final arrow from James. I need to make sure he never harms anyone else ever again.

"I just… I just," he wheezes, coughing up blood as he does. "I-I…" And then his eyes close.

My eyes find James who limps towards me. A wave of relief floods through my body, but suddenly his eyes go wide, as he shouts my name, "Katherine!"

But I am too slow to react. A searing pain of heat floods my side. My hand rests against my waist, but when I pull away all I can see is blood. I inhale the cool air around me, my mind running blank. I stumble backwards, hitting the floor, my brain scrambling to make sense of the pain.

"No one else… can have… you, Katherine Turner of Leicester. You… are my… my… rose," Lord Tyrell wheezes, barely conscious as he gets to his feet again.

Clutching at the final arrow, now red with my blood, he gasps for air that will no longer sustain him, leaning against the lower part of the wall. As if time has slowed, our eyes meet. The anger in his face is replaced with sadness then peace. His once-happy, heart-warming smile returns, before, eventually, he loses his grip. He falls backwards several feet to the ground below, landing with a bone-crunching thud onto the riverbank. I use all my remaining strength to haul my body up onto the ramparts and look at the ground below where a broken Lord Henry Tyrell now lies in a pool of his own blood.

It's over. It's finally over.

James's voice becomes distant, like petals scattered to the four winds. "Katherine! Stay with me! It's going to be…"

Thirty-eight

The door to the king's Council Chamber is closed silently behind us as I am ushered into a plush, ornate chair. The room is much larger than mine back home, candles flickering at the slightest movement, heavy expensive drapes framing the tall windows around the room. It is quiet. I am thankful for the peace, a contrast to the tremors and raised eyebrows of the world outside this room. One of the king's men offers me a welcoming goblet of honey mead, which I sip with a deep sigh, my throat incredibly dry. I lean back and close my eyes, breathing deeply.

I gingerly place my hand at my side, a healing scar permanently etched across my skin as a grim reminder of all that happened the day Lord Tyrell was finally removed from this world. I awoke to searing pain, in and out of nightmares; places I thought I would never escape. But that was only the beginning.

News quickly spread across the kingdom of what took place, the truth beginning to twist one way or the other, separating itself from reality. I was summoned to the King's Court as soon as I had recovered to give my own account of what happened. I have attended many gatherings and hearings at Westminster Palace, but to be on the other side of it all is something else entirely. The eyes of every nobleman bored into mine, and it took everything in me not to shrink away. The sudden death of Lord Tyrell had a mixed response: anger, shock, denial, rage, but also relief, delight and peace. I didn't care for what his supporters had to say; they wouldn't believe the evil he had committed, even when the evidence against him was unquestionable.

My uncle, Sir Francis, James, and two of my surviving men, Johnson and Taylor, all gave their own accounts of what happened that day. Lord Thame, being the only survivor from Lord Tyrell's crew of bandits, was the last to give his account. I was anxious, scared, uneasy as to what he would say, knowing that he is the type of man to throw his own wife and children into the fire to save his own skin. However, to my surprise, he told the truth, openly admitting his own part in it all, including when he nearly killed James and the part he played in my kidnapping. The truth stunned the court into silence. I could see the Earl of Nottingham smile broadly, nodding his head when King Richard decreed that I was innocent of any crime, and that the death of Lord Tyrell was by his own hand. I was free to leave.

When I stepped outside the Great Hall, I nearly broke down in tears, pent-up emotion exhausting every muscle in my body, but I will never shed a tear for the likes of Lord Henry Tyrell ever again.

"I trust my mead is to your liking, Lady Turner?" King Richard asks, gently pulling me from my thoughts.

"It is, Your Majesty, thank you." I sit up a little straighter, almost forgetting where I am.

"Then I must gift you a basket for your long journey home. I know it is your uncle's favourite after all." He smiles warmly, his crystal-blue eyes gazing intently. "I must thank you again, my lady, for informing me in your own words as to what happened at your home. I can only acknowledge how truly traumatic it must have been for all of you."

I nod, swallowing hard at the memories that still haunt me. Images of blood, death and destruction… I close my eyes again to try to centre myself, but the dull ache in my side won't allow my mind to rid itself of this nightmare too easily.

The king leans forwards in his chair, his brown hair covering his face slightly. Though he is only a few years older than me, he has the scars and lines to show the difficulties he has had to overcome in his short life so far. He does not show the pressures his sudden rise to the throne has exerted upon him, as he looks at ease, as if he was born to rule.

"I want you to know that I do not blame you for Lord Tyrell's death. He was a shadow upon your light for too long; and mine, if truth be told. The murder of your lady's maid, Lady Hargreaves, is unforgiveable!" King Richard breathes heavily and forms a deathly grip in his right fist.

Bess. Fragments of her face flutter into my mind, her life leaving her body completely. We buried her in Greyfriars. It is going to be strange without her; for all her faults and brashness, she was family. Many others would blame her: she knew what she was doing. If they truly believe that, then they do not know what it is to be manipulated and abused by those you trust, those who supposedly love you. I could have saved her… if only I was given more time.

"I have to ask, Lady Turner." King Richard leans forwards across the desk between us. "You say Lord William Thame should be pardoned for his part in the event that took place at Leicester. Now, I am a man who believes in undying loyalty to those around themselves, but to a man who had a hand in plotting my demise… *that* I cannot understand, my lady."

He is right. Lord Thame is partly to blame for all that happened, and more, but I just couldn't see him sentenced to death or imprisonment. I told myself over and over that he knew what he was doing, selfishly plotting and scheming for his own ill-gotten gains. So, why did I ask the king's court to pardon him? I was informed when I awoke that Lord Thame had helped to dispose of the rest of Lord Tyrell's men. They were lured into the kitchens by my uncle, Sir Francis, Johnson and Taylor who had survived the onslaught that killed Giles and the majority of my men. I know that his actions do not outweigh all the terrible deeds he performed, but he will soon become an extension of my family once James and I wed, and I cannot see him hanged because of me. I couldn't save Bess, but perhaps I can allow Lord Thame's redemption.

"There has been too much death, and Lord Thame helped save the lives of my uncle and dear friend, Sir Francis Grey," I reply as evenly as I can before taking another sip from my goblet to hide the slight tremor in my hand. If King Richard notices, he does not show it. "I am aware that many want someone to pay for Lord Tyrell's death – he was a powerful nobleman after all – but we cannot sentence someone to death to appease those who choose to ignore the truth behind Lord Tyrell and his selfish actions. Lord Thame has his own demons to face. Now that Lord Tyrell cannot blackmail or threaten Lord Thame's family's lives, we should give him a chance to prove that a man can change."

King Richard mulls over my words for a minute or so, leaning back in his ornate chair and clasping his hands together, each silent second that ticks by becoming increasingly unbearable.

"Very well, Lady Turner, I trust your judgement, as I always have."

He leans back in his chair once more and steeples his fingers together, whilst I lean back with a huge sigh of relief. If Lord Thame was sentenced to death for his crimes, it would destroy his family, James included, and I cannot allow another family to be torn apart because of Lord Tyrell's actions.

King Richard's lips form a thin line, which then morph into a tight smile as he gazes outside to the city below. "It's such a lovely day. I think we should take a walk about the palace gardens, don't you?" he suggests, the change in topic of conversation surprising me.

"Of course, Your Majesty, I would like that."

The air outside has a slight chill, refreshing from the stuffiness of the palace, a place I dread going to every time I am summoned. It is surprisingly quiet out here, though;

only the occasional shout from the people outside the palace walls reaches us. It is rare to be alone in the king's company like this, with just a couple of the king's personal guards following us a few paces behind.

I catch King Richard observing me whilst we walk into a rose garden, a place I never knew existed amongst the heavy stone and towering turrets. "I have heard your castle boasts a much finer collection of roses than mine, Lady Turner."

"Would it be treason for me to agree with you, Your Majesty?" I ask, as we both laugh lightly.

"For you, my lady, I will make an exception."

"I do love my flowers so, but it is more than mere roses that make my garden a peaceful and happy place for me. I can remember fondly as my brother, William, chased me through the newly planted bushes. I see my friend Isabelle and me laughing with one another on our favourite bench, chatting into the late hours of the afternoon. My aunt oversaw my embroidery classes in that garden, making sure that I had the colour of the roses just right. I can even imagine a future where James and I can finally rest, grow old together, perhaps even raise a child of our own." I catch myself before I say another ridiculous fancy in front of the King of England. "Apologies, I misplaced myself, Your Majesty."

"Don't be. It is a pleasure to see a smile upon your face again, Lady Turner."

I look up at him with a shy grin. It is high praise to hear him say such things.

"I have many ears and eyes around the kingdom watching everything for me… Whenever they report on

Leicestershire, I only hear good things. You are a great leader with a kind heart. You put your people first above all others and won't bow down to anyone unworthy. They are great attributes to have, my lady, and ones I value highly myself."

"Thank you. I can thank my family and friends for that."

He pauses for a second and studies me. My cheeks flush under his gaze, and for the first time today, I look away.

"You have something that a lot of nobles wish they had. A loyal and loving family. A lot of nobles, my house included, always have to watch their own backs, and not just from those on the outside. If it's not their own son that is plotting to steal from them, it is their brother or even their wife!" He chuckles to himself. "You have strong allies, my lady, you have a power over people that some envy, and some may even want to take from you."

We carry on walking, his words leaving a strange caution behind them.

"Lord Henry Tyrell was just one example. I will do my utmost to protect you and your family, for as long as I live, but know this: you are an exceptional woman and leader, Lady Turner."

I try not to shy away, but I am not used to such compliments, especially from a man such as he. So many have doubted my position here; it is odd to hear such high praise. We pause by the edge of the garden.

King Richard leans in slightly, his voice prickling my ear. "I could do with someone like you at court. You could set a shining example to the men who squander and gloat about their wealth. It would be refreshing to have a woman such as yourself by my side, with the other men within my close confidence, of course. I know my wife, Queen Anne, would find your presence refreshing."

My breath catches in my lungs. To be a close confidante of the King and Queen of England is something I should accept straight away, but yet I hesitate. My mother and aunt were the former queen's ladies-in-waiting, serving the court by looking beautiful and marrying advantageously. If my aunt were alive, she would push me to take up the offer, but I am not made for a life of following in another's shadow. My position would be questioned at every turn, I would never feel comfortable here, no matter if I had the king's seal of approval. As soon as King Richard's back is turned or, heaven forbid, something happened to him, I would be in grave danger, and I cannot put my family through that again.

"I thank you for your offer, Your Majesty, but I am needed in Leicester more," I reply, hoping my words are not a disappointment to him. "I finally have my happy ending with Lord Stanford by my side. If we are blessed with a happy marriage and an heir, I want to show them all that they can achieve, but I want to do that at home, rather than far away in London. It is something that my father regretted. We are strong because of those around us, not because we are born to a noble house."

The sounds of laughter and boots crunching on gravel fractures our train of conversation, but when I look up to see who the noise belongs to, my heart softens as James makes his way towards us. He is joined by Lord John McNally, who was keen to join the rest of the court to hear my account. A close friend and ally, he was one of the first to congratulate me for ridding the world of the 'devil's own'.

James greets King Richard first with a low bow, soon followed by a gentle but longing kiss on my cheek. The king smiles humbly, watching us both with a warm look upon his face.

"I see, Lady Turner," he continues, "and I don't blame you. If I had the choice, maybe I would do the same. I love my wife dearly, she means the world to me, even more so as queen by my side. I hope that I can count on you both as strong allies, however. I will not lie. My reign thus far has been… interesting. The more support I have, the easier it will be to obtain an everlasting peace."

"Of course, Your Majesty," I reply with a confident smile, happy to be a close ally and friend to one of the most powerful men in the world.

"And, erm… more importantly, I *am* invited to your wedding, yes? Your uncle told me you are due to wed next year – is that correct?" he teases, but with a hint of seriousness.

I laugh wholeheartedly. "Of course, I would be honoured if you and Queen Anne would attend our wedding, whenever it may be."

"Excellent! Do you hear that, McNally? We'd best prepare our queen with the finest cloth and jewels." He chuckles deeply, Lord McNally nodding along with interest.

James and I leave London that evening, arriving back in Leicester in the late afternoon the next day. As we enter the courtyard, I look up at the fortifications around me, the grey stone standing tall, protecting all who seek shelter within. The heavy oak doors that lead to the heart of the castle stand proudly. The sway of the winter breeze, the sound of crunching feet upon gravel, the whinnying of horses in the stables, alongside the babbling of the River Soar just on the other side of the wall, all tell me I'm home. Kitchen maids, groundsmen, and stableboys all go about their usual duties with smiles on their faces. More importantly, I can hear the laughter of my uncle and Sir Francis coming from an open window that must be the library. Then there is James, my heart, my love, my future. With him by my side, I know that I can achieve anything, *we* can achieve anything, as now I know, I do not have to do this alone.

"So, what next, m'lady?" James whispers in my ear, his arm encircling my waist.

"Hmmm." I pretend to think, tapping my finger on my chin. "How about we escape from here for a little while?"

"I would never say no, but what about after that?" He kisses my cheek, warming me against the winter chill.

"A peaceful future with my handsome husband by my side?" I question with a smirk upon my lips.

"I couldn't think of anything more perfect, m'lady."

I turn to face him, placing a longing kiss on his lips as the rest of the world melts away like rose petals scattered on the wind.

Laura Johnson-Smith has always been captivated by storytelling, driven by her deep love of history, and the overlooked tales of women throughout time. This passion led to the creation of her debut novel, *The Rose Amongst the Thorns.*

She lives in Leicestershire with her husband and two cats. When she's not crafting her next novel, she escapes into the immersive world of video games, a hidden spark and inspiration for her writing.